Praise for
#1 *New York Times* and *USA TODAY* bestselling author

NORA ROBERTS

"Roberts' bestselling novels are some of the best in the romance
genre. They are thoughtfully plotted, well-written stories
featuring fascinating characters."
—*USA TODAY*

"Some estimates have [Nora Roberts] selling 12 books an hour,
24 hours a day, 7 days a week, 52 weeks a year."
—*New York Times*

"Roberts has a warm feel for her characters
and an eye for the evocative detail."
—*Chicago Tribune*

"There's no mystery about why Roberts is a bestselling author
of romances and mainstream novels:
she delivers the goods with panache and wit."
—*Publishers Weekly*

"Roberts is deservedly one of the best known
and most widely read of all romance writers."
—*Library Journal*

"Nora Roberts is among the best."
—*Washington Post Book World*

"Romance will never die
as long as the megaselling Roberts keeps writing."
—*Kirkus Reviews*

Dear Reader,

What is the most powerful thing in the world? What can change a person…change a life? Love. Nobody knows this better than the master of romance, Nora Roberts. In this collection, Nora weaves two tales about love's ability to conquer all.

Certified charmer Sam Weaver is instantly enchanted by Johanna Patterson, but the feeling isn't quite mutual. Undeterred by her rebuffs, Sam realizes that he must first earn Johanna's trust, if he wants a chance at her heart. And when "The Name of the Game" is love, he will put it all on the line!

It's been five years since musician/composer Brandon Carstairs left Raven Williams without a word. Now he wants the talented singer back—but only to work with him on a project. Yet the fire between Raven and Brandon has never died. They know they can make beautiful music together "Once More with Feeling," but this time will they get it right?

Love is never easy, but always worth it. Happy reading!

The Editors
Silhouette Books

NORA ROBERTS

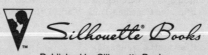

Published by Silhouette Books

America's Publisher of Contemporary Romance

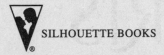

SILHOUETTE BOOKS

DUETS

ISBN-13: 978-0-373-28585-3

Copyright © 2010 by Harlequin Books S.A.

The publisher acknowledges the copyright holder of the individual works as follows:

THE NAME OF THE GAME
Copyright © 1988 by Nora Roberts

ONCE MORE WITH FEELING
Copyright © 1983 by Nora Roberts

Visit Silhouette Books at www.eHarlequin.com

Printed in U.S.A.

CONTENTS

The Name
of the Game

To Faye Ashley.
Now you'll have to leave me the bracelet.

1

"Marge Whittier, this is your chance to win *ten thousand dollars*. Are you ready?"

Marge Whittier, a forty-eight-year-old schoolteacher and grandmother of two from Kansas City, squirmed in her chair. The lights were on, the drum was rolling and the possibility of her being sick was building. "Yes, I'm ready."

"Good luck, Marge. The clock will start with your first pick. Begin."

Marge swallowed a lump of panic, shuddered with excitement and chose number six. Her sixty seconds began to dwindle, and the tension grew as she and her celebrity partner picked their brains for the right answers. They leaped over such questions as who founded psychoanalysis and how many yards in a mile, then came to a screeching halt. What element do all organic compounds contain?

Marge went pale, and her lips quivered. She was an English teacher and a bit of a history and movie buff, but science wasn't her long suit. She looked pleadingly at her partner, who was better known for her wit than for her wisdom. Precious seconds ticked away. As they fumbled, the buzzer sounded. Ten thousand dollars flowed through Marge's sweaty fingers.

The studio audience groaned their disappointment.

"Too bad, Marge." John Jay Johnson, the tall, sleekly polished host, laid a sympathetic hand on her shoulder. His rich, rolling voice expressed just the right combination of disappointment and hope. "You were so close. But with eight correct answers you add another eight hundred dollars to your total. An impressive one." He smiled at the camera. "We'll be back after this break to total up Marge's winnings and to give you the correct answer to the stumper. Stay with us."

The music was cued. John Jay kept his avuncular smile handy. He used the timed ninety-second break to come on to the pretty celebrity panelist.

"Pompous jerk," Johanna muttered. The pity was that she was too aware his smooth looks and slick manner were keeping *Trivia Alert* up in the ratings. As producer, she'd learned to accept John Jay as part of the set. She checked the second hand of her watch before walking over to the losers. Putting on a smile of her own, she commiserated and congratulated as she eased them along. She needed them in camera range for the finish.

"Coming up on five," she announced, and signaled for applause and music. "And cue."

John Jay, his arm around Marge and his three-thousand-dollar caps gleaming, closed the show.

They were one big happy family as the assistant director shut off his stopwatch. "That's a wrap."

Kiki Wilson, Marge's partner and the current star of a popular situation comedy, chatted a few moments longer with Marge in a way that would have the schoolteacher remembering her warmly for years to come. When Kiki rose, her smile was still firmly in place as she walked the few steps to John Jay.

"If you ever pull something like that again," she said quietly, "you'll need a paramedic."

Knowing she was referring to his quick—and, if he did say so, clever—hand maneuver just before the end of the break, John Jay smiled. "Just part of the service. About that drink, sweetheart…"

"Kiki." In a smooth move that didn't appear nearly as rushed and harassed as it was, Johanna swung over and scooted the actress away. "I want to thank you again for agreeing to do the show. I know how hectic your schedule must be."

Johanna's warm voice and soothing manner brought Kiki's blood pressure down slightly. "I enjoyed it." Kiki pulled out a cigarette and tapped it absently against an enameled case. "It's a cute show, moves fast. And God knows the exposure never hurts."

Though Johanna didn't smoke, she carried a small gold lighter. Pulling it out, she lit Kiki's cigarette. "You were wonderful. I hope you'll consider coming back."

Kiki blew out smoke and regarded Johanna. The lady knew her job, Kiki admitted. Even though she looked like some cuddly little model for shampoo or yogurt. It had been a long day, but the catered dinner break had been first-class, the studio audience generous with their applause. In any case, her agent had told her that *Trivia Alert* was *the* up-and-coming game show of the year. Considering that, and the fact that Kiki had a good sense of humor, she smiled.

"I just might. You've got a good crew, with one notable exception."

Johanna didn't have to turn to know where Kiki's narrowed

gaze had landed. With John Jay it was either love or disgust, with little middle ground. "I have to apologize for any annoyance."

"Don't bother. There are plenty of jerks in the business." Kiki studied Johanna again. Quite a face, she decided, even with the minimal makeup. "I'm surprised you don't have a few fang marks."

Johanna smiled. "I have very thick skin."

Anyone who knew her would have attested to that. Johanna Patterson might have looked soft and creamy, but she had the energy of an Amazon. For eighteen months she had slaved, hustled and bargained to get and keep *Trivia Alert* on the air. She wasn't a novice in the entertainment business, and that made her all the more aware that behind the scenes and in the boardrooms it was still a man's world.

That would change eventually, but eventually was too long a wait. Johanna wasn't patient enough to wait for doors to open. When she wanted something badly enough, she gave them a push. For that she was willing to make certain adjustments herself. The business of entertainment was no mystery to her; nor were the deals, the concessions or the compromises. As long as the end product was quality, it didn't matter.

She'd had to swallow pride and sacrifice a principle or two to get her baby off and running. For example, it wasn't her name, but her father's logo that flashed importantly at the end of the show: Carl W. Patterson Productions

His was the name the network brass related to, and his was the one they trusted. So she used it—grudgingly—then ran things her way.

Thus far, the uneasy marriage was into its second year and

holding its own. Johanna knew the business—and her father—too well to take for granted that it would continue.

So she worked hard, tying up loose ends, hammering out solutions to problems and delegating carefully what couldn't be handled personally. The success or failure of the show wouldn't make or break her, financially or professionally, but she had more than money and reputation tied up with it. She had her hopes and her self-esteem.

The studio audience had been cleared. A few technicians remained on the set, either gossiping or tidying up last-minute business. It was just past eight o'clock, and moving into hour fourteen for Johanna.

"Bill, do you have the dupes?" She accepted the copies of the day's tape from her editor. Five shows were produced and recorded in one full-day session. Five costume changes for the celebrity panelists—Johanna had a policy against referring to them as guest stars. Five wardrobe trips for John Jay, who insisted on a change from underwear out for each show. His natty suits and coordinated ties would be sent back to the Beverly Hills tailor who provided them free in exchange for the plug at the end of each show.

His job was over, but Johanna's was just beginning. The tapes would be reviewed, edited and carefully timed. Johanna would oversee each step. There would be mail to go through, letters from home viewers who hoped to be chosen as contestants, more letters from people who disagreed with certain answers. She'd go head-to-head with her research coordinator to check facts and select new questions for upcoming shows. Though she couldn't personally interview and screen each potential contestant, she would go over her contestant coordinator's selections.

The game-show scandals of the fifties were long over, but no one wanted a repeat of them. Standards and Practices was very strict, their rules and regulations very clear. Johanna made it a habit never to relax her own, and to check each detail herself.

When screened contestants arrived at the studio for a day's taping, they were turned over to staff members who sequestered them from the crew, the audience and their prospective partners. They were entertained and soothed, literally cut off from the show until their turn came to participate.

Questions were locked in a safe. Only Johanna and her personal assistant had the combination.

Then, of course, there were the celebrities to deal with. They would want their favorite flowers and choice of beverage in their dressing rooms. Some would go with the flow and make her life easier, and others would be difficult just to show they were important. She knew—and they knew she knew—that most of them appeared on morning game shows not for the money or the fun but for the exposure. They were plugging series and specials, placating their networks or scrambling to keep their face familiar to the public.

Fortunately, a good percentage of them had fun once the ball was rolling. There were still more, however, who required pampering, cajoling and flattery. She was willing, as long as they helped her keep her show on the air. When a woman had grown up with artistic temperaments and the wheeling and dealing of the entertainment business, very little surprised her.

"Johanna."

Regretfully Johanna put her fantasy of a hot bath and a foot massage on hold. "Yes, Beth?" She slipped the tapes into her oversize tote and waited for her assistant. Bethany Landman was young, sharp and energetic. Just now she seemed to be bubbling over. "Make it good. My feet are killing me."

"It's good." A bouncy dark contrast to Johanna's cool blond looks, Bethany gripped her clipboard and all but danced. "We've got him."

Johanna secured the tote on the shoulder of her slim violet-blue jacket. "Who have we got and what are we going to do with him?"

"Sam Weaver." Beth caught her lower lip between her teeth as she grinned. "And I can think of a lot of things we could do with him."

The fact that Bethany was still innocent enough to be impressed by a hard body and tough good looks made Johanna feel old and cynical. More, it made her feel as though she'd been born that way. Sam Weaver was every woman's dream. Johanna wouldn't have denied him his talent, but she was long past the point where sexy eyes and a cocky grin made her pulse flutter. "Why don't you give me the most plausible?"

"Johanna, you have no romance in your soul."

"No, I don't. Can we do this walking, Beth? I want to see if the sky's still there."

"You read that Sam Weaver's done his first TV spot?"

"A miniseries," Johanna added as they wound down the studio corridor.

"They aren't calling it a miniseries. Promotion calls it a four-hour movie event."

"I love Hollywood."

With a chuckle, Bethany shifted her clipboard. "Anyway, I took a chance and contacted his agent. The movie's on our network."

Johanna pushed open the studio door and breathed in the

air. Though it was Burbank air and therefore far from fresh, it was welcome. "I'm beginning to see the master plan."

"The agent was very noncommittal, but…"

Johanna stretched her shoulders, then searched for her keys. "I think I'm going to like this *but.*"

"I just got a call from upstairs. They want him to do it. We'll have to run the shows the week before the movie and give him time to plug it every day." She paused just long enough to give Johanna a chance to nod. "With that guarantee they'll put on the pressure and we've got him."

"Sam Weaver," Johanna murmured. There was no denying his drawing power. Being tall, lanky and handsome in a rough sort of way didn't hurt, but he had more than that. A bit part in a feature film five, maybe six years before had been a springboard. He'd been top-billed and hot box office ever since. It was more than likely he'd be a pain in the neck to work with, but it might be worth it. She thought of the millions of televisions across the country, and the ratings. It would definitely be worth it.

"Good work, Beth. Let's get it firmed up."

"As good as done." Bethany stood by the spiffy little Mercedes as Johanna climbed in. "Will you fire me if I drool?"

"Absolutely." Johanna flashed a grin as she turned the key. "See you in the morning." She drove the car out of the lot like a bullet. Sam Weaver, she thought as she turned the radio up and let the wind whip her hair. Not a bad catch, she decided. Not bad at all.

Sam felt like a fish with a hook through his mouth, and he didn't enjoy the sensation. He slumped in his agent's overstuffed chair, his long, booted legs stretched out and a pained scowl on the face women loved to love.

"Good Lord, Marv. A game show? Why don't you tell me to dress like a banana and do a commercial?"

Marvin Jablonski chomped a candied almond, his current substitute for cigarettes. He admitted to being forty-three, which made him a decade older than his client. He was trim and dressed with a subtle flair that spoke of wealth and confidence. When his office had consisted of a phone booth and a briefcase, he'd dressed the same. He knew how vital illusions were in this town. Just as he knew it was vital to keep a client happy while you were manipulating him.

"I thought it was too much to expect that you'd be open-minded."

Sam recognized the touch of hurt in Marv's tone—the poor, self sacrificing agent, just trying to do his job. Marv was far from poor and he'd never been into personal sacrifice. But it worked. With something like a sigh, Sam rose and paced the length of Marv's glitzy Century City office. "I was open-minded when I agreed to do the talk-show circuit."

Sam's easy baritone carried a hint of his native rural Virginia, but his reputation in Los Angeles wasn't that of a country gentleman. As he paced, his long-legged stride made the observer think of a man who knew exactly where he was going.

And so he did, Marv thought. Otherwise, as a selective and very successful theatrical agent he would never have taken the struggling young actor on six years before. Instinct, Marv was wont to say, was every bit as important as the power breakfast. "Promotion's part of the business, Sam."

"Yeah, and I'll do my bit. But a game show? How is guessing what's behind door number three going to boost the ratings for *Roses*?"

"There aren't any doors on *Trivia*."

"Thank God."

Marv let the sarcasm pass. He was one of the few in the business who knew that Sam Weaver could be maneuvered with words like *responsibility* and *obligation*. "And it'll boost the ratings because millions of sets are tuned in to that half-hour spot five days a week. People love games, Sam. They like to play, they like to watch and they like to see other people walk out with a free lunch. I've got miles of facts and figures, but let's just say that most of those sets are controlled by women." His smile spread easily, shifting his trim, gray-flecked mustache. "Women, Sam, the ones who buy the bulk of the products the sponsors are hyping. And that fizzy little soft drink that's the major sponsor for *Roses* also buys time on *Trivia*. The network likes that, Sam. Keeps things in the family."

"That's fine." Sam hooked his thumbs in the pockets of his jeans. "But we both know I didn't take the TV deal to sell soda pop."

Marv smiled and ran a hand over his hair. His new toupee was a work of art. "Why did you take the deal?"

"You know why. The script was gold. We needed the four hours to do it right. A two-hour feature would have meant hacking it to bits."

"So you used TV." Marv closed his fingers together lightly, as if he were shutting a trap. "Now TV wants to use you. It's only fair, Sam."

Fair was another word Sam had a weakness for.

A short four-letter epithet was Sam's opinion. Then he said nothing as he stared out at his agent's lofty view of the city. He wasn't so many years off the pavement that he'd forgotten what it felt like to have the heat bake through his sneakers and frustration run through his blood. Marv had taken a chance on him. A calculated risk, but a risk nonetheless. Sam believed in paying his dues. But he hated making a fool of himself.

"I don't like to play games," he muttered, "unless I set the rules."

Marv ignored the buzzer on his desk; it was the prerogative of a man in demand. "You talking politics or the show?"

"Sounds to me like they've been lumped together."

Marv only smiled again. "You're a sharp boy, Sam."

Sam turned his head just a fraction. Marv had been hit by the power of those eyes before. They were one of the reasons he'd signed an unknown when he'd been in a position to refuse the business of well-established luminaries. The eyes were big, heavy lidded and blue. Electric blue, with the power of a lightning bolt. Intense, like his long-boned, narrow face and firm mouth. The chin wasn't so much cleft as sculpted. The kind of chin that looked as though it could take a punch. The nose was a bit crooked, because it had.

California sun had tanned the skin a deep brown and added the interest of faint lines. The kind that made a woman shiver, imagining the experiences that had etched them there. There was a mystery about his face that appealed to females, and a toughness that drew approval from other men. His hair was dark and left long enough to go its own way.

It wasn't a face for a poster in a teenager's room, but it was the kind that haunted a woman's secret dreams.

"How much choice do I have on this?" Sam asked.

"Next to none." Because he knew his client, Marv decided it was time to bare the truth. "Your contract with the network ties you to promotion work. We could get around it, but it wouldn't be good for you, this project or any future ones."

Sam didn't give a damn if it was good for him. He rarely did. But the project was important. "When?"

"Two weeks from today, I'll move the paperwork through. Keep it in perspective, Sam. It's one day out of your life."

"Yeah." One day, he thought, could hardly make much difference. And it wasn't easy to forget that a decade before he'd have considered an offer to do a game show as much of a miracle as manna from heaven. "Marv…" He paused at the door. "If I make an ass out of myself, I'm going to dump Krazy Glue on your hairpiece."

It was strange that two people could have business in the same building, often ride the same elevator, but never cross paths. Sam didn't make the trip from Malibu to his agent's office often. Now that his career was on the rise he was usually tied up in rehearsals, script meetings or location shoots. When he had a few weeks, as he did now, he didn't waste it battling L.A.'s traffic or closing himself up inside Century City's impressive walls. He preferred the seclusion of his ranch.

Johanna, on the other hand, made the trip to her Century City office daily. She hadn't taken a personal vacation in two years, and she put in an average of sixty hours a week on her show. If anyone had tagged her as a workaholic she would have shrugged off the label. Work wasn't an illness, as far as Johanna was concerned; it was a means to an end. The long hours and dedication justified her success. She was determined that no one accuse her of riding on Carl Patterson's coattails.

The offices maintained by *Trivia*'s staff were comfortable but understated. Her own was large enough to prevent her from feeling claustrophobic and practical enough to make the statement that this was a place of business. She arrived like clockwork at eight-thirty, broke for lunch only if it included a meeting, then worked straight through until she was finished. Besides her almost maternal devotion to *Trivia*, she had another concept on the back burner. A word game this time, an idea that was nearly refined enough to take to the network brass.

Now she had her jacket slung over her chair and her nose buried in a week's worth of potential questions passed on to her by Research. She had to get close to the words because she refused to wear the reading glasses she needed.

"Johanna?"

With little more than a grunt, Johanna continued to read. "Did you know Howdy Doody had a twin brother?"

"We were never close," Bethany said apologetically.

"Double Doody," Johanna informed her with a nod. "I think it's a great one for the speed round. Did you catch today's show?"

"Most of it."

"I really think we should try to lure Hank Loman back. Soap stars are a big draw."

"Speaking of big draws…" Bethany set a stack of papers on Johanna's desk. "Here's the contract for Sam Weaver. I thought you'd like to look it over before I run it up to his agent."

"Fine." She shuffled papers before drawing the contract close enough to focus on it. "Let's send him a tape of the show."

"The usual fruit and cheese for the dressing room?"

"Mmm-hmm. Is the coffee machine fixed?"

"Just."

"Good." She took a casual glance at her watch. It was a simple affair with a black leather band. The diamond-encrusted one her father's secretary had picked out for her last

birthday was still in its box. "Listen, you go on to lunch. I'll
run these up."

"Johanna, you're forgetting how to delegate again."

"No, I'm just delegating me." Rising, she shook the creases
out of her pale rose jacket. After picking up the remote channel
changer from her desk, she aimed it at the television across the
room. Both picture and sound winked off. "Are you still seeing
that struggling screenwriter?"

"Every chance I get."

Johanna grinned as she shrugged into her jacket. "Then
you'd better hurry. This afternoon we need to brainstorm over
the home viewer's contest. I want that rolling by next month."
She picked up the contracts and slipped them and a cassette
into a leather portfolio. "Oh, and make a note for me to slap
John Jay's wrist, will you? He charged a case of champagne to
the show again."

Bethany wrote that down enthusiastically and in capital
letters. "Glad to do it."

Johanna chuckled as she swung out the door. "Results of
the contestant screening by three," she continued. "That tech's
wife—Randy's wife—she's in Cedars of Lebanon for minor
surgery. Send flowers." Johanna grinned over her shoulder.
"Who says I can't delegate?"

On the ride up in the elevator, Johanna smiled to herself.
She was lucky to have Beth, she thought, though she could
already foresee the time when her assistant would be moving
up and out. Brains and talent rarely settled for someone else's
dream. She liked to think she'd proved that theory for herself.
In any case, Johanna had Beth now, and with the rest of her
bright young staff, Johanna was on her way to establishing her
own niche in the competitive world of daytime television.

If she could get her new concept as far as a pilot, she had no doubt she could sell it. Then maybe a daytime drama, something with as much action as heartache. That story was already in its beginning stages. In addition to that, she was determined to have a nighttime version of *Trivia* syndicated to the independents. She was already on the way to achieving her five-year goal of forming her own production company.

As the elevator rose, Johanna automatically smoothed down her hair and straightened the hem of her jacket. Appearances, she knew, were as important as talent.

When the doors opened, she was satisfied that she looked brisk and professional. She passed through the wide glass doors into Jablonski's offices. He didn't believe in understatement. There were huge Chinese-red urns filled with feathers and fans. A sculpture of what might have been a human torso gleamed in brushed brass. The carpet was an unrelieved white and, Johanna's practical mind thought, must be the devil to keep clean.

Wide chairs in black and red leather were arranged beside glass tables. Trade magazines and the day's papers were set in neat piles. The setup told her Jablonski didn't mind keeping clients waiting.

The desks in the reception area followed the theme in glossy red and black. Johanna saw an attractive brunette seated at one. Perched on the corner of the desk and leaning close to the brunette was Sam Weaver. Johanna's brow lifted only slightly.

She wasn't surprised to see him flirting with one of the staff. Indeed, she expected that kind of thing from him and others like him. After all, her father had had an affair with every secretary, receptionist and assistant who had ever worked for him.

He'd been the tall, dark and handsome type, too, she thought. Still was. Her only real surprise at running into Sam

Weaver was that he was one of that rare breed of actor who actually looked better in the flesh than on the screen.

He packed a punch, an immediate one.

Snug jeans suited him, she acknowledged, as did the plain cotton shirt of a working man. No gold flashed, no diamonds winked. He didn't need them, Johanna decided. A man who could look at the receptionist the way Sam was looking at that brunette didn't need artifice to draw attention to him.

"She's beautiful, Gloria." Sam bent closer to the snapshots the receptionist was showing off. From Johanna's angle it looked as though he were whispering endearments. "You're lucky."

"She's six months old today." Gloria smiled down at the photograph of her daughter, then up at Sam. "I was lucky Mr. Jablonski gave me such a liberal maternity leave, and it's nice to be back at work, but boy, I miss her already."

"She looks like you."

The brunette's cheeks flushed with pride and pleasure. "You think so?"

"Sure. Look at that chin." Sam tapped a finger on Gloria's chin. He wasn't just being kind. The truth was, he'd always gotten a kick out of kids. "I bet she keeps you busy."

"You wouldn't believe—" The still-new mother might have been off and running if she hadn't glanced up and seen Johanna. Embarrassed, she slid the pictures into her drawer. Mr. Jablonski had been generous and understanding, but she didn't think he'd care to have her spending her first day back on the job showing off her daughter. "Good afternoon. May I help you?"

With a slight inclination of her head, Johanna crossed the room. As she did, Sam swiveled on the desk and watched her. He didn't quite do a double take, but damn near.

She was beautiful. He wasn't immune to beauty, though he

was often surrounded by it. At first glance she might have been taken for one of the hordes of slim and leggy California blondes who haunted the beaches and adorned glossy posters. Her skin was gold—not bronzed, but a very pale and lovely gold. It set off the smoky blond hair that fluffed out to tease the shoulders of her jacket. Her face was oval, the classic shape given drama by prominent cheekbones and a full mouth. Her eyes, delicately shaded with rose and violet, were the clear blue of a mountain lake.

She was sexy. Subtly sexy. He was used to that in women as well. Maybe it was the way she moved, the way she carried herself inside the long loose jacket and straight skirt, that made her seem so special. Her shoes were ivory and low-heeled. He found himself noticing even them and the small, narrow feet they covered.

She didn't even glance at him, and he was glad. It gave him the chance to stare at her, to absorb the sight of her, before she recognized him and spoiled the moment.

"I have a delivery for Mr. Jablonski."

Even her voice was perfect, Sam decided. Soft, smooth, just edging toward cool.

"I'll be happy to take it." Gloria gave her most cooperative smile.

Johanna unzipped her portfolio and took out the contracts and tape. She still didn't look at Sam, though she was very aware he was staring. "These are the Weaver contracts and a tape of *Trivia Alert*."

"Oh, well—"

Sam cut her off neatly. "Why don't you take them in to him, Gloria? I'll wait."

Gloria opened her mouth, then shut it again to clear her

throat as she rose. "All right. If you'd just give me a moment," she said to Johanna, then headed down the corridor.

"Do you work for the show?" Sam asked her.

"Yes." Johanna gave him a small and purposefully disinterested smile. "Are you a fan, Mr.——?"

She didn't recognize him. Sam had a moment to be both surprised and disconcerted before he saw the humor of it and grinned. "It's Sam." He held out a hand, trapping her into an introduction.

"Johanna," she told him, and accepted the handshake. His easy reaction made her feel petty. She was on the verge of explaining when she realized he hadn't released her hand. His was hard and strong. Like his face, like his voice. It was her reaction to them, her quick and intensely personal reaction to them, that drove her to continue the pretense and blame it on him.

"Do you work for Mr. Jablonski?"

Sam grinned again. It was a fast, crooked grin that warned a woman not to trust him. "In a manner of speaking. What do you do on the show?"

"A little of this, a little of that," she said, truthfully enough. "Don't let me keep you."

"I'd rather you did." But he released her hand because she was tugging at it. "Would you like to have lunch?"

Her brow lifted. Five minutes ago he'd been cuddling up to the brunette; now he was inviting the first woman who came along to lunch. Typical. "Sorry. I'm booked."

"For how long?"

"Long enough." Johanna glanced past him to the receptionist.

"Mr. Jablonski will have the contracts signed and returned to Ms. Patterson by tomorrow afternoon."

"Thank you." Johanna shifted her portfolio and turned. Sam laid a hand on her arm and waited until she looked back at him.

"See you."

She smiled at him, again disinterestedly, before she walked away. She was chuckling when she reached the elevators, unaware that she'd tucked the hand he'd held into her pocket.

Sam watched her until she'd turned the corner. "You know, Gloria," he said, half to himself, "I think I'm going to enjoy playing this game after all."

2

On the day of a taping, Johanna was always on the set by nine. It wasn't that she didn't trust her staff. She did. She simply trusted herself more. Besides, last week they'd had a few mechanical glitches with the moving set that swung the contestants and their counters stage center for play, then off again for the championship round. Small problems like that could delay taping anywhere from five minutes to two hours. By checking everything through personally beforehand, she sweetened the odds.

All the lights on the display board had to be tested, and the dressing rooms had to be primped and fresh coffee and cookies arranged for the prospective contestants.

They weren't due until one, but experience told Johanna that most would arrive early so they could chew their nails in the studio. Soothing them was one job she gladly delegated. The celebrities were also due at one so they could do a run-through and still have plenty of time for hair, makeup and wardrobe.

John Jay would arrive at two to complain about the suits that had been selected for him. Then he would close himself in his dressing room to sulk before his makeup call. When he was suited up, powdered and sprayed he would emerge, ready to shine for the cameras. Johanna had learned to ignore his artistic temperament—for the most part—and to tolerate the rest. There was no arguing with his popularity quotient. It was largely due to him that the line would form outside the studio for tickets for the day's taping.

Johanna checked off her duties one by one, then double-checked everyone else's. Over the years, efficiency had grown from a habit to an obsession. At noon she downed something that resembled a shrimp salad. The taping should start at three and, if God was in his heaven, be over by eight.

Fortunately, the female celebrity was a repeater who had done *Trivia* at least a dozen times, along with numerous other game shows. That gave Johanna one less headache. She hadn't given Sam Weaver a thought.

So she told herself.

When he arrived, she would turn him and his entourage over to Bethany. It would give her assistant a thrill and keep God's gift to women out of her hair.

She only hoped he could handle the game. The questions were fun, for the most part, but they weren't always easy. More than once she'd had a celebrity grumble and complain because an inability to answer had made him or her look stupid. Johanna made it a policy to see that each show's batch of questions contained the obvious and amusing, as well as the challenging.

It wouldn't be her fault if Sam Weaver turned out to have an empty head. He would only have to smile to gain the audience's forgiveness.

She remembered the way he'd smiled at her when she'd asked if he worked for Jablonski. Yes, that was all it would take to make every woman at home and in the studio turn to putty—except her, of course.

"Check the bell." Johanna stood in the middle of the set and directed her sound technician. At her signal the bright, cheery beep of the winning bell rang. "And the buzzer." The flat drone of the loser sounded. "Bring up the lights in the winner's circle." She nodded in satisfaction as the bulbs flashed.

"The contestants?"

"Sequestered." Bethany checked her clipboard. "We have the accountant from Venice returning from last week. He's a three-game winner. First challenger's a housewife from Ohio in town visiting her sister. Nervous as hell."

"Okay, see if you can help Dottie keep them calm. I'll give the dressing rooms a last check."

Mentally calculating her time as she went, Johanna scooted down the corridor. Her female celebrity was Marsha Tuckett, a comfortable, motherly type who was part of the ensemble of a family series in its third year. A nice contrast for Sam Weaver, she thought. Johanna made sure there were fresh pink roses on the dressing table and plenty of club soda on ice. Satisfied the room was in order, she walked across the narrow hall to the next room.

Because she hadn't thought roses appropriate for Sam Weaver, she'd settled on a nice leafy fern for the corner. As a matter of course she checked the lights, plumped the pillows on the narrow daybed and made certain the towels were fresh and plentiful. A last look showed her nothing he could find fault with. Carelessly she stole a mint from the bowl on the table and popped it into her mouth, then turned.

He was in the doorway.

"Hello again." He'd already decided to make it his business to find her, but he hadn't expected to be quite so lucky. He stepped into the room and dropped a garment bag negligently over a chair.

Johanna pushed the candy into the corner of her mouth. The dressing room was small, but she couldn't recall feeling trapped in it before. "Mr. Weaver." She put on her best at-your-service smile as she offered a hand.

"It's Sam. Remember?" He took her hand and stepped just close enough to make her uncomfortable. They both knew it wasn't an accident.

"Of course. Sam. We're all delighted you could join us. We'll have our run-through shortly. In the meantime, you can let me or one of the staff know if you need anything." She looked past him, puzzled. "Are you alone?"

"Was I supposed to bring someone?"

"No." Where was his secretary, his assistant, his gofer? His current lover?

"According to my instructions, all I needed was five changes. Casual. Will this do to start?"

She studied the navy crewneck and the buff-colored slacks as though it mattered. "You look fine."

She'd known who he was all along, Sam thought. He wasn't so much annoyed as curious. And she wasn't comfortable with him now. That was something else to think about. Making a woman comfortable wasn't always a goal. After reaching for a mint himself, he rested a hip against the dressing table. It was a move that brought him just a little closer. Her lipstick had worn off, he noticed. He found the generous and unpainted shape of her mouth appealing.

"I watched the tape you sent."

"Good. You'll have more fun if you're familiar with the format. Make yourself comfortable." She spoke quickly but not hurriedly. That was training. But she wanted out, and she wanted out now. That was instinct. "One of the staff will be along to take you to Makeup."

"I also read credits." He blocked the door in an offhand way. "I noticed that a Johanna Patterson is executive producer. You?"

"Yes." Damn it, he was making her jittery. She couldn't remember the last time anyone had been able to make her nervous. Cool, controlled and capable. Anyone who knew her would have given that description. She glanced deliberately at her watch. "I'm sorry I can't stay and chat, but we're on a schedule."

He didn't budge. "Most producers don't hand-deliver contracts."

She smiled. Though on the surface it was sweet, he saw the ice underneath and wondered at it. "I'm not most producers."

"I won't argue with that." It was more than attraction now, it was a puzzle that had to be solved. He'd managed to resist any number of women, but he'd never been able to resist a puzzle. "Since we missed lunch before, how about dinner?"

"I'm sorry. I'm—"

"Booked. Yeah, so you said." He tilted his head just a bit, as if to study her from a new angle. It was more than the fact that he was used to women being available. It was the fact that she seemed bound and determined to brush him off, and not very tactfully. "You're not wearing any rings."

"You're observant."

"Involved?"

"With what?"

He had to laugh. His ego wasn't so inflated that he couldn't take no for an answer. He simply preferred a reason for it. "What's the problem, Johanna? Didn't you like my last movie?"

"Sorry. I missed it," she lied, smiling. "Now if you'll excuse me, I've got a show to see to."

He was still standing at the door, but this time she brushed past him. And against him. Both felt a jolt, unexpected and tingling.

Annoyed, Johanna kept walking.

Intrigued, Sam kept watching.

She had to admit, he was a pro. By the middle of the taping of the first show, Sam had gotten in a casual and very competent plug for his new miniseries *No Roses for Sarah*. So effective, that Johanna knew she'd tune in herself. The sponsors and the network brass would be delighted. He'd charmed his partner, the mother of two from Columbus, who had walked onto the set so tense that her voice had come out in squeaks. He'd even managed to answer a few questions correctly.

It was hard not to be impressed, though she worked at it. When the lights were on and the tape was rolling he was the embodiment of that elusive and too often casually used word: *star*. John Jay's posturing and flashing incisors shifted to the background.

Not all entertainers were at ease in front of a live audience. He was. Johanna noted that he was able to turn on just the right amount of enthusiasm and enjoyment when the cameras were rolling, but also that he played to the studio audience during breaks by joking with his competitor and occasionally answering a question someone shouted out at him.

He even seemed to be genuinely pleased when his partner won five hundred in cash in the bonus speed round.

Even if he was just putting on a good face, Johanna couldn't fault him for it. Five hundred dollars meant a great deal to the mother of two from Columbus. Just as much as her moment in the sun with a celebrated heartthrob.

"We've got a very tight game going here, folks." John Jay smiled importantly at the camera. "This final question will determine today's champion, who will then go to the winner's circle and try for ten thousand dollars. Hands on your buzzers." He drew the card from the slot on his dais. "And the final question, for the championship, is…who created Winnie the Pooh?"

Sam's finger was quick on the trigger. The woman from Columbus looked at him pleadingly. John Jay called for a dramatic silence.

"A. A. Milne."

"Ladies and gentlemen, we have a new champion!"

As the cheers got louder and his partner threw her arms around his neck, Sam caught Johanna's look of surprise. It was easy to read her mind and come up with the fact that she didn't see him as a man who could read and remember storybooks—especially not classic children's books.

John Jay said the official goodbyes to the accountant from Venice and broke for a commercial. Sam had to all but carry his partner to the winner's circle. As he settled back in his chair, he glanced at Johanna.

"How'm I doing?"

"Sixty seconds," she said, but her voice was friendlier because she saw he was holding his partner's hand to calm her.

When the minute was up, John Jay managed to make the woman twice as nervous as he ran down the rules and the possibilities. The clock started on the first question. They weren't so difficult, Sam realized. It was the pressure that made them hard. He wasn't immune to it himself. He really wanted her to win. When he saw she was beginning to fumble, he blanked out the lights and the camera the way he did during any important scene. The rules said he could answer only two questions for her. Once he did, letting her keep her viselike grip on his hand, she was over the hump.

There were ten seconds left when John Jay, his voice pitched to the correct level of excitement, posed the last question. "Where was Napoleon's final defeat?"

She knew it. Of course she knew it. The problem was to get the word out. Sam inched forward in the impossibly uncomfortable swivel chair and all but willed her to spit out the word.

"Waterloo!" she shouted, beating the buzzer by a heartbeat. Above their heads, *10,000* began to flash in bold red lights. His partner screamed, kissed him full on the mouth, then screamed again. While they were breaking for a commercial, Sam was holding her head between her knees and telling her to take deep breaths.

"Mrs. Cook?" Johanna knelt down beside them and monitored the woman's pulse. This wasn't the first time a contestant had reacted so radically. "Are you going to be all right?"

"I won. I won ten thousand dollars."

"Congratulations." Johanna lifted the woman's head far enough to be certain it was merely a case of hyperventilation. "We're going to take a fifteen-minute break. Would you like to lie down?"

"No. I'm sorry." Mrs. Cook's color was coming back. "I'm all right."

"Why don't you go with Beth? She'll get you some water."

"Okay. I'm fine, really." Too excited to be embarrassed, Mrs. Cook managed to stand, with Johanna taking one arm and Sam the other. "It's just that I've never won anything before. My husband didn't even come. He took the kids to the beach."

"You'll have a wonderful surprise for him," Johanna said soothingly, and kept walking. "Take a little breather, then you can start thinking about how you're going to spend that money."

"Ten thousand dollars," Mrs. Cook said faintly as she was passed over to Beth.

"Do you get a lot of fainters?" Sam asked.

"Our share. Once we had to stop taping because a construction worker slid right out of his seat during the speed round." She watched a moment longer until she was satisfied Bethany had Mrs. Cook under control. "Thanks. You acted quickly."

"No problem. I've had some practice."

She thought of women fainting at his feet. "I'll bet. There'll be cold drinks and fresh fruit in your dressing room. As long as Mrs. Cook's recovered, we'll start the tape in ten minutes."

He took her arm before she could move away. "If it wasn't my last movie, what is it?"

"What is what?"

"All these little barbs I feel sticking into my heart. You have a problem with me being here?"

"Of course not. We're thrilled to have you."

"Not we. You."

"I'm thrilled to have you here," she corrected, wishing he didn't make it a habit to stand almost on top of her. Her low heels brought her eyes level with his mouth. She discovered it wasn't the most comfortable view. "This series of contests, like your movie, will be shown during the May sweeps. What could be better?"

"A friendly conversation, over dinner."

"You're persistent, Mr. Weaver."

"I'm puzzled, Ms. Patterson."

Her lips very nearly twitched. There was something cute about the way he drawled her last name. "A simple no shouldn't puzzle a man who obviously thinks so well on his feet." Deliberately she looked at her watch. "Half your break's up. You'd better change."

Because things ran smoothly, they were able to tape three shows before the dinner break. Johanna began to have fantasies about finishing on time. She kept them to herself, knowing how easy it was to jinx success. The dinner spread wasn't elaborate, but it was plentiful. Johanna didn't believe in pinching pennies over such minor matters as food. She wanted to keep her celebrities happy and her contestants at ease.

During the break she didn't sit, but grabbed a plate and a few essentials and kept herself available. The audience had been cleared, and new ticketholders would be allowed in for the two final tapings. All she had to do was avoid any crises, keep the energy level up and make certain John Jay didn't proposition any of the females on set.

With the first in mind, Johanna kept her eyes on the new challenger, a young woman from Orange County who appeared to be about six months pregnant.

"Problem?"

She'd forgotten that her other prerequisite had been to avoid Sam Weaver. Reminding herself to keep the celebrities happy, she turned to him as she plucked a small chilled shrimp from her plate. "No, why?"

"You don't relax, do you?" Without expecting an answer, he chose a slim carrot stick from her plate. "I've noticed you're watching Audrey like a hawk."

She wasn't surprised that he already knew the expectant

mother by her first name. "Just being cautious." She bit into the shrimp and unbent enough to smile at him. After all, the day was nearly over. "During one of my early shows we had an expectant mother go into labor in the winner's circle. It's not an experience you forget."

"What did she have?" he asked, testing.

"A boy." Her smile became more generous as her eyes met his. It was one of her best memories. "By the time she was halfway to the hospital the staff had a pool going." She swallowed the last of the shrimp. "I won."

So she liked to bet. He'd keep that in mind. "I don't think you have to worry about Audrey. She's not due until the first part of August." He caught Johanna's curious look. "I asked," he explained. "Now, can I ask you a question? Professional," he added when he sensed her withdrawal.

"Of course."

"How often do you have to wind John Jay up?"

She had to laugh, and she didn't bother to object when he snitched a cube of cheddar from her plate. "Wind down's more like it. He's harmless, really. Only he thinks he's irresistible."

"He told me the two of you were…cozy."

"Really?" She glanced briefly over in the show's host's direction. The haughty look was so casual and innate that Sam grinned. "He's also an optimist."

He was glad to hear it. Very glad. "Well, he does his job. Somehow he manages to hit the note between cheerleader and father confessor."

Covering her personal opinion with her professional one was an old habit. To her, entertainment was first and last a business. "Actually, we're lucky to have him. He hosted another show about five years back, so he's not only familiar but also has a strong appeal to the home viewer."

"Are you going to eat that sandwich?"

Without answering, Johanna took half of the roast-beef-and-Swiss and handed it to him. "Are you enjoying yourself so far?"

"More than I'd expected." He took a bite. So she had a taste for hot mustard. He was fond of spice himself, and in more than food. "Will you be offended if I tell you I kicked a bit about doing it?"

"No. I'm the first to admit that the show isn't Shakespeare, but it serves its purpose." Leaning against a wall, she watched one of the crew heap on a second helping. "What have you found appealing about it?"

He avoided the obvious answer. Her. The one he gave was equally true. "I got a kick out of seeing those people win. Of course, I developed a soft spot for Mrs. Cook. Why do you do it?"

She avoided several possible answers. The one she settled on was true enough. "I enjoy it." When he offered her his glass of sparkling water and lime, she accepted without thinking. She was relaxed, optimistic about the rest of the day and, though she didn't realize it, comfortable in his company.

"I hesitate to point this out, but it looks like we're having dinner after all."

She looked at him again, slowly, gauging him and her reaction to him. If she'd had a different background, different memories, fewer disillusionments, she would have been flattered. More, she would have been tempted. He had a way of looking at her as though they were alone; as though, if they'd been in a room with hundreds of other people, he would have picked her, and only her, out.

Trick of the trade, she told herself, disliking her own cynicism.

"Isn't it handy we got that out of the way?" She handed him back his glass.

"Yeah. It should make it easier for us to do it again."

Casually she signaled to the crew to begin clearing up. "I don't want to rush you, but we'll start taping again in fifteen minutes."

"I never miss my cue." He shifted his body just enough to prevent her from walking by him. He had the moves, Johanna thought. Very smooth. Very slick. "I get the impression you like to play games, Johanna."

There was a dare in his voice. She caught it, and was trapped. Though her voice was cool again, she stood her ground and met his gaze. "Depends on the stakes."

"Okay, how's this? If I win the next two games you'll have dinner with me. I set the time and the place."

"I don't like those stakes."

"I haven't finished. If I lose I come back on the show within six months. No fee." That had her attention, he noted, pleased with himself. He hadn't misjudged her dedication to her show or her weakness for a dare.

"Within six months," she repeated, studying him to assess whether he could be trusted. Not an inch, she decided, on many matters. But she didn't see him as a man to welsh on a bet.

"Deal?" He made his voice deliberately challenging as he held out a hand.

It was too good a bet to turn down. His eyes were too mocking to ignore. "Deal." She set her palm against his, then removed it and stepped away. "Ten minutes, Mr. Weaver."

Johanna had a very bad feeling when Sam and his teammate took the first game. Since the conception of the show, she'd

The Name of the Game

had a strict personal policy against rooting for either side. It didn't matter that no one could read her thoughts. She knew them, and prejudice of any kind was unprofessional. She certainly would never have imagined herself actually rooting against a certain team. She did now.

It was because she wanted him back on the show, she told herself when the last taping of the day began. The producer, not the woman, had made the bet. It was ridiculous to think that she was afraid, even uneasy, about having a meal with him. That would only be a small annoyance—like a spoonful of bad-tasting medicine.

But she stood behind camera two and cheered inwardly when the opposing team took the lead.

He didn't show nerves. Sam was much too skilled an actor to show nerves in front of a camera. But they dogged him. It was the principle, he told himself. That was the only reason he was so determined to win and make Johanna pay the price. He certainly wasn't infatuated. He'd been around too long to be infatuated just because a woman was beautiful. And aloof, his mind added. And contrary and stubborn. And damn sexy.

He wasn't infatuated. He just hated to lose.

By the beginning of the final round, the two teams were neck and neck. The studio audience was loud and raucous, the contestants wired. Johanna's stomach was in knots. When Sam turned and winked at her during the commercial break she nearly bared her teeth.

Positions jockeyed back and forth. Professionally Johanna knew that when the show aired it would pull the television audience in. That was, after all, the name of the game. Personally, she'd hoped for a landslide, however boring.

When the final question came up, she held her breath. Sam

was quick to push the button, but his partner was quicker. He nearly swore. The expectant mother from Orange County had more than her own fate in her hands.

"Surrender, Dorothy!" she shouted. When the lights went on, Sam took her face in his hands and kissed her. Hard. Audrey would be able to dine out on the moment for months. Sam kept his arm around her as they walked toward the winner's circle. Once she was settled, he strolled casually over to Johanna and bent closer to her ear.

"Saturday night, seven. I'll pick you up."

She only nodded. It was hard to speak when your teeth were clenched.

Johanna found several vital tasks to perform after the taping was completed. She did not, as was her habit, say a personal thank-you to both guest stars. That job was handed over to Bethany. She made herself scarce for thirty minutes so that she could be sure Sam Weaver was off and out of her hair. Until Saturday.

She couldn't quite drum up the job-well-done mood the end of the day usually brought her. Instead she made a list of details to see to the following day that would keep her occupied from the time she got up until she crawled back home again. Business as usual, she told herself, and broke the tip off her pencil.

"Everybody's happy," Beth told her. "The questions we didn't use in the speed round are locked back in the safe. The contestants we didn't get to are ready and willing to come back next week. Your dupes." She handed Johanna the tapes. "We've got some great shows. Especially the last one. Even the techs were getting into it. They loved Sam." Bethany pushed back a lock of hair. "And you know how jaded techs can be.

Anyway, it's nice to know that besides being gorgeous and sexy he's got some smarts."

Johanna grunted and dropped the tapes in her carryall.

Bethany tilted her head. "I was going to ask you if you wanted to take some of the leftover fruit home, but it looks more like you'd prefer raw meat."

"It's been a long day."

"Uh-huh." Beth knew her boss better. Johanna had pulled a roll of antacids out of her bag and had popped two of them. A sure sign of trouble. "Want to have a drink and talk about it?"

Johanna had never made it a habit to confide in anyone. There simply hadn't been enough people in her life she could trust. Johanna knew Beth. Her assistant was young and energetic, but she was also trustworthy. She was also the closest thing Johanna had ever had to a foul-weather friend.

"I'll pass on the drink, but how about walking me out to my car?"

"Sure."

The sun hadn't set. Johanna found something reassuring about that after having been inside all day. She'd put the top down, she thought, and take the drive home through the Hills fast. Maybe a bit recklessly. She had a taste for the reckless, a taste she usually controlled. It came from her father. But tonight it might do her good to give in to it for a little while.

"What did you think of Sam Weaver?"

Bethany cocked a brow. "Before or after I stopped drooling?"

"After."

"I liked him," she said simply. "He didn't expect the red carpet, he wasn't condescending and he wasn't snickering behind his hand at the contestants."

"Those are all negative virtues," Johanna pointed out.

"Okay, I liked the way he joked around with the crew. And the way he signed autographs as though he wanted to instead of acting as though he were granting a favor." She didn't add that she'd asked for one herself. "He acted like somebody without making sure everybody remembered that *somebody* was in all capital letters."

"Interestingly said," Johanna murmured. "Are you still keeping that little book with the list of celebrity panelists?"

Beth colored a bit. She was in the business, but that didn't stop her from being a fan. "Yeah. Sam gets five stars."

Johanna's lips twitched a bit at her assistant's top rating. "I guess I should be relieved to hear it. I'm having dinner with him on Saturday."

Bethany's mouth went into the O position. There were stars in her eyes. She simply couldn't help it. "Wow."

"It's confidential."

"Okay," Bethany said, and Johanna knew she was as good as her word. "Johanna, I know you were raised in the business and Cary Grant probably bounced you on his knee, but doesn't it give you a tingle?"

"It gives me a pain," Johanna stated bluntly as she pulled open her car door. "Actors aren't my type."

"Too general."

"Okay, blue-eyed lanky actors with a drawl aren't my type."

"You're sick, Johanna. Very, very sick. You want me to go as proxy?"

She chuckled as she lowered herself into the car. "No. I can handle Sam Weaver."

"Lucky you. Listen, not to pry or anything…"

"But?"

"You will remember the details? I might want to write a book or something."

"Go home, Beth." The engine sprang to life as she twisted the key. Yes, she definitely wanted power and speed tonight.

"Okay, just let me know if he always smells so good. I can live on that."

Shaking her head, Johanna roared out of the lot. She hadn't been interested enough to notice what Sam Weaver had smelled like.

Like a man, her memory informed her. He'd smelled very much like a man.

3

It was only dinner. Nothing to worry about. Certainly nothing, after several days to put it in perspective, to be annoyed about. They would no doubt go to one of L.A.'s flashier restaurants, where Sam could see and be seen. Between the pâté and the double chocolate mousse he would greet and chat with the other glamorous types who patronized that kind of eatery.

Meat houses, her second stepmother had called such places. Not because of the menu but because of the flesh exposed. Darlene had been one of the most honest and least affected of her father's attachments.

If she wanted to stretch a point, Johanna could consider it a business dinner. She found she wanted to stretch a point. She could tolerate this, as she had tolerated many other meals, as a part of the game everyone who wanted to remain part of the business learned to play. Since it was business, she would be charming and chatty, even gracious, until it was over and she could close the door on the entire episode.

She didn't like persistent men.

She didn't like men with reputations.

She didn't like Sam Weaver.

That was before the flowers arrived.

Johanna had spent Saturday morning gardening and half-hoping Sam Weaver wouldn't find her address. He hadn't called to ask her for it or to confirm plans. Waiting for him to do just that had left her jumpy and out of sorts all week. That was just one more sin to lay at his door.

It was her habit whenever she worked outside to take her cordless phone with her. Business could crop up even on weekends. Today, however, she pretended to have forgotten it and spent a warm and pleasant morning tending a plot of columbine.

This was her respite, even her vice, in a way. The flowers she planted were nurtured and cared for. They rewarded her by renewing themselves year after year. Their continuity soothed her. This, as was the case in other areas of her life, was something she'd done with her own hands. Whatever rewards she reaped, whatever failures she suffered, were her own.

The flowers lasted. The people in her life rarely did.

Her jeans were scruffy at the knees and her hands stained with mulch when the delivery man pulled up. Johanna shaded her eyes as she rose.

"Miz Patterson?"

"Yes."

"Sign here, please." The deliveryman met her halfway across her lawn, handing her first his clipboard and then a long white box embossed with a florist's name and tied with a red satin ribbon. "Nice garden you got there," he said with a tip of his hat as he climbed back into the truck.

She was a sucker for flowers. Without waiting to go in and wash up, Johanna opened the box. They were roses. Not a dozen red or two dozen pink, but one long-stemmed sample of every color she'd ever seen, from the purest white to the deepest red, and all the pinks and golds between. Charmed, she lowered her face to the box to draw in their scent.

Heady. Roses were always heady, lush and unashamedly sensual.

It wasn't her birthday. In any case, her father—or rather her father's secretary—wasn't imaginative enough to have thought of such a sweet and charming gift. Though her fingertips were soiled, she pulled open the card that had come with the box. I don't know your favorite color. Yet. Sam.

She wanted to shrug it off. Pretty gestures came so easily to some. It would have taken only a casual order to an assistant to have them delivered. How well she knew it. So he'd found her, she thought with a shrug as she started back across the lawn. The deal was still on, and she'd live up to her end of it.

She tried, really tried, to set them aside and go back to work on the buds she'd planted herself. But she couldn't dismiss the roses, didn't have the heart to dampen her own pleasure. She was smiling when she sniffed the flowers again. Smiling still when she went into the house to arrange them.

He hadn't looked forward to an evening quite so much in a long time. It was easy to compare it to a winning poker hand or a successful day at the track. He'd never cared half as much for the purse as for the winning. He'd have preferred to think of it in those terms, but the truth was that he was looking forward to spending a few hours in Johanna Patterson's company.

Maybe he was intrigued because she was so disinterested. Sam took a turn sharp and fast while the radio blared through the open windows. What man didn't appreciate a challenge? If she'd taken him at his word on their first meeting, they might have enjoyed a pleasant lunch and an easy hour. He'd never know if that would have been the end of it. The fact that she'd refused, and had continued to refuse, only made him more determined to wear her down.

Women came easily to him. Too easily. Sam wouldn't deny he'd gone through a stage when he'd taken advantage of that. But his background, and what many might have considered the rather quaint and traditional values that had gone into it, had surfaced again.

The press could beat the drum of his romantic adventures all they liked. The truth was, he *was* a romantic. Rolling from one bed to the next had never been his style.

There were two Sam Weavers. One was intensely private, guarded about matters like family and relationships, the things that really mattered. The other was an actor, a realist who accepted that the price of fame was public consumption. He gave interviews, didn't bother to dodge the paparazzi and was always willing to sign an autograph. He'd learned to shrug off whatever reports were exaggerations or outright lies. They were the public Sam's problem. The private one couldn't have cared less.

He wondered, given what he now knew about Johanna Patterson's background, which Sam Weaver she would understand.

She was the only child of the respected producer Carl Patterson, the product of his first, and reportedly most tempestuous marriage. Her mother had disappeared or, as some reports put it, "gone into seclusion," after the marriage had failed. Johanna had grown up in the luxury of Beverly Hills, had attended the best schools. Some rumors stated that she adored her father, others that there was no love lost between them. In either case, she was the only offspring Patterson had after four marriages and numerous affairs.

He was surprised that she lived back in the Hills. He'd expected some slick condo in the city or a wing in her father's Beverly Hills estate. The sharp professional woman he'd met seemed out of place so far from the action. He was more surprised when he found the house.

It was tiny. Like a dollhouse, but without the gingerbread. Hardly more than a cabin, it was rustic and sturdy, with the wood unpainted and the panes of glass sparkling in the evening sun. There wasn't much land before the trees and the hills took it over. What was there was uneven and rocky. To compensate—more, to enhance it—flowers and budding vines were everywhere. The dashing little Mercedes parked in the driveway looked as though it had been left there by mistake.

Hands in pockets, he stood beside his own car and looked again. She didn't have any close neighbors, and the view was nothing to write home about, but it seemed as though she'd carved out her own corner of the mountainside. He knew about that. Appreciated it.

When he reached the door, he caught the scent of sweet peas. His mother planted them each spring, outside the kitchen windows. Johanna opened the door and found him smiling.

"Brigadoon," he said, and watched her polite smile turn to an expression of puzzlement. "I was trying to think what your place reminded me of. Brigadoon. Like it's only here once every hundred years."

Damn him, she thought, feeling almost resigned. She'd barely managed to put the roses in perspective and here he was, charming her again. "I wasn't sure you'd find it."

"I have a good sense of direction. Most of the time." He glanced toward the flowers that flanked both sides of her house. "From the looks of things, the roses were overkill."

"No." It would have been petty not to let him know they'd pleased her. "It was sweet of you to send them." He wasn't wearing a dinner suit, but a breezy linen shirt and pleated slacks. Johanna was glad she'd guessed right when she'd bypassed glitz for the subtler lines of a slim-skirted white dress. "If you'd like to come in a minute, I'll get my jacket."

He did, though he thought it would be a shame to cover up her arms and shoulders. The living room was small enough to be cozy. She'd arranged deep chairs by a white bricked fireplace and had added dozens of pillows. It made Sam think that when Johanna was finished with work she liked to take off her shoes and snuggle in.

"This isn't what I expected."

"No?" She pulled on a sizzling tomato-red jacket. "I like it."

"I didn't say I didn't like it, I said it wasn't what I expected." He noted his roses had been given a place of honor on the mantel, tucked prettily in a clear, widemouthed vase that glinted at the bottom with colored pebbles. "Do you have a favorite?"

She glanced at the roses. "No. I just like flowers." The clusters of rubies at her ears glinted as she adjusted them. "Shall we go?"

"In a minute." He crossed to her, noticing with some interest the way she stiffened up. Despite it, he took her hand. "Are you going to be a good sport about this?"

She let out a little sigh. "I've thought about it."

"And?" It was the easy curving of his lips that made her relax.

"I decided I might as well."

"Are you hungry?"

"Some."

"Mind a bit of a ride?"

Curious, she tilted her head. "No, I suppose not."

"Good." He kept her hand in his as they walked outside.

She should have known he was up to something. They didn't drive into the city as she'd expected. Rather than comment, Johanna let the conversation flow as she wondered how to handle him. Actors were a tricky bunch. They knew how to set the stage, how to read their lines, how to put on whatever face was most appropriate to the situation. At the moment, it seemed Sam had chosen to be the casually friendly companion a woman could relax with. Johanna wasn't ready to give him an inch.

He drove fast, just faster than the law allowed and just under the edge of safety. Even when they left the freeway for a road that was rough and sparsely populated, he continued at the same steady clip.

"Mind if I ask where we're going?"

Sam negotiated a lazy turn. He'd wondered how long it would take before she asked. "To dinner."

Johanna turned to study the landscape. The land rolled by, wide and dusty. "Something over an open fire?"

He smiled. She'd used her haughty tone again, and damned if he didn't enjoy hearing it. "No, I thought we'd eat at my place."

His place. The thought of dining privately with him didn't alarm her. She was too confident of her ability to handle whatever situation cropped up. She was more curious about the fact that he would have a *place* this far from the glitz. "You have a cave?"

Because there was amusement in her voice now, his smile

widened. "I can do a little better than that. I only eat in restaurants when it's necessary."

"Why?"

"Because you end up doing business, or being stared at. I wasn't in the mood for either tonight." Pebbles spit from under the tires as he turned to drive through a plain wooden gate.

"That's part of the game, isn't it?"

"Sure, but there has to be a reason to play it." He whizzed by a pretty white house with blue shutters, giving two blasts of his horn. "My foreman and his family live there. If he knows it's me he won't come looking for trespassers."

They passed barns and sheds, and she was surprised that they looked as though they had a purpose other than a decorative one. She spotted paddocks with split rail fencing and dark, rich dirt. A dog—or what sounded like a pair of them—began to bark.

The road forked, and then she saw the ranch house. It, too, was white, but the shutters were gray and the three chimneys it boasted were brick weathered to a dusky rose. It was low and spreading, shaped like an H turned on its side. For all its size, it didn't overpower. There were rockers on the porch, sturdy wooden ones that gave the impression that someone sat in them often. Window boxes had been freshly painted a bright, sassy red. Tumbling out of them were pansies and bushy impatiens. Though the air here was hot and dry, they were thriving and well tended.

Johanna stepped out of the car to turn a slow circle. It certainly looked like a working ranch. "Quite a place."

"I like it," he said, mimicking her earlier remark.

She acknowledged that with a quick, though cautious, smile. "It must be inconvenient to commute."

"I keep a place in L.A." He shrugged it off as though it were no more than a storage closet. "The best thing about finishing a film is being able to come back here and dig in for a while. Before I got hooked on acting, I'd wanted to come west and work on a ranch." He took her arm as they walked up the two wooden steps to the porch. They creaked. For some reason, Johanna found that endearing. "I was lucky enough to do both."

She glanced at the pansies, with their arrogant Alice-in-Wonderland faces. "Do you raise cattle?"

"Horses." He'd left the door unlocked. It was a habit he'd grown up with. "I bought the place about three years ago. Convinced my accountant that it'd be a great tax shelter. It made him feel better."

The hardwood floors were polished to a high gloss, scattered with hand-hooked rugs in muted pastels. In the entrance a collection of pewter—bowls, spoons, mugs, even a dented candlestick—was arranged on a waist-high table. The early twilight crept through the windows.

It had a good feel, a solid feel. Though she would never had admitted it out loud, Johanna had always felt strongly that houses had their own personalities. She'd selected her own house because it had made her feel warm and comfortable. She'd left her father's because it had been possessive and dishonest.

"Do you get to stay here often?" she asked him.

"Not often enough." He glanced around at the walls, which he'd painted himself. The house, like his career, was something he never took for granted. Though he'd never known poverty, he'd been taught to appreciate security, and that nothing replaced sweat for earning it. "Would you like a drink, or would you rather go for dinner?"

"Dinner," she said firmly. She knew better than to drink, socially or otherwise, on an empty stomach.

"I was hoping you'd say that." In the casual way he had, he took her hand and led her down the hall. The wing of the house ran straight. At the end it opened up into a large country kitchen. Copper pots hung from hooks over a center island. The room was flanked by counters and cabinets on one side and a small stone hearth on the other. A ribbon of windows gave an open view of dusk settling over a brick terrace and a mosaic pool. She'd thought to find a servant or two busily preparing the evening meal. Instead, all she found was the scent of cooking.

"It smells wonderful."

"Good." Scooping up two hot pads, Sam bent down to the oven. "I left it on warm." He drew out a casserole of bubbly lasagna.

Food wasn't something that usually excited her, but now the scent alone drew her over to his side. How long had it been since she'd seen someone take a homemade meal out of an oven? "It looks wonderful, too."

"My mother always told me food tastes better if it looks good." He picked up a long loaf of Italian bread and began slicing.

"You didn't cook this."

"Why not?" He glanced over his shoulder, amused that she was frowning again. She looked so thoughtful that he was tempted to run a fingertip down the faint line that formed between her brows. "Cooking's a very manageable skill if you approach it properly and have the right incentive."

Johanna stuck with carryout or prepackaged microwave meals. "And you have both?"

"I wanted to be an actor, but I didn't have any desire to be a starving actor." He poured garlic butter over the bread, set the oven, then slid it in. "After I came to California, I kicked around from audition to audition and from greasy spoon to greasy spoon. A couple of months of that and I called home and asked my mother for some recipes. She's a great cook." Sam drew the cork from a bottle of wine, then set it aside to breathe. "Anyway, it took me a lot less time to figure out how to sauté trout than it did for me to get a memorable part."

"Now that you've had a number of memorable parts, what's your incentive?"

"To cook?" He shrugged and took a leafy spinach salad from the refrigerator. "I like it. We're about ready here. You want to grab the wine? I thought we'd eat outside."

The trouble with Hollywood, Johanna thought as she followed him out, was that things were never what they seemed. She'd been sure she had Sam Weaver pegged. But the man she'd assessed and dismissed wouldn't have copied recipes from his mother.

Nor was he the type, she thought as she set the wine down, who would have prepared a charming dinner for two, alfresco, with pretty blue stoneware plates and thick yellow candles. It was every bit as friendly as it was romantic. The romance she'd expected, and she knew just how to discourage it. The offer of friendship was another matter.

"Light those candles, will you?" He glanced around briefly, checking the way a man did when he was already certain things were just as he wanted them to be. "I'll get the rest."

Johanna watched him go back inside. Did someone who walked like that, she wondered—as though he were heading toward a shoot-out—really prepare spinach salad? She struck a match and held it to the wick of the first candle. Apparently so. There were more important things to lie about than cooking. She held the match to the second candle, then deliberately blew it out. She wouldn't have called avoiding three on a match superstitious. Just practical.

She heard the music he put on, something low and bluesy, with a lot of sax. While he brought out the rest of the meal, she poured the wine.

His instincts had been right, Sam thought as they settled at the wicker table. He'd been on the verge of making dinner reservations at some tony restaurant when he'd pulled back. He'd cooked for women before, but never here. He never brought anyone to the ranch, because the ranch was home. Private. Off limits to the press and the public, it was both refuge and sanctuary from a world he was a voluntary member of—when he chose to be. At the time, he hadn't been sure why he'd wanted to break his own rule with Johanna. Now he began to understand.

At the ranch he could be himself—no pretenses, no roles. Here he was Sam Weaver from Virginia, and here he was most comfortable. He didn't have to be *on* here. And he wanted to be himself with Johanna.

She wasn't without pretenses, he mused as he watched her. Not entirely. Unless he missed his guess, most of her resentment had faded, but not her distrust. He'd already decided to ease his curiosity and find the reason for it.

Maybe she'd been stung in an affair that had gone sour. Broken hearts often mended jaggedly. If she had been betrayed by a man she'd cared for and trusted, it would be logical that she would put up some defences. It might take some time before he could wear them down, but he had a feeling it would be worth it. He'd start with what he believed was the focus of her life: her work.

"Were you happy with the taping the other day?"

"More than." She was too fair-minded not to give him his due. "You were really good, not just as far as the answers went, but overall. A lot of times you can have people zip right through the questions and be a dead bore." She broke off a piece of bread, then nibbled at the crust. He'd hit the right tone. It was always easy for her to relax when the subject was business. "And, of course, it was a coup to have you."

"I'm flattered."

She studied him again with those cool blue eyes. "I doubt it would be that easy to flatter you."

"An actor always wants to be wanted. Well, to a point, anyway," he added with another quick grin. "Do you know how many game shows I've turned down in the last couple of days?"

She smiled and sipped her wine. "Oh, I could hazard a guess."

"How'd you get into it? Producing?"

"Heredity." Her lips tightened only briefly. After taking a second sip, she set her glass down. "I guess you could say I like pulling the strings."

"You'd have learned young with Carl Patterson as your father." He saw it, very briefly but very clearly. More than resentment, less than pain. "He's produced some of the best, and most successful television shows, as well as an impressive number of features. Being second-generation can be a strain, I imagine."

"You get past it." The lasagna was cheesy and rich with spices. Johanna concentrated on it. "This really is terrific. Your mother's recipe?"

"With some variations." So her father was off limits. He could respect that—for now. "How about the show itself? How did that get started?"

"With the flu." At ease again, she smiled and took another bite.
"Care to elaborate?"

"I had the flu, a nasty bout of it, a couple of years ago. I had to stay in bed for a week, and since it hurt my eyes to read, I lay there hour after hour and watched television. The game shows hooked me." She didn't object when he topped off her glass. The wine was very mellow and dry, and she knew her limit right down to the swallow. "You get involved, you know, in the games, and the people playing them. After a while you start rooting for them, tensing up in an effort to help them. When someone wins, the vicarious thrill is automatic. And then you have the advantage of almost always being smarter at home, because there's no pressure. That's a nice smug feeling."

He watched her as she spoke. She was animated now, the way she'd been while she'd rushed around the set making sure things fell into place. "So after your bout with the flu you decided to produce one."

"More or less." She could remember running into the brick wall of the network brass and ultimately having to appeal to her father. "In any case, I had the concept, and the experience in producing. I'd done a couple of documentaries for public television and had worked on a prime-time special. With a little string-pulling, we got a pilot done. Now we're only a couple of ratings points from being on top. I'm waiting for the go-ahead to start evening syndication."

"What happens then?"

"The demographics open. You get the kids who've finished their homework, the business crowd who want to put their feet up for a half hour. You up the ante. Give away some cars, bigger bucks."

She was surprised to discover she'd cleared her plate. Usually she ate a few bites, then ended up picking at the rest, impatient for the meal—and the time sitting down—to be over.

"Want some more?"

"No. Thanks." She picked up her wine as she studied him. "I know I lost the bet, but it looks as though I got the best part of the deal."

"Not from where I'm sitting."

The shades came down. Just like that. One compliment, however offhand, and she pulled back. Seeing it, Sam rose and offered a hand. "Want to walk? There's enough moonlight."

There was no point in being ungracious, Johanna told herself. She hated it when she became prickly over something unimportant. "All right. The only ranches I've ever seen have been on the back lot."

He bundled up the last of the bread, then handed it to her. "We'll go by the pond. You can feed the ducks."

"You have ducks?"

"Several overfed ducks." He slipped an arm around her shoulders to steer her. She smelled like the evening they walked through, quiet and promising. "I like looking at them in the morning."

"Your Jake in *Half-Breed* would have eaten them for breakfast."

"So you did see my last movie."

She took a quick nip at the tip of her tongue. "Oh, was that your last one?"

"Too late. You've already boosted my ego."

When she looked at him, his smile was appealing and too easy to respond to. *He* was too easy to respond to. In self-defense she looked back at the house.

"It's lovely from out here, too. You live all alone?"

"I like a little solitude now and then. Of course, I've got a few hands who look after things while I'm working, and Mae comes in a couple times a week to scoop at the dust." His hand slipped down to take hers. "My family comes out a few times a year and shakes everything up."

"Your parents visit you here?"

"Them, my brother, my two sisters, their families. Assorted cousins. The Weavers are a large and loud bunch."

"I see." But she didn't. She could only imagine. And envy. "They must be proud of you."

"They were always supportive, even when they thought I was crazy."

The pond was almost a quarter mile from the house, but the going was easy. It was obvious he walked the path often. She caught the scent of citrus, then the stronger scent of water. The moonlight struck it, highlighting the grass which had been left to grow ankle-high. Sensing an audience, several brown and speckled ducks paddled over to the water's edge.

"I've never had the nerve to come out here empty-handed," he told her. "I think they'd follow me home."

Johanna opened the linen cloth and broke off a crust of bread. It didn't even hit the water before it was gobbled up. She laughed; it was a low, delighted sound deep in her throat. Immediately she tore off another piece and, tossing this one farther out, watched a drake zoom in on it.

"I've always wanted to watch them from underneath so I could see their feet scramble." She continued to break off and toss. Ducks pursued the bread in groups and squabbled over it with bad-tempered quacks and competitive pecks. "My mother and I used to go out and feed the ducks. We'd give them silly names, then see if we could tell them apart the next time."

She caught herself, amazed that the memory had surfaced, stunned that she'd shared it. Her hand closed into a fist over the bread.

"There was a pond about five miles away when I was a kid," Sam said, as if he hadn't noticed her change in mood. "We used to ride our bikes to it during the summer, after we'd stolen a pack of crackers or whatever from the kitchen. We'd toss it out for the ducks—and a couple of pushy swans—and accidentally fall in as often as possible." He glanced out over the water. "Looks like someone's had a family."

She followed his gaze and saw a brown duck gliding along, trailed by a long shadow. As it came closer, Johanna saw that the shadow wasn't a shadow, it was fluffy ducklings. "Oh, aren't they sweet?" She crouched down for a closer look, forgetting about the hem of her skirt. The babies followed Mama on their evening swim, straight as an arrow. "I wish there was more light," she murmured.

"Come back when there is."

Johanna tilted her head up. In the moonlight his face was stronger, more attractive, than it had a right to be. The eyes, eyes that invariably drew women in, were as dark as the water. And, as with the water, Johanna didn't know what lay beneath the surface. Turning away again, she continued shredding the bread and tossing it.

He liked the way her hair haloed around her face, stopping just inches from her shoulders. A man could fill his hands with it. It would be soft, like the hand she rarely offered but he continued to take. It would carry that same subtle scent.

Her skin would be like that, on the back of her neck beneath all that heavy blond hair. He had an urge to touch it now, to skim his fingers over it and see if she trembled.

The ducks stopped their chatter when the last of the bread was consumed. A few hopefuls hung around the edge of the pond for a minute longer, then, satisfied the treat was done, glided away. Into the sudden silence came a night bird's song, and the rustle of a rabbit running into the brush.

"It's a lovely spot," she said, rising and brushing the crumbs from her fingers. "I can see why you like it so much."

"I want you to come back."

It was said very simply, so it shouldn't have meant so much. Johanna didn't back away, because that would have been admitting it did. If her heart was beating a little faster, she could pretend otherwise. She reminded herself that things often seemed more important in the moonlight than they did in the day.

"We had a bet. I lost." She said it lightly, already aware that the tone wouldn't matter. "But that's been paid up tonight."

"This has nothing to do with bets or games." He touched her hair as he'd wanted to. "I want you to come back."

She should have been able to shrug it off, to nip it before whatever was beginning to grow would blossom. It wasn't as easy as it should have been to dredge up the cool smile and the careless refusal. She looked at him, really looked at him, and could think of only one thing to say.

"Why?"

His lips curved. She watched the smile move slowly over his face, the angles shifting, the shadows playing. "Damned if I know. But when you do come back, maybe we'll both have an answer. Meanwhile, why don't we get this one question out of the way?"

He leaned toward her. She'd told herself she didn't want to be kissed. She wouldn't like it. She wasn't a demonstrative person, and for her a kiss wasn't merely a touching of lips. Even though she'd grown up in a world where a kiss was nothing more than a handshake—and often less binding—to her it was a personal thing that meant affection, trust, warmth.

She'd told herself she wouldn't be kissed. But that had been before the moonlight and the bird's song. That had been before he'd touched her.

Her eyes were wary. He saw that even as he brushed his lips lightly over hers. He'd meant it to be light, casual, hardly more than a peace offering. She was so cool and lovely, and so firmly on guard, that he'd been unable to resist.

An easy kiss. A friendly kiss. That was where he'd meant to begin and end it. That was before he'd tasted her.

He drew back, not quite sure of his footing. He hadn't been prepared for whatever had rushed into him, not for the punch of it. With the water lapping beside them, he stared down at her. Moonlight was on her face, and he touched her cheek where the light played. She didn't move. He couldn't know that her own stunned reaction had left her rooted to the spot.

He touched her again, drawing his fingers back through her hair until they gripped it. Still she didn't move. But when his lips came to hers again, hard, hungry, she met passion with passion.

She'd never wanted it to be like this. Desire raced through her, pushing her to keep pace with it. His mouth ran along her jaw, across her face, making her shiver with pleasure, but she twisted until their lips joined again.

A craving she'd never known she had…a dream she'd never allowed into her waking hours…that was what he was. Wherever his hands touched, they lingered, as if he couldn't get enough. Lost in the first wave of pleasure, she pressed against him.

No, he couldn't get enough. He pulled her head back and deepened the kiss. She tasted like the night, dark, haunted. The thin silk under her jacket teased and shifted until he had to force back the urge to tear it away. He wanted her, all of her. There, in the tall, damp grass, he wanted to discover all her secrets and make them his own.

She was breathless when they drew apart. That frightened her. Caution and control had been hard-learned lessons, and she always, without exception, applied them to all the areas of her life. She'd lost them both in the flash of an instant, in the brush of his lips.

She had to remember what he was: an artist, both in his craft and with his women. More, she had to remember what she was. There was no room in her life for reckless passion In the moonlight.

He reached for her again, just to trace his knuckles along her cheek. Because even that affected her, she moved aside.

"This isn't the answer for either of us." She didn't like hearing the strain in her own voice, or the lingering huskiness he'd caused.

"It was a lot more than I bargained for," he admitted. The defenses were going up again. He took her hand before she could withdraw behind them completely. "I felt something the first time I saw you. Now I begin to see why."

"Lust at first sight?"

"Damn it, Johanna."

She'd hated herself the moment she'd said it, but she couldn't back down. If she backed down, she'd give in. "Let's let it go, Sam. I'll be honest and say that was more than nice, but I'm just not interested in the sequel."

Anger stirred. He knew his own temper well enough to take

things slow. He'd never decked a woman. Yet. "What are you interested in?"

She recognized barely restrained fury when she heard it. It was almost a relief. If he'd been kind, if he'd been the least bit persuasive, she would have crumbled. "My job." She tried for a smile and almost managed it. "That's really enough complications for me."

"Lady, anybody who can kiss like that is just asking for complications."

She hadn't known she could kiss like that. She certainly hadn't known she'd wanted to. And what was even more unnerving was that she wanted to kiss him again. "I suppose that's a compliment. Shall we just say it was an interesting evening and leave it at that?"

"No."

"That's the best I can do."

He touched her hair again. It wasn't a testing gesture this time, it was a possessive one. "Okay. You'll learn as you go along."

She couldn't pretend to be amused, because he was frightening her. It wasn't a fear that he would drag her to the ground and finish what they'd both started, but it was a fear that he would prove to be stronger-willed and much more determined than she.

Stay out of his way, her mind warned her. And get started on it now.

"It was much too nice an evening to end it with an argument. I appreciate the meal and the walk. Now it's getting late, and since it's a long drive, we should be going."

"All right." He was much too annoyed to fight with her. Better, he thought, that he do exactly as she asked, then reevaluate the situation. Turning homeward, he reached out to guide her so that she wouldn't stumble. When she jerked at his touch, he smiled again, and most of his annoyance left him.

"The longest trips are often the most eventful, don't you think?"

She thought it best to leave that question unanswered.

4

"Just how many cases of Diet Zing do we have?" Johanna waited for Bethany to run down her list.

"Considering what the crew pinched, about a hundred and fifty cases. We're square on the porto-vacs and the gift certificates and, of course, the encyclopedias." Bethany turned over the list of parting gifts. Though she thought it odd that Johanna was staring out the window rather than checking off her own list, she didn't comment. "About the home viewers' contest," Bethany began.

"Hmmm?"

"The home viewers' contest?"

"Oh." Johanna swore at herself, then pulled her gaze away from the window and her mind away from Sam Weaver. Daydreaming was always a waste of time, but it was a sin during office hours. "I want to get that nailed down this morning." She unlocked the top drawer of her desk and pulled out a file. "I have several potential questions. Research put in a lot of extra time on it last week. The idea is to have John Jay announce a different one every day, somewhere during the program." She glanced down the list again to satisfy herself. "I don't want him to do it at the same time every day, particularly not at the beginning. If we're going to draw people in, I want them to watch all day, all week. Is the deal on the car set?"

"Almost. We're going with the American product and tying it in with the drawing the week of the Fourth of July."

"Fine, but I want two."

"Two what?"

"Two cars, Beth. Watch *Trivia Alert* and win." She smiled a bit and tapped the end of her pencil on the desk. "Two luxury cars. One should be a convertible. People in Omaha with two kids don't usually buy convertibles. Let's make it a red one, at least for the ads. We'll have the full-sized car in white and John Jay in a blue suit."

"Hit them over the head with patriotism?"

"Something like that. See if we can bring the total value up to fifty thousand."

"Sure." Bethany blew her bangs away from her eyes. "I'll use charm. And if that doesn't work I'll use Mongo the enforcer."

"Use the ratings," Johanna suggested. "I want a big ad in the *TV Guide* and the Sunday supplements. Black and white for the guide, color for the supplements." She waited while Bethany made her notes. "The ten-second spot at ten is already set. We'll tape it as soon as the cars are delivered. We have to pick five questions from the list." She handed Bethany a copy. "And the list doesn't go out of this office."

Bethany skimmed down. "Where did Betty meet the leader of the pack?" Lips pursed, she glanced up. "Betty who?"

"Brush up on your girl groups. Early-sixties rock and roll."

Bethany merely made a face. "These are pretty tough."

That was exactly what she'd wanted to hear. "They're worth fifty thousand."

Giving a quiet murmur of agreement, she checked another question. "Johanna, how could anyone know how many witches were burned at the stake in Salem?"

"None." Sitting back, Johanna ran the pencil through her fingers. "They were hanged."

"Oh. Well, so far I'm batting a thousand." When Johanna's phone rang, Bethany took another hard look at the questions.

"Mr. Weaver's on the line, Ms. Patterson."

Johanna opened her mouth and was surprised when nothing came out.

"Ms. Patterson?"

"What? Oh, tell Mr. Weaver I'm in a meeting."

When she hung up, Beth glanced over. "I wouldn't have minded waiting."

"I doubt he's calling to discuss the show." Telling herself to dismiss it, Johanna picked up her list and made her eyes focus. "What do you think about number six?"

"I don't know that answer, either. Johanna…" Outgoing and candid herself, Bethany nonetheless understood and respected her boss's restraint. "Did everything go okay the other night?"

It would have been foolish to pretend to misunderstand. "It went fine. Very pleasant." Johanna dug into her pocket for a roll of antacids. "I'm leaning toward numbers one, four, six, nine and thirteen."

Beth looked at each one, decided she might have an inkling about question thirteen, then nodded. "Let's go for them." She handed the list back so that Johanna could lock them up. "Could we pretend we're out of the office, maybe at home with our feet up and a nice bottle of wine already half-gone?"

Johanna turned the key and pocketed it. "Do you have a problem, Beth?"

"No, but I'd swear you did."

"I'm fine." Johanna began to stack and straighten papers on her desk. "We had a friendly dinner, some pleasant conversation, and that was that. I have no idea why Sam's calling me at the office, but I don't have time to chat with him."

"I didn't mention Sam," Bethany pointed out. "You did. I only mentioned a problem." She smiled sympathetically. "I get the feeling they're the same thing."

Johanna rose and, with her hands in the deep pockets of her skirt, walked to the window. "He just can't get it through his head that I'm not interested."

"Are you? Not interested, I mean," Bethany supplied when Johanna turned her head.

"I don't want to be interested. It's the same thing."

"No. If you weren't interested you'd be able to smile, maybe pat him on the head and say thanks but no thanks. Not wanting to be interested means you are and you get around it by avoiding phone calls and making excuses."

Johanna pushed a thumb into the ivy geranium hanging in a basket at her window. The soil was moist. She'd watered it herself that morning. "How did you get to be an expert?"

"Unfortunately, most of it comes from observation rather than execution. He seems like a nice guy, Johanna."

"Maybe, but I don't have room for men right now, and less than none for actors."

"That's a hard line."

"It's a hard town."

Bethany wasn't willing to buy that. True, she'd only lived in L.A. for three years, but it still fascinated her. To her it remained the town where dreams could be chased and caught. "I hope you're not going to break my heart and tell me he's a jerk."

"No." With a reluctant smile, Johanna turned again. "No, he's not a jerk. Actually, you're right, he's a very nice guy, charming, easy to talk to—" She caught herself. "For an actor."

"He makes my insides tingle," Bethany confessed, unashamed and artless.

Mine, too, Johanna thought. Which was precisely why she wasn't going to see him again. "You're supposed to be concentrating on your screenwriter," she said briskly, then stopped when she saw Beth's expression. "Trouble?"

"He dumped me." She shrugged her shoulders in an unconcerned gesture. Johanna only had to look at Beth's eyes to see how much she was hurting. "It's no big deal, really. We weren't serious."

Maybe he wasn't, Johanna thought with a mixture of sympathy and resignation. "I'm sorry. Everyone has spats, Beth."

Bethany understood that, had even expected it. She hadn't expected deceit. "We went a little beyond that. It's better this way, really it is. I thought he was interested in me, you know, but when I found out he was more interested in my position—" She caught herself, swore silently, then smiled. "Doesn't matter. He was just one of the many toads you have to go through to find the prince."

"What about your position?" It never took Johanna long to put two and two together. Screenwriter, assistant producer. Toss in ambition and it added up perfectly. "Did he want you to hawk a script?"

Uncomfortable, Bethany shifted. "Not exactly."

"Spit it out, Beth."

"All right. He had the idea that I could influence you to influence your father to produce his screenplay. When I told him it wouldn't work, he got mad, then I got mad, and one thing led to another." She didn't add that it had been ugly. She didn't have to.

"I see." Why were there so many creeps in this world? Johanna wondered. So many users. "I am sorry, Beth."

"Bruises fade," Beth said easily, though she was aware hers would last a long time. "Besides, I've got the satisfaction of hoping he sells nothing but commercial jingles for the next ten or twenty years."

"Do yourself a favor," Johanna advised her. "Fall in love with an insurance salesman." She glanced toward the door as her secretary popped a head in.

"Telegram, Ms. Patterson."

With a murmured thank-you, Johanna took it. Stupid, she told herself as her fingers tensed on the paper. It had been almost twenty-five years since she'd gotten that brief and heartbreaking telegram from her mother. She hadn't even been old enough to read it herself. Shoving back the memory, she tore the envelope open.

I can be as stubborn as you. Sam.

Johanna scowled at the single line, read it twice, then crumpled it into a ball. But instead of tossing it in the waste-basket, she shoved it into her pocket.

"Bad news?" Bethany asked.

"A weak threat," Johanna said, picking up her remote. "The show's starting."

The damn woman was making him crazy. Sam groomed the mare, who'd been bred only hours before to his prize stud. She was still skittish and prone to nip. High-strung, pedigreed and temperamental, she reminded Sam of Johanna. That made him smile, if a bit grimly. He didn't think Johanna would appreciate being compared to a horse, not even a purebred.

She hadn't returned one of his calls. *Miss Patterson is unavailable. Miss Patterson is in a meeting.*

Miss Patterson is avoiding you like the plague.

He was beginning to feel like a gawky teenager with a crush on the class princess. More than once he'd told himself to write her off, to find some less complicated woman to spend an evening with.

The mare turned her head and took aim at his shoulder. Sam merely shifted out of range and continued to stroke and soothe. He didn't want to spend the evening with a less complicated woman. He wanted to spend it with Johanna. Just a test, he told himself, to see if whatever had happened by the pond would happen again. And if it did, what the hell was he going to do about it?

He was better off not seeing her again. A man had a lot more freedom when he cluttered up his life with many women than when he found himself concentrating on only one. He wasn't trying to concentrate on her, he reminded himself. He just couldn't get her out of his head.

What secrets did she have tucked away inside her? He had to find out.

When she'd kissed him…there had been no secrets there. She'd been open, passionate and as honest as a man could hope for. It hadn't been ordinary. He knew what it was to kiss a woman for pleasure, for obligation or because the script called for it. That moment with Johanna had been nothing so simple as pleasure, and it had been nothing so casual as obligation. The reaction—his *and* hers—hadn't been in any script.

She'd been as stunned as he was, and as unnerved. Didn't she want to know why?

The hell with what she wanted, Sam decided as he shut the stall door. *He* had to know why. Whether she wanted to or not, Johanna was going along for the ride.

She was beat. Johanna downed two aspirin and a carton of yogurt at her kitchen sink. Her afternoon had been taken up by back-to-back meetings, and though she should have been celebrating the nighttime syndication of *Trivia*, she'd opted for a quiet evening at home. She'd have to set up a party for the crew next week. They deserved it. And she'd see that Beth got a raise. For tonight, she didn't want to think about production meetings or sponsors. Her flowers needed tending.

The sun was warm on her face and arms as she walked outside to her garden. The roses that climbed the trellis along the side of the house needed pinching off. Snapdragons and hollyhocks needed weeding. Some of the taller and heavier-bloomed plants would require staking. Pleased with the scents and colors, she dug in.

She'd spent many quiet afternoons with the gardener on her father's estate, learning the names of the plants and the care they required. He'd let her have a plot of her own and had shown her how to turn soil and plant seeds, how to separate at the roots and prune. She'd learned how to blend plants for color, texture, height and flowering periods from him. On rainy days, or during cold snaps, he'd let her explore the greenhouse, where fragile seedlings had been nursed or exotic bulbs forced for early blooming.

The scents there had never been forgotten, the sultriness,

the heat, even the damp smell of watered soil. He'd been a kind man, a little stoop-shouldered and thick through the middle. During one brief fantasy she'd imagined he was her father and they'd gone into business together.

She hadn't known until she'd heard him talking with another servant that he'd felt sorry for her.

All the servants had felt sorry for her—the little girl who was only brought out and paraded at her father's whim. She'd had a three-story dollhouse, a tea set of English china and a white fur coat. There had been ballet lessons and piano lessons and French taught by a private tutor. Other little girls would have dreamed of having what Johanna had only had to lift a hand for.

At six, her picture had been splashed across the press. She'd worn a red velvet dress that had skimmed her ankles and a tiny diamond tiara as flower girl at her father's second wedding. A Hollywood princess.

The bride had been an Italian actress who enjoyed having tantrums. Her father had spent a good deal of that two-year union on the Italian Riviera. Johanna had spent most of it in the gardens of his Beverly Hills estate.

There had been a scandal and a mudslinging divorce. The actress had kept the Italian villa, and her father had had a blistering affair with the lead in his next production. Johanna, at age eight, had already developed a cool and all-too-adult view of relationships.

She preferred her flowers. She didn't like wearing gloves. She felt that she got a better sense of the soil and the fragile roots with her hands uncovered. When she managed to squeeze in time for a manicure, she was usually met with shock and dismay. As a matter of routine, Johanna kept her nails clipped short and didn't bother with enamel.

Unfeminine. That was what Lydia had called her. Lydia had been one of her father's more vocal and longer-lasting distractions. Lydia had been palely beautiful and unceasingly selfish. Fortunately, she hadn't wanted to marry Carl Patterson any more than he had wanted to marry her.

Send the girl to the nuns in Switzerland, darling. Nothing like nuns for teaching a girl a little femininity and grace.

Johanna, at twelve, had lived in terror that she would be sent away, but Lydia had been replaced before she'd managed to pressure Carl into paying the tuition.

Unfeminine. The word still cropped up in Johanna's head from time to time. She usually ignored it; she'd found her own style of womanhood. But now and again, like an old scar, the word caused an itch.

On her hands and knees, she brushed through her patio dahlias, back to the freesia that would bloom in another few weeks. With care and precision, she pulled out any weeds that had had the audacity to sprout. It had been a dry spring, and after testing the soil she decided she'd give everything a good soak before calling it a day.

She heard the car but didn't bother to glance up, because she expected it to drive by. When it didn't, Johanna had just enough time to look around before Sam swung out of the driver's side.

She said nothing and remained kneeling, speechless.

He was furious. The long drive from his ranch had given him plenty of time to work on his temper. Here he was chasing after some cool-eyed go-to-hell blonde and all he could think of when he saw her was how she'd looked in the moonlight.

It was dusk now, the light soft and tenuous. She was kneeling in front of a bank of flowers like some pagan virgin sacrifice.

She didn't rise, and her hands were stained with soil and grass. The air smelled like sin, dark and rich.

"Why the hell do you have a secretary and an answering machine if you don't intend to answer messages?"

"I've been busy."

"What you are is rude."

She hated that. Hated knowing it was true. "I'm sorry." She put on her coolest and most professional smile. "The show's going into syndication and I've been tied up with meetings and paperwork. Was there something important?"

"You know damn well it's important."

She spent the next ten seconds carefully wiping the worst of the dirt from her hands onto her jeans and staring at his boots. "If there's a problem with your contract—"

"Cut it, Johanna. We've done our business. That's over."

She looked at him then. "Yes, that's right."

He stuck his hands in his pockets. If he'd had them free much longer he might have throttled her. "I don't like feeling like a fool."

"I'm sure you don't." She rose, careful to keep an arm's length of distance between them. "I'm losing the light, Sam. If there's nothing else…" The rest of the words slid down her throat when he grabbed her by her shirtfront.

"You're going to turn away from me once too often," he said quietly. Much too quietly. "I've always considered myself fairly even-tempered. Seems I was wrong."

"Your temperament's not my problem."

"The hell it isn't." To prove his point, he yanked her against him. Her hands came up automatically for balance and defense. But his mouth was already on hers.

There was no testing kiss this time, no friendly overture.

There was only the outpouring of urgency and demand that had clawed inside him for days. She didn't struggle. He hated to think of what he might have done if she had. Instead, she went very still, and for a moment nearly fooled them both into thinking she was unaffected.

Then she moaned. The sound went from her mouth into his, filled with surrender and despair. Before the sound had died her arms were around him, her fingers digging into his shoulders.

Twilight deepened, cooling the air, but she felt only the heat from his body as she pressed against him. He smelled of horses and leather. Dazed, she thought that the scent must be part of some deeply buried fantasy. Knight on white charger. But she didn't want to be rescued. Like a fool, she'd thought she could escape, from him, from herself. It only took a moment to show her how firmly she was already bound.

He brushed his mouth across her face, drawing in the taste, the softness. Her lips skimmed his jaw as she, too, searched for more. He tightened his arms around her. He'd thought he'd understood what it was to ache for a woman. Nothing had ever come close to this. He hurt everywhere, with a pain more erotic than anything he'd ever imagined. The more he touched, the more he hurt. The more he hurt, the more he was driven to touch.

"I want you, Johanna." His hands were in her hair now, as if he couldn't trust them to wander over her again. "I haven't been able to stop thinking about you for days. For nights. I want to be with you. Now."

She wanted it, too. A shudder ran through her as she clung to him. She wanted him. She wanted to let go of her control, of her caution, and just feel—the way he could make her feel.

Somehow she already knew that he could bring her things she'd never believed in. Once he did, she'd never be the same.

For a moment longer, she held on. Regret, more than she'd ever known, replaced desire as she drew away. With an effort she managed a smile as she glanced at the smudges on his shoulders. "My hands were dirty."

He took them both. "Let's go inside."

"No." Gently she drew her hands from his. "It wouldn't work, Sam. *We* wouldn't work."

"Why?"

"Because I wouldn't want it to. I wouldn't let it work."

He took her chin in his hand. "Bull."

"I wouldn't." She wrapped her fingers around his wrist. The pulse was fast there, as fast as her own. "I'm attracted to you, I won't deny that. But it can't lead anywhere."

"It already has."

"Then it can't lead any farther. Believe me when I say I'm sorry, but we're both better off facing up to it now."

"I'm sorry, too, but I can't accept it." He moved his hand to her cheek in a gesture that pierced her with its tenderness. "If you're expecting me to walk away and leave you alone, you're going to be disappointed."

She took a deep breath and met his eyes squarely. "I'm not going to sleep with you."

His brow lifted. "Now, or ever?"

The last thing she'd expected to do was laugh, but the chuckle bubbled out. "Good night, Sam."

"Hold on. We're not finished." There was amusement in his voice as he gestured toward her front steps. "Why don't we sit down? It's a nice night." When she hesitated, he lifted his hands, palms out. "No contact."

"All right." She wasn't completely at ease with it but felt perhaps she owed them both that much. "Would you like a drink?"

"What have you got?"

"This morning's coffee."

"I'll skip it, thanks." He settled comfortably next to her, hip to hip. "I do like your place, Johanna," he began, wondering if he would be able to understand her better through it. "It's quiet, private, well looked-after. How long have you had it?"

"About five years."

"Did you plant all this?"

"Yes."

"What are those?"

She looked over to the edge of one of her borders. "Soapwort."

"Ugly name for such a pretty thing." The little pink flowers looked delicate, but he could see that they spread exactly as they chose. "You know, it occurs to me that we don't know each other very well." He leaned back against the next step, stretching his legs out. Johanna thought he looked very much at home.

"No," she said cautiously. "I suppose we don't."

"You believe in dating?"

She hooked her hands around her knees and smiled. "It's a nice occupation for teenagers."

"You don't figure adults can pull it off?"

On guard again, she moved her shoulders. "Most people I know have lovers, not boyfriends."

"And you don't have either."

"I like it that way."

The way she said it made him glance back at the little pink flowers again. "Why don't we shoot for another term, like

companion?" He turned to study her profile. "We could try
being companions for a while. That's an easy, uncomplicated
term. No strings."

It sounded that way, but she knew better. "I meant what I
said before."

"I'm sure you did." He crossed his feet at the ankles. "That's
why I figured you wouldn't be afraid to get to know me
better."

"I'm not afraid," she said immediately, showing him that
he'd hit the right button.

"Good. There's a benefit Friday night at the Beverly
Wilshire. I'll pick you up at seven."

"I don't—"

"You support raising funds for the homeless, don't you?"

"Of course I do, but—"

"And since you're not afraid, it wouldn't bother you to be
my companion. It's formal," he continued smoothly. "I don't
care much for that kind of evening myself, but it's for a good
cause."

"I appreciate the offer, but I simply couldn't manage to get
home from work and change in time for a formal function at
the Wilshire by seven." And that, she thought, should be the
end of that.

"All right, I'll pick you up at your office. That way we can
make it seven-thirty."

She let out a huge breath, then shifted so that she could
look at him directly. "Sam, why are you trying to maneuver
me this way?"

"Johanna…" He took her hand and kissed her fingers, too
quickly for her to object. "I can maneuver much better than this."

"I'll just bet."

Delighted, he grinned. "I love it when you use that tone. It's so proper. Makes me want to muss you up."

"You didn't answer my question."

"Which question? Oh, that one," he finished when she narrowed her eyes. "I'm not trying to maneuver you, I'm trying to make a date with you. No, not a date," he corrected. "No dates for adults. We can't call it a meeting, that's too businesslike. How about encounter? You like encounter?"

"I don't think so."

"One thing I've found out about you already, Johanna, is that you're a hard woman to please." He stretched out again with a sigh. "But that's all right. I can sit right here until you come up with the right choice of words. Stars are coming out."

Involuntarily she glanced up. She often sat out by herself in the evening. She'd been content to look at the stars alone. Somehow the night seemed more appealing with him there, and that worried her. Depending on someone else for your contentment was a big mistake.

"It's getting chilly," she murmured.

"Are you asking me in?"

She smiled, then rested her elbow on her knee. "It's not that chilly." They were silent for a moment. Then the silence was broken by a nighthawk. "Why aren't you down in the city at some club being seen with some up-and-coming actress with lots of teeth?"

As if he were thinking it through, Sam rested his elbows on the back of the step. "I don't know. Why aren't you down in the city at some club being seen with some hotshot director with a perfect tan?"

Still pouting a bit, she kept her head still but shifted her gaze over to him. "I asked you first."

"I love acting," he said after a moment. His voice was so calm and serious that she turned her head again. "I really love it when it all comes together—the script, the moves, the crew. And I don't mind being paid well for it, either. I've got a couple of weeks before we start shooting. Once we do, there are going to be a lot of very long and very demanding days. I don't want to waste the little time I have in a club." He touched her hair. They both remembered he'd promised there would be no contact, but she didn't object. "Are you going to come back and feed my ducks, Johanna?"

It was a mistake, she told herself as she smiled at him. A stupid one. At least she was making it with her eyes open. "I think I can make it Friday night, if you don't mind leaving the benefit a bit early. I'll have put in a full day at the office."

"Seven-thirty, at your office?"

"Fine. No strings?"

"Deal."

The minute he leaned toward her, she held up a hand. "Don't kiss me, Sam."

He backed off, not without effort. "Now, or ever?"

She rose and brushed off the seat of her jeans. "Now, anyway. I'll see you tomorrow."

"Johanna." She paused at the top of the steps and looked back. "Nothing," he told her. "I just wanted to look at you again. Night."

"Drive carefully. It's a long trip."

He threw her a grin over his shoulder. "It's getting shorter all the time."

5

By five-thirty the offices were like a tomb. Johanna was happy enough to have an extra hour to herself. Paperwork that never seemed to diminish during the normal working day could be gotten through in an uninterrupted hour. Questions for Monday's taping had been chosen and checked, but Johanna took the time to go over them herself to be certain they were as entertaining as they were educational.

She answered a pile of memos, read and signed letters and approved a stack of bills. The beauty of game shows, she thought as she worked, was that they were cheap to produce. In a big week they could give away over fifty thousand dollars and still come in at a fraction of the cost of a thirty-minute situation comedy.

She was still determined to get her other concept on the air, and was ready to make her pitch for the pilot so that when things clicked the show could debut in the fall. And they would click, Johanna promised herself. One more success, one more solid success, and her own production company could begin its struggle for survival.

Garden Variety Productions. She could already see the logo. Within two years others would see it, as well. And remember it.

She'd continue to do the games, of course, but she'd begin to expand her own horizons, as well. A daytime drama, a couple of prime-time movies, a weekly series. She could already see it building, step by step. But for now she had to concentrate on getting through the rest of the day. And the evening.

After her desk was cleared, Johanna brought out her secret. She'd hidden the bag in her bottom drawer, behind the office stationery. There'd been enough commotion over her bringing an evening dress to the office. Now Johanna pulled the box from the bag, opened it, then read the instructions through twice. It didn't seem that complicated. She'd make it an adventure, she told herself, even if it was silly. She'd told herself it was silly even as she'd let the clerk talk her into buying them.

Johanna set her equipment in orderly lines, with the instructions handy, then examined her hands, back, then palms. The clerk hadn't been wrong about her nails being a mess. And what was wrong with trying something new? Johanna picked up the first fake fingernail and began to file it. She tested it often, placing it on her short, unpainted thumbnail until she was satisfied that the length wasn't extravagant. Only nine more to go, she thought, and began to attack the rest.

As she worked, she slipped out of her shoes and curled her legs under her. It was a position she never would have permitted herself to take if anyone had been in the office. Alone, she switched to it without thinking. Once she had ten uniformly filed nails on her blotter, she went on to the next stage.

The instructions told her it was easy, quick and neat. Johanna peeled off the adhesive and pressed it against her nail. Easy. With the tweezers she carefully caught the tip of the backing and began to peel it off. The adhesive rolled into a ball. Patiently Johanna removed it and tried again. The third time she managed to make it stick. Pleased, she picked up the first nail and aligned it carefully over her own. After pressing down, she examined the result.

It didn't look like her thumb, but it was rather elegant. After she painted it with the Shell-Pink Fizz enamel the clerk had sold her, no one would know the difference.

It took her twenty minutes to complete one hand, and she had to resort to digging out her reading glasses—something else she never would have done unless completely alone. She was swearing at the clerk, at herself and at the manufacturer when the phone rang. Johanna hit line one and popped the nail off her index finger.

"Johanna Patterson," she said between her teeth.

"It's John Jay, honey. I'm so glad you're a workaholic."

Johanna glared at her naked index finger. "What is it?"

"I've got a teeny little problem, sweetheart, and need you to come to my rescue." When she said nothing, he cleared his throat. "Listen, it seems my credit card's at the limit and I'm in a bit of an embarrassment. Would you mind talking to the manager here at Chasen's? He says he knows you."

"Put him on." Disgusted, she ran her hand through her hair and popped off another nail. It took less than two minutes to squeeze John Jay out of his embarrassment. After she hung up the phone, Johanna looked at her hand. Two of the nails she'd meticulously placed were gone, and her fingers were smeared with adhesive. Letting out a long breath, she began to remove the rest.

She was an intelligent, capable woman, she reminded herself. She was a hop and a skip away from being thirty and she held down a complex and demanding job. She was also probably the only woman in the country who couldn't attach fake nails.

The hell with it. She dumped everything, including the bottle of enamel, into the trash.

She did what she could with her hair in the women's lounge. Then, because she was feeling unfeminine and klutzy, she went dramatic with her makeup. Dressed only in thigh-high stockings and tap pants, she unzipped the garment bag. She'd only worn the gown once before, a year ago. It was strapless and clingy, a far cry from her usual style. With a shrug, Johanna stepped into it, and shimmied it up, then fought to reach the zipper. She swore again and wondered why she'd allowed herself to be talked into going out at all. Once the dress was secured, she tried to see as much of herself as possible in the waist-high mirrors.

It was a good fit, she decided as she turned to the side. And the color—which, she remembered grimly, would have matched the enamel now in the trash—was flattering. Though she couldn't see it, the hem skimmed her knees in the front, then graduated down to full-length in the back. Johanna changed her everyday earrings for pearl-and-diamond circles, then clasped on a matching choker.

As good as it gets, she thought, and zipped her office clothes in the bag. She'd have her secretary send them to the cleaners on Monday. With the bag slung over her arm, she started back to her office. She'd been wise to have Sam meet her here, Johanna decided. Not only did it make it less like a date, there was the added security that she'd have to be dropped off back in the parking garage so that she could drive herself home.

The coward's way. She shrugged her shoulders with a touch of annoyance as she walked. The safe way, she corrected.

Whatever she was feeling for Sam was a little too fast and a little too intense. Having an affair wasn't in her plans, professionally or personally. She'd simply lived through too many of her father's.

Her life would never be like his.

As far as Sam Weaver was concerned, she would be sensible, cautious and, above all, in complete control of the situation.

Oh, God, he looked wonderful.

He was standing in her office by the window, his hands in the pockets of his tux and his thoughts on something she couldn't see. Pleasure, hardly comfortable, slammed into her. If she'd believed in happily-ever-afters, she would have believed in him.

He hadn't heard her, but he'd been thinking about her hard enough, deeply enough, that he'd known the moment she'd stepped into the doorway. He turned, and his image of her dissolved and reassembled.

She looked so fragile with her hair swept up off her neck and her shoulders bare. The business-first office had suited the woman he'd first met. The pretty garden and isolated house had suited the woman who'd laughed with him beside the pond. But this was a new Johanna, one who seemed too delicate to touch.

As ridiculous as it made him feel, he had to catch his breath. "I thought you'd skipped out."

"No." When she realized her knuckles were turning white clutching her summer bag, she relaxed them. "I was changing." Because she wanted badly to act natural, she made herself move to the closet. "I'm sorry if I'm a bit behind. I got caught up. Work," she said, and with a quick glance made certain the fiasco of plastic nails and polish was out of sight.

"You look wonderful, Johanna."

"Thanks." She shut the closet door, trying to take the compliment with the same ease with which it was given. "So do you. I'm ready whenever you are."

"I need another minute." He crossed to her, catching the quick surprise in her eyes just before he covered her bare shoulders with his hands and kissed her. He lingered over the kiss, struggling to keep the pressure light, the demand minimal. "Just wanted to see if you were real," he murmured.

She was real, all right, so real that she could feel her own blood pumping hot and quick. "We should go."

"I'd rather stay here and neck. Well, maybe some other time," he added when he saw her brow lift. With her hand in his, he started out of the office toward the elevators. "Listen, if this is really boring we could leave early. Take a drive."

"Hollywood galas are never boring." She said it so dryly that he laughed.

"You don't like them."

"I don't often find it necessary to attend them." She stepped into the elevator as the door opened.

"It's hard to be a part of a world and ignore it at the same time."

"No, it's not." She'd been doing it for years. "Some of us do better behind the scenes. I saw one of the early ads for your miniseries," she continued, changing the subject before he had a chance to probe. "It looked good, very classy, very sexy."

"That's marketing," he said dismissively as the elevator reached the underground parking garage. "It's not really sexy. It's romantic. There's a difference."

There was indeed, but it surprised her that he knew it. "When you've got your shirt off and your chest is gleaming, people think sex."

"Is that all it takes?" He opened the passenger door of his car. "I can be out of this cummerbund in under five seconds."

She swung her legs into the car. "Thanks, but I've already seen your chest. Why television?" she asked when he'd joined her. "At this point in your career, I mean."

"Because the majority of people won't sit still in a theater for four hours, and I wanted to do this movie. The small screen's more personal, more intimate, and so was this script." The car's engine echoed in the nearly empty garage as he backed up and began to drive out. "The character of Sarah is so fragile, so tragic. She's so absolutely trusting and naive. It knocked me out the way Lauren pulled it off," he added, referring to his co-star. "She really found the essence of that innocence."

And, according to the press, he and Lauren had had as many love scenes away from the cameras as they had in front of them. It would be wise, Johanna reminded herself, to remember that. "It's not usual to hear an actor talk about a character other than his own."

"Luke's a bastard," Sam said simply as he stopped at a light. "An opportunist, a womanizer and a heel. A very charming, glib-tongued one."

"Did you capture his essence?"

He studied Johanna before the light changed. "You'll have to watch and tell me."

Deliberately she turned away. "What's your next project?"

"It's a comedy."

"I didn't know you did comedy."

"Obviously you missed my tour de force as the Raisin Crunch man a few years ago."

The chuckle welled up. "I'm embarrassed to say I did."

"That's all right. I'm embarrassed to say I didn't. That was right before I did the Mano cologne commercials. 'What woman can resist a man who smells like a man?'"

She would have laughed again if she hadn't remembered her own reaction to everything about him, including his scent. "Well, no one can say you haven't paid your dues."

"I like to think I have, and I'm also aware that the Mano campaign got me a reading for *Undercover*."

She was sure it had. Johanna hadn't missed those particular ads. In them, Sam had been blood-pumpingly sexy, intensely male and cocky enough to make a woman's mouth water. His character in *Undercover* had been precisely the same, but with an underlying depth that had surprised both the audience and the critics.

"Those kind of breaks don't happen very often," she said aloud. "When they do, they're usually deserved."

"Well…" He drew the word out. "I think that was a compliment."

She shrugged. "I've never said you weren't good at what you do."

"Maybe we could turn that around and say the problem from the outset has been that I am." She said nothing, but he thought that was answer enough.

Her brow creased a bit as they drove up to the well-lit limousine-adorned Beverly Wilshire. "Looks like quite a crowd."

"We can still go back to your office and neck."

She gave him a brief, very bland look as one of the uniformed staff opened her door. The moment she was on the curb, strobe lights and cameras flashed.

She hated that. She didn't have the words to explain even to herself how much she hated it. With a gesture that could be taken for one of aloofness rather than panic, she turned away. Sam slipped an arm around her and by doing so caused a dozen more flashes.

"They hound you less if you smile and cooperate," he murmured in her ear.

"Mr. Weaver! Mr. Weaver! What can you tell us about your upcoming television miniseries?"

Sam aimed his answer at the crowd of reporters and personalized it with a smile even as he started to walk. "With a quality script and a cast that includes Lauren Spencer, I think it speaks for itself."

"Is your engagement to Miss Spencer off?"

"It was never on."

One of the reporters got close enough to grab Johanna's arm. "Could we have your name, Miss?"

"Patterson," she said, and shook him off.

"Carl Patterson's girl," she heard someone in the crowd say. "That's the old man's daughter. Ms. Patterson, is it true your father's marriage is on the rocks? How do you feel about him being linked with a woman half his age?"

Saying nothing, Johanna swept through the front doors into the lobby.

"Sorry." Sam kept his arm around her. She was trembling a bit with what he took for anger.

"You had nothing to do with it." She only needed a moment, she thought, to calm down. Yes, there was anger, but there was also that stomach-churning distress that swooped down on her whenever she was confronted with cameras and demanding questions about her father. It had happened before and would happen again, as long as she was the daughter of Carl W. Patterson.

"You want to slip into the bar and get a drink? Sit in a dark corner for a minute?"

"No. No, really, I'm fine." As the tension eased, she smiled up at him. "I'd hate to go through that as often as you must."

"It's part of the job." But he lifted her chin with a finger. "Are you sure you're okay?"

"Of course. I think I'll just—"

But her plans for a brief escape were scotched when several people walked over to greet Sam.

She knew them, some by sight, others by reputation. Sam's co-star in his last feature was with her husband and happily pregnant with her first child. The elite of the press who had been permitted inside took the photo opportunity.

As they inched their way to the ballroom, others came by to renew an acquaintance or be introduced. Through her father she knew a great many of them herself. There were cheeks to be kissed, hugs to be given, hands to be shaken. A veteran actor with a silver mane of hair and a face that still graced billboards squeezed her. With an affection she felt for few, Johanna hugged him back. She'd never forgotten how he had come up to her room and entertained her with stories long ago, during one of her father's parties.

"Uncle Max, you're even more handsome than ever."

His laugh was low and gravelly as he kept his arm around her. "Jo-Jo. Looking at you makes me feel old."

"You'll never be old."

"Mary will want to see you," he said, speaking of his longtime and only wife. "She's run off with a safari to the ladies' room." He kissed her cheek again, then turned to size up Sam. "So you've finally broken down and taken on an actor. At least you've chosen a good one. I've admired your work."

"Thank you." After six years in the business, Sam had thought he was immune to being starstruck. "It's an honor to meet you, Mr. Heddison," he said, and he meant it. "I've seen everything you've ever done."

"Little Jo-Jo always had taste. I'd like to work with you sometime. Not many of this generation I'd say that to."

"Tell me when and where."

With his eyes narrowed, Max gave a slow nod. "I've a script I've been considering. Maybe I'll send it along and let you have a look. Jo-Jo, I'd like to see your pretty face more often." He kissed her again, then strode off to find his wife.

"I believe you're speechless," Johanna commented when Sam only continued to watch Max's back.

"There's not another actor alive I admire more than Max Heddison. He doesn't socialize much, and the couple of times I've seen him I didn't have the nerve to wangle an introduction."

"You, shy?"

"Intimidated is a mild way to put it."

Johanna took his hand again, touched that he could be. "He's the kindest man I know. Once for my birthday he gave me a puppy. My father was furious—he hates dogs—but he couldn't say anything because it was from Uncle Max."

"Jo-Jo?"

She shot him a look. "Uncle Max is the only one who has ever, or who will ever, call me that."

"I like it." He ran a finger down her nose. "It makes me wonder how you'd look in pigtails and a straw hat. Oh, God." She saw his expression change from one of amusement to resignation just before he was enveloped by slim white arms.

"Oh, Sam, I just can't believe how long it's been." The woman with the gypsy mane of red curls turned her face just enough to let the camera get her best side. "Darling, where *have* you been hiding?"

"Here and there." He managed, with considerable skill, to untangle himself. "How are you, Toni?"

"Well, how do I look?" She threw back her magnificent head and laughed. Johanna noted that her dress was cut to the lowest degree that the law would allow. "I've been so terribly busy I've lost touch. I've just started filming and could barely fit this little event into my schedule. It's so boring not being able to see friends."

"Johanna Patterson, Toni DuMonde."

"It's nice to meet you." Johanna knew DuMonde's reputation as a mediocre actress who traded more on sex appeal than talent. She'd married well twice, and both husbands had boosted her career.

"Any friend of Sam's—" she began, then stopped. "You aren't Carl's daughter, are you?" Before Johanna could answer, she threw her head back again, making sure her hair cascaded as she laughed. "What a riot! Darling, I've just been dying to meet you!" Placing a hand on Johanna's shoulder, she scanned the room. Her eyes, sharp and tawny, skimmed over minor celebrities, smiled at those worth noticing and narrowed when focused on a rival. When she found her objective, her smile turned up several hundred kilowatts. Johanna noticed the flashy diamond on her left hand as she signaled.

"This is such a happy coincidence," Toni continued. "I'm sure you'll understand how very delighted I am. Sweetheart, look who I found."

Johanna looked at her father as Toni snuggled against him. The move was calculated so that the diamond on her finger winked hard and cold and in plain sight.

"Johanna, I didn't realize you were attending." Carl brushed his cheek against hers, as he would have with any of his hundreds of acquaintances.

He was a tall man, with broad shoulders and a flat stomach.

He'd allowed his face to line because he had a fear of going under the knife, even cosmetically. But he'd never permitted his body to sag. At fifty-five, Carl W. Patterson was in his prime. Women were as drawn to him now as they had been thirty years before. Perhaps more, as power added to his sex appeal.

"You're looking well," Johanna told him. Sam noted that there was none of the warmth here that there had been when she'd greeted Max Heddison. "Carl Patterson, Sam Weaver."

"A pleasure." Carl took Sam's hand in his hefty, well-manicured one. "I've kept my eye on your career. Word is you're starting a film with Berlitz soon. We go back a ways."

"I'm looking forward to it."

"Isn't this cozy?" Toni put in, clipping her free hand through Sam's arm. "The four of us running into each other this way. We'll have to get a table together, won't we, Carl? After all, I'll want to get to know your daughter, now that we're going to be family."

Johanna didn't freeze. She didn't even react. By this time she was past being surprised by her father. "Congratulations." She winced only slightly when a camera flashed, catching the four of them together.

"We haven't set the date yet." Toni beamed up at Carl. "But we plan to make it soon—well, as soon as a few minor matters are taken care of."

Which would be the legal disposal of his fourth wife, Johanna surmised. Fortunately, she was no longer affected by the whims or variable presence of stepmothers. "I'm sure you'll be very happy."

"We intend to be." Carl patted Toni's hand, looking at her rather than at his daughter.

"Do let's get a table, Carl, and have a drink to celebrate."

Toni kept a casual grip on both men. So casual that it was barely noticeable when Sam removed her hand and took Johanna's. Hers was ice-cold and rigid.

"I'm sorry, we can't stay long." Sam's smile was charming and faintly apologetic.

"Oh, pooh, you've time for one quick drink before this place turns into a zoo." Toni trailed her fingertips up Carl's arm. "Darling, you'll have to insist."

"No need to insist." She wouldn't be ill, Johanna told herself. She wouldn't even be upset. Neither did she smile as she looked up at her father. "The least I can do is drink to your happiness."

"Wonderful." Toni thought it more than wonderful to be seen with a man as important as Carl and a man as attractive as Sam at the same time. "Now, Johanna darling, you mustn't believe all those naughty things you must have read about Sam and me. You know how people in this town love to talk." She turned to be escorted inside and shot a smile over her shoulder, daring Johanna not to believe every word.

"Why in the hell are you doing this?" Sam demanded.

"Because it's part of the game." Chin up, Johanna stepped into the ballroom.

The room was full of babble. It glittered as such events are meant to, and it would make excellent copy in *People*. It would raise a great deal of money—a hundred, perhaps a hundred and fifty thousand dollars—while making the evening worth the price of the meal. And the food was lavish.

She didn't eat. Johanna barely noticed what was placed in front of her, though Toni cooed over each course and made noises about calories. The ring on her hand flashed triumphantly every time she moved her fingers. She made coy little remarks about Sam behaving like a gentleman with her almost-step-daughter, giggled delightedly about having a daughter the same age as herself and snuggled kisses on Carl's cheek when she wasn't flirting elsewhere.

He was dazzled by her. Johanna sipped champagne and watched her father preen whenever the redhead stroked his ego. She'd never known him to be dazzled by a woman before. Desirous, covetous, infuriated, but never dazzled.

"Just a teeny bit more," Toni said when Carl poured more wine. "You know how silly I get when I drink too much." She shot him an intimate look that promised she could get a great deal more than silly. "Isn't this a wild crowd?" She waved cheerily to someone at another table. "God, what a hideous dress. All those diamonds don't make up for plain bad taste, do they? Sam, darling, I heard Lauren's seeing some French race-car driver. Did she break your heart?"

"No," he said flatly, and shifted away when she patted his knee.

"That's because you always do the heartbreaking. Be very careful with this man, Johanna dear, better women than I have shed a tear over him."

"I'm certain," Johanna said sweetly, and sipped more champagne.

"Tell me, why haven't you had your daddy put you in the movies?" Toni gave her a cool woman-to-woman look over her glass.

"I don't act."

"What do you do?"

"Johanna produces daytime television," Carl put in. "The latest reports that crossed my desk were excellent, by the way."

"Thank you."

"Evening syndication is moving forward?"

"Yes, we just finalized it. I would have sent you a memo, but I thought you were out of town."

"We just spent two weeks on the most dismal location shoot in Arizona." Toni patted Carl's hand. "Thank God Carl was there to be sure I wasn't worn to a frazzle. Sam, I've heard the most marvelous things about your television thing. That'll be aired in a couple of weeks, won't it?"

He smiled at her again and nodded. He knew she'd tested for the part of Sarah and had yet to forgive him for not pulling strings to get it for her.

"We really should do a movie together, with Carl producing."

When hell freezes over, Sam thought. "I really hate to cut this short, but Johanna and I are already late." He rose before anyone could protest and offered a hand. "A pleasure meeting you, Mr. Patterson, and my compliments on your finest production." Taking Johanna by the hand, he grinned at Toni. "Don't ever change, darling."

"Good night," Johanna said to her father. "Best wishes." She didn't object to Sam's supporting arm as he guided her out of the ballroom. "You didn't have to cut your evening short on my account," she began.

"I didn't cut it short, and I'm not leaving only on your account. I don't like socializing with piranhas like Toni." He drew out the claim check for his car and handed it to the boy on the curb. "Besides, you look like you could use some fresh air."

"I'm not drunk."

"No, but you were heading there."

"I never get drunk, because I don't like to be out of control."

Truer words had never been spoken, he was certain. "Fine, but I'm going to get you something to eat anyway." He handed the boy who brought his car a twenty and ushered Johanna in himself. "Could you handle a burger?"

"I'm not hungry."

Stubborn, he thought, and just this side of sulking. "Okay, I want a burger."

She started to snap and realized just in time that she was being nasty. "Sam, I appreciate it, but I really don't want anything. Why don't you just drop me off so I can get my car?"

"You had five glasses of wine. I counted." He'd nursed one the moment he'd seen what kind of mood she was in. "I'm driving you home—after we eat."

"I can't leave my car in town."

"I'll have someone drop it off to you tomorrow."

"That's too much trouble. I can—"

"Johanna…" He pulled over to the curb and waited until she looked at him. "Let me be a friend, okay?"

She shut her eyes, wanting badly to do something else she never allowed herself. To cry, hard and long and for no reason at all. "Thanks. I guess I could use some food and some air."

In his tux, Sam ran into a bright fast-food restaurant, ordered burgers, fries and coffee, signed half a dozen autographs and ran out again. "Life's rarely simple anymore," he told Johanna as he tucked the bag between her feet. "The little girl behind the counter wanted to pay for them, and I know damn well she stuck her phone number in the bag. She must have been all of nineteen."

"You should have let me go in."

"We all have our crosses to bear." He headed out. "Johanna, I don't make it a habit to pay attention to what's said about me in print—unless it's a review—but I'd like to make an exception and tell you that Toni and I were never together."

"Sam, it's none of my business."

"Whether you think it's your business or not, I'd like you to believe me. If you've already got a picture of her and me, it's bad enough. When you add that to the fact that she's apparently going to marry your father, it's ludicrous."

Johanna opened her eyes and studied him as he drove. It hadn't occurred to her before. She'd been too wrapped up in her own thoughts and feelings to notice. But she saw it now. "She embarrassed you. I'm sorry."

"I just didn't like her implying—" Implying, hell, he thought. She'd practically taken out an ad. "I'd feel better if you understood there'd never been anything between us." He wanted to say more but found it difficult to say what he thought about the woman who was going to become a part of Johanna's family. "Anyway, it wasn't quite the evening I had in mind."

In a little while he pulled up at the crest of a hill. Below, spread out like a game of lights, was the Los Angeles Basin. He put the top down. Far off in the distance she heard the call of a coyote.

"We're not dressed for burgers, but I got plenty of napkins." He reached down for the bag and the back of his hand brushed her calf. "Johanna, I have to tell you something."

"What?"

"You have incredible legs."

"Give me a hamburger, Sam," she said, and took off her shoes.

"Smells better than the veal medallions."

"Is that what we had?"

"No, that's what you didn't have. Here's the ketchup." He passed her a handful of little plastic bags, then waited until he was satisfied she was eating. If he'd ever seen anyone more miserable than Johanna had been at that pretty, flower-bedecked table with stars glittering in every corner, he couldn't remember. The worst of it was that she'd been struggling to be valiant about it.

"Want to talk about it?" When she only shrugged, he pressed a little harder. "I take it you didn't know your father was planning to get married again."

"I didn't know he was planning to get divorced again. He doesn't check these things through with me."

"Are you fond of your current stepmother?"

"My father's current wife," she corrected automatically, which told him a great deal. "I don't know, I've only met her a couple of times. I think she moved back to New York a few weeks ago. I was just surprised because he doesn't usually stack one marriage on top of the other. Generally there's a space of a year or two between legal contracts."

"He'll have a few months to get to know Toni better. He could change his mind."

"I'm sure he knows exactly what she is. One thing Carl isn't is stupid."

"Sometimes if you tell someone when you're angry with them it loosens things up."

"I'm not angry with him, not really."

He brushed his knuckles along her cheek. "Hurt?"

She shook her head, unable to trust herself to speak for a moment. "He lives his own life. He always has. And that makes it easier for me to live mine."

"You know, I had some real matches with my father." He shook the bag of fries, urging them on her.

"Did you?"

"God, did we fight." With a laugh, Sam opened his coffee and began to sip. "The Weavers have tempers. We like to yell. I think I spent most of the years between fifteen and twenty going head-to-head with my old man. I mean, just because I plowed the car through Greenley's fence was no reason to confiscate my license for six weeks, was it?"

"I imagine Greenley thought it was. Did you ever get your own way?"

"I figure that was about seventy-five, twenty-five, with him holding the lion's share. I probably got as much as I did because he was busy yelling at my brother or one of my sisters."

"It must be different, having a big family. I always imagined…"

"What?"

The wine cushioned embarrassment. Without it, she might never have said it out loud. "I sometimes thought it would be nice when I was little to have brothers and sisters… I don't know, grandparents to visit, family squabbles. Of course, I had stepsiblings from time to time. Things were usually finished before we'd gotten used to each other."

"Come here." He shifted over so he could put an arm around her. "Feel any better?"

"A lot." She sighed and rested her head. "I appreciate it."

Her hair smelled like the air outside the windows. Clean, quiet. The urge to turn his face into it was natural, and he did it without thinking. "I wish you hadn't had so much wine."

"Why?"

"Then it wouldn't be against the rules for me to seduce you."

She surprised herself by turning her face to his. She didn't like the word "seduce." It implied a lack of will. But just now it sounded liberating, and more than tempting. "You live by the rules?"

"Not many of them." He brought his hand to her hair. "I want to make love with you, Johanna, but when I do I want you to have your wits about you. So for now I'll settle for a little less."

He nipped at her lower lip, testing its softness, experimenting with tastes. Here was warmth, just edging toward heat, and acceptance, only a step away from surrender.

Of all the visions and fantasies he'd already had of being with her, the one that was the strongest was of him just holding her like this, with the stars overhead and the night breezes blowing cool and clean.

She could have pulled away. His touch was so gentle she knew he would never have pushed. Not this time. There would be others. She already accepted that. On another night when the breeze was just ruffling the leaves he'd hold her like this, and his mood wouldn't be as patient. Nor, she was afraid, would hers. Something had taken root, no matter how hard she'd tried to pull it free. With a little sigh, she brought a hand to his face.

It was torture, but he ran his hand along her bare shoulders. He wanted to take the feel of her with him when he drew away. Just as he would take the taste of her, the scent of her skin, with him on the long, lonely trip home.

"I wish I knew what I was feeling," she murmured when she could speak again. It wasn't the wine. It would have been a lie to blame it on anything so ordinary. Her eyes were heavy, a bit dazed. Her mouth was soft. Just by looking at her Sam knew he could have her. One more easy nudge and they would be lovers.

He reminded himself about rules and fragile women.

"We're going to have to talk about it." He kissed her again, briefly. "Then we're going to have to do something about it. But right now I'm going to take you home."

6

Johanna considered Saturdays the day the work force had been given to catch up on everything their jobs had forced them to ignore during the week. Rather than a day off, she thought of it as an alternate. Saturdays weren't for sleeping late—even if you were slightly hung over and punchy. They were for weeding the garden, marketing, dealing with personal correspondence and bookkeeping. Her Saturdays, like the rest of her days, had a routine she rarely varied. Johanna depended on organization because a well-ordered life was a safe one.

She dealt with the cleaning first. Though she'd never thought of herself as particularly domestic, Johanna had never considered hiring someone to do the housekeeping. The house was her personal life, and as in all areas of that life, she preferred to handle it herself.

The vacuuming and dusting, the scrubbing down and polishing up, were never mundane chores. There was a certain basic pleasure in them, but more compelling was the feeling that her house, her things, deserved her attention. It was as simple as that. She could haul a bucket and dust rags from room to room with the same dedication and enjoyment she put into reading contracts or balancing budgets.

She preferred the radio loud so that she could hear it in whatever corner of the house she decided to tackle first. This was a day for both production and solitude. Over the years, Johanna had developed a dependency on both.

She did think about the car, and thinking of that naturally turned her thoughts to Sam. She hoped he didn't forget his promise to have someone drop it off, but if he did she'd simply forgo her Saturday marketing and have Bethany pick her up on Monday morning.

Johanna never depended on promises or other people's memories.

But she did think of him, and if her thoughts weren't completely comfortable she couldn't forget that he'd been kind, and gentler than she'd expected. She remembered, a little too well, how she'd felt when she'd kissed him. Full, edgy, tempted. Just a little more tempted each time she was with him to throw away the pact she'd made with herself so many years ago. The pact said no relationships that couldn't be controlled, by her, from the outset—no dependencies, no promises, long- or short-term.

It was a sensible pact, unwritten but binding. The fact that Sam had nearly lured her into forgetting it worried her. But it made her wonder more.

Just what was it about him that made her lose a bit of ground every time they were together? She could discount his looks, however delightful they were. She might appreciate a great physique, but she wouldn't swoon over one.

Not that she was swooning over Sam Weaver, Johanna reminded herself as she poured hot water into her bucket. She thought very little of women who built fantasies or relationships around cleft chins and bulging biceps.

Nor was it his reputation. That, in fact, worked against him. Johanna dunked her mop in hot, soapy water, then began to wash her kitchen floor. The fact that he was an actor was a strike against him. The fact that he was an actor with a reputation with women was a bigger one.

Of course, she knew that such reports were usually exaggerated and often outright lies. But there were times… There were times, Johanna thought as she swiped the mop back and forth, that the press didn't even come close to making rumor as outrageous as the truth.

The press had never known her truth. Her mother's truth. With the care and firmness of experience, she locked that thought away.

So it wasn't his looks or his reputed way with women. It certainly wasn't his fame. Growing up as she had, Johanna had had to tolerate vicarious fame all her life. It wasn't his talent, either, though she certainly respected that. She knew people were often drawn to talent and power. Her father, and the stream of women in his life, were proof of that. They were also drawn to wealth and position. Johanna was too ambitious and had spent too much time trying to perfect her own skills to be swayed by anyone else's.

So if it wasn't one of the attributes he was so obviously endowed with, just what was it that was making her think about him when she shouldn't?

It hadn't started with that first kiss. It would have been easy to blame it on basic sexual attraction, but Johanna preferred honest self-analysis. The seed of something had been there from that first meeting. If not, she wouldn't have gone out of her way to give him a hard time.

Defense mechanism, Johanna thought, recognizing and acknowledging it.

There was his charm, of course. She wrung out the mop and began to rinse. It wasn't stylized or deliberate. That she would have been immune to. It was natural, easy, even friendly. The roses had managed to turn the key in an old, well-guarded lock. The kiss had managed to blow it open briefly, just long enough to give her cause for alarm.

Alarm. Yes, that was what she'd felt overlaying every other emotion he'd drawn out of her. Now that she'd admitted it, she had to decide what to do about it.

She could ignore him. But she didn't believe that would do much good. She could—cautiously—go along with his suggestion that they get to know each other better. Slowly. And she could stick to her guns and not get involved beyond a wary friendship.

The solution had to be in there somewhere, she thought. She'd come up with it, and the next time she had to deal with him she'd be prepared.

She was incredible. Sam stood in the kitchen doorway and watched her mop the kitchen floor. He'd knocked, but the music she had blaring in the other room had drowned out the sound. Since the door hadn't been locked, he'd simply walked in and wandered through until he'd found her.

Johanna Patterson. She was just a bit different every time he saw her. Sophisticated one minute, wonderfully simple the next. Alluring, then cool. Nervous, then tough. A man could take years getting to know all of her. Sam figured he had time.

Right now she was dressed in faded cotton pants rolled up at the ankles and a big man-styled shirt pushed to her elbows. Her feet were bare, and her hair was pinned up untidily. She handled the mop with smooth, easy strokes, not skimming over the job and not swearing over it. He imagined she took to such things as housekeeping with the same steady drive she took to everything else. He liked that, and he liked her for it.

He knew exactly why he was attracted to Johanna. She was beautiful, but that wouldn't have been enough. She was smart, but though he respected a sharp mind that wouldn't have kept him coming back. She was vulnerable. Normally that would have made him take a cautious step back instead of these continued steps forward. She had an edge to her that in another few years might become hard. But now, just now, Johanna was a cautious woman with a few bruises who wasn't easily impressed by status. The combination was more than enough to keep pulling him toward her.

And she'd rather he didn't, Sam thought. On the surface, at least, she'd have preferred that he step out of her life and stay out. But deep down, he believed, she was looking for someone, for something, just as he was.

He wasn't naive enough to believe it was so just because that was what he wanted, but he was determined to find out.

He stood where he was as the strokes of the mop brought her closer. When she rammed into him, he took her arm to keep her from overbalancing.

Johanna whirled around, automatically gripping the mop like a weapon. The relief when she saw him turned quickly to anger.

"How the hell did you get in here?"

"The door," he told her easily. "It wasn't locked. I did knock. I guess you didn't hear me."

"No, I didn't." She was shouting to be heard over the music. "Apparently you took that as an invitation."

"I took it to mean you didn't hear me." He held up the

keys she'd given him the night before. "I thought you'd want your car back."

"Thanks." She stuffed them in her pocket. It wasn't anger nearly as much as it was embarrassment. She didn't care to be sneaked up on unaware.

"You're welcome." He handed her a bouquet of painted daisies and snapdragons. As he'd suspected they would, her eyes softened. "I stole them from Mae's garden. I figured she wouldn't notice."

"They're pretty." With a sigh that was only partially one of resignation, she took them. "I do appreciate you bringing my car back." She knew she was weakening, and she struggled not to. "You've caught me at a bad time. I can't even offer you a drink because the floor's wet, and I'm really busy."

"I'll take you out for one. Better, let's go have some lunch."

"I can't. I've only half finished here, and I'm not dressed to go out. Besides, I—"

"Look fine," he finished for her. "You'd better put those in water. They're starting to droop."

She could have been rude. Johanna knew she was capable of it, but she found she hadn't the heart. Instead, she said nothing. She plucked an old square bottle from a shelf and went into the bathroom to fill it. As she did, she heard the volume of the music go down several notches. He was in the living room studying her collection of antique glass when she came back.

"My mother used to have some plates like this green stuff here. Depression glass, right?"

"Yes."

"I thought that meant it made her sad. I could never figure out why she kept it."

She wouldn't be amused, Johanna told herself. At least not

very. "Sam, you really shouldn't keep whoever followed you up waiting outside."

"No one followed me up." He hooked his thumbs in his pockets and smiled. Some might have thought the look sheepish, but Johanna wasn't fooled.

"Now I suppose you want me to drive you back."

"Sooner or later."

"I'll call you a cab," she said, turning to the phone. "I'll even pay for it."

He put his hand over hers on the receiver. "Johanna, you're being unfriendly again."

"You're being pushy."

"Yeah, but subtleties don't work with you." He reached over to stick a loose pin back in her hair. He'd have preferred to have pulled it out, and the rest of them besides, but bided his time. "So how about lunch?"

"I'm not hungry."

"So, we'll take a drive first." He skimmed his hand from her hair to her cheek. "I really think we should, because if we stay in here too much longer I'm going to want to make love with you, and since I figure you're not ready, a drive's a better idea."

Johanna cleared her throat and took another stab at persuasion. "I appreciate your logic, but I don't have time for a drive, either."

"You've got an appointment?"

"No," she said, then wished she could bite off her tongue. "That is, I—"

"You already said no." He watched her eyes narrow and thought she was almost as pretty annoyed as she was amused. You're already sunk waist-deep, Sam, he told himself. Another few steps and you're over your head. But what the hell. "It's too nice a day to stay indoors cleaning a house that's already clean enough."

"That's my business."

"Okay, then I'll wait for you to finish before we go out."

"Sam—"

"I'm persistent, Johanna. You told me so yourself."

"I'll drive you home," she said, giving up.

"Not good enough." He caught her again, this time by the shoulders. There was something about the way he spread his fingers over her, about the way his palm fit so truly over her. His expression had changed just enough to make her uneasy. The amusement was gone, but it hadn't been replaced by anger. She wouldn't have been uneasy about anger. This was determination, solid and unshakable. "I want to spend the day with you. You know damn well I want to spend the night with you, as well, but I'll settle for the day. Give me five reasons why not and I'll walk down to the freeway and hitch a ride."

"Because I don't want to."

"That's a statement, not a reason. And I don't buy it, anyway."

"Your ego won't buy it."

"Suit yourself." Refusing to be annoyed, he sat on the arm of her couch, absently picked up one of her pillows and began to toss it. "Look, I've got all day. I don't mind sitting around until you've stopped fussing with your imaginary dust. Hell, I'll even give you a hand, but then we're going to have to get out of here, because being alone with you for long periods of time isn't easy." She opened her mouth, but he continued before she could make a suggestion. "I keep wanting to touch you, Johanna, in all kinds of interesting places."

"We'll go out," she said quickly, before she could admit she wanted it, too.

"Good idea. Listen, why don't I drive?"

She started to protest even that—on principle—then decided he'd be less likely to give her trouble if he had his eyes on the road. "Fine." After switching off the radio, she dumped the keys back in his hands. "It'll take me a few minutes to change."

"You look fine," he said again, and took her hand. "I happen to like this Johanna every bit as much as the others I've met over the last couple of weeks."

She decided not to ask him what he was talking about. "We'll have to make it a very informal lunch, then."

"It will be." He opened the door of the car for her. "I promise."

He was as good as his word.

The hot dog dripped mustard, and the noise level was intense. Johanna sat almost in the shade and watched pink elephants circle overhead. It wasn't a dream, or the last remnants of a hangover. It was Disneyland.

"I don't believe this." She took another bite of the hot dog as a boy in mouse ears dashed by, yelling for his parents to hurry up.

"Pretty great, isn't it?" Sam wore sunglasses and a low-brimmed cowboy hat that Johanna was forced to admit suited him. So did the chinos and the simple T-shirt. The disguise wasn't very imaginative, and it would have been transparent as glass if anyone had looked closely enough. Sam had told her that the best place to be anonymous was a crowd. They certainly had one.

"You come here for lunch often?"

"Great hot dogs in Fantasyland." He took an enormous bite to prove his point. "Besides, I'm hooked on the Haunted Mansion. It's terrific, don't you think?"

"I don't know. I've never been in it."

"Never?" His tone of quick astonishment wasn't feigned. Wanting a better look, he tipped down his tinted glasses and studied her. "You grew up here, didn't you?"

She only shrugged. Yes, she'd grown up a short drive from Anaheim, but neither her father nor her succession of step-mothers or "aunts," as she'd been taught to call the other women in her father's life, had been inclined to take a day trip to an amusement park.

"You're not telling me you've never been to Disneyland at all?"

"It's not a requirement."

He pushed his glasses back on his nose as she wiped her hands on a napkin. He remembered the impersonal non-kiss her father had given her the night before. His family was always, had always been, demonstrative, both physically and vocally. No, Disneyland, like other small pleasures, wasn't a re-quirement. But it should be.

"Come on, your education's lacking."

"Where are we going?"

"To take Mr. Toad's Wild Ride. You're going to love it."

Oddly enough, she did.

It was fast and foolish and certainly designed for the younger set, but Johanna found herself gasping and giggling as the car swerved and twisted through the tunnels. She'd barely put her foot on the ground again before Sam was dragging her off to the next line.

They rode down a mountain in a raft, and the final water-fall drop surprised a scream out of her. Wet and breathless, she didn't even protest when he pulled her along again. By the time they'd done Fantasyland to his satisfaction, she'd been spun, twirled, flown and floated. The Mad Hatter's Tea Party had left her giddy and weak-kneed and without the least notion that she was being educated.

He bought her mouse ears with her name stitched across the front, using her own hairpins to secure it even when she grumbled.

"Looks cute," he decided, then kissed her. She might not have known it, Sam thought, but she was more relaxed than he'd ever seen her. "I think you're ready for the Haunted Mansion."

"Does it spin?"

"No, it strikes terror into your heart. That's why you're going to hang on to me and make me feel brave." He swung an arm around her shoulders and began to walk. Johanna had already discovered he knew the park very well.

"You really do come here a lot, don't you?"

"When I first came to California I had two priorities. Get a job—an acting job—and go to Disneyland. Whenever my family comes out we always spend at least one day here."

Johanna looked around as they walked. There were families, so many families. Infants and toddlers pushed in strollers, children with sticky faces riding piggyback and pointing toward the next adventure.

"I guess it is an amazing place. Everything seems real while it's going on."

"It is real when it's going on." He stepped to the back of the line, undaunted by its length. After a moment's hesitation, he took a chance. "I was Pluto for six weeks."

"Pluto?"

"The dog, not the planet."

"I know who Pluto is," she murmured. Absently adjusting her hat, she frowned at him. "You actually worked here?"

"In a dog suit. A very hot dog suit—no pun intended. It paid my first month's rent."

"What exactly did you do?" The line shifted up.

"Marched in the parade, posed for pictures, waved and sweated a lot. I really wanted to be Captain Hook, because he gets to have sword fights and look evil, but Pluto was all that was open."

Johanna tried to imagine it, and nearly could. "I always thought he was cute."

"I was a terrific Pluto. Very lovable and loyal. I did cut it from my résumé after a while, but that was on Marv's suggestion."

"Marv? Oh, your agent?"

"He thought playing a six-foot dog was the wrong image to project."

While Johanna thought that one through, they were ushered inside. The spiel was camp and full of bad puns, but she couldn't help being pulled in. The pictures on the walls changed, the room shrank, the lights went out. There was no turning back.

By the time they were in their tram and starting on the tour she was, so to speak, entering into the spirit of things.

The producer in her couldn't fail to be impressed by the show. Holograms, music and elaborate props were blended to entertain, to raise goose pimples and nervous chuckles. Not so scary that the toddlers in the group would go home with nightmares, but not so tame that the adults felt cheated out of the price of a ticket, Johanna decided as she watched ghosts and spirits whirl around in a dilapidated, cobweb-draped dining room.

Sam had been right about one thing. It was real while it was going on. Not everything in life could be trusted to be the same.

She didn't have to be prodded any further, not to visit a pirate's den and dodge cannon fire, nor to take a cruise up the Amazon or a train ride through Indian territory. She watched mechanical bears perform, ate dripping ice cream and forgot she was a grown woman who had been to Paris and dined in an English manor but had never been to Disneyland.

By the time they started back to the car she was exhausted, but in the most pleasant way she could remember.

"I did not scream," she insisted, holding the small stuffed Pluto he'd bought her in a headlock.

"You never stopped screaming," Sam corrected. "From the minute that car started moving through Space Mountain until it stopped again. You've got excellent lungs."

"Everyone else was screaming." In truth, she hadn't a clue whether she'd screamed or not. The car had taken its first dive, and planets had raced toward her. Johanna had simply squeezed her eyes shut and held on.

"Want to go back and do it again?"

"No," she said definitely. "Once was quite enough."

Sam opened the car door but turned before she could climb in. "Don't you like thrills, Johanna?"

"Now and again."

"How about now?" He cupped her face in his hands. "And again later."

He kissed her as he'd wanted to do since he'd seen her studiously mopping her floor that morning. Her lips were warm, as he'd known they would be, but softer, incredibly softer, than he'd remembered. They hesitated. There was a sweetness in that, a sweetness that was its own allure.

So he lingered, longer than he'd intended. He wanted, more than was wise. When she started to back away, he gathered her closer and took, more than either of them had expected.

It wasn't supposed to be like this, Johanna told herself even as she stopped resisting both of them. She was supposed to be strong, in charge, reachable only when and if she chose to be. With him, he only had to touch... No, he only had to look and she began losing ground.

All her careful analysis that morning was blown to dust the minute his mouth was on hers.

I don't want this. Her mind tried to cling to that thought while her heart beat out steadily: But you do, yes, you do. She could almost feel herself separating into two parts, one aloof, one almost pitifully vulnerable. The most frightening thing was that this time she was more than afraid that vulnerability would be the stronger.

"I want to be alone with you, Johanna." He said it against her lips, then again against her cheek as he trailed kisses there. "Anywhere, anywhere at all as long as it's only you and me. I haven't been able to get you out of my system."

"I don't think you've been trying."

"You're wrong." He kissed her again, feeling her renewed resistance swerve toward passion. That was the most exciting, the most irresistible thing about her, the way she wanted, held back and wanted again. "I've actually given it a hell of a shot. I kept telling myself you're too complicated, too uptight, too driven." He felt her lips move into a frown and was seduced into nibbling on them. "Then I find ways to see you again."

"I'm not uptight."

He sensed her change of mood but could only be amused by it. Johanna, outraged, was fascinating. "Lady, half the time you're like a spring that's wound to the limit and just waiting to bust out. And I damn well intend to be there when you do."

"That's ridiculous. And don't call me lady." She snatched the keys from him, decided she'd do the driving this time.

"We'll see about that." He climbed into the car and nearly managed to stretch out his legs and get comfortable. "Going to give me a lift home?"

She was tempted, more than tempted, to order him out and strand him in the parking lot, right under Donald Duck's cheerful beak. Instead, she decided to give him the ride of his life. "Sure." Johanna put the car in gear.

She drove cautiously enough through the lot. It was, after all, full of pedestrians, many of them children. Things changed when she hit the freeway. She whipped around three cars, settled in the fast lane and rammed down on the gas pedal.

Drives like she's ready to bust, too, Sam thought, but said nothing. Her speedometer might have been hovering around ninety, but her hands were competent on the wheel. And she might, he thought, burn off that temper that had fired up when he'd called her uptight.

She hated it that he was right. That was the worst of it. She knew very well that she was full of nerves and hang-ups and insecurities. Didn't she spend most of her time fighting them off or blanketing them over? It didn't do her any good to hear Sam pinpoint it so casually.

When she'd made the conscious and very calculated decision to make love with a fellow college student, he, too, had called her uptight. Sexually. "Loosen up" had been his sage advice. She hadn't been able to, not with him, who she'd been fond of, nor with any of the men she'd developed careful relationships with. So she'd stopped trying.

She wasn't a man-hater. That would be absurd. She simply didn't want to be tied to one, emotionally or sexually. Her eyes had been opened young, and she'd never forgotten how those two tools could be used. So perhaps she was uptight, though she detested the word. Better that than loose enough to tumble for a pair of wonderful blue eyes or a lazy drawl.

Mad as hell, Sam thought. That was fine. He preferred strong emotion. As a matter of fact, he preferred any emotion at all when it came from Johanna. He didn't mind her being angry with him, because if she was angry she was thinking. About him. He wanted her to do a lot of that.

God knew he'd been thinking about her. Constantly. He'd been telling her no less than the truth when he'd said he'd tried to get her out of his system. When it hadn't worked, he'd decided to stop beating his head against the wall and see where the road would lead.

It was a bumpy ride, but he was enjoying every minute of it.

He was going to have her, sooner or later. Sooner, he hoped for the sake of his sanity. But for now he'd let her drive awhile.

When he saw she was going to miss the exit, he gestured. "You want to get off here."

Johanna switched lanes, aggressively challenging traffic, and breezed onto the ramp.

"How about dinner next week?" He said it casually, as though the interlude in the parking lot had been as make-believe as the rest of the day. When she said nothing, he fought back a grin and tossed his arm over the seat. "Wednesday's good for me. I can pick you up at your office."

"I'm busy next week."

"You've got to eat. Let's make it six."

She downshifted for a turn. "You're going to have to learn to take no for an answer."

"I don't think so. Take the left fork."

"I remember," she said between her teeth, though she didn't.

She drove in silence, slowing down only slightly when she passed through the gate of his ranch. Sam leaned over casually and tooted her horn. When she stopped in front of his house he sat there a moment, as though gathering his thoughts.

"Want to come in?"

"No."

"Want to fight?"

She would not be amused or charmed or soothed. "No."

"All right, we can fight some other time. Want to hear a theory of mine? Never mind," he said before she could answer. "Listen anyway. The way I figure it, there are three stages to a relationship. First you like somebody. Then, if things work out, you start to care for them. When the big guns hit, you fall in love with them."

She kept her hands on the wheel because they'd gone damp all at once. "That's very interesting. If only life worked that neatly."

"I've always thought it does—if you let it. Anyway, Johanna, I went past liking you last night and went straight into the second stage. A woman like you wants reasons for that kind of thing, but I haven't got a handle on them yet."

Her hands had stopped sweating and were now as cold as ice, though the heat was baking right through the windshield. "Sam, I said before I don't think this is a good idea. I still believe that."

"No, you still want to believe that." He waited patiently until she looked at him. "There's a difference, Johanna. A big one. I care for you, and I figured we'd do better if I let you know." He leaned over to kiss her. A very gentle threat. "You've got until Wednesday to think about it."

He got out of the car, then leaned in through the window. "Drive carefully, will you? You can always kick something when you get home if you're still mad."

7

It had been a long day. In fact, it had been several long days. Johanna didn't mind. The pressure to solve problems and work through a few minor crises had kept her mind off her personal life.

Her lighting director had chosen Monday, taping day, to have an appendectomy. She sent flowers and wished him—not for totally altruistic reasons—a speedy recovery. John Jay, in the middle of contract negotiations, had decided to have laryngitis. Johanna had been forced to pamper and cajole—and make a few veiled threats—to work an instant and miraculous cure. Her assistant lighting man had proven to be competent and unruffled, even after three technical hitches. Still, the day had been lengthened by two hours.

Tuesday had stretched even further with meetings to discuss the photo sessions for the ads and the final preparations for the following week's contest. Security had been strengthened to guard that set of questions. A special safe had been purchased, and only she had the combination. Only she and Bethany knew which five questions had been sealed inside. Johanna began to feel like the head of the CIA.

A meeting with her father had been draining and difficult. They'd both been professional, executive producer to producer, as they'd discussed the show's status and plans for expansion. He'd absently mentioned an engagement party and told her his secretary would be in touch.

And, of course, because she considered it part of her job, Johanna watched *Trivia* every morning. It was just a nasty trick of fate that Sam's appearance ran this week. It was difficult enough not to think of him, and impossible when she was forced to watch him every day—long shots, close-ups. By Wednesday they had already received a stack of mail from delighted viewers.

Wednesday.

He'd given her until Wednesday to think about it. To think about him. Them. She just hadn't had the time, Johanna told herself as she turned up the volume and prepared to watch the day's segment. If she'd allowed herself to think about it she would have come up with a way, a polite and reasonable way, to get out of a dinner she hadn't even accepted.

The bright, bouncy opening theme came on, the lights flashed. The two celebrity panelists walked through the arch, then paused for applause before they took their seats. Johanna struggled to look at the big picture, but she kept focusing on him.

Relaxed. He always looked so relaxed, so confident about who he was. That was something she couldn't help but admire about him. He was at ease and put his partner at ease while still maintaining that larger-than-life quality people expected from stars.

So he was good at his job, Johanna told herself as she paced back and forth during the commercial break. That didn't mean she was infatuated with him.

When the show came back on, she took her chair again, wishing she didn't need to have that very small and indirect contact with him.

It's my job, Johanna reminded herself. But she lost track of the game as she watched him. And she remembered, a bit too clearly, that after this segment had been taped she had had her first real conversation with him. She'd taken a dare, and had lost. Since that one miscalculation, nothing had been the same.

She wanted it to be the same. The quick panic surprised her, but she fought it back and tried to think logically. She did want it to be the same as it had been before, when her life had been focused on career and nudged by ambition, both heated and cooled by pride. There hadn't been any sleepless nights then. Tension and self-doubt, perhaps, but no sleepless nights.

And there hadn't been any rides down a mountain on a raft, either, her mind echoed.

She didn't need them. Sam could keep his thrills. All she required was peace of mind.

He was in the winner's circle, surrounded by lights and the audience's total support. Johanna remembered that the quick, cocky grin had been for her benefit. The minute the congratulatory applause began, she snapped off the set.

On impulse, she went to the phone. Rather than going through her secretary, Johanna dialed direct. Such minor precautions were a bit late, since her picture—with Sam—had already been in the paper, and the speculation about them as a couple had already begun. Johanna had decided there was no use adding to the gossip that was already buzzing around the office.

She was calm, she told herself even as she wound the phone

cord around her fingers. She wasn't being stubborn or spiteful, but sensible.

A woman's voice answered. Hearing it gave Johanna all the justification she needed. A man like Sam would always have women around. And a man like that was precisely what she wanted to avoid.

"I'd like to speak with Mr. Weaver. This is Johanna Patterson calling."

"Sam's not in. I'd be happy to take a message." On the other end of the line, Mae was digging for the notepad she always carried in her apron pocket. "Patterson?" she repeated, then shifted the phone and grinned. "Sam's spoken about you. You're the one who does *Trivia Alert*."

Johanna frowned for a moment at the idea of Sam talking about her to one of his women. "Yes, I am. Would you mind—"

"I never miss it," Mae continued conversationally. "I always keep it on when I'm cleaning. Then I see if Joe can answer any of the questions that night at dinner. Joe's my husband. I'm Mae Block."

So this was Mae, the one who shoveled out the dust and grew the snapdragons. Johanna's vision of a pretty morning visitor faded and left her more than a little ashamed. "I'm glad you like the show."

"Crazy about it," Mae assured her. "As a matter of fact, I just had it on. Got a real kick out of seeing our Sam on it. Thought he did real good, too. I even put it on the VCR so Joe could see it later. We're all just crazy about Sam. He speaks real kindly of you, too. Did you like your flowers?"

Having at last found a space in Mae's rapid-fire conversation for a word, Johanna managed to insert one. "Flowers?"

"Sam doesn't think I saw him snitch them."

"They were lovely." Despite all her resolutions, Johanna felt herself soften. "I hope you didn't mind."

"Plenty more where they came from. I figure flowers should be enjoyed, don't you?"

"Yes. Yes, I do. Mrs. Block—"

"Mae. Just Mae, honey."

"Mae, if you could tell Sam I called." Coward, her mind said all too clearly. Johanna closed herself off from it and continued. "And that—"

"Well, you can tell him yourself, honey, 'cause he just this minute walked in. Hold on now."

Before Johanna could babble an excuse, she heard Mae yelling. "Sam, that lady you've been mooning about's on the phone. And I'd like to know what you're thinking of wearing a white shirt when you're wrestling with horses. How you expect me to get out those stains is more than I can understand. Did you wipe your feet? I just washed that kitchen floor."

"Yes, ma'am. It's an old shirt," he added in a half apology Johanna recognized even over the wire.

"Old or not, it's a dust rag now. A boy your age oughta know better. Don't keep your lady waiting all day. I'll make you a sandwich."

"Thanks. Hello, Johanna."

Mae hadn't mentioned her name. *The lady you've been mooning about.* That was something Johanna would have to think about later. "I'm sorry to bother you in the middle of the day. You must be busy."

"Having my wrist slapped." He pulled out a bandanna and wiped the line of sweat from his temple. "I'm glad you called. I've been thinking about you."

"Yes, well…" Where were all the neat excuses she'd thought up? "About tonight."

"Yes?"

Very carefully she unwrapped the cord from around her fingers. "We'd left things a bit unstructured, and as it turns out, I have a late meeting. I can't be sure what time I'll wrap things up, so—"

"So why don't you drive out here when you're finished?" He recognized a lie when he heard one. "You should know the way by now."

"Yes, but it might run late. I don't want to mess up your evening."

"The only way you'd mess it up is not to come."

She hadn't a clue as to how to respond to that. "I never actually agreed to come." Her conscience insisted on reminding her she hadn't stuck by a refusal, either. "Why don't we make it some other time?"

"Johanna," he said, very patiently, "you don't want me to camp on your doorstep, do you?"

"I just think it would be better—"

"Safer."

Yes. "Better," she insisted.

"Whatever. If you don't show up by eight I'm coming after you. Take your choice."

Bristling wasn't nearly as effective over the phone. "I don't like ultimatums."

"That's a pity. I'll see you when you get here. Don't work too hard."

Johanna scowled at the dial tone, then dropped the phone on the hook. She wouldn't go. She would be damned if she did.

Of course, she went.

Only to prove that she wasn't a coward, Johanna assured herself. In any case, avoiding a situation didn't solve anything, it only postponed things. Loose ends were something she invariably tied up.

It was true that she enjoyed his company, so there was no reason to be out of sorts. Except for the fact that she'd been maneuvered again. No, he hadn't done the maneuvering, she corrected. She'd done that all by herself, thank you very much. If she hadn't wanted to go, she would never have called him to say she wasn't going to. Deep down she'd wanted to keep the engagement because she'd always had a need to face up to whatever could be faced.

She could certainly face Sam Weaver.

A simple dinner, she decided. Between friends. They could, cautiously, be called friends by this time. A little conversation never hurt, particularly between two people who were in the same business. Game shows or movies, it all came down to entertainment. She picked up speed a bit, and the plastic bags over this week's dry cleaning snapped and rustled on their hangers behind her.

At least this time she had her own transportation. She would leave when she was ready to leave. There was some security in that.

When she passed through the gates leading to the ranch, she promised herself that she would enjoy the evening for what it was. A simple dinner with a friend. She stopped her car in front of his house and stepped out, refusing to glance in the visor mirror. She wouldn't fuss with or freshen her makeup any more than she had fussed with her outfit. Her gray suit was stylish but certainly businesslike, as were the three hanging in the car. Her low-heeled pumps were comfortable, purchased as much for that as for fashion.

She glanced at her watch and was pleased with the time. Seven-thirty. Not so early that it would appear that she'd been cowed, nor so late that it made her look spiteful.

She looked as she had on that first day, Sam thought. Composed, coolheaded, subtly sexy. His reaction to her now was exactly the same as it had been then. Instant fascination. Stepping out on the porch, he smiled at her.

"Hi."

"Hello." She didn't want to be unnerved, not again, not the way she seemed to be every time she saw him. She answered his smile, though cautiously, and started up the steps. His next move was so unexpected that she had no chance to block it.

He cupped a hand around the base of her neck and kissed her, not passionately, not urgently, but with a casual intimacy that shot straight through her. Welcome home, it seemed to say, and left her speechless.

"I love the way you wear a suit, Johanna."

"I didn't have time to change."

"I'm glad." He glanced beyond her at the sound of a truck. With a half smile, he shaded his eyes. "You forgot to blow your horn," he told her.

"Everything all right here, Sam?" In the cab of a pickup was a man of about fifty with shoulders like cinder blocks.

"Everything's fine." Sam slipped an arm around Johanna's waist.

The man in the truck chuckled, then spun the wheel and made a U-turn. "I can see that. Night."

"That was Joe," Sam explained as they watched the truck cruise down the hard-packed road. "He and Mae keep an eye on the place. And me."

"So I see." It was entirely too easy, standing on the porch, his arm around her, as the sun lowered. Johanna didn't deliberately step away. The move was automatic. "Your housekeeper told me she watches *Trivia.*"

She also said you were mooning over me. Johanna kept the fact that she'd overheard that little piece of information to herself. It was ridiculous, of course. Men like Sam Weaver didn't moon over anyone.

"Religiously," he murmured, studying her. She was nervous. He'd thought they'd passed that point, and he wasn't sure whether to be pleased or frustrated to discover otherwise. "In fact, Mae considers my, ah…performance so far this week the height of my career."

The smile came quickly. Her fingers relaxed their grip on the railing. "Emmy material, I'm sure."

"Is that a smirk?"

"I never smirk, and especially not about my show. I suppose I'll have to risk inflating your ego, but we've already gotten a tremendous amount of mail. 'Sam Weaver is the cutest thing on two legs,'" Johanna quoted, and was amused when he grimaced. "That was from a seventy-five-year-old woman in Tucson."

"Yeah." He took her hand and drew her inside. "When you've finished smirking—"

"I told you, I never smirk."

"Right, and when you're finished we'll see about dinner. I figured we'd barbecue, since I wasn't sure when you'd wind up that meeting."

"Meeting?" The lie had slipped away from her. Remembering, Johanna did something else she couldn't remember having done before. She blushed. Just a little, but enough. "Oh, well, it moved along faster than I'd expected."

"Lucky for both of us." He could have pinned her on it, Sam mused, but decided to let her escape. If he understood Johanna as well as he believed he was coming to understand her, she was already berating herself for the excuse, and for botching it. "I've got some swordfish. Why don't you pour yourself some wine and I'll heat up the grill?"

"All right." The bottle was already open. Johanna filled the two glasses he'd set on the kitchen counter as he breezed through the back door.

He'd known the meeting was nothing more than a weak excuse. She couldn't remember ever having been quite so transparent. Johanna sighed, sipped, then sighed again. He was letting it go so that she wouldn't be embarrassed. That only made it worse. The least she could do, she thought as she picked up his glass, was to be pleasant company for the rest of the evening.

The pool looked cool and delightfully inviting. Swimming had been a daily habit when she'd lived in her father's house. Now she couldn't seem to find time for the health club she'd conscientiously joined. She skirted around the pool to where Sam stood by the stone barbecue pit with two fish steaks on a platter, but she did glance at the water rather wistfully.

"You want to take a quick swim before dinner?" he asked.

It was tempting. Johanna found herself tempted too often when around him. "No, thanks."

"There's always after." He set the steaks on the grill, where they sizzled. Taking his glass from her, he clinked it lightly against hers, then drank. "Go ahead and sit down. These won't take long."

Instead, she wandered a short distance away, looking at his land, the tidy outbuildings, the isolation. He seemed so comfortable here, she thought, so much at home. He could be anybody, an ordinary person. But she remembered that she'd read about him just that morning.

"There's a very hot write-up in this week's *TV Guide* about *No Roses for Sarah*."

"I saw it." He saw, too, how the sun bounced off the water of the pool and onto her skin, making her seem like an illusion. The trim gray suit didn't make him think of offices or board meetings, but of quiet evenings after the day was over.

"*Variety* was equally enthusiastic. 'Gripping, not to be missed,' and so on." She smiled a little as she turned to him again. "What was the adjective used to describe you…" She trailed off as if she couldn't quite remember, though the exact quote had engraved itself on her brain. "'Weaver executes a'— Was it 'sterling performance'?"

Sam flipped the steaks, and they hissed. Smoke rose up, hot and sultry. "'Sizzling,'" he corrected, knowing when he was being strung along.

"Yes, sizzling." She paused to touch her tongue to her upper lip. "'A sizzling performance as a down-on-his-luck drifter who seduces Sarah and the audience with equal panache.' Panache," she repeated. "That one rolls around on the tongue, doesn't it?"

"I didn't realize you were such a smart aleck, Johanna."

She laughed and crossed over to him. "I'm also human. Nothing could drag me away from my set on Sunday night when the first part's aired."

"And Monday?"

"That'll depend, won't it?" She sipped her drink and sniffed appreciatively at the mesquite smoke. "On how *sizzling* you were on Sunday."

The grin was fast and crooked, as if he had no doubt where she would be at nine o'clock Monday night. "Keep an eye on these, will you? I'll be right back."

She'd keep an eye on them, but she hoped the steaks didn't do anything they weren't supposed to do until he got back. Alone, she stretched her arms and worked the muscles in her back. The late meeting had been a lie, but the long day hadn't. Wistfully she glanced at the pool again. It really was tempting.

If she were just anyone—if he were just anyone—she could share this meal with him, laugh a little over something that had happened during the day. Afterward, while the wine was still cool and the air still hot, they could slide into the water and relax together. Just two people who enjoyed each other and a quiet evening.

Later, when the moon came out, they might stay in the water, talking quietly, touching, easing gently into a more intimate form of relaxation. He would have music on again, and the candles on the table would burn down and drown in their own melted wax.

When something brushed against her legs, she jolted, sloshing wine over her hand. The fantasy had come through a bit too clearly, too compellingly, and that wasn't like her. Johanna turned away from the pool and the ideas it had had stirring inside her. With a hand to her heart, she looked down at a fat gray cat. He rubbed up against her calf again, sent her a long, shrewd look, then settled down to wash.

"Where did you come from?" Johanna wondered as she bent to scratch his ears.

"The barn," Sam told her, coming up from behind her. "Silas is one of the barn cats, and I'd guess he got a whiff of the fish and came down to see if he could charm any out of us."

She didn't look at Sam right away, concentrating on the cat instead. The daydream was still a bit too real. "I thought barn cats were fast and skinny."

Not when someone was always taking them down scraps, Sam thought ruefully as he set the bowl of pasta salad on the table and flipped the fish onto a platter. "Silas can be pretty charming," he said, and pulled out a chair for Johanna.

"Silas is pretty huge."

"You don't like cats?"

"No, actually, I do. I've even thought of getting one myself. Why Silas?"

"Marner," Sam explained easily as he served her. "You know how he hoarded gold. Well, this Silas hoards mice."

"Oh."

He laughed at her expression and topped off her wine. "You wanted to know. I've been meaning to ask you," he said, thinking she deserved a change of subject, "when you go on nighttime."

"Two weeks." Johanna told herself she wasn't nervous, not nervous at all. "We tape in two weeks, actually, and go on in four."

"Adding more crew?"

"Some. For the most part it just means that we'll be taping two days a week instead of one. Interested in making another appearance?"

"I'm going to be a bit tied up for a while."

"The new movie." She relaxed a few more degrees. This was how her practical mind had imagined the evening. Shoptalk, nothing more. "When do you start?"

"Any day, theoretically. Realistically, in a week or two. After some preproduction and studio work here, we'll head east.

They figure about three weeks on location in Maryland, in and around Baltimore."

"You must be anxious to begin."

"I always get lazy between pictures. Nothing like a few 6:00 a.m. calls to get you back in gear. How's your fish?"

"It's wonderful." And once again, she'd all but cleared her plate without realizing it. "I bought a grill a few months ago, but I burned everything I put on it."

"A low flame," he said, and something in his voice made her skin tingle. "A careful eye." He took her hand, linking their fingers. "And patience."

"I—" He brought her hand to his lips, watching her over it as he kissed her fingers. "I'll have to give it another try."

"Your skin always smells as though you've walked through the rain. Even when you're not here I can't help thinking about that."

"We should—" Stop pretending, she thought. Acquiesce. Take what we want. "Go for a walk," she managed. "I'd like to see your pond again."

"All right." Patience, Sam reminded himself. But the flame wasn't as low as it had been. "Hold on a minute." He tossed a few scraps onto the grass before gathering up the dishes. She knew she should have offered her help, but she wanted, needed—badly needed—a moment alone.

She watched the cat saunter over to the fish with an arrogance that told her he'd been certain all along he'd get what he'd come for. Sam walked like that, Johanna thought, and suddenly cold, she rubbed her hands over her arms.

She wasn't afraid of him. She reminded herself of that to boost her confidence. But it was no less than the truth. She wasn't afraid of Sam: fear of herself, however, was another matter.

She was here because she wanted to be here. Wasn't it time to face that one fact? She'd already admitted that she hadn't come because he'd maneuvered her. She'd maneuvered herself, or that part of herself that was still determined to stand apart.

There was another part of herself, a part that was slowly taking charge, that knew exactly what she wanted. Who she wanted. That was a part that had already made an enormous mistake by falling in love with Sam.

Before she had a chance to deal with the enormity of that realization, he was back, carrying a plastic bag filled with crackers.

"They'll expect to be— Are you all right?"

She was pale, and her eyes were huge. If Sam hadn't known better he would have sworn someone had come along and given her a fast, unexpected backhand.

"I'm fine." Thank God her voice was steady. She still had that much under control. "Your pets keep you under their thumb, don't they?"

Her smile didn't quite reach her eyes, but he nodded. "It looks that way." He touched her face. She didn't flinch, but he felt the muscles of her jaw tense. "You look a little dazed, Johanna."

Terrified was the word. In love with him, her mind repeated. Good Lord, when, how and, most of all, *why?* "It's probably the wine. I'll walk it off."

It had nothing to do with the wine, but he let it go. Taking her hand firmly in his, he started toward the path. "Next time you come, you're going to have to dress for this. As sensible as those shoes are, boots or sneakers are better for the hike."

Sensible. Frowning, Johanna looked down at her trim, low-heeled Italian pumps. Damn it, they were sensible. She managed to bite off the sigh. Sensible. Like her. "I told you I didn't have time to change."

"That's okay, I can always carry you."

"That won't be necessary."

There it was again, that low, cool tone. He didn't bother to fight back the smile as he steered her along.

The sun was nearly down, so the light was soft and pearly. There were wildflowers along the path that hadn't yet bloomed the last time they'd taken this walk. He imagined Johanna could name them for him if he asked, but he preferred to let them pop out of the ground anonymously.

He could smell the water now, and could just hear its faint lap against the high grass. Every time he'd walked there in the last few weeks he'd thought of her. The birds were quiet now, settling down for the night. Those that called the night their own had yet to stir. He liked the quiet of dusk, the aloneness of it, and wondered if she felt the same. He remembered how she'd knelt in front of a bank of flowers at sundown and figured that she did.

The water of the pond was darkening, like the sky. The shadows of the trees were long and dim across it. It still made her smile to see the ducks gliding over it, preening a bit in anticipation of an audience.

"I take it Silas and his companions don't bother them."

"Too much effort to come all the way out here and get wet when they've got the barn. Here." He handed her the bag. As she had before, Johanna laughed at the ducks' antics as she tossed the crackers to them.

"I guess no one spoils them like this when you're away."

"Mae does. She wouldn't admit it, though."

"Oh, I didn't see the drake close up before." She skimmed

a cracker to him. "He's beautiful. And look how the babies have grown." She scattered crumbs on the water until the bag was empty. Without thinking, she tucked it into her pocket. "It's so nice here," she murmured. "Just the water, and the grass." And you, she thought. But she didn't look at him, not until his hand was on her cheek, gently urging her to.

It was just as it had been the first time. And yet it was nothing like it. This time she knew exactly how she would feel, how she would want, when he kissed her. She knew he would touch her hair before he drew her close. She knew her mind would cloud and her pulse would quicken.

She knew, but it still stunned her.

He felt as though he'd waited forever. It hadn't been merely weeks since he'd first seen her. She'd been under his skin, inside his heart, for as long as he could remember. A dream, a half-formed wish that had only taken one look at her to click solidly into place. It was so right. Somehow it was exactly right when his mouth found hers.

She still wasn't sure. He could feel the hesitation even as he felt the passion that drummed beneath it. But he was sure enough for both of them.

It was meant to be here, here where those first shock waves had passed through both of them. It was meant to be now, before night fell.

She tightened her grip on his shirt, holding on, holding back. In a moment, she knew, she wouldn't be able to think clearly. It would be wise to withdraw now, to leave things as they had been. But his lips coaxed her to stay. To trust.

She murmured, tensing up when she felt him slip the jacket from her shoulders. A step was being taken. Then he was soothing her, giving her time, plenty of time, but no choice at all. The buttons that ran down her back were loosened one by one in an agony of sweetness and promise. When she felt his fingers brush her skin, she shuddered at the contact and searched for the will to end it.

But his lips skimmed her throat as he peeled the blouse from her. She was helpless, but the sensation was no longer frightening.

Is this what it felt like to give in, at last, fully, completely give in to something not quite known but only sensed? Hadn't she waited for it, anticipated it, even while she'd struggled against it? Now the struggle was almost over.

He had to use every ounce of self-control not to rush her. He knew she needed time and care, even as his own needs balled like fists inside him. He'd already imagined what it would be like to touch her like this, to feel her tremble when he did. Her skirt slid down her hips. His hands followed it.

The sun had dropped away, but he could see her, her hair haloed around her face, her eyes wide and uncertain. He kissed her again, slowly, trailing his lips over her jaw as he shrugged out of his shirt. He saw her start to reach for him, then hesitate just short of contact. Taking her hand, he brought it, palm up, to his lips and felt her go limp.

He lowered her to the grass.

It was cool, soft and damp with early dew—a sensation Johanna knew she would remember always. He was over her, so she could only see his face, then only his eyes. She heard the first owl call before he bent to her. Then there was only him.

He touched. She shuddered, no longer from fear or from doubt, but from a pleasure so pure she could never have described it. He tasted. She floated, no longer helpless, but a willing partner. And when she reached for him, drew him closer, the world was shut off for both of them.

She was so soft, so generous. He wondered that he could still be surprised by how many facets there were to her. She'd opened to him now, as completely as he could have hoped.

If her touch was still shy, it was only more endearing. He wanted it to be sweet for her, memorable, and as special as he already knew it would be for him. Somewhere along the line she had stopped being a woman, however desirable, however fascinating, and had become his woman.

He took her, gently, higher.

When she moaned, desire thrummed in him, hard, demanding. He fought it back, wanting her to ride the wave as long as they could both stand it. Slowly, drawing out the process, he slipped her teddy down to her waist, then to her hips, letting the hunger build inside him.

Her fingers dug into the grass as he brushed his lips over her. She could feel her skin tremble wherever he chose to linger. Then, abruptly, the pleasure rocketed up, beyond anything she'd dreamed possible. She cried out his name, her body arching up. Pleasure doubled back, and he was with her again. Now her fingers dug into his shoulders desperately.

Stars began to wink to life above them.

The breath was dragging in and out of his lungs when he filled her. Now he was helpless, his face buried in her hair, his body more her prisoner than she had ever been his. Need expanded and became the focus of his world, and then even that shattered, leaving only her.

8

He couldn't speak. At the moment Sam wasn't sure his mind would ever be able to direct that basic function again. He knew he should shift his weight from her but couldn't bear to break the bond.

Whatever else it had been—passion, desire, chemistry—it had forged a bond.

Overhead, the stars were still coming out. Johanna could see them now, but all she could think of was the way Sam's heart still raced against hers. She hadn't known she was capable of giving or receiving that kind of pleasure. Though the heat had eased, his body was still warm, a continuing contrast to the cool grass that waved around them. The water, pushed by the night breezes, lapped only a few feet away.

It had been a shock to realize she was capable of feeling anything this intensely, but more, she had seen his eyes, felt his body shudder, and had known for the first time in her life that she could give.

Hardly realizing she was doing so, she lifted a hand to stroke his hair. Sam was aware, even if she wasn't, that it was the first time she'd touched him without being backed into a corner.

He closed his eyes and held on to that thought. What would once have been a small thing to him was now an enormous one. He'd slipped into the third phase, into love, almost painlessly.

"Johanna." When he could speak, her name was the first thing that formed. Because he wanted to see her, he found the strength to raise himself onto his elbows. Her hair was spread out on the grass that had bent under them. Her eyes were half-closed, but what he could see was still dazed with pleasure. "You're so lovely."

Her lips curved a bit, and she touched him again, her fingers on his face. "I didn't think this would happen. I didn't think it could."

"I imagined it, here, just like this." He lowered his head, just to brush his lips against hers. "But my fantasy didn't even come close to the real thing. Nothing ever has." He felt her withdraw at that, just a fraction, but enough that he felt compelled to take her face in his hand. "Nothing and no one, Johanna."

His eyes insisted that she believe him, and she wanted to, but there was still too much of a block within her to make that possible. "I've wanted you." At least she could be honest with both of them. "I can't think about what happens next."

"We're both going to have to. I've no intention of letting you go." She opened her mouth to protest, to make some excuse, and only managed to moan as she felt him harden inside her. "Not a chance," he murmured, before desire clouded his mind completely.

When she could think again, she tried to draw away. She was going to need time to put this in perspective, to work out the steps. The first was to be an adult, and not to expect.

They had shared something. Perhaps it hadn't been casual for her, but she'd always understood that every relationship had its limitations. Better to remember that now and face it from the outset. She cared, too much for her own good, but she still knew better than to cuddle up at his side and start thinking about tomorrows.

"It's late." She pulled her hands through her hair as she sat up. "I have to go."

He'd have been surprised if he could have moved again for eight hours. "Go where?"

"I have to go home." She reached for her teddy but missed by an inch when his hand braceleted her wrist.

"If you expect me to let you go anywhere tonight, you're crazy."

"I don't know what you're talking about." Her voice was amused as she tugged on her hand. "In the first place, it's not a matter of you *letting* me go anywhere." After picking up her teddy, she shook it out. "And I can hardly sleep in the grass all night."

"You're absolutely right." If she hadn't been so relaxed, she would have realized he'd given in too easily. "Here, put on my shirt. It'll be easier for you to dress inside."

Because it made sense, Johanna allowed him to bundle her into it. It carried his scent. Unconsciously she rubbed her cheek against the collar as Sam pulled on his jeans.

"Let me give you a hand with those." Sam took her now-folded clothes and draped them over his arm. "Better let me go first. There isn't much light tonight."

Johanna followed him down the path, hoping she seemed as casual and at ease as he. What had happened by the pond, weeks ago and now tonight, had been beautiful. She didn't want to lose the importance of it. But she didn't want to exaggerate its importance, either.

Nothing and no one else.

No, she'd be a fool to believe it—to hope for it. He might have meant it at the moment he'd said it. She could believe that because she'd come to understand that Sam wasn't a man for lies, even pretty ones. She could believe, too, that he cared for her—again, for the moment.

Intense feelings rarely lasted, and all the hopes and promises built on those feelings eventually crumbled. So she didn't allow herself to hope and refused to make promises.

They still had a long way to go, Sam mused. She wasn't ready to take what he'd discovered he was ready to give. The trouble was, now that he was in love with her he wouldn't be able to be so patient. Johanna was just going to have to keep pace.

As they stepped onto the terrace, he set her clothes neatly on the table. A frown formed between her brows as he casually stripped off his jeans.

"What are you doing?"

He stood before her, undeniably magnificent in the light of the moon. With a smile that warned her an instant too late, he hauled her into his arms.

"It's what *we're* doing," he said simply, and jumped into the pool.

The water was several degrees warmer than the night air, but it was still a shock. Before it closed over her head, she had time for one surprised shriek. Her legs tangled with his as the plunge separated them and the shirt billowed up around her head. Then her feet touched bottom, and instinctively she pushed upward. Gasping, she surfaced, blinking water from her eyes.

"Damn it!" She drew her arm through the water, hand fisted, and shot a spray into his grinning face.

"Nothing like a midnight swim, is there, Jo-Jo?"

"Don't call me that. You must be out of your mind."

"Only about you," he told her, then sent an unloverly splash in her direction.

Johanna dodged it, barely, telling herself she wasn't amused. "What the hell would you have done if I couldn't swim?"

"Saved you." He trod water with little effort. "I was born to be a hero."

"Jerk," she corrected. She turned, and in two strokes had reached the side. Before she could haul herself out, Sam caught her by the waist.

"When you stop being mad, you'll admit you like it." He nuzzled the back of her neck. "Want to race?"

"What I want to do is—" She turned—another miscalculation. His hands slid up her wet skin to her breasts as he bent his lips to her throat.

"Me too," he murmured.

She lifted a hand to his shoulder where it skimmed over cool skin just beginning to heat. "Sam, I can't."

"That's okay. I can." He slid into her.

Johanna woke with a faint grumble and tried to roll over. It took her several confusing seconds to realize that Sam's arm had her pinned. Lying still, she turned her head cautiously to look at him.

He slept more on her pillow than on his own. No, they were both his pillows, Johanna reminded herself. His bed, his house. Would he think her a fool or a freak if she told him this was the first time she'd ever woken up in a man's bed? It didn't matter; she wouldn't tell him. How could she tell him he was the first man she'd cared for enough, trusted enough, to share that private vulnerability called sleep?

She still wasn't quite sure how he'd managed to nudge her into it. One minute she'd been standing, naked and dripping, by the side of the pool, and the next… They hadn't even made love there, but had simply fallen into bed much like two exhausted children.

He'd made her laugh, too, and he'd given her, all unknowing, the sweet daydream of her own making.

Now it was morning and she had to remind herself again that she was an adult. They had wanted each other, enjoyed each other. It was important not to add complications to that simple formula. There wouldn't be regret. Regret usually meant blame, and she didn't want that, either. Wisely or not, she'd made a decision. The decision had taken her into intimacy with Sam. She wouldn't use the word *affair*.

Now that it was done, she had to be realistic. This intensity, this flash of feeling, would fade, and when that happened, she'd be hurt. It couldn't be prevented, only prepared for.

Her emotions had already deepened beyond her control, but she still had her strength and her sense. No strings. He'd said it. She'd meant it.

Despite that, she lifted a fingertip to brush the hair from his forehead.

Oh, God, I'm in love with him, I'm so ridiculously in love with him, and I'm bound to make a fool of myself.

When he opened his eyes, those dark, heavy-lidded eyes, she didn't give a damn.

"Hi."

She lowered her hand, flustered because he'd caught her petting him. "Good morning."

It was there, even after their incredible night together. The trace of shyness he found so appealing. So exciting. Because he didn't want to give her time to layer it over with composure, he rolled on top of her.

"Sam—"

"It occurs to me," he began as he drew longer, lazier kisses from her, "that we never made love in bed." He ran his hand down her side, from shoulder to hip, from hip to thigh. "I'm feeling traditional this morning."

She didn't have time to analyze what she was feeling. Even as she tried to say his name again, her breath caught. This morning he wasn't so patient—or perhaps she, knowing what could be, was more sensitive.

She curled around him and let herself go.

Time had gotten away from her. Everything had gotten away from her, Johanna corrected as she stepped out of the shower and began to towel off quickly. If she threw on her clothes, let her hair air-dry on the way to work and pushed the speed limit, she might just make it.

She grabbed a few basic cosmetics out of her purse. The effort would be sketchy, but it was all she could afford. In the bedroom she ripped the plastic off the first suit Sam had brought up from her car. Yesterday's blouse would have to work with it. Cursing herself for not having planned properly, she zipped the skirt and ran down the hall carrying her shoes.

"Where's the fire?" Sam asked her as she rested a hand against the wall and struggled into her shoes.

"I'm running late."

He lifted a brow. "Do you get demerits for being tardy?"

"I'm never late."

"Good, then you can afford to be. Have some coffee."

She took the cup he offered, grateful. "Thanks. I really have to run."

"You haven't eaten anything."

"I never eat breakfast."

"Today you do." He had her arm. To prevent the contents of the cup sloshing all over her freshly laundered suit, she kept up with him. "Five minutes, Johanna. Catch your breath, drink your coffee. If you argue, it'll take ten."

She swore, but downed more coffee as he pulled her into the kitchen. "Sam, you're the one who's on vacation, not me. I've got a full day scheduled that might, if I'm lucky, end before six."

"All the more reason you should have a decent breakfast." He couldn't remember ever having felt better in the morning, more alive or full of energy. Briefly he wished he was in the middle of filming so that he could pour some of that energy into a part. "Sit. I'll fix you some eggs."

Because her temper was beginning to fray, she drank more coffee. "I appreciate it, really I do, but I don't have time. We're shooting ads today for the home viewers' contest, and I'm the only one who can handle John Jay."

"A dubious talent." The English muffin he'd dropped in the toaster popped up. "You can at least eat this."

Annoyed, she snatched it from him, ignored the butter and jam on the table and bit into it. "There," she said, and swallowed. "Satisfied?"

Her hair was still dripping around her face, and she'd forgotten her lipstick. Eyes still shadowed from the long night glared at him. He grinned and flicked a crumb off her chin. "I love you, Johanna."

If he'd drawn back and planted his fist on her chin she would have been no less shocked. She stared at him as the muffin slipped out of her boneless fingers onto the table. Her step back was instinctive, defensive. Sam lifted his brow at it, but that was all.

"Don't say that to me," she managed at length. "I don't need to hear that. I don't want to hear it."

She needed to hear it all right, he thought. She might not have wanted to, but she needed to. He was going to see that she did, at regular intervals, but right now she'd gone pale again. "All right," he said slowly. "It doesn't change the facts one way or the other."

"I—I have to go." She ransacked her purse almost desperately for her keys. "I'm really running late." What was she supposed to say? What was supposed to be said on the morning after the night? With her keys clutched in her hand, she looked up. "Goodbye."

"I'll walk you out." His arm went around her shoulders. She tried not to tense. She tried not to lean against him. She could feel the tug-of-war as they walked. "There's something I'd like to tell you, Johanna."

"Please, it isn't necessary. We agreed even before—before last night—that there wouldn't be any promises."

"Did we?" Damned if he remembered that, but if he had agreed, that was one agreement that would have to be broken. He pushed the front door open and stepped onto the porch before turning her to him. "We'll have to talk about that."

"All right." She would have agreed to almost anything if it had meant he'd let her go. Because she wanted to stay. More than she'd ever wanted anything, she wanted to toss her keys over her shoulder, throw herself into his arms and stay as long as he'd have her.

"In the meantime, I want you to know that I've never had another woman in that bed." He saw the flash of doubt in her eyes before she was able to mask it. And before he could stop himself, he'd hauled her up by the lapels. "Damn it, a man gets tired of having everything he says dissected in that brain of yours. I didn't say there haven't been other women, Johanna, but there's never been another woman here. Because here's special to me. It's important. And so are you." He let her go. "Chew on that for a while."

Johanna thumbed another antacid tablet from the roll. She'd told Sam no less than the truth when she'd said she was the only one who could handle John Jay. It just so happened that today she wasn't doing a good job of it. The two-hour photo session had stretched into three, and tempers were fraying. If she didn't have the crew, equipment and two cars out of the studio in another forty-five minutes she was going to have the producer of *Noon with Nina* on her back.

Resigned, Johanna chewed the antacid and prayed it did its job better than she was doing hers. She signaled for a halt and hoped the five-minute break would keep the photographer from strangling her host.

"John Jay." She knew the game. Johanna pasted a smile on her face as she crossed to him. "Can I have a minute?" Her voice was calm, her touch light and friendly, as she took his arm to guide him to a corner. "Sessions like this are so annoying, aren't they?"

He literally pounced on the sympathy. "You have no idea,

Johanna. You know I want what's best for the show, darling, but that man…" He glanced over at the photographer with loathing. "He has no conception of mood or image."

"That man" was one of the tops in his business and was being paid by the incredibly expensive hour. Johanna bit off an oath in time to have it slip out as a sigh. "I know, but unfortunately we have to work with him. We're running behind schedule, and the last thing I want is to have him take shots of the cars only." She let the threat hang until she was certain it had sunk in. "After all, there are three stars here. The cars, the show itself and, of course, you. The teasers went beautifully, by the way."

"I was fresh." He fussed with the knot of his tie.

"I understand perfectly. But I have to ask you to keep the energy up for just a few more minutes. That suit's very becoming, John Jay."

"It is, isn't it?" He held out an arm, turning it over to study the sleeve.

"These shots are going to make quite a statement." If she didn't strangle him herself first. "All I want you to do is stand between those two cars and flash the smile America loves."

"For you, darling." He squeezed her hand, ready to sacrifice himself to the masses. "You know, you're looking a little dragged-out."

Her smile didn't fade, only froze. "It's lucky I'm not having my picture taken."

"It certainly is," he agreed, patting Johanna's head. He already knew his producer could grow fangs if he patted her elsewhere. "You have to try to relax more, Johanna, and take those vitamins I told you about. God knows I couldn't get through the day without them." He watched the photographer come back on the set. With a sniff, John Jay signaled for makeup. "Johanna, there's a rumor running rampant that you're seeing Sam Weaver."

"Is there?" Johanna ground her teeth as John Jay got a dusting of powder. "It's amazing how these things get started."

"What a town." Satisfied that he was perfect, John Jay strode over to do his duty.

It took only twenty minutes more. The moment she'd sent her host on his way, Johanna apologized to the photographer, offered him and his assistant lunch on her and handed out tickets to Monday night's taping.

By the time she drove from the studio in Burbank back to her offices in Century City, she was two hours behind schedule and had consumed almost half the roll of antacids in her pocket.

"You've got a half-dozen messages," Bethany told her the moment she walked in. "Only two of which require answers yesterday. I contacted Tom Bradley's agent. He's interested in doing the pilot."

"Good. Let's set it up." In her office, Johanna dropped her briefcase, accepted the cup of coffee Beth was already offering and sat on the edge of her desk. "I've thought of twenty-seven ways to successfully murder John Jay Johnson."

"Would you like me to type them up?"

"Not yet. I want to wait until I have an even thirty." Johanna sipped her coffee and wished for five minutes, five full minutes to be completely alone, so that she could take her shoes off, put her feet up and close her eyes. "Bradley has a reputation as being very professional."

"A veteran. Did his first show in '72, when he was still wet behind the ears. It ran for five years, and he slid right into the old classic *Word Bingo*. That was on the air from '77 to '85. Pretty amazing. He retired as sort of the guru of game shows, but his face is still recognizable from occasional appearances on other daytime shows and grand-marshaling parades. Luring him back to the fold would be no small accomplishment."

She stopped because Johanna was drinking coffee and staring out the window. There were shadows under her eyes, Bethany noted, and a definite look of melancholy in them. "Johanna, you look terrible."

Taken aback, Johanna set her coffee aside. "So I've been told."

"Is everything all right?"

"Everything's fine." Except that Sam said he was in love with her and she was so terrified she wanted to get in her car and keep driving. She drew out her roll of tablets.

Frowning, Beth eyed it. "Was that a new roll this morning?"

"It was, before I spent most of it with John Jay."

"Have any lunch?"

"Don't ask."

"Johanna, why don't you take the rest of the day off, go home, take a nap, watch the soaps?"

With a small smile, Johanna rose to move behind her desk. "I've got to answer those questions yesterday. Beth, let's see if we can set that pilot up for the week after next. Be sure to notify Patterson Productions."

Bethany shrugged and stood. "You're the boss," she said, and set the stack of messages on Johanna's desk.

Absolutely true, Johanna thought as Bethany closed the door behind her. She was the boss. Johanna rubbed at the headache behind her temple and wondered why she felt as though someone else were pulling the strings.

* * *

He didn't know what he was doing there, sitting on her front steps like a lovesick teenager. Because he was lovesick, Sam told himself as he crossed his booted ankles.

He hadn't felt this stupid about a woman since he'd fallen like a ton of bricks for Mary Alice Reeder. She'd been an older woman, sophisticated, wise and like most sixteen-year-old girls, not very interested in a fourteen-year-old pest. But he'd loved pretty little Mary Alice with a kind of worshipful devotion that had lasted nearly nine months.

Calf love, his mother had called it, not unkindly.

Since then he'd fallen into the second stage, the care-for stage, with a number of women. But he hadn't loved anyone else since Mary Alice Reeder. Until Johanna.

He almost wished he could go back to that calf love. However painful it was, it passed, and it left a man with sweet and rather filmy memories. Hearts and initials carved surreptitiously in a tree trunk, daydreams that always ended with him saving his girl from some horrendous disaster that opened her eyes to his charm and bravery.

Sam laughed at himself and looked at a spiky blue flower that was just beginning to bloom in Johanna's garden. Times changed. Mary Alice had slipped through his shaky fingers. But he wasn't fourteen anymore, and Johanna, like it or not, was going nowhere.

He wanted her. Just sitting there in front of her quiet, empty house, with a basket beside him and her flowers sleeping in the evening sun, he wanted her. For good. It wasn't a decision he'd made with a snap of his fingers, though she might think so. It was something that had happened to him, and not entirely in a way he liked. The only plans he'd counted on, the only pressure he'd expected, had been career-oriented.

If he'd had his choice, he would have cruised along for another few months, a year. Ten years. Time didn't have a damn thing to do with it. He'd looked at her, he'd touched her, and the decision had been made for him.

Hadn't he sat right here not so long before and told her they should get to know each other better? Companions, with no strings. He'd meant it, every bit as honestly as he'd meant it when he'd told her he loved her.

She'd accepted the first—warily, but she had accepted it. The second had been met with pure panic.

What was it that made Johanna so skittish? Another man? She'd never mentioned one, never even hinted at one. Unless he was completely obtuse, the woman he'd made love with the night before had been almost frighteningly innocent. If she'd been hurt, he felt it must be buried deep in the past, and it was time for her to let it go.

Time. He didn't have much of that, he thought as he lifted the lid of the basket to check on his gift. Any day he could get the call that would send him three thousand miles away. It would be weeks before he could be with her again. He could handle that. He thought he could handle that, but only if she gave him something to take with him.

When he heard the car he set the lid carefully back in place. Lovesick, he thought as his stomach knotted and his nerves began to jangle. It was a very apt phrase.

Johanna pulled in behind his car and wondered what the hell she was going to do. She'd been so sure she would be able to come home, close herself in, maybe dive into bed and sleep for hours without thinking at all. But he was here, invading her privacy, stealing away her quiet hours. The worst of it was, she was glad, so glad to see him.

"You put in a long day." He rose but didn't cross to her.

"A lot of things are coming to a head at once."

He waited until she stood in front of him. "I know what you mean." He touched her then, just a light stroke down her cheek. "You look tired."

"So I've been informed, with annoying regularity."

"Are you going to let me come in?"

"All right." He hadn't kissed her. Johanna had expected it this time, had been prepared for it. As she turned toward the house she suspected that was exactly why he hadn't done it. She spotted the wicker basket and paused as he scooped it up. "What did you do, bring sandwiches in case I was late?"

"Not exactly." He followed her inside. It was precisely as it had been the last time, neat, homey, smelling faintly of potpourri and fresh flowers. They were peonies this time, fat red blooms in a dark blue jar.

Johanna started to slip out of her shoes, caught herself and set down her briefcase.

"Can I get you a drink?"

"Why don't you sit down and I'll fix you one?" He set the basket down next to the jar of flowers. "I'm the one on vacation, remember?"

"I usually just get some coffee, but—"

"Fine. I'll get it."

"But—"

"Relax, Johanna. It'll just take a minute."

He strode off as she stood where she was. As far as she could remember, no one had ever cut her off in the middle of so many sentences. Well, he'd invited himself, she decided. He could heat up the coffee as well as she. And she did want to sit down, for just a minute.

She chose the corner of the sofa and thought she might rest her eyes until she heard Sam coming back. Johanna stifled a yawn, shut her eyes and was asleep in seconds.

She awoke the same way, instantly. Somehow she'd snuggled down and had pulled an afghan up to her chin. Sitting up, Johanna dragged her hands through her hair just before she spotted Sam sitting across from her drinking coffee.

"I'm sorry." She cleared the huskiness out of her voice. "I must have dozed off."

She'd slept like a rock for half an hour. He'd tucked her up himself. "How do you feel?"

"Embarrassed."

He smiled and rose to go to the coffeepot he'd set on a warmer. "Want this now?"

"Yes, thanks."

"You didn't get much sleep last night."

"No." She took the coffee, studying the little painted cup as though it fascinated her. "Neither did you."

"I didn't put in a ten-hour day." He sat beside her. She was up like a spring.

"I'm starving," she said quickly. "There isn't much out in the kitchen, but I can put together a couple of sandwiches."

"I'll give you a hand."

Even as he rose, she was shrugging out of her jacket. "That's all right, it's no trouble." Nervous, she turned the jacket over, spilling out the contents of the pockets. Sam bent over and picked up loose change, a hairpin and what was left of the roll of antacids.

"What do you need these for?"

"Survival." Taking everything from him, she set them on the table.

"You put yourself under too much pressure. How many of these do you take?"

"For heaven's sake, Sam, they're more candy than medicine."

Her defensive tone had his eyes narrowing. Too many, he decided. "I'm entitled to worry about you." When she started to shake her head, he cupped her chin in his hand. "Yes, I am. I love you, Johanna, whether you can deal with it yet or not."

"You're pushing me too fast."

"I haven't even started to push yet."

With her face still caught in his hand, he kissed her. His lips demanded response, nothing timid, nothing cool. She could taste the trace of anger on them, the hint of frustration. Desire, kicked into high gear by other emotions, held sway. If it had been possible, she would have pulled back, ended it then and there. But it wasn't possible.

She touched a hand to his cheek, not even aware that she sought to soothe. As the kiss deepened, she slid her hand up into his hair. His name was like a sigh from her lips to his. Then she was locked close.

It was the whirlwind again, fast and furious. This time it was she who tugged at his shirt, wanting that contact, that intimate, secret feel of flesh against flesh. Her need was a springboard for his. Tangled, groping at buttons, they tumbled onto the couch.

Even last night, in that first burgeoning passion, she hadn't been like this. She trembled as she had trembled before, but now it was anticipation, even impatience, that shivered through her. To be swept away wasn't what she looked for now; to be taken wasn't enough. It had only taken one night for her to realize her own power. Now she was driven to test it again.

He struggled to keep his hands gentle as the insistence of hers had desire clawing at him. Her mouth, open and hungry, sought the taste of him, chest, shoulders, throat, while she tugged at the snap of his jeans and sent his stomach muscles dancing.

"Johanna." As much for her preservation as his own, he tried to slow the pace. Then her mouth was back on his, silencing him, ripping the last shreds of control.

The last light of day streamed through the windows of a room scented by flowers in a house tucked almost secretly in the hills. As long as he lived he would think of her that way—in soft light, in fresh scents, alone.

She hadn't known she could be like this, so full of need, so desperate to be filled. Heedless, daring, reckless. She felt the teddy he'd slipped so carefully from her the night before tear as he yanked aside the barrier.

Then she captured him, drawing him in, arching high as pleasure arrowed into her. Fast, then faster still, she drove them both in a race for that final dazzling release.

He held on to her, even after her body went lax, after his own emptied. Her shyness had delighted him, lured him, but this Johanna, the one who could flash with white heat, could make him a slave. He wasn't certain what he'd done, he only remembered the grasping, titanic lunge into delirium.

"Did I hurt you?" he murmured.

"No." She was too stunned by her own behavior to notice any bruises. "Did I hurt you?"

He grinned against her throat. "I didn't feel a thing." He tried to shift her to a more comfortable position and spotted the remains of her teddy on the floor. "I owe you some lingerie," he murmured as he lifted it up.

Johanna studied the torn strap and rent seam. Abruptly she began to laugh. She felt like that, torn open, and God only knew what would pour through the holes. "I've never attacked a man before," she managed.

"You can practice on me anytime. Here." He picked up his shirt and slipped it over her shoulders. "I always seem to be lending you a shirt. Johanna, I want you to tell me how you feel. I need you to."

Slowly, hoping to gather up some of her scattered senses, she buttoned the shirt. "There are reasons... I can't talk about them, Sam, but there are reasons why I don't want things to get serious."

"Things already are serious."

He was right. She knew he was right even before she looked into his eyes and felt it. "How serious?"

"I think you know. But I'm willing to spell it out for you again."

She wasn't being fair. It was so important, and sometimes so impossible, to be fair. There was too much she couldn't tell him, she thought. Too much he'd never be able to understand even if she could. "I need time."

"I've got a couple of hours."

"Please."

"All right." It wasn't easy, but he promised himself he'd give her time, even though he felt it slipping away. He tugged on his jeans, then remembered the basket. "I almost forgot. I brought you a present." He plucked up the basket and set it in her lap.

He wasn't going to push. She shot him a quick look of gratitude, then added a smile. "What, a picnic?" She flipped back the lid, but instead of cold chicken she saw a small dozing kitten. Johanna drew her out and was instantly in love. "Oh, Sam! She's adorable." The kitten mewed sleepily as she rubbed its rust-colored fur against her cheek.

"Blanche had a litter last month." He tickled the kitten's ears.

"Blanche? As in Dubois?"

"Now you're catching on. She's sort of a faded Southern belle who likes to pit the toms against each other. This one's weaned, and there's enough cat food in the basket to get you through about a week."

The kitten climbed down the front of her skirt and began to fight with one of the buttons. "Thank you." Johanna turned to him as he stroked the kitten's head. For the first time, she threw her arms around Sam's neck and hugged him.

9

He knew he shouldn't be nervous. It was an excellent production, with a quality script, top-notch casting and a talented director. He'd already seen the rushes, as well as a preview of the press screening. He knew he'd done a good job. But still he paced and watched the clock and wished like hell it was nine.

No, he wished it was eleven and the damn thing was over.

It was worse because Johanna was engrossed in the script Max Heddison had sent him. So Sam was left to worry, nurse the brandy he had no desire for and pace her living room. Even the redheaded kitten, which Johanna had christened Lucy, was too busy to bother with him. She was involved with wrestling a ball of yarn under Johanna's feet.

Sam made himself sit, poked at the Sunday paper, then was up again.

"You could take a walk outside for a change of scenery," Johanna suggested from across the room.

"She speaks! Johanna, why don't we go for a ride?"

"I have to finish this. Sam, Michael's a wonderful part for you, a really wonderful part."

He'd already decided that, but it was Luke, the character

who would be exposed to millions of eyes in a matter of thirty minutes, who worried him. If he took on Michael, that would be another worry at another time. "Yeah. Johanna, it's lousy for your eyes to hold papers that close."

She moved them back automatically. In less than a minute she had her nose against them again. "This is wonderful, really wonderful. You're going to take it, aren't you?"

"For a chance to work with Max Heddison, I'd take it if it was garbage."

"Then you're lucky it shines. God, this scene here, the one on Christmas Eve, just leaves you limp."

He stopped pacing long enough to glance at her again. She was rereading it as avidly as she'd read it the first time. And the papers were an inch from her face.

"You keep that up, you're going to need glasses." He saw the frown come and go and was distracted enough to smile. "Unless you already do."

Without bothering to glance up, she turned a page. "Shut up, Sam, you're breaking my concentration."

Instead, he pulled the script away and held it at a reasonable distance. "Read me some dialogue."

"You already know what it says." She made a grab for the script, but he inched it away.

"You can't, can you? Where are your glasses, Johanna?"

"I don't need glasses."

"Then read me some dialogue."

She squinted, but the words ran together. "My eyes are just tired."

"Like hell." He set the script down to take her hands. "Don't tell me my sensible Johanna's too vain to wear reading glasses."

"I'm not vain, and I don't need glasses."

"You'd look cute in them." When she pulled her hands away, he made two circles out of his index fingers and thumbs and held them over her eyes. "Studiously sexy. Dark frames—yes, that would be best. Very conservative. I'd love to take you to bed while you were wearing them."

"I never wear them."

"Ah, but you do have them. Where?"

She made a grab for the script, but he blocked her. "You're just trying to distract yourself."

"You're right. Johanna, I'm dying in here."

She softened enough to touch his face. It was something she still did rarely. Automatically he lifted his hand to her wrist and held it there. "The reviews couldn't have been better, Sam. America waits for nine o'clock with bated breath."

"And America might be snoring by nine-fifteen."

"Not a chance." Reaching over, she picked up the remote to turn on the set. "Sit down. We'll watch something else until it starts."

He eased into the chair with her, shifting her until she stretched across his lap. "I'd rather nibble on your ear until it starts."

"Then we'll miss the first scene." Content, she rested her head against his shoulder.

It had been an odd weekend, she thought. He'd stayed with her. After her first unease, they'd fallen into a simple routine that was no routine at all. Lovemaking, sleep, walks, the little chores a house required, even a trip to the market to fuss over fresh vegetables.

She hadn't felt like a producer for forty-eight hours, nor had she thought of Sam as an actor. Or a celebrity. He'd been her lover—or, as he had once put it, her companion. How lovely life would be if it could be that simple. It had been difficult, even for these short two days, to pretend it could be. It had been much less difficult to wish.

She'd changed his life. He didn't know how to explain it, or how to put it into words she might understand, but change it she had. He'd known that for certain when he'd gotten the script.

Max Heddison had been as good as his word. Sam had felt like a first-year drama student being offered the lead in a summer-stock production. It had come through Marv, of course, along with Marv's opinion about potential, the old school and the new, a million five plus percentages. Sam had taken it all in. It was never wise to forget that show business remained a business. Then he had devoured the script.

There was a part of him, a part he hoped would always be there, that could break out in a sweat at the chance to take on a new role. The character of Michael was complex, confused, desperately trying to unravel the mystery of his much-loved, much-detested father. He could already see Max Heddison in that role. Slowly, trying to see the script as a whole, as well as a vehicle, he'd read it again.

And he'd known he wanted to do it. Had to do it.

If Marv could get a million five, fine and dandy. If he could get peanuts and a keg of beer, that was all right, too. But rather than picking up the phone and calling his agent with a go-ahead, he'd bundled up the script and taken it to Johanna.

He'd needed her to read it. He'd needed her opinion, though throughout his career he'd always gone on his own gut instinct. Agent or not, the final decision had always been his. Now that had changed.

In a matter of weeks she'd become entwined with his life,

his thoughts, his motives. Though he'd never thought of himself as a solitary person, he'd stopped being alone. She was there now, to share with—the big things, like the script, and the small things, like a new litter of kittens. It might have been true that she still held back from him, but in the last two days he'd seen her relax. Degree by degree, certainly, but he'd been able to see the change. That morning she'd seemed almost used to waking beside him.

He was giving her time, Sam thought as he brushed his lips over her hair. But he was also making his moves.

"Here come the teasers," Johanna murmured, and he was jerked back to the present. His stomach clenched. He swore at himself, but it tightened anyway, as it did whenever he prepared to watch himself on-screen. He flashed on, wearing only faded jeans, a battered panama and a grin, while the voice-over promised the sultry and the shocking.

"It is a nice chest." She smiled and kissed him on the cheek.

"They spent half the time spraying it so it'd have that nice jungle-fatigue shine. Do women really pant over a sweaty chest?"

"You bet," she told him, and settled down to watch the opening credits.

She was drawn in before the first five minutes were over. Luke drifted into town with two dollars in his pocket, a reputation on his back and an eye for the ladies. She knew it was Sam, pulling bits and pieces of his art together to meld with the writer's, but it rang true. You could almost smell the sweat and boredom of the sleepy little town in Georgia.

During the first commercial he slid down to the floor to give her the chair. He didn't want to ask her now, didn't want to break the rhythm. But he rested a hand on her calf.

For two hours they said nothing. She rose once and came back with cold drinks, but they didn't exchange words. On screen she watched the man she'd slept with, the man she'd loved, seduce another woman. She watched him talk himself out of one fight and raise his fists for another. He got drunk. He bled. He lied.

But she'd stopped thinking of him as Sam. The man she watched was Luke. She felt the slight pressure of Sam's fingers against her leg and kept her eyes on Luke.

He was irresistible. He was unforgivable.

When the segment ended, it left her hanging and Sarah's roses dying in the bowl.

Sam still said nothing. His instincts told him it was good. It was better than good. It was the best he'd ever done. Everything had fallen into place—the performances, the atmosphere, those lazy two-edged words that had first caught his imagination and his ambition. But he wanted to hear it from her.

Rising, he shifted to sit on the arm of her chair. Johanna, his Johanna, was still frowning at the screen. "How could he do that to her?" she demanded. "How could he use her that way?"

Sam waited a moment, still careful. "He's a user. It's all he knows."

"But she trusts him. She knows he's lied and cheated, but she still trusts him. And he's—"

"What?"

"He's a bastard, but— Damn, there's something compelling about him, something likable. You want to believe he could change, that she could change him." Unsettled, moved, she looked up at him. "What are you grinning at?"

"It worked." He hauled her up and kissed her. "It worked, Johanna."

She backed up enough to breathe. "I didn't tell you how good I thought you were."

"You just did." He kissed her again, then began tugging up her shirt.

"Sam—"

"I suddenly find myself with all this energy—incredible energy. Let me show you." He slid back into the chair, taking her with him.

"Wait a minute." She laughed, then moaned when his hands began to wander. "Sam, give me a minute."

"I've got hours for you. Hours and hours."

"Sam." With one laughing shove, she held him off. "I want to talk to you."

"Is it going to take long?" He tugged at the waistband of her slacks.

"No." To stop him, she framed his face with her hands. "I want to tell you how really exceptional you were. I pretended once that I didn't pay attention to your films, but I have. And you were never better than tonight."

"Thanks. It means a lot coming from you."

She took a deep breath, managing to push herself out of the chair. "You put a lot into that part."

She was leading somewhere. Though he wasn't sure he'd like the destination, he let her take the lead. "A part's not worth anything unless you do. Nothing is."

No, nothing was. "I, ah...I almost forget, when we're like this, who you are. These past few weeks, here, at the ranch, it hasn't been like being with Sam Weaver in capital letters."

Puzzled, he rose with her. "Johanna, you're not going to try to tell me you're intimidated by actors? You've been around the business all your life."

"All my life," she murmured. She didn't want to love him. She didn't want to love anyone, but most particularly not an actor, a movie star, a household name. The trouble was, she already did. "It's not a matter of being intimidated, it's just that it's been easy to forget you're not just an ordinary man who I ran into and grew fond of."

"Fond of," he repeated, drawing out the phrase. "Well, we're improving." He had her by the shoulders. That lazy drawl of a voice could fool you into forgetting how quick he was. "I don't know what the hell this is about, but we'll get to it in a minute. Right now, I want you to look at me. Really look at me, Johanna," he repeated, adding a little shake. "And tell me if you're in love with me."

"I never said—"

"No one knows better than I what you've never said." He drew her a little closer, insisting that her eyes stay on his. "I want to hear it now, and it has nothing to do with how I make my living, what the critics say or how much I'm worth at the box office. Do you love me?"

She started to shake her head but simply couldn't force it to move. How could she lie when he was looking at her, when he was touching her? She drew a deep breath to be certain her voice was calm. "Yes."

He wanted to take her then, just gather her close and hold on. But he knew that not only did he have to hear the words, she had to say them. "Yes, what?"

"Yes, I love you."

He looked at her for a long time. She was trembling a little, so he lowered his head and pressed his lips to her forehead. He didn't know why it was so difficult for her to say.

Not yet. But he was determined to find out.

"That should make things easier."

"But it doesn't," she murmured. "It doesn't change anything."

"We'll talk about it. Let's sit down."

She nodded. She didn't know what there was to say, but there had to be something. Trying to make it seem normal, she started to the front door to lock up for the night. Then she heard the quick report on the evening news.

"Sources report that Carl W. Patterson, respected producer, has suffered a heart attack this evening. Paramedics were summoned to his Beverly Hills estate, which he shares with his fiancée, Toni DuMonde. His condition at this hour remains critical."

"Johanna." Sam laid a hand on her arm. She hadn't gasped or cried out. There were no tears in her eyes. She had simply stopped in her tracks as though she'd run into a wall. "Get your purse. I'll take you to the hospital."

"What?"

"I'll drive you." He switched off the set and went to get her bag himself. "Come on."

She only nodded and let him lead her out.

No one had called her. The oddness of it struck Sam as they rode the elevator up to Cardiac Care. Her father had had a heart attack, and she hadn't been notified.

The year before, when his mother had broken her ankle in a nasty fall on the ice, he'd received three calls in a matter of hours. One from his sister, another from his father and the last from his mother, telling him that his sister and father were fuss-budgets.

Nonetheless the ankle had worried him enough to have him do some quick scheduling adjustments so that he could make the trip back east. He'd only had thirty-six hours to spare, but it had been time enough to see his mother for himself, sign her cast and put his mind at rest.

And a broken ankle was a far cry from a heart attack.

Johanna was Patterson's only child, yet she'd had to hear about her father's illness on the eleven-o'clock news. Even if they weren't close, as he'd already deduced, they were family. In Sam's experience, families stuck together in times of crisis.

She'd barely said a word since they'd left the house. He'd tried to comfort her, to offer both hope and support, but she hadn't responded. It seemed to him that she was just going through the motions, pale, a little dazed, but with the automatic control that had slipped effortlessly back into place. He watched her approach the nurse's station. Her hands were steady, her voice was calm and unwavering when she spoke.

"Carl Patterson was admitted this evening. They told me downstairs he's in CCU."

The nurse—sturdy, mid-forties and used to the night shift— barely glanced up. "I'm sorry, we're not permitted to give out patient information."

"He's my father," Johanna said flatly.

The nurse looked up. Reporters and the curious used all kinds of ploys to glean information on the famous. She'd already discouraged a few of them that evening. The woman on the other side of the counter didn't look like a reporter— the nurse prided herself on having a nose for them—but she hadn't been told to expect family, either. Recognizing doubt, Johanna drew out her wallet and identification.

"I'd like to see him, if that's possible, and speak with his doctor."

The nurse felt a stirring of sympathy. Her gaze shifted and locked on Sam. She recognized him, and though seeing him face-to-face would give her something to tell her husband when they passed over the breakfast table, she wasn't overly impressed. After twenty years of nursing in Beverly Hills she was accustomed to seeing celebrities, often naked, sick and vulnerable. But she did remember reading that Sam Weaver was having a fling with Carl Patterson's daughter.

"I'll be happy to page the doctor for you, Miss Patterson. There's a waiting room down the hall and to the left. Miss Dumonde is already there."

"Thank you." She turned and started down, refusing to think past the moment, refusing to think past the action required to get beyond that moment. She heard a bell ding quietly, almost secretively, then the soft slap of crepe-soled shoes.

The panic was gone, that first thunder of panic that had filled her head when she'd heard the news report. Replacing it was the knowledge that she had to put one foot in front of the other and do whatever needed to be done. She was used to doing such things alone.

"Sam, I have no idea how long this might take. Why don't you go home? I can take a cab back when I'm ready."

"Don't be ridiculous," was all he said.

It was enough, more than enough to cause her breath to hitch. She wanted to turn to him, to press her face against his chest. She wanted to be held, to be passive, to let him handle whatever had to be done. Instead, she turned into the waiting room.

"Sam!" Toni's eyes, already damp, spilled over. She sprang out of her chair and launched herself into his arms. "Oh, Sam, I'm so glad you're here. I've been so frightened. It's a nightmare. I'm just sick with worry, Sam. I don't know what I'll do if Carl dies."

"Pull yourself together." Sam led her back to a chair, then lit one of the cigarettes she'd spilled from a pack onto the table. He stuck it between her fingers. "What did the doctor say?"

"I don't know. He was so technical and grim faced." She held out a hand to a blond man in a dinner jacket. "I never would have survived this without Jack. He's been a wall, an absolute wall. Hello, Johanna." She sniffled into a lacy hand-kerchief.

"Sam." Jack Vandear nodded as he patted Toni's hand. He'd directed two of Patterson's productions and had run into Sam at least a half-dozen times on the party circuit. "It's been a rough night."

"So we heard. This is Patterson's daughter."

"Oh." Jack rose and offered a hand.

"I'd like to know what happened."

"It was horrible." Toni looked up at Johanna through an attractive veil of tears. "Just horrible."

Jack sent her a look that was three parts impatient, one part sympathetic. He hadn't minded comforting her, but the truth was, he'd come for Carl. It went through his mind that with Sam here, the soggy-eyed Toni could be passed along.

"We were having a small dinner party. Carl looked a bit tired, but I took it to mean he'd been working too hard, as usual. Then it seemed he couldn't get his breath. He collapsed into a chair. He complained of pain in his chest and his arm. We called the paramedics." He started to skim over the rest, then decided Johanna looked strong enough to handle it. "They had to bring him back once." At that Toni put up a low, heartbreaking sob and was ignored. "The doctor said it was a massive coronary. They've been working to stabilize him."

Her legs were shaking. She could keep her hands steady and

her face impassive, but she couldn't stop her legs from trembling. Massive coronary. Darlene, her father's wry and witty
third wife, would have said that Carl W. Patterson never did
anything halfway.

"Did they tell you his chances?"

"They haven't told us much of anything."

"We've been waiting forever." Toni dabbed at her eyes again,
then drew on her cigarette. In her own way, she was fond of
Carl. She wanted to marry him even though she knew that
divorce would be at the end of the rainbow. Divorce was easy.
Death was another matter. "The press was here five minutes
after we were. I knew how much Carl would hate having them
report this."

Johanna sat and for the first time looked, really looked, at her
father's fiancée. Whatever she was, the woman obviously knew
Carl. The heart attack was a weakness, and he would detest
having it made public knowledge. "I'll handle the press," she said
tonelessly. "It might be best if you, both of you," she said, including Jack, "told them as little as possible. Have you seen
him?"

"Not since they took him in." Toni took another drag as
she looked out into the corridor. "I hate hospitals." After
crushing out the cigarette, she began to pleat the handkerchief.
The silver sequins on her evening dress sparkled opulently in
the dim waiting room. "We were supposed to go to Monaco
next week. Carl had some business there, but for the most part
it was to be a kind of prehoneymoon. He seemed so...well,
so virile." The tears started again when the doctor came into
the waiting room.

"Miss DuMonde."

She was up and clutching at both his hands, the picture of

the distressed lover barely holding back hysteria. It surprised her to discover it was only half an act. "He's all right. Tell me Carl's all right."

"His condition's stabilized. We're running tests to determine the extent of the damage. He's a strong man, Miss DuMonde, and overall his health seems excellent."

He looked tired, Johanna thought as she studied the doctor. Unbearably tired, but she recognized the truth. She rose as he glanced her way.

"You're Mr. Patterson's daughter?"

"I'm Johanna Patterson. How serious is his condition?"

"I have to tell you it's very serious. However, he's getting the best care possible."

"I'd like to see him."

"For a few moments. Miss DuMonde?"

"He wouldn't want me to see him this way. He'd hate it."

Because Johanna could only agree, she ignored the little stab of resentment and followed the doctor out. "He's sedated," she was told. "And he's being monitored very closely. The next twenty-four hours will tell the tale, but your father's relatively young, Miss Patterson. An incident like this is often a warning, to slow down, to take a hard look at your own mortality."

It had to be said, just once out loud, though she knew she would get no absolutes. "Is he going to die?"

"Not if we can help it." The doctor pushed open a glass door.

There was her father. She'd lived in his house, eaten his food, obeyed his rules. And she barely knew him. The machines that eased his breathing and monitored his vital signs hummed. His eyes were shut, his face pasty under his tan. He looked old. It occurred to her that she'd never thought of him as old, even when she'd been a child. He'd always been handsome, ageless, virile.

She remembered Toni using that word. Virile. That was so important to Carl. He'd often been described as a man's man— salty tongued, strong shouldered, reckless with women. He'd always been impatient with weaknesses, excuses, illnesses. Perhaps that was why, when he'd reached the middle of his life, the women he'd brought into it had become younger and younger.

He was a hard man, even a cold one, but he'd always been full of life. There was a genius in him, a genius she'd admired as much as she'd feared it. He was an honest man, a man of his word, but never one to give an inch more than he chose.

She touched him once, just a hand over his. It was a gesture she would never have considered making had he been awake.

"Will it happen again?"

"He has an excellent chance of full recovery, if he throws away the cigars, watches his alcohol intake and cuts back on his schedule. There's his diet, of course," the doctor went on, but Johanna was already shaking her head.

"I can't imagine him doing any of those things."

"People often do what others can't imagine after they end up in CCU. It'll be his choice, of course, but he's not a stupid man."

"No, he's not." She removed her hand. "We'll need a press release. I can take care of that. When will he be awake?"

"You should be able to talk to him in the morning."

"I'd appreciate a call if there's any change before then. I'll leave my number at the nurses' station."

"I should be able to tell you more in the morning." The doctor pushed open the door again. "You'd do well to get some rest yourself. A recovering cardiac patient can be wearing."

"Thank you." Alone, she started back down the hall. In self-defense, she blocked out the image of her father in the hospital bed. The moment she walked back in, Toni was up and grabbing both her hands.

"How is he, Johanna? Tell me the truth, tell me everything."

"He's resting. The doctor's very optimistic."

"Thank God."

"Carl will have to make some adjustments—diet, work load, that sort of thing. You'll be able to see him tomorrow."

"Oh, I must look a wreck." The need to check was so ingrained that Toni was already reaching for her compact. "I'll have to take care of that by tomorrow. I wouldn't want him to see me with my eyes all red and my hair a fright."

Again, because it was true, Johanna held back her sarcasm. "He won't wake up until tomorrow, according to the doctor. I'm going to handle the press—through a hospital spokesman, I think—and make certain his publicist has time to work up a statement. It might be a day or two before he's able to make those decisions for himself."

She wavered there a moment, trying to imagine her father unable to make any decision. "The important thing for you to do is to keep him calm. Go home and get some rest. They'll call if there's any change before morning."

"How about you?" Sam asked her when Jack had taken Toni down the corridor. "Are you all right?"

"Yes, I'm fine."

Wanting to judge for himself, he took her chin in his hand. There was something about the eyes, he thought. More than shock, certainly different than grief. Big secrets, he decided. Big fears. "Talk to me, Johanna."

"I've told you everything."

"About your father's condition." Though she tried to draw away, he held on. "I want to know about yours."

"I'm a little tired. I'd like to go home."

"Okay." Better, he thought, that they hash this, whatever it was, out at home. "We'll go back. But I'm staying with you."

"Sam, there's no need."

"There's every need. Let's go home."

10

It was after one a.m. when they arrived at Johanna's house, but she went straight to the phone. With a pen in one hand, she began to flip through her address book. "It shouldn't take long for me to set this up," she told Sam, "but you don't have to wait up."

"I'll wait." There were things that had to be said, and he wanted them said before she had a chance to build the barricades again. Though she looked steady, perhaps too steady, he was coming to understand her. Still, he left her alone as she began to dial.

There was little enough she could do. She was certain her father would tolerate only the slightest interference from her, but he would want his people informed. Johanna fed information to his publicist, then hashed out a simple, straightforward press release.

While she was calming her father's assistant and making sure that the daily business of Patterson Productions would run as smoothly as possible, Sam handed her a mug. Grateful, Johanna sipped, expecting coffee. Instead she tasted the soothing herbal tea she'd bought on impulse and brewed occasionally after a particularly long day.

"I'll be able to tell you more tomorrow, Whitfield. No, whatever can't be handled by you or another member of the staff will have to be canceled. That would appear to be your problem, wouldn't it?"

Across the room, Sam had no choice but to smile at her tone. As producers went, he'd never heard better.

"Where's Loman? Well, call him back." She made a quick notation on a pad. "Yes, that's right, but I'm sure he'll be giving you instructions himself in a couple of days. You'll have to check with the doctor on that, but I don't think you'll be able to discuss that or anything else with Carl for at least forty-eight hours." Her voice changed, went frigid. "That's not really the issue here, Whitfield. You'll have to consider Carl unavailable until further notice. No, I won't take the responsibility, you will. That's what you're paid for."

She hung up, incensed by the man's insensitivity. "Idiot," she muttered as she picked up her tea again. "His main concern is that Carl insisted on supervising the editing of *Fields of Fire*, and the heart attack is going to put the project behind schedule."

"Are you finished?"

Still frowning, she skimmed down her notes. "I don't think there's any more I can do."

"Come and sit down." He waited until she'd joined him on the sofa, then poured more tea into her cup from the pot he'd brewed. Sensing tension even before he touched her, Sam began to massage her shoulders. "It's hard, only being able to wait."

"Yes."

"You handle yourself well, Johanna."

She sipped tea and stared straight ahead. "I had a good teacher."

"Tell me about your father."

"I told you everything the doctor told me."

"I don't mean that." She was tensing up again, even as he massaged the muscles. "Tell me about him, about you and him."

"There's really nothing to tell. We've never been particularly close."

"Because of your mother?"

She went stiff at that. "What does my mother have to do with it?"

"I don't know. You tell me." He'd been shooting in the dark, but he wasn't surprised that he'd hit the target. "Johanna, you don't have to be a gossip buff to know that your parents divorced when you were, what—four?"

"I'd just turned five." It still hurt. No matter how often she told herself it was foolish, even unhealthy, the child's pain and confusion leaked into the woman. "That's history, Sam."

He didn't think so. Instinct told him it was as much a part of the present as he was. "She went back to England," he prompted. "And your father retained custody of you."

"He didn't have much choice." The bitterness leaked out. She made a conscientious and difficult effort to bury it again. "It really isn't relevant."

"I'm not Whitfield, Johanna," he murmured. "Humor me."

She was silent for so long he decided to try another tactic. Then she sighed and began. "My mother went back to England to try to pick up the stage career she felt she'd sacrificed when she'd married. I didn't have a place there."

"You must have missed her."

"I got over it."

He didn't think so. "I don't suppose divorce is ever easy on a kid, but it's got to be worse when one of the parents ends up several thousand miles away."

"It was better that way, for everyone. They always fought terribly. Neither of them were happy with their marriage or..." She trailed off before she could say what was in her mind. *Me. Neither of them wanted me.* "With the situation," she finished.

"You'd have been pretty young to have known that." He'd begun to get a picture of five-year-old Johanna, dealing with the inexplicable ups and downs of a rocky marriage.

"You don't have to be very old to recognize turmoil. In any case, my mother explained it to me. She sent me a telegram from the airport." Her tea had gone cold, but she sipped automatically.

A telegram's just like a letter, the pretty young maid had told Johanna. If the maid hadn't been new, the telegram would have been handed over to Carl and disposed of. But the maid had been avid to know the contents, and more than willing to help Johanna struggle over the words.

> My darling girl. I'm devastated to leave you like this, but I have no choice. My situation, my life, has become desperate. Believe me, I have tried, but I've come to understand that divorce and a complete separation from what was, is the only way I can survive. I despise myself for leaving you in your father's hands, but for now mine are too frail to hold on to you. One day you'll understand and forgive. Love. Mother.

She remembered it still, word for word, though at the time all she had understood was that her mother was leaving her because she wasn't happy.

Sam was staring at her, amazed that she could be so matter-of-fact. "She sent you a telegram?"

"Yes. I wasn't old enough to fully understand, but I caught the drift. She was miserably unhappy and desperate to find a way out."

Bitch. The word rose up in his throat, hotly, and he had to swallow it. He couldn't imagine anyone being so self-absorbed and selfish as to say goodbye to her only child by telegram. He tried to remember that Johanna had told him how her mother had taken her to feed the ducks, but he couldn't equate the two acts with the same woman.

"It must have been rough on you." He put his arm around her, as if he could find a way to protect her from what had already happened.

"Children are resilient." She rose, knowing that if he offered comfort she would break. She hadn't broken in over twenty years. "She did what she had to do, but I don't think she was ever happy. She died about ten years ago."

Suicide. He swore at himself for not remembering it before. Glenna Howard, Johanna's unhappy mother, had never quite achieved the sparkling comeback she'd sought. Disappointment had been eased by pills and alcohol until she'd taken a deliberate overdose of both.

"I'm sorry, Johanna. Losing her twice. It must have been hell for you."

"I never knew her that well." She reached for her tea again, for something to keep her hands busy. "And it was a long time ago."

He went to her, though she turned away. Patient but determined, he drew her back. "I don't think things like that ever stop hurting. Don't back off from me, Johanna."

"There's no use dredging all this up."

"I think there is." He took her shoulders, firmly enough to let her know he wasn't easing off. "I've wondered all along why you held off. I thought at first it was because you'd had a bad experience with another man. But it goes back farther than that, and deeper."

She looked at him then, her face set but her eyes desperate. She'd said too much, more than she'd ever said before. In saying it, the memories became all too clear. "I'm not my mother."

"No." He lifted a hand to brush at her hair. "No, you're not. And you're not your father either."

"I don't even know if he *is* my father."

The moment it was said, she went white. The hands she had fisted unballed and went limp. Not once in all of her life had she said it out loud. The knowledge had been there, locked tight but never completely silent. Now she heard her words echo back to her and was afraid, terribly afraid, she'd be ill.

"Johanna, what are you talking about?"

His voice was calm and quiet, but it shot like a bullet through her shock. "Nothing, nothing. I'm upset. I'm tired. Tomorrow's going to be a difficult day, Sam. I need to sleep."

"We both know you're too wired to sleep." He could feel the violent shudders begin as he held her there. "And you will be until you get the rest of it out. Tell me about your father, Johanna. About Carl."

"Will you leave me alone?" There were tears in her voice that only frightened her more. She could feel the walls cracking, the foundation giving way, but didn't have the strength to shore it up again. "For God's sake, can't you see I've had all I can manage? I don't want to talk about my mother. I don't want to talk about him. He could be dying." The tears spilled out, and she knew she'd lost. "He could be dying, and I should feel something. But I don't. I don't even know who he is. I don't know who I am."

She fought him, pushing away as he gathered her to him, swearing at him as he held her there. Then she collapsed in a storm of weeping.

He didn't offer comforting words. He hadn't a clue which ones to choose. Instead, he lifted her into his arms. With her sobs muffled against his throat, he sat down, cradling her to him. Sam stroked her hair and let her purge herself. He hadn't known it was possible to hold that many tears inside.

She felt ill. Her throat and eyes burned, her stomach heaved. Even when the tears were over, the raw, sick feeling remained. Her strength had been sapped, as if someone had pulled a plug and let it drain away. She didn't object when Sam shifted her, nor when he rose. He was going away. It was something she accepted even as her own battered heart suffered another crack.

Then he was sitting beside her again, placing a snifter in her hands. "It might help some," he murmured. "Take it slow."

If there'd been any left, more tears would have fallen. She nodded, took a sip of brandy and let it coat the raw wounds.

"I was always in awe of him," Johanna began without looking up. "I don't know even now if I loved him as a child, but he was always the largest and most important figure in my life. After my mother left—" she paused to sip again "—after my mother left I was terrified that he'd leave, too, or send me away. I didn't understand then how important it was to him to keep his private affairs private. The public could accept and be entertained by his romances and marriages, but if he'd shipped off his only child without a blink, they'd have taken a different view. No one forgot that he'd been married to Glenna Howard and that she'd had his child. No one except him."

How could she explain how lost she had been? How confusing it had been to see her father entertain other women as though her mother had never existed.

"When he married again it was horrible. There was a big, splashy wedding, lots of photographers, microphones, strangers. They dressed me up and told me to smile. I hated it—the stares and innuendos about my mother. The whispers about her. He could ignore it. He'd always had that kind of presence, but all I could think was that my mother was being replaced with someone I didn't even know. And I had to smile."

Insensitive, selfish idiots. Even as he thought it, he tightened his arms around her. "Wasn't there anyone else...any family?"

"His parents had died years before. I remember hearing or being told somewhere along the line that he'd been raised by his grandmother. By that time she was gone, too. I'd never met her. I had what you'd call a governess, who would have literally died for my father. Women react that way to him," she said wearily. "Nothing could have stopped it—my being in the wedding was important. Impressions, photo opportunities, that kind of thing. After it was over, I didn't see him again for three months. He was spending a lot of time in Italy."

"You stayed behind."

"I was in school." She pulled a hand through her hair, then clasped them in her lap. "It was perfectly legitimate for him to leave me behind with my tutors and instructors. In any case, his second wife had little tolerance for children. Few of his liaisons did."

Because she could feel his sympathy reaching out to her, she shook her head. "I was happier here. I spent a lot of time with the Heddisons. They were wonderful to me."

"I'm glad for that." He drew her hand into his. "Go on."

"It was after his second divorce, when he was involved with…it doesn't matter who. Anyway, I was out of school and feeling sorry for myself. I went up to his room. I don't even know why, except to be there, to see if I could solve the mystery of my father. I solved it.

"I'd always felt inadequate, awkward around him. There seemed to be something lacking in me that kept him from loving me the way that he should. He had this wonderful old desk in his room, one with all these fascinating cubbyholes and compartments. He was away again, so I didn't have to worry about him catching me poking around. I found letters. Some of them were from his women, and I was old enough to be embarrassed, so I put them away again. Then I found one from my mother. An old one, one she'd written right after she'd gone back to England. Holding it was like seeing her again. Sometimes I hadn't been able to bring the picture of her into my head, but the minute I had that letter, I saw her exactly as she'd been. God, she was beautiful, so fragile and haunted. I could even hear her voice, that trained, extraordinary voice. I'd loved her so much."

He took the snifter from her and set it on the table. "You read the letter?"

"I wish to God I hadn't." She squeezed her eyes shut for a moment, but it was now, as it had been then, too late to turn back. "I was so hungry for anything she'd touched, any part of her, that I didn't even realize at first when I was reading. She must have been furious when she wrote it. It came across, the anger, the bitterness, the need to punish. I'd known, even as a child, that their marriage hadn't been smooth. But until I'd read the letter I'd had no idea how much hate had been built up between them."

"People say things they don't mean, or at least things that shouldn't be said under those kind of circumstances."

"Well, she's gone, has been gone, and there's no way of knowing if she meant what she'd said. No way for me to know, no way for my father—for Carl to know."

Her mouth was dry, but she no longer wanted the brandy. Johanna pressed her lips together and continued. "She brought up every hurt, every broken promise, every real or imagined infidelity. Then she brought out the big guns. Leaving me with him was the biggest payback she could think of. She was saddling him with a child who wasn't even his own. Not that he could ever prove it, or that she would ever tell him who had fathered the child he'd given a name to. There was, of course, the possibility that the child was his, but... She wished him a lifetime of hell wondering. And because I read the letter, she gave me the same."

Sam stared out the darkened window for a long time. The rage was so keen, so close to the surface, he was afraid to speak. She'd been a child, innocent, helpless. And no one had given a damn.

"Did you ever speak to him about it?"

"No, there was no reason to. He didn't change toward me. I was well tended, well educated and allowed to pursue my own interests as long as I didn't embarrass him."

"They didn't deserve you. Either of them."

"It doesn't matter," she said wearily. "I'm not a child anymore." Nor had she been from the moment she'd read the letter.

"It matters to me." He cupped her face in his hands. "You matter to me, Johanna."

"I never meant to tell you, or anyone. But now that I have,

you must understand why I can't let what's between us go too far."

"No."

"Sam—"

"What I understand is that you had a lousy childhood, and that things went on around you that no kid should ever be a part of. And I understand that there're bound to be scars."

"Scars?" She gave a quick, brittle laugh as she rose. "Don't you see, my mother was ill. Oh, it was kept quiet, out of the press, but I managed to dig it up. She was in and out of sanitariums the last few years of her life. Manic depression, instability, alcohol addiction. And the drugs…" Johanna pressed her fingers to her eyes and struggled to get a grip on herself. "She didn't raise me, and I can't be sure who my father is, but she was my mother. I can't forget that, or what I may have inherited from her."

He rose slowly. His first instinct was to tread carefully, but then he realized it was the wrong one. She needed to be brought up short, and quickly. "It's not like you to be melodramatic, Johanna."

His words had exactly the effect he'd hoped for. Anger flashed into her eyes and whipped color back into her cheeks. "How dare you say that to me?"

"How dare you stand there and make up insufficient excuses why you can't commit to me?"

"They're not excuses, they're facts."

"I don't give a damn who your mother was, or your father. I'm in love with you, Johanna. Sooner or later you're going to have to swallow it and take the next step."

"I've told you all along that it couldn't lead anywhere. Now I'm telling you why. And that's only half of it. My half."

"There's more?" He hooked his thumbs in his pockets and rocked back on his heels. "Okay, give me the rest."

"You're an actor."

"Right the first time, but you're not going to set any bells ringing with that answer."

"I've been around actors all of my life," she continued, searching for patience. "I understand the strain and demands of the job, the impossibility, especially for a talented actor, of maintaining a private life that keeps anything truly private. And I know that even with the best of intentions and effort relationships suffer. If I believed in marriage—which I don't—I still wouldn't believe in marriage to an actor."

"I see." It was difficult enough not to be angry with her, and it was impossible not to be furious with the people who had had the major hand in forming her beliefs. "Then you're saying that because I'm an actor—worse yet, a good one—I'm too big a risk."

"I'm saying that what there is between us can't go any further." She stopped, wanting to be strong. "And that if you don't want to see me again, I'll understand."

"Will you?" For a moment he studied her, as though he were considering it. A few steps away, Johanna prepared herself. She'd known it would hurt when it ended, but even her worst fears hadn't come close to this. When he crossed to her, she made herself look in his eyes. She could read nothing in them.

"You're an idiot, Johanna." He yanked her against him so hard that her breath whistled out in surprise. "Do you think I can turn my feelings for you on and off? Damn it, you do, don't you? I can see it in your face. Well, I'm not going to step neatly out of your life, and if you think you can push me out, you're going to be disappointed."

"I don't want you to go." Tears clouded her eyes, though she'd thought she was through with them. "I just don't think—"

"Then don't think." He swept her up into his arms. "You do too much thinking."

She didn't protest when he carried her upstairs. She was through with arguing, with excuses, with reasons. Perhaps it was a weakness to want to be taken care of, but she couldn't find the strength to stand on her own tonight. She didn't want to think. He was right about that. She didn't want to think at all for whatever hours of the night were left. For once, feelings took no effort and she could let them dominate.

She needed him. If she hadn't been so drained it would have frightened her to realize it.

The bedroom was dark, but he didn't turn on the light. The fragrances from her garden were carried up and through the windows on the night air. In silence he laid her on the bed and sat beside her.

There was too much to say to speak at all just yet. He'd once thought her cool, tough and self-sufficient. That woman had attracted and intrigued him. Intrigued him enough, Sam thought, to have caused him to dig deeper. The more he knew about her, the more layers he'd discovered.

She was tough, in the best sense of the word. She'd taken the blows, the disappointments, and had worked her way through them. Some people, he knew, would have buckled under, found a crutch or given up. But Johanna, his Johanna, had carved a place for herself and had made it work.

Underneath the toughness he'd found passion. He'd sensed and now was certain that it had gone untapped. Whether it was fate, blind luck or timing, he'd found the key that had released it. He wouldn't allow it to be locked again, or to be opened by anyone but himself.

Beneath the passion was a touching shyness. A sweetness that was a miracle in itself, considering her childhood and the disillusionments she'd faced so early in life.

Now, beneath all the rest, he'd found a core of fragility. He was determined to protect that vulnerability. And it was to the fragile Johanna that he would make love tonight.

In kindness as much as love. In compassion, as well as desire.

Softly, his touch barely a whisper, he brushed her hair away from her face. There were tears still drying on her cheeks. With his fingertips, he wiped them away. He wouldn't be able to prevent more from being shed, but he would do whatever he could to see that she didn't shed them alone.

He kissed her once, then twice, where the tears had lain. Then he kissed her again, tenderly. Night shadows shifted across her face, but he could see her eyes, half closed with fatigue but very aware, as she watched him.

"Do you want to sleep?" he asked her.

"No." She put her hand over his. "No, I don't want to sleep. And I don't want you to go."

"Then relax." He brought her hand to his lips. His eyes, so dark and intense, seemed to absorb everything she was. "And let me love you."

It was just that easy.

She hadn't known love could be soothing. He hadn't shown her that before. Tonight, when her emotions were raw and her self-esteem at its lowest ebb, he showed her another side of desire. A desire to please, and one to nurture. A desire to have, and one to heal. He touched her as though she alone mattered.

He drew off her shirt so that the material trailed over her skin before it was discarded, but he didn't take what she would have given. With his eyes on hers, he removed his own. When she reached for him, he took her hands, pressing them both to his lips.

He undressed her slowly, carefully, as though she were asleep and he didn't want to disturb her. The tenderness of it brought its own strange ache. Though she was naked and totally open to him, he contented himself with long, lazy kisses and the feel of her hair under his hands.

Her skin looked so white against the dark spread. He ran his hand down her arm, watching the movement. The moon had waned to a thin crescent, shedding little light, but he already knew her so well. Still, he traced her face with his fingertip, outlining her features for his own pleasure.

He'd never treated her like this before. Johanna closed her eyes as she began to drift into contentment. Even through passion and hunger, he'd always shown her an unexpected sweetness. But this…this was what it meant to be cherished. This was the way promises were given when they were meant to be kept. It made her eyes swim and her heart break, just a little, at the beauty of it.

He felt stronger somehow, being gentle. He'd never wanted her more than he did at this moment, and yet he had never felt less need to rush. The passion was there, and growing, but it was filled with a need to comfort.

Time passed unnoticed, unheeded. In the darkest hours of the morning, he led her gently higher.

The rhythm of her heart beat under his lips, fast, unsteady, but not yet desperate. Her arms were around him, holding him close, but there was no urgent press of fingers. She moved with him, willing to let him set the pace, grateful that he had understood, even if she hadn't, that she needed care.

Had she ever noticed how strong he was? How the muscles

of his back and shoulders flexed and rippled with his movements? She'd touched him before, held him just like this, but
each time she had she'd been driven close to the edge. Now
the ride was quiet and unhurried, like floating on a raft on a
still lake.

Inspired by love, she sought to give him the same gentleness he showed her. Her touch was easy, her demands few. She
heard in the murmur of her name that he felt as she did. They
might never come together so perfectly, so unselfishly, again.

Her sigh was quiet as she opened for him. They merged
without heat but with much warmth.

Later, much later, she lay beside him, sleepless as the sky
began to lighten.

11

He could have strangled her. When Sam woke, he found himself alone in bed and the house empty. In the bath, her still-damp towel hung tidily over the rail. The room carried, very faintly, the scent of her. The clothes he'd removed from her the night before had been put away. Downstairs, he saw that her briefcase was gone and the flowers freshened. Her phone machine had been cleared of messages and reset.

In crisis or in control, Johanna was always organized.

He was sure he would strangle her.

In the kitchen he found the glasses they'd used the night before conscientiously rinsed and draining. Propped against the coffeepot was a note in Johanna's neat handwriting. *I didn't want to wake you. I needed to get to the hospital early, then to the studio. The coffee's fresh.*

She'd written something else, crossed it out, then signed the note simply *Johanna.*

His mother could have written it, Sam thought as he skimmed it a second time. Only she might have added, *Leave the kitchen the way you found it.* Damn it, Johanna.

He stood in the kitchen dressed only in jeans and tossed her note onto the counter. No one would ever accuse Johanna of not having her feet firmly on the ground. But there were times when it was better, even necessary, to keep them planted beside someone else's. She still needed to accept that he was that someone else. He'd been sure he'd gotten through, but he'd forgotten how incredibly stubborn she could be.

Absently he bent down and picked up the kitten, who was doing figure eights between his legs. She wasn't hungry. Johanna had left Lucy well taken care of, with a full dish in the corner. She only wanted some affection. Most creatures did, Sam mused as he stroked her fur. Apparently that wasn't enough to make Johanna purr and settle trustingly in his arms.

It looked as if he still had a fight on his hands. Sam gave the kitten's ears a last scratch before he set her down again. He could be hardheaded, as well.

She was thinking of him. Sam would have been amazed if he had known how hard and long she'd struggled over those few brief lines she'd left him. She'd wanted to thank him for being with her and to tell him how much it had meant to her that he'd been kind and understanding when she'd been down for the count. She'd wanted to tell him that she loved him in a way she had never before and would never again love. But the words had seemed so empty and inadequate on paper.

It was hard to need someone, really need him, when you'd spent your entire life making certain you could handle anything and everything on your own. How would he have felt if he'd known how close she'd come to waking him and asking him to come with her because she'd been dreading the thought of facing this day alone? She couldn't ask, any more than she could forget that she now had no secrets from him, physically or emotionally. Dealing with this day alone was imperative if she was ever to face another without him.

The nurse on duty this morning was younger and more approachable than the one the night before. She told Johanna that her father was resting comfortably, then asked her to have a seat until Dr. Merritt could be located.

Johanna chose the waiting room because the corridors seemed so public. She'd managed to evade the reporters outside but didn't want to take any chances on having to deal with any who'd been clever enough to sneak in.

Inside, an elderly woman and a boy of about twenty sat half dozing on a sofa, hands linked. On the wall-mounted television a morning show flashed cheerfully, showing a demonstration of gourmet cooking. Johanna moved to a table where twin pots of coffee and hot water sat on warmers. She bypassed the tea bags, ignored the little bags of powdered cream and sugar and poured a cup black. As she took the first sip, she heard the break for local news.

Carl W. Patterson was the top story. Dispassionately she listened to the newscaster recite the press release she and the publicist had written over the phone the night before. It gave a great deal more information on Carl's career than it did on his illness, and she knew Carl would have given it his nod of approval. The report ended by saying that Toni DuMonde, Patterson's housemate and fiancée, could not be reached for comment.

At least the woman wasn't a fool, Johanna thought as she chose a seat. There were some, she knew, who would have spilled their guts to the press and enjoyed the melodrama. And if Toni had, Johanna imagined, Carl would have cut whatever strings tied them together as soon as he was able.

"Miss Patterson?"

Johanna rose automatically. The moment she saw the doctor, her calm fled. The nurse had said Carl was resting comfortably, but that was hospital talk. She fought back the touch of fear and offered her hand.

"Dr. Merritt, I hope I'm not too early." Or too late.

"No, as a matter of fact your father's awake and stable. As a matter of precaution we'll keep him in CCU for another twenty-four hours. If he continues to progress, he can be moved to a private room."

"The prognosis?"

"The prognosis is good, if he cooperates. A lighter work load is essential. How much influence do you have over him?"

Her smile was almost amused. "None at all."

"Well, then, he might find himself confined to the hospital a day or two longer than he's counting on." Merritt took off his glasses to polish the lenses on the hem of his coat. "As I explained to you last night, certain adjustments will have to be made. Mr. Patterson will have to realize that, like the rest of us, he has certain limitations."

"I understand. And I wish you the best of luck explaining the same to him."

"I've already spoken to him briefly." Merritt slid the glasses back on his nose. He gave Johanna a smile that was gone almost before it formed. "At the moment, it's more important to reassure him. We'll speak about future care soon enough. He's asked to see Miss DuMonde and someone named Whitfield. It may be good for him to see his fiancée, but—"

"Don't worry about Whitfield. I'll handle it."

Merritt only nodded. He'd already decided Patterson's

daughter had a good head on her shoulders. "Your father's a fortunate man. If he's sensible, there isn't any reason why he shouldn't lead a full and productive life."

"Can I see him?"

"Fifteen minutes only. He needs calm and quiet."

She was both as she walked into the small curtained-off room in CCU. Her father was as he'd been the night before, eyes closed, wired to machines. But his color was better. She stood by the bed, studying him, until his eyes flickered open.

It took him a moment to focus. It occurred to Johanna that this was certainly the longest their eyes had ever held. When she saw recognition in his, she bent to brush his cheek with hers.

"Good morning," she said, keeping her voice carefully neutral. "You gave us a scare."

"Johanna." He took her hand, surprising her. He'd never been quite so alone or quite so weak. "What have they told you?"

Why, he's frightened, she thought, and felt a stirring of sympathy. It had never occurred to her that he could be frightened. "That you're a fortunate man," she said briskly. "And that if you're sensible the world will still see quite a number of Carl W. Patterson productions."

It was exactly the right thing to say. She hadn't realized she'd known him so well. "Damned inconvenient time for my body to set booby traps for me." He glanced around the room, and the moment of closeness vanished.

"The hospital's contacting Toni," Johanna told him. "I'm sure she'll be here soon."

Satisfied, Carl looked back at his daughter. "They say they intend to keep me strapped down here another day."

"Yes. More if you make a fuss."

"I've work to do that can't be done from a hospital bed."

"Fine. I'll tell them to release you. You might be able to edit *Fields of Fire* before you keel over again."

His expression changed from impatience to astonishment, then to something she'd rarely seen directed at her—amusement. "I suppose I could spare a few days. But I don't want that ham-handed Whitfield to get his hands on it."

"I've sent for Loman." His expression tightened immediately, and he became the cool, disapproving man she'd lived with most of her life. "I'm sorry if I overstepped my bounds, but when I contacted Whitfield last night and saw how things were, I thought you'd prefer Loman."

"All right, all right." He waved away her apology. "I do prefer Loman. Whitfield has his place, but God knows it's not in an editing room. What about the press?"

He'd forgotten to be frightened. Johanna thought, and bit back a sigh. It was business as usual. "Under control. Your publicist issued a release this morning and will update it as becomes necessary."

"Good, good. I'll meet with Loman this afternoon. Set that up for me, Johanna."

"No."

The effort of making plans had already sapped his strength, and that only made him more furious. "No? What the hell do you mean, no?"

"It's out of the question." Her voice was calm, which pleased her. There had been a time he could have used that tone and made her quake. "It should be all right in a day or two, once you're in a private room and stronger."

"I run my own life."

"No one's more aware of that than I."

"If you've got some idea about taking over while I'm down—"

The fury leaped into her eyes and stopped him cold. He'd never seen that look before, or the power behind it. Or, if it had been there, he'd never bothered to look. "I don't want anything from you. I did once, but I learned to live without it. Now, if you'll excuse me, I've got a show of my own to produce."

"Johanna." She started to whip the curtain aside. It was the tremor in his voice that stopped her.

"Yes?"

"I apologize."

Another first, she thought, and made herself turn back. "All right. The doctor told me not to stay long, and I've probably already overtired you."

"I almost died."

He said it like an old man, an old, frightened man. "You're going to be fine."

"I almost died," he repeated. "And though I can't say my life flashed in front of my eyes, I did screen a few clips." He closed his eyes. It infuriated him that he had to stop just to gather the strength to speak. "I remember getting in the back of the limo—on my way to the airport, I think. You were standing on the steps with that dog Max forced on me. You looked as though you wanted to call me back."

Johanna didn't remember that particular incident because there'd been so many of them. "If I had, would you have stayed?"

"No." He sighed, not with regret but with acknowledgement. "Work has always come first. I've never been able to put a marriage together the way I could a film. Your mother—"

"I don't want to talk about my mother."

Carl opened his eyes again. "She could have loved you more if she'd hated me less."

It hurt. Even having known it all these years, it hurt to hear it said aloud. "And you?"

"Work has always come first," he repeated. He was tired, much too tired for regrets or apologies. "Will you come back?"

"Yes. I'll come back after the taping."

He was asleep before she drew the curtain aside.

Max Heddison's estate was as distinguished and well-tended as the man. Sam was ushered through the thirty-room house the actor had purchased a quarter of a century before. On the terrace were thickly padded chaises and half a dozen wicker chairs that invited company to spread out and be comfortable. An aging golden retriever was curled up in one, snoring.

In the sparkling L-shaped pool beyond the terrace, Max Heddison was doing laps. Across the sloping lawn, partially hidden by squared-off hedges, were tennis courts. To the east, identifiable only by a distant flag, was a putting green.

A houseboy in a spotless white jacket offered Sam his choice of chairs. Sun or shade. Sam chose the sun. As he watched, Sam counted ten laps, cleanly stroked and paced, and wondered idly how many Max had done before he'd arrived. The official bio said Max was seventy. It could have taken off fifteen years and still have been believable.

He accepted coffee and waited while Max hauled himself out of the pool.

"Good to see you again." Max dragged a towel over his hair before he shrugged into a robe.

"I appreciate you letting me drop by this way." Sam had risen automatically.

"Sit down, boy, you make me feel like a king about to be deposed. Had breakfast?"

"Yes, thanks."

The moment Max sat, the houseboy was back with a tray of fresh fruit and dry toast. "Thank you, Jose. Bring Mr. Weaver some juice. Straight from our own oranges," he told Sam. "I figure it only costs me about three dollars a glass." With a grin, he dug into his breakfast. "My wife's the health nut. No additives, no preservatives. Enough to drive a man to drink. She's at her morning class, which means I'll have time to sneak a cigarette before she gets back."

Sam's juice was served in cut crystal. He sipped, letting Max fall into a conversation about pruning and organic sprays.

"Well, I don't suppose you came here to discuss fertilizers." Max pushed his tray aside and reached in his pocket for a pack of unfiltered cigarettes. "What did you think of the script?"

"Who do I have to kill to get the part?"

Max chuckled and drew in smoke with great pleasure. "I'll hold that in reserve. You know, I don't care too much for today's moviemakers—money-makers, I should say. In the old days, men like Mayer might have been despots, but they knew how to make films. Today they're a bunch of damn accountants running around with ledgers and red pencils—more interested in profit than entertainment. But my gut tells me we might be able to give them both with this one."

"It made my palms sweat," Sam said simply.

"I know the feeling." Max settled back, regretting only that his cigarette was nearly done. "I've been making movies since before you were born. Over eighty of them, and only a handful ever made me feel that way."

"I want to thank you for thinking of me."

"No need for that. Ten pages into the script and your name popped into my head. It was still there when I finished." He crushed out his cigarette, sighing. "And, of course, I went straight to my consultant with it—my wife." He grinned, drank more coffee and thought it a pity his wife had ordered decaf. "I've relied on her opinion for over forty years."

It made Sam remember how important it had been for him to hear Johanna's.

"She finished it, handed it back to me and said if I didn't do it I was crazy. Then she told me to get young Sam Weaver to play Michael. By the way, she admires your…build," Max said. "My sainted wife's an earthy woman."

The grin came quickly and lingered. "I'd love to meet her."

"We'll arrange it. Did I mention that Kincaid's been signed to direct?"

"No." Sam's interest was piqued again. "You don't get much better."

"Thought the same myself." Max watched Sam thoughtfully from under his bushy white brows. "Patterson's producing." He saw Sam's eyes sharpen and reached casually for more coffee. "Problem?"

"There might be." He wanted the part, more than he could remember wanting any other. But not at the cost of his still-too-tenuous relationship with Johanna.

"If you're concerned about Jo-Jo, I don't think it's necessary. The complete professional, our Jo-Jo. And she respects her father's work." He saw the dull anger in Sam's eyes and nodded. "So, it's gotten that far, has it? I wasn't sure Johanna would ever let anyone get that close."

"It wasn't so much a matter of choice as circumstance." He hadn't come just to talk about the script. When Sam had called to make the appointment, he'd already decided to dig for whatever Max might have buried. "I take it you haven't heard that Patterson had a heart attack last night."

"No." The concern came automatically. The friendship went back a quarter of a century. "I haven't so much as flicked the news on today. I go for days at a time without it. How bad?"

"Bad enough. As far as I know, he's stable. Johanna went back to the hospital this morning."

"He lives hard," Max mused. "Carl never seemed to be able to settle down long enough to enjoy what he was working for. I hope he still gets the chance." Max tipped back in his chair and looked out over the pool, the grounds. "You know, I have three children of my own. Five grandchildren now, and the first great-grandchild on the way. There were times I wasn't there for them, and I'll always regret it. Holding a family and a career together in this business is like juggling eggs. There's always some breakage."

"Some people juggle better than others."

"True enough. It takes a lot of effort and more than a few concessions to make it work."

"It seems to me that in Johanna's case she made all the concessions."

Max said nothing for a moment. He considered having another cigarette but decided his wife's sensitive nose would find him out. "I hate old men who poke into young people's business. Ought to be out playing checkers or feeding pigeons. But...just how serious are you about Jo-Jo?"

"We're going to get married," Sam heard himself say, to his own astonishment. "As soon as I talk her into it."

"Good luck. And that comes from the heart. I've always had

a soft spot for that girl." Max poured another cup of coffee and knew he was a long way from ready to feed pigeons. "How much did she tell you?"

"Enough to make me understand I've got an uphill battle."

"And how much do you love her?"

"Enough to keep climbing."

Max decided to risk a second cigarette. If his wife came sniffing around, he could always blame it on Sam. He lit it slowly, savoring the taste. "I'm going to tell you things she wouldn't appreciate me saying. Whether it'll give you an edge or not I can't say. I can tell you I hope it does."

"I appreciate it."

With the smoke trailing lazily from between his fingers, Max looked back. A long way. "I knew her mother well. A beautiful woman. A glorious face. Bone structure always makes the difference. Johanna favors her physically, but it ends there. I can say I've never known anyone more completely her own woman than Johanna."

"Neither have I," Sam murmured. "It doesn't always make it easy."

"You're too young to want things easy," Max told him from the comfortable perspective of seven decades. "When something comes easy, you usually let it go the same way. That's my philosophy for the day. Now, Glenna was selfish, driven by her own demons. She married Carl after a brief and very torrid affair. Affairs were just as torrid thirty years ago, only a bit more discreet."

He drew in smoke and remembered a few of his own. Though he'd let them go without regret upon his marriage, he could still be grateful for the experience.

"They were a golden couple, the photographers' darlings.

Carl was dark, ruggedly handsome, broad shouldered. Glenna was almost waiflike, pale, fragile. They threw incredible parties and incredible tantrums. To be honest, I quite enjoyed both. You may have heard I was a hellion in my youth."

"I heard you were a hellion," Sam agreed. "But I didn't hear it was something in the past."

"We'll work well together," Max declared. He took one last drag before crushing the second cigarette out. "When Glenna was pregnant, she spent thousands decorating the nursery. Then she started to lose her figure and went on a rampage. She could sit for a photographer like a Madonna, then toss back a Scotch and curse like a sailor. Glenna had no middle ground."

"Johanna told me she was ill, a manic-depressive."

"Perhaps. I don't pretend to understand psychiatry. I will say she was weak—not weak-minded, but weak-spirited—and tormented by the fact that she was never as successful as she needed to be. There was talent in her, real talent, but she didn't have the drive or the grit to stay on top. It became easy for her to blame Carl for that, and the marriage. Then it became easier to blame the child. After Johanna was born, Glenna went through phases of being a devoted, loving mother. Then she'd be almost obscenely neglectful. The marriage was crumbling. Carl had affairs, she had affairs, and neither of them ever considered putting the child first. Not in their nature, Sam," he added when he saw the fury flare. "That's not an excuse, of course, but it is a reason. Carl wouldn't have cared if Glenna had had one child or thirty. He'd had no more than a passing interest. When the break finally came, Glenna used the child as a weapon. I don't mean to make Carl a hero, but at least he never used Johanna. Unfortunately, she was never that important to him."

"How could two people like that ever have someone like Johanna?"

"Another question for the ages."

"Is Patterson her father?"

Max lifted both brows. "Why do you ask?"

It was a confidence he felt he had to break. Not for himself. Sam had already decided her parentage meant less than nothing to him, but the truth would be important to Johanna.

"Because when she was still a child, Johanna found a letter her mother had written to Patterson right after she'd gone back to England. She told him she'd never been sure if he was Johanna's father."

"Good God." Max ran a hand over his face. "I had no idea about that. It's a wonder it didn't destroy Johanna."

"No, she wasn't destroyed, but it did plenty of damage."

"Poor little Jo-Jo," Max murmured. "She was always such a lonely little girl. Spent more time with the gardener than anyone else. It might not have mattered if Carl had been different. I wish she'd come to me with this."

"I don't think she's told anyone about it until last night."

"You'd better not let her down."

"I don't intend to."

Max fell silent for a time, thinking. Johanna's parents had been his friends. He'd been able to accept them for what they were and for what they weren't, all the while regretting it for the child's sake.

"For what it's worth, I'd say the letter was pure spite and total nonsense. If another man had fathered Johanna, Glenna would have blurted it out long before the separation. She could never keep a secret for more than two hours. Make that two minutes if you added a drink. Carl knew that." His face clouded as he hunched over the table. "I'm sorry to say that if Carl had suspected Johanna wasn't his flesh and blood he never would have kept her under his roof. He'd have put her on a plane to her mother without a backward glance."

"That doesn't make him a saint."

"No, but it does make him Johanna's father."

"We have something special for our home audience," John Jay began, giving the camera a brilliant smile. "If you've been listening this week, you know that our Drive American contest is already underway. We at *Trivia Alert* are very excited about having the chance to show all of you at home how much we appreciate you. To win, all you have to do is watch and answer. Every day this week, sometime during the show, I'll be asking questions. Today it's time to tell you at home what you have a chance to win."

He paused, giving the announcer the time to describe the cars and eligibility requirements. As requested, the studio audience applauded and cheered.

"The week of Fourth of July," John Jay continued on cue, "one of you at home will win not one but both luxury cars. All you have to do is answer five questions in order. Send your answers to Trivia Alert, Drive American, Post Office Box 1776, Burbank, California 91501. Now for today's question."

There was a dramatic pause as he drew the sealed envelope from the slot. "Question number three. What is the name of Captain America's alter ego? Write down your answer and be sure to tune in tomorrow for the fourth question. All complete sets of correct answers will be part of a random drawing. Now, back to our game."

Johanna checked her watch and wondered how she could

get through two more segments. They were already behind schedule due to a delay caused by an overenthusiastic member of the studio audience who had called out answers during the speed round. They'd had to stop, reset, calm the contestant and begin again with a new batch of questions. Usually she took that sort of thing in stride, but somewhere along the way her stride had broken. For the past few hours, Johanna had been struggling to find her pace again.

When the segment ended, she nearly groaned with relief. She had fifteen minutes before they would begin again. "Beth, I have to make a call. I'll be in the office if a crisis comes up."

Without waiting for a response, she hurried off the set. At the end of the corridor a small room was set up with the essentials. A phone, a desk and a chair. Making use of all three, Johanna called the hospital. She still had ten minutes left when she learned that Carl had been downgraded from critical to serious condition. She was rubbing her eyes and thinking about another cup of coffee when the door opened.

"Beth, if it isn't a matter of life and death, put it on hold."

"It might be."

She straightened immediately at the sound of Sam's voice. "Oh, hello. I didn't expect you."

"You don't expect me nearly often enough." He closed the door behind him. "How are you doing?"

"Not bad."

"Your father?"

"Better. They think he can be moved out of CCU tomorrow."

"That's good." He came over to the desk and sat on the edge before giving her a long, critical study. "You're dead on your feet, Johanna. Let me take you home."

"We haven't finished, and I promised to stop by the hospital after the taping."

"Okay, I'll go with you."

"No, please. It's not necessary, and I'd be lousy company tonight."

He looked down at her hands. They were linked together tightly. Deliberately he took them in his own and separated them. "Are you trying to pull back, Johanna?"

"No. I don't know." She took a long breath, and her hands relaxed in his. "Sam, I appreciate what you did for me last night more than I can ever tell you—the way you listened and didn't judge. You were there when I needed you, and I'll never forget it."

"Sounds like a kiss-off," he murmured.

"No, of course it isn't. But you should understand now why I feel so strongly about being involved with you. Why it won't work."

"I must be pretty stupid, because I don't. I do understand why you're scared. Johanna, we have to talk."

"I have to get back. There's only a few more minutes."

"Sit down," he told her as she started to rise. She might have ignored the order, but the look in his eyes had her sitting again. "I'll try to make it quick. Time's either a blessing or a curse now, anyway. I've got to fly East the day after tomorrow to start filming."

"Oh." She dug deep for a smile. "Well, that's good. I know you've been anxious to start."

"I'll be gone three weeks, probably more. It isn't possible for me to put this off."

"Of course not. I hope—well, I hope you let me know how it's going."

"Johanna, I want you to come with me."

"What?"

"I said I want you to come with me."

"I—I can't. How could I? I have my job, and—"

"I'm not asking you to make a choice between your job and us. Any more than I'd expect you to ask me to make one between mine and the way I feel about you."

"No, of course I wouldn't."

"I'd like to think you meant that." He paused a moment, searching her face. "The script that Max sent me—I want to do it."

"You should do it. It's perfect for you."

"Maybe, but I want to know if it's perfect for you. Your father's producing it, Johanna."

"Oh." She looked down at her hands a moment, hands that were still caught in his. "Well, then, you've got the best."

"I want to know how you feel about it, Johanna. How you really feel."

"It's more a matter of how you feel."

"Not this time. Don't make me use pliers."

"Sam, your professional choices have to be yours, but I'd say you'd be a fool not to grab a chance to work with Max and Patterson Productions. That script might have been written for you, and I'd be disappointed if I didn't see you in it."

"Always sensible."

"I hope so."

"Then be sensible about this. Take a few days off and come east with me." Before she could protest again, he was continuing. "You've got a tight crew, Johanna. I've seen them work firsthand. You know they could run things for a couple of weeks."

"I suppose, but not without any notice. Then there's my father…" She let her words trail off. There must have been dozens of reasons, but they seemed to slide away before she could get a grip on them.

"All right. Take a week to make sure your crew is on top of things and that your father's recovering. Then fly out and meet me."

"Why?"

"I wondered when you'd ask." He reached in his pocket to pull out a box. Through his life he'd done a great many things on impulse. This wasn't one of them. He'd thought it through carefully, and had kept coming up with one answer. He needed her. "Things like this usually speak for themselves." After opening the lid, he took her hand and set the box in her palm. "I want you to marry me."

She stared at the single flawless diamond. It was square-cut, very classic and simple. The kind of ring, Johanna thought, girls dreamed about when they thought of white chargers and castles in the sky.

"I can't."

"Can't what?"

"I can't marry you. You know I can't. I had no idea you'd started thinking like this."

"Neither had I, until today. When Marv called I knew I had two choices. I could go East and stew about it or I could take the step and let you stew about it." He touched her hair, just the tips. "I'm sure, Johanna."

"I'm sorry." She offered the box back to him. When he didn't take it, she set it on the desk. "I don't want to hurt you, you know I don't. That's why I can't."

"It's about time you unloaded some of the baggage you've

been carrying around, Johanna." Rising, he drew her up with him. "We both know what we've got doesn't come along every day. You might think you're doing me a favor by turning me down, but you're wrong. Dead wrong."

His fingers tangled in her hair as he kissed her. Unable to deny him—or herself—she curled her arms up his back until she gripped his shoulders. She held on to him even while her mind whirled with dozens of questions.

"Do you believe me when I tell you I love you?" he demanded.

"Yes." She held him tighter, burying her face against his shoulder to absorb his scent. "Sam, I don't want you to go. I know you have to, and I know how much I'll miss you, but I can't give you what you want. If I could...if I could you're the only one I'd give it to."

He hadn't expected to hear even that much. Another man might have been discouraged, but he'd run into too many walls in his life to be put off by one more. Particularly since he had every intention of tearing this one down, brick by brick.

He pressed a kiss to her temple. "I already know what I need and what I want." He drew her away until their eyes met. "You'd better start thinking about yourself, Johanna. About what you want, what you need. Just you. I figure you're smart enough to come up with an answer before too long." He kissed her again until she was breathless. "Keep in touch."

She didn't have the strength to do anything but sink into the chair when he left her. The show was starting, but she continued to sit, staring at the ring he'd left behind.

12

The man was playing games. Johanna knew it, and though she tried not to nibble at the bait, she was already being reeled in. He'd been gone two weeks, and she hadn't gotten a single phone call.

But there had been flowers.

They'd arrived every evening. Black-eyed Susans one day, white orchids another. She couldn't walk into any room of her house without thinking of him. After the first week they'd begun to arrive at her office—a small clutch of violets, a huge bouquet of tea roses. She couldn't even escape from him there.

The man was definitely playing, and he wasn't playing fair.

Of course, she wasn't going to marry him. That was absurd. She didn't believe people could love, honor and cherish for a lifetime. She'd told him so, and she'd been sorry, but she had no intention of changing her mind.

She might carry the ring with her—for safekeeping, that is—but she hadn't taken it out of its box. At least not more than two or three times.

She was grateful that her work load had intensified so that she was unceasingly busy. It didn't leave much time to mope around missing him. Unless you counted the long, solitary nights when she kept listening for the phone.

He'd told her to keep in touch, but he hadn't told her where he'd be staying. If she'd wanted to, she could have found out easily enough. It did happen that a few discreet inquiries had put the name and address of his hotel in her hands, but that didn't mean she would call him. If she called, he'd know she'd gone to some trouble—damn it, a great deal of trouble—to find out where he was.

Then he would know she'd not only nibbled at the bait but swallowed it whole.

By the end of the second week, she was furious with him. He'd pushed her into a corner where she didn't want to be, wedged her in and then strolled off, leaving her trapped. A man didn't ask a woman to marry him, drop a ring in her hand, then waltz off.

Once she'd considered putting the ring in the mail and shipping it off to him. That had been at three o'clock in the morning on the fifteenth day. Johanna had rolled over, slammed the pillow a few satisfactory times and vowed to do just that the minute the post office opened in the morning.

She would have, too, if she hadn't been running a few minutes late. Then she'd been tied up at lunchtime and unable to get five free minutes until after six. She decided against mailing it, thinking it would be more civil and courteous to throw it in his face when he got back into town.

It was just her bad luck he'd chosen to send forget-me-nots that day. They happened to be one of her particular favorites.

As the third week approached, she was a wreck. Johanna knew she deserved the wary glances of her staff. She pushed through Monday's taping, growling at every interruption. Her excuse was that she'd agreed to take duplicates to her father that evening.

He wasn't particularly interested in the show, she knew, but his recuperation wasn't sitting well with him. He wanted to live badly enough to follow his doctor's orders, but that didn't mean he couldn't review everything Patterson Productions had a part in. Johanna waited impatiently for the copies, pacing the set and toying with the ring box in her pocket.

"Here you go." Bethany put on an exaggerated smile. "Try not to gnaw on them on the way home."

Johanna dumped them in her bag. "I'll need you here by nine. We can work until it's time to set up for taping."

"Whatever you say."

Johanna narrowed her eyes at the overbright tone. "Have you got a problem?"

"Me?" All innocence, Bethany opened her eyes wide. "No, not me. Well, there is my back."

"Your back? What's wrong with it?"

"It's nothing really. It always aches a bit when I've been flogged."

Johanna opened her mouth, then shut it again on a puff of air. "I'm sorry. I guess I've been a little edgy."

"Just a tad. Funny, if someone had been sending me flowers every day for weeks I'd be a bit more cheerful."

"He thinks that's all it takes to twist me around his finger."

"There are worse positions to be in. Forget I said it," Bethany said immediately, holding up a hand. "There's nothing more diabolical than sending a basket of tiger lilies. The man's obviously slime."

For the first time in days, Johanna smiled. "He's wonderful."

The smile confirmed what Johanna's scowls had already told her. "You miss him?"

"Yes, I miss him. Just like he knew I would."

Bethany looked at romance in the most straightforward of terms. If you cared, you showed it, then put all your energy into making it work. Her solution for Johanna was just as simple. "You know, Johanna, it's the same distance from the West to the East Coast as it is from East to West."

She'd already thought of going. Not that she'd *considered* it, but she had thought of it. "No, I can't." She fingered the box in her pocket. "It wouldn't be fair to him."

"Because?"

"Because I won't…can't…" On impulse she pulled the box out and opened it. "Because of this."

"Oh, my." Bethany couldn't help the long-drawn-out sigh. "My, oh, my," she managed, already smelling orange blossoms. "Congratulations, best wishes and bon voyage. Where's a bottle of champagne when you need it?"

"No, I didn't accept it. I'm not going to. I told him no."

"Then why do you still have it?"

Because the question was so reasonable, Johanna could only frown and stare at the diamond while it winked at her. "He just dropped it in my hand and walked off."

"Romantic devil, isn't he?"

"Well, it wasn't exactly— That's close enough," she decided. "It was more of an ultimatum than a proposal, but either way, I told him no."

It sounded wonderfully romantic to Bethany. She stuck her tongue in her cheek. "So you just decided to walk around with it in your pocket for a few days."

"No, I…" There had to be a reasonable excuse. "I wanted to have it handy so I could give it back to him."

Bethany thought that over, then tilted her head. "I think that's the first lie I've ever heard you tell."

"I don't know why I've still got it." Johanna closed the box with a snap, then pushed it into her pocket. "It's not important."

"No, I've never thought proposals of marriage or gorgeous engagement rings were anything to get excited about." She put a hand on Johanna's shoulder. "What you need is some fresh air."

"I don't believe in marriage."

"That's like not believing in Santa Claus." At Johanna's lifted brow, Bethany shook her head. "Johanna, don't tell me you don't believe in him, either? He might be something of a fantasy, but he's been around a while, and he's going to stay around."

It was hard to argue with that kind of logic. Johanna decided she was too tired to try. "We'll talk about the logic of that some other time. I have to drop off these tapes." With Bethany beside her, she started out. "I'd like you to keep this to yourself."

"It goes with me to the grave."

"You're good for me," Johanna said with a laugh. "I'm going to be sorry to lose you."

"Am I fired?"

"Sooner or later you're going to fire me. You won't be content to be anyone's assistant for long." Outside, Johanna took a deep breath. So much had changed since she'd walked with Bethany from the studio weeks before. "Leaving Santa Claus out of it, do you believe in marriage, Beth?"

"I'm just an old-fashioned girl with strong feminist under-pinnings. Yeah, I believe in marriage as long as two people are willing to give it their best shot."

"You know what the odds are of a marriage making it in this town?"

"Lousy. But strikeout or home run, you've got to step up to bat. See you tomorrow."

"Good night, Beth."

She did a great deal of thinking as she drove to Beverly Hills. Not all of it was clear, but every thought circled back to Sam. Johanna was coming to realize that her thoughts would, whether she was with or without him.

The gates were locked, as they always were. Reaching out, she pressed the button on the intercom and waited for her father's housekeeper to ask her name. In moments the gates opened soundlessly.

The drive toward the house didn't stir any childish memories. She saw the estate as an adult. Perhaps she always had. It was stunning—the white columns, the terraces and balconies. The exterior had changed little from her earliest recollections.

Inside, it had gone through major overhauls, depending on its mistress. Her mother had preferred the feminine and delicate look of *Louis Quinze.* Darlene had chosen art nouveau, right down to the light fixtures. Its last mistress had gone for the opulently elegant. Johanna didn't think it would take Toni long to put her stamp on it.

The door was opened for her by the gray-uniformed maid before she'd reached the top of the wide, curved steps.

"Good evening, Miss Patterson."

"Good evening. Is Mr. Patterson expecting me?"

"He and Miss DuMonde are in the sitting room."

"Thank you."

Johanna crossed the glossy tiles, skirting the fish pond her father's last wife had installed. She found her father looking well, and impatient, in a dark blue smoking jacket. Toni sprawled lazily on the sofa across from him, sipping wine and flipping through a magazine. Johanna nearly smiled when she saw that it was one on home fashion and decoration.

"I expected you an hour ago," Carl said without preamble.

"We ran late." She took the tapes from her bag to set them on the table beside him. "You're looking well."

"There's nothing wrong with me."

"Carl's a bit bored." Toni stretched herself into a sitting position. She wore silk lounging pajamas the color of ripe peaches. The pout she wore went with them beautifully. "Perhaps you can entertain him better than I." Rising, she stalked gracefully out of the room.

Johanna lifted a brow. "Have I come at a bad time?"

"No." Carl pushed himself up and headed for the bar. Johanna bit back a protest and was relieved when he poured club soda. "Do you want anything?"

"No, thank you. I can't stay."

Carl halfheartedly added a twist of lime. "I assumed you'd stay until I'd previewed the tapes."

"You don't need me for that." He wanted company, she realized. Because she remembered how old and alone he'd looked in the hospital, she relented. "I could put them in for you, answer whatever questions you might have about the first segment or two."

"I've seen the show before, Johanna. I doubt I'd have any questions about my own show."

"No." She picked up the bag she'd just set down. "Then I'll leave you to it."

"Johanna." He cleared his throat and he turned back, then took his seat again. "You've done a good job with it."

This time both brows rose. "Thank you." She set her bag down again and checked her watch.

"If you've got some damn appointment, go on, then."

"No, actually, I was just marking the time. Since it's the first time in my life you've ever complimented me on anything, I want to remember when it happened."

"There's no need to be sarcastic."

"Maybe not." She crossed the room to sit but stayed on the edge of her chair. She'd never been comfortable in this house. "I'm glad you're doing so well. If you're interested, I can see that you get dupes of tomorrow's taping for the evening shows. We're giving away a trip for two to Puerto Vallarta during the speed round."

He only grunted at that. Johanna folded her hands and continued. "If a contestant reaches the winner's circle and can answer all of the questions himself, without deferring to his partner, he'll win a car. We're using a sedan this week. Four-door."

"I'm not interested in the prizes."

"I thought not, but you might prefer a different angle or see a flaw when you preview. I'm sure you know that you can accomplish as much here as most men can in an office."

"I won't be sitting here forever."

"There's no question of that." No, he would be back, full steam, very soon. Maybe this was the time, the only time. "Before I go, I'd like to ask you something."

"If it has to do with the new pilot, I've already seen it and approved it."

"No, it's personal."

He sat, cradling his glass. He didn't mind giving up liquor half so much as doing without his cigars. Rather than answer, he simply nodded for her to go on.

"Why do you want to marry Toni DuMonde?"

As far as Carl was concerned, the question had come out

of left field. No one questioned his motives or his reasons. "I'd say that was between Toni and myself. If you're uncomfortable with the age difference—"

"It would hardly matter to me if there was twice as much difference as there already is," Johanna said. "I'm just curious."

"I'm marrying her because I want to."

Johanna sat for a minute, studying him. Maybe it was just that simple with Carl. I want, I do. I covet, I take. "Do you plan to stay married to her?"

"As long as it suits both of us."

She smiled a little and nodded. That, at least, was the unvarnished truth. "Why did you marry my mother?"

If her first question had surprised him, this one left him speechless. Staring at Johanna, he saw the resemblance he'd always ignored. But there was more character in this face. More courage. "Why are you bringing this up now? You never asked about her before."

"Maybe I should have. We began to talk about her when you were in the hospital, but I suppose I wasn't ready. Now I have a decision of my own to make, and I can't do it until I understand a little better. Did you love her?"

"Of course. She was beautiful, fascinating. We were both building our careers. There wasn't a man who met Glenna in those days who didn't love her."

She didn't find reasons for love and fidelity in those answers. "But you're the only one who married her. And the only one who divorced her."

"The marriage was a mistake," he said, abruptly uncomfortable. "We both realized it before the first year was out. Not that we weren't attracted to each other. As I said, she was beautiful, very delicate. You favor her." His glass paused halfway to his lips when he saw her expression. Perhaps he'd never been a loving father, but he'd always been an astute man. "If you're concerned about her health, don't be. Glenna was always erratic. Drinking made her more so, but I've never seen any part of that in you. Believe me, I've watched for it."

"Have you?" Johanna murmured.

"You've never been one for extremes," he went on. "Apparently you inherited enough from me to offset the rest."

"Did I?" This time her voice was firm and her eyes level. "I've always wondered what, if anything, I inherited from you."

His look was so blank that she couldn't believe he feigned it. "You're a producer, aren't you? And a good one. That should say something. The Pattersons have always been strong, practical people. Ambitious. I'd say, now that I think of it, that you take after my grandmother. She was strong minded, never one to sit around and let the world go by. Got the hair from her, too," he decided, looking thoroughly at his daughter for the first time in years.

A little dazed, Johanna reached up to touch her hair. "*Your* grandmother?"

"Didn't get it from your mother," he said with a sour laugh. "Got hers from her hairdresser. That was one of her most prized secrets. Hers was brown, mousy brown. God knows you didn't get your drive from her. That's the Patterson in you." He didn't say it with pride, just stated it as fact.

So this was her father after all. Johanna sat, waiting for a flood of feeling. When none came, she sighed. Nothing had really changed. Then her lips curved. Then again, maybe everything had.

"I'd like to hear about her sometime. Your grandmother."

She rose, taking a look at her watch in earnest. "I really have to go. I'm going to be out of town. Everything should run smoothly enough without me for a few days."

"Out of town? When?"

"Tonight."

Johanna caught the last plane out. She'd had just enough time before final boarding to call Bethany and give her quick and not completely coherent instructions about the next day's business and the care and feeding of her cat. Bethany had been awakened out of a sound sleep, but she could be depended on.

Strapped in, Johanna watched L.A., and the resolutions she'd lived with all of her life, slip away. She'd taken a step, the largest one of her life, without even being sure she would land on solid ground.

Somewhere over Nevada she dozed, then woke over New Mexico in a kind of blind panic. What in God's name was she doing, traveling thousands of miles without so much as a toothbrush? It wasn't like her not to plan or make lists. They were taping the next day. Who would handle the details, check the staff? Who would deal with John Jay?

Someone else, she told herself. For once it would just have to be someone else.

She traveled from one coast to the other, sleeping in fits and starts and wondering if she'd lost her mind. In Houston she nearly lost her nerve, as well. But she changed planes and strapped in a second time, determined to see it through.

Perhaps she wasn't being smart or responsible, but everyone was entitled to do something on impulse once. Even if they lived to regret it.

Almost certain she would, she arrived in Baltimore just after
dawn. The terminal was deserted except for a few napping pas-
sengers waiting for connections. The air was cool in Maryland,
and she was grateful for her suit jacket. The same jacket,
Johanna remembered, that she'd put on that morning when
she'd still been sane. The sky, full of pewter clouds, promised
rain as she climbed into a cab and gave the driver the name of
Sam's hotel.

This was it, she told herself. It helped a little to close her
eyes and ignore the unfamiliar landscape. If she didn't watch
it, she wouldn't think too much about being on the other side
of the country. In L.A. people were rolling over in bed, snuggling into pillows with morning still hours away. Here they
were waking up, preparing to face the day.

So was she.

She paid off the driver and tried not to think. The rain
began as she walked into the lobby.

Suite 621. At least she knew the number, so she'd be spared
the embarrassment of going to the desk and convincing the
clerk she wasn't a fan. Clutching the strap of her bag, she rode
to the sixth floor. It was easy enough to step from the elevator.
She even managed to walk down the hall to his door.

Then she stared at it.

What if he didn't want her there? What if he wasn't alone?
After all, she had no claim on him, had made no promises.
She'd refused to accept, even to listen to, his promises. He was
free to…to do whatever he wanted, with whomever he
wanted.

Certain she couldn't go through with it, she turned away
and took two steps back from the door.

It was absurd, she told herself. She'd just spent hours in a plane, traveled thousands of miles, and now she couldn't even get up the nerve to knock on a door.

With her shoulders straight and her chin up, she knocked. When her stomach rolled, she reached in her pocket automatically for her antacids. Her fingers closed over the small velvet box. She drummed up her courage and knocked again.

He woke swearing. They'd worked until after two, and he'd barely had the energy to strip before tumbling into bed. Now the damn assistant director was banging on the door. Any idiot knew they couldn't film any of the scheduled outside shots in the rain.

Groggy and full of the desire for vengeance, Sam dragged the top sheet from the bed and wrapped it around him. He tripped over the hem, cursed again, then yanked open the door.

"Goddamn it—" His mouth dried up. He had to be dreaming. Johanna was a continent away, snuggled under the covers. Then he saw her lips curve before she began to stumble out an apology.

"I'm sorry I woke you. I should have…waited. Called." *Stayed away,* she thought desperately.

Then she didn't think at all, because he was dragging her inside. The door slammed and she was pressed back against it, her mouth captive.

"Don't say a word," he ordered when she sucked in her breath. "Not a word. Not yet."

It would have been impossible to speak. Even as he pulled her through the sitting room, he was peeling off her jacket, fighting the buttons on her blouse. With a throaty laugh, she tugged at the sheet. It was left behind in a stream of white as they worked their way to the bedroom.

Her skirt slid down to her hips, and he lifted her out of it.

While his hands played over her, she stepped out of one shoe. They were nearly at the bedroom door before she managed to rid herself of the other.

He wasn't even awake. Sam clung to the drowsy fingers of sleep as they fell onto the bed.

She was here. Dream or reality, she was here. Her skin was just as soft under his hands, just as fragrant. Her lips as they parted for his had the same unique flavor he'd craved since he'd tasted them last. At her sigh, as her arms locked around him, he heard everything he needed to hear.

Delighted with each other, they rolled over the already rumpled bed as the rain grew heavy and streaked the windows.

She'd been right to come. Whatever had happened before, whatever happened after, she'd been right to take this moment. And to give this time to him. There would be no questions, no need for explanations or excuses, just gladness that was racing harder and faster toward dazzling pleasure.

In tune, body and mind, they came together, taking that pleasure to its pinnacle.

The thunder started as he gathered her against him again. Or perhaps it had been there all along but they hadn't heard it. Now, as the storm rattled over the city, they were together and alone and in love. Sometimes that really was all that mattered.

She kept her hand on his heart and her head on his shoulder as they floated down to solid ground. The gloom kept the room dim, but for Johanna there had never been a more beautiful morning.

"Were you just passing through?" Sam murmured.

She spread her fingers over his chest, watching the movement. "I had urgent and unexpected business on the East Coast."

"I see." He hoped he did, but he could afford to wait. "You on a contestant search?"

"Not exactly." The nerves began leaking back. "I take it you don't have an early call today."

"If the rain keeps up, please God, I won't have one at all." Slowly, like a man who had all the time in the world, he stretched. "We were scheduled to shoot down at the Inner Harbor. Terrific place. Best crab I've ever eaten." He was already imagining showing it to her himself. "Once that's wrapped, we'll be finished here."

A pout, something she never allowed herself, formed on her lips. "You've run a little over your three weeks."

He certainly hoped it was annoyance he detected in her voice. "A little."

"I guess you've been too busy to call and let me know how things were going."

"No."

"No?" She propped herself on her elbow to frown at him.

"No, I haven't been too busy to call. I didn't call."

"Oh, I see." She started to push herself up and found herself flat on her back again with Sam leaning over her.

"I hope you don't think you're getting out of this room."

"I told you I have business."

"So you did. Is it a coincidence that you have business in Baltimore and just happen to be staying at the same hotel— apparently in my room?"

"I'm not staying."

"Guess again." He nipped her gently on the jaw. "Why did you come, Johanna?"

"I'd rather not discuss it. I'd like my clothes," she said stiffly.

"Sure. Let me get them for you." He strolled out, leaving

Johanna with the dubious cover of a pillow. She started to rise when he came back in with her suit bundled in his arms. Then she could only gape, openmouthed, as he opened the window and tossed them out.

"What in the hell are you doing?" She forgot the pillow as she leaped up and ran to the window. "You threw out my clothes." Dumbfounded, she could only stare at him. "You threw them out the window."

"Sure looks that way."

"Are you out of your mind? I flew out here with the shirt on my back, and now it's six floors down and soaked. I don't have anything to wear out of here but my shoes."

"I was counting on that. Seemed like the best way to guarantee your staying put."

"You *are* out of your mind." She started to crane out of the window, remembered she was naked, then dropped on the bed. "What am I supposed to do now?"

"Borrow another of my shirts, I guess. Help yourself." He gestured toward the closet. "You might toss me a pair of jeans while you're at it. It's hard for me to talk to you reasonably when we're not wearing anything but smiles."

"I'm not smiling," she told him between her teeth as she heaved jeans in his direction. "That was one of my best suits, and I—" Her fingers froze on the buttons of the shirt she'd pulled on. "Oh, God. Oh, my God, in the jacket. I had it in the jacket." With the shirt still half buttoned she jumped for the door. Sam was just quick enough to slam it closed before she ran out.

"I don't think you're dressed for a stroll, Johanna. Not that you don't look terrific. In fact, you look so terrific I think I'd like you to give me my shirt back."

"Will you stop being an idiot?" She tried to shove him aside but met with solid resistance. "You threw it out the window. I can't believe what a complete fool you are. You threw my ring out the window."

"Whose ring?"

"My ring, the one you gave me. Oh, for God's sake." She ducked under his arm to run to the window again. "Someone's going to take it."

"Your suit?"

"No, I don't care about the suit. The hell with the suit. I want my ring."

"All right. Here." Sam drew it off his pinky and offered it. "The box must have dropped out of your pocket when—when I said hello." Johanna had given a cry of relief and grabbed for it before she realized she'd been taken.

"Damn it, Sam, you had it all the time and you let me think it was gone."

"It was nice to know it was important to you." He held it between them. "Are you going to let me put it on you?"

"You can take it and—"

"I'm open to suggestions." Then he smiled at her in a way she found completely unfair. Even her temper failed her.

"I'd like to sit down a minute." She did, sinking into the bed. The relief was gone, and the anger. She'd come for a purpose. and it was time to see it through. "I came to see you."

"No? Really?"

"Don't make fun of me."

"All right." He sat beside her, draping an arm over her shoulders. "Then I guess I can tell you that if you hadn't come, or called within the next twenty-four hours, I was heading back, movie or no movie."

"You didn't call me."

"No, I didn't, because I think we both knew you had to make the next move. And I hope you suffered as much as I did." He pressed his lips to her hair. "So what's it going to be?"

"I want to tell you that I spoke with my father last night." She tilted her head so that she could look at him. "He is my father."

Gently he brushed her hair back from her face. "Is everything all right?"

"It's not like a story where everything turns out beautifully at the end, but it's all right. I don't suppose we'll ever be close, and I can accept that now. I'm not like him, nor like my mother, either. It's taken me all this time to figure out that that's okay. I'm okay."

He kissed her hair again, enjoying the fragrance as much as the familiarity. "I could have told you that, if you'd listened."

"I can listen now, now that I've told myself." With a long breath, she took his hands in hers. "I need to ask you something, Sam. You could almost say it was the championship question."

"I work best under pressure."

But her eyes didn't smile. "Why do you want to marry me?"

"That's it?" His brows rose, and then he was laughing and holding her close. "I thought you were going to ask me a tough one. I want to marry you because I love you and I need you in my life. It changed when you walked into it."

"And tomorrow?"

"A two-part question," he murmured. "I could promise you anything." He drew her away to kiss her cheek, then her brow, then her lips. "I wish there were guarantees, but there aren't. I can only tell you that when I think about tomorrow, when I think about ten years from tomorrow, I think about you. I think about us."

He couldn't have said it better, she thought as she touched his face. No, there weren't any guarantees, but they had a chance. A good one.

"Can I ask you one more thing?"

"As long as I'm going to get an answer eventually."

"Do you believe in Santa Claus?"

What made it perfect, even more than perfect, was that he didn't even hesitate. "Sure. Doesn't everyone?"

Now she smiled, completely. "I love you, Sam."

"That's the answer I wanted."

"Looks like you win." She held out her hand so that he could slip the ring on her finger. It felt as though it belonged, and so did she. "Looks like we both do."

* * * * *

Once More
with Feeling

To Ran,
for all the songs yet unwritten,
for all the songs yet unsung.

1

He stood out of view as he watched her. His first thought was how little she had changed in five years. Time, it seemed, hadn't rushed or dragged but had merely hung suspended.

Raven Williams was a small, slender woman who moved quickly, with a thin, underlying nervousness that was unaccountably appealing. She was tanned deep gold from the California sun, but at twenty-five her skin was as smooth and dewy soft as a child's. She pampered it when she remembered and ignored it when she forgot. It never seemed to make any difference. Her long hair was thick and straight and true black. She wore it simply, parted in the center. The ends brushed her hips and it swirled and floated as she walked.

Her face was pixielike, with its cheekbones well-defined and the chin slightly pointed. Her mouth smiled easily, but her eyes reflected her emotions. They were smoky gray and round. Whatever Raven felt would be reflected there. She had an overwhelming need to love and be loved. Her own need was one of the reasons for her tremendous success. The other was her voice—the rich, dark, velvet voice that had catapulted her to fame.

Raven always felt a little strange in a recording studio: insulated, sealed off from the rest of the world by the glass and the soundproofing. It had been more than six years since she had cut her first record, but she was still never completely comfortable in a studio. Raven was made for the stage, for the live audience that pumped the blood and heat into the music. She considered the studio too tame, too mechanical. When she worked in the studio, as she did now, she thought of it exclusively as a job. And she worked hard.

The recording session was going well. Raven listened to a playback with a single-mindedness that blocked out her surroundings. There was only the music. It was good, she decided, but it could be better. She'd missed something in the last song, left something out. Without knowing precisely what it was, Raven was certain she could find it. She signaled the engineers to stop the playback.

"Marc?"

A sandy-haired man with the solid frame of a lightweight wrestler entered the booth. "Problem?" he said simply, touching her shoulder.

"The last number, it's a little…" Raven searched for the word. "Empty," she decided at length. "What do you think?" She respected Marc Ridgely as a musician and depended on him as a friend. He was a man of few words who had a passion for old westerns and Jordan almonds. He was also one of the finest guitarists in the country.

Marc reached up to stroke his beard, a gesture, Raven had always thought, that took the place of several sentences. "Do it again," he advised. "The instrumental's fine."

She laughed, producing a sound as warm and rich as her singing voice. "Cruel but true," she murmured, slipping the headset back on. She went back to the microphone. "Another vocal on 'Love and Lose,' please," she instructed the engineers. "I have it on the best authority that it's the singer, not the musicians." She saw Marc grin before she turned to the mike. Then the music washed over her.

Raven closed her eyes and poured herself into the song. It was a slow, aching ballad suited to the smoky depths of her voice. The lyrics were hers, ones she had written long before. It had only been recently that she had felt strong enough to sing them publicly. There was only the music in her head now, an arrangement of notes she herself had produced. And as she added her voice, she knew that what had been missing before had been her emotions. She had restricted them on the other recordings, afraid to risk them. Now she let them out. Her voice flowed with them.

An ache passed through her, a shadow of a pain buried for years. She sang as though the words would bring her relief. The hurt was there, still with her when the song was finished.

For a moment there was silence, but Raven was too dazed to note the admiration of her colleagues. She pulled off the headset, suddenly sharply conscious of its weight.

"Okay?" Marc entered the booth and slipped his arm around her. He felt her tremble lightly.

"Yes." Raven pressed her fingers to her temple a moment and gave a surprised laugh. "Yes, of course. I got a bit wrapped up in that one."

He tilted her face to his, and in a rare show of public affection for a shy man, kissed her. "You were fantastic."

Her eyes warmed, and the tears that had threatened were banished. "I needed that."

"The kiss or the compliment?"

"Both." She laughed and tossed her hair behind her back. "Stars need constant admiration, you know."

"Where's the star?" a backup vocalist wanted to know.

Raven tried for a haughty look as she glanced over. "You," she said ominously, "can be replaced." The vocalist grinned in return, too used to Raven's lack of pretentions to be intimidated.

"Who'd carry you through the session?"

Raven turned to Marc. "Take that one out and shoot him," she requested mildly, then looked up at the booth. "That's a wrap," she called out before her eyes locked on the man now standing in full view behind the glass.

The blood drained from her face. The remnants of emotion from the song surged back in full force. She nearly swayed from the power of it. "Brandon." It was a thought to be spoken aloud but only in a whisper. It was a dream she thought had finally run its course. Then his eyes were on hers, and Raven knew it was real. He'd come back.

Years of performing had taught her to act. It was always an effort for her to slip a mask into place, but by the time Brand Carstairs had come down from the booth, Raven wore a professionally untroubled face. She'd deal with the storm inside later.

"Brandon, it's wonderful to see you again." She held out both hands and tilted her face up to his for the expected, meaningless kiss of strangers who happen to be in the same business.

Her composure startled him. He'd seen her pale, seen the shock in her eyes. Now she wore a façade she'd never had before. It was slick, bright and practiced. Brand realized he'd been wrong; she *had* changed.

"Raven." He kissed her lightly and took both her hands.

"You're more beautiful than anyone has a right to be." There was the lightest touch of brogue in his speech, a mist of Ireland over the more formal British. Raven allowed herself a moment to look at him, really look at him.

He was tall and now, as always, seemed a bit too thin. His hair was as dark as her own but waved where hers was needle straight. It was thick and full over his ears and down to the collar of his shirt. His face hadn't changed; it was still the same face that drove girls and women to scream and swoon at his concerts. It was raw-boned and tanned, more intriguing than handsome, as the features were not altogether even. There was something of the dreamer there, from his mother's Irish half. Perhaps that was what drew women to him, though they were just as fascinated by the occasional British reserve. And the eyes. Even now Raven felt the pull of his large, heavy-lidded aquamarine eyes. They were unsettling eyes for as easygoing a man as Brand Carstairs. The blue and green seemed constantly at odds. But it was the charm he wore so easily that tilted the scales, Raven realized. Charm and blatant sex appeal were an irresistible combination.

"You haven't changed, have you, Brandon?" The question was quiet, the first and only sign of Raven's distress.

"Funny." He smiled, not the quick, flashing grin he was capable of, but a slow, considering smile. "I thought the same of you when I first saw you. I don't suppose it's true of either of us."

"No." God, how she wished he would release her hands. "What brings you to L.A., Brandon?"

"Business, love," he answered carelessly, though his eyes were taking in every inch of her face. "And, of course, the chance to see you again."

"Of course." Her voice was coldly polite, and the smile never reached her eyes.

The sarcasm surprised him. The Raven he remembered hadn't known the meaning of the word. She saw his brow lift into consideration. "I do want to see you, Raven," Brand told her with his sudden, disarming sincerity. "Very much. Can we have dinner?"

Her pulse had accelerated at his change of tone. Just reflex, just an old habit, she told herself and struggled to keep her hands passive in his. "I'm sorry, Brandon," she answered with perfect calm. "I'm booked." Her eyes slipped past him in search of Marc, whose head was bent over his guitar as he jammed with another musician. Raven could have sworn with frustration. Brand followed the direction of her gaze. Briefly his eyes narrowed.

"Tomorrow, then," he said. His tone was still light and casual. "I want to talk to you." He smiled as to an old friend. "I'll just drop by the house awhile."

"Brandon," Raven began and tugged on her hands.

"You still have Julie, don't you?" Brand smiled and held on to her hands, unaware of—or ignoring—her resistance.

"Yes, I..."

"I'd like to see her again. I'll come by around four. I know the way." He grinned, then kissed her again, a quick, friendly brushing of lips before he released her hands, turned and walked away.

"Yes," she murmured to herself. "You know the way."

An hour later Raven drove through the electric gates that led to her house. The one thing she hadn't allowed Julie or her agent to thrust on her was a chauffeur. Raven enjoyed driving, having control of the low, sleek foreign car and indulging from time to time in an excess of speed. She claimed it cleared her head. It obviously hadn't done the job, she thought as she pulled up in front of the house with a short, peevish squeal of the brakes. Distracted, she left her purse sitting on the seat beside her as she sprang from the car and jogged up the three stone steps that led to the front door. It was locked. Her frustration only mounted when she was forced to go back and rip the keys from the ignition.

Slamming into the house, Raven went directly to the music room. She flung herself down on the silk-covered Victorian sofa and stared straight ahead without seeing anything. A gleaming mahogany grand piano dominated the room. It was played often and at odd hours. There were Tiffany lamps and Persian rugs and a dime-store flowerpot with a struggling African violet. An old, scarred music cabinet was filled to overflowing. Sheet music spilled onto the floor. A priceless Fabergé box sat next to the brass unicorn she had found in a thrift shop and had fallen in love with. One wall was crowded with awards: Grammys, gold and platinum records, plaques and statues and the keys to a few cities. On another was the framed sheet music from the first song she had written and a breathtaking Picasso. The sofa on which she sat had a bad spring.

It was a strange hodgepodge of cultures and tastes and uniquely Raven's own. She would have thought *eclectic* a pretentious word. She had allowed Julie her exacting taste everywhere else in the house, but here she had expressed herself. Raven needed the room the same way she needed to drive her own car. It kept her sane and helped her remember exactly who Raven Williams was. But the room, like the drive, hadn't calmed her nerves. She walked to the piano.

She pounded out Mozart fiercely. Like her eyes, her music

reflected her moods. Now it was tormented, volatile. Even when she'd finished, anger seemed to hover in the air.

"Well, I see you're home." Julie's voice, mild and unruffled, came from the doorway. Julie walked into the room as she had walked into Raven's life: poised and confident. When Raven had met her nearly six years before, Julie had been rich and bored, a party-goer born into old money. Their relationship had given them both something of importance: friendship and a dual dependence. Julie handled the myriad details attached to Raven's career. Raven gave Julie a purpose that the glittery world of wealth had lacked.

"Didn't the recording go well?" Julie was tall and blond, with an elegant body and that exquisitely casual California chic.

Raven lifted her head, and the smile fled from Julie's face. It had been a long time since she'd seen that helpless, ravaged look. "What happened?"

Raven let out a long breath. "He's back."

"Where did you see him?" There was no need for Julie to ask for names. In all the years of their association only two things had had the power to put that look on Raven's face. One of them was a man.

"At the studio." Raven combed her fingers through her hair. "He was up in the booth. I don't know how long he'd been there before I saw him."

Julie pursed her lightly tinted lips. "I wonder what Brand Carstairs is doing in California."

"I don't know." Raven shook her head. "He said business. Maybe he's going to tour again." In an effort to release the tension, she rubbed her hand over the back of her neck. "He's coming here tomorrow."

Julie's brows rose. "I see."

"Don't turn secretary on me, Julie," Raven pleaded. She shut her eyes. "Help me."

"Do you want to see him?" The question was practical. Julie, Raven knew, was practical. She was organized, logical and a stickler for details—all the things Raven wasn't. They needed each other.

"No," Raven began almost fiercely. "Yes..." She swore then and pressed both hands to her temples. "I don't know." Now her tone was quiet and weary. "You know what he's like, Julie. Oh, God, I thought it was over. I thought it was finished!"

With something like a moan, she jumped from the stool to pace around the room. She didn't look like a star in jeans and a simple linen blouse. Her closet held everything from bib overalls to sables. The sables were for the performer; the overalls were for her.

"I'd buried all the hurts. I was so sure." Her voice was low and a little desperate. It was still impossible for her to believe that she had remained this vulnerable after five years. She had only to see him again, and she felt it once more. "I knew sooner or later that I'd run into him somewhere." She ran her fingers through her hair as she roamed the room. "I think I'd always pictured it would be in Europe—London—probably at a party or a benefit. I'd have expected him there; maybe that would have been easier. But today I just looked up and there he was. It all came back. I didn't have any time to stop it. I'd been singing that damn song that I'd written right after he'd left." Raven laughed and shook her head. "Isn't that wild?" She took a deep breath and repeated softly, wonderingly, "Isn't that wild?"

The room was silent for nearly a full minute before Julie spoke. "What are you going to do?"

"Do?" Raven spun back to her. Her hair flew out to follow the sudden movement. "I'm not going to *do* anything. I'm not a child looking for happy-ever-after anymore." Her eyes were still dark with emotion, but her voice had grown gradually steadier. "I was barely twenty when I met Brandon, and I was blindly in love with his talent. He was kind to me at a time when I badly needed kindness. I was overwhelmed by him and with my own success."

She lifted a hand to her hair and carefully pushed it behind her shoulders. "I couldn't cope with what he wanted from me. I wasn't ready for a physical relationship." She walked to the brass unicorn and ran a fingertip down its withers. "So he left," she said softly. "And I was hurt. All I could see—maybe all I wanted to see—was that he didn't understand, didn't care enough to want to know why I said no. But that was unrealistic." She turned to Julie then with a frustrated sigh. "Why don't you say something?"

"You're doing fine without me."

"All right, then." Raven thrust her hands in her pockets and stalked to the window. "One of the things I've learned is that if you don't want to get hurt, you don't get too close. You're the only person I've never applied that rule to, and you're the only one who hasn't let me down." She took a deep breath.

"I was infatuated with Brandon years ago. Perhaps it was a kind of love, but a girl's love, easily brushed aside. It was a shock seeing him today, especially right after I finished that song. The coincidence was..." Raven pushed the feelings away and turned back from the window. "Brandon will come over tomorrow, and he'll say whatever it is that he has to say, then he'll go. That'll be the end of it."

Julie studied Raven's face. "Will it?"

"Oh, yes." Raven smiled. She was a bit weary after the emotional outburst but more confident. She had regained her control. "I like my life just as it is, Julie. He's not going to change it. No one is, not this time."

2

Raven had dressed carefully, telling herself it was because of the fittings she had scheduled and the luncheon meeting with her agent. She knew it was a lie, but the smart, sophisticated clothes made her feel confident. Who could feel vulnerable dressed in a St. Laurent?

Her coat was white silk and full cut with batwing sleeves that made it seem almost like a cape. She wore it over matching pants with an orchid cowlneck blouse and a thick, gold belt. With the flat-brimmed hat and the carefully selected earrings, she felt invulnerable. You've come a long way, she had thought as she had studied herself in the bedroom mirror.

Now, standing in Wayne Metcalf's elaborate fitting room, she thought the same thing again—about both of them. Wayne and Raven had started the rise to fame together, she scratching out a living singing in seamy clubs and smoky piano bars and he waiting tables and sketching designs no one had the time to look at. But Raven had looked and admired and remembered.

Wayne had just begun to eke out a living in his trade when plans had begun for Raven's first concert tour. The first professional decision she made without advice was the choice of her costume designer. She had never regretted it. Like Julie, Wayne was a friend close enough to know something about Raven's early personal life. And like Julie, he was fiercely, unquestionably loyal.

Raven wandered around the room, a much plusher room, she mused, than the first offices of Metcalf Designs. There'd been no carpet on that floor, no signed lithographs on laquered walls, no panoramic view of Beverly Hills. It had been a cramped, airless little room above a Greek restaurant. Raven could still remember the strange, heavy aromas that would seep through the walls. She could still hear the exotic music that had vibrated through the bare wood floor.

Raven's star had not risen with that first concert tour, it had rocketed. The initial taste of fame had been so heady and so quick, she had hardly had the time to savor it all: tours, rehearsals, hotel rooms, reporters, mobs of fans, unbelievable amounts of money and impossible demands. She had loved it, although the traveling had sometimes left her weak and disoriented and the fans could be as frightening as they were wonderful. Still she had loved it.

Wayne, deluged with offers after the publicity of that first tour, had soon moved out of the one-room office above the *moussaka* and *souvlaki*. He'd been Raven's designer for six years, and although he now had a large staff and a huge workload, he still saw to every detail of her designs himself.

While she waited for him, Raven wandered to the bar and poured herself a ginger ale. Through all the years of luncheon meetings, elegant brunches and recording sessions, she had never taken more than an occasional drink. In this respect, at least, she would control her life.

The past, she mused, was never very far away, at least not

while she still had to worry about her mother. Raven shut her eyes and wished that she could shut off her thoughts as easily. How long had it been that she had lived with that constant anxiety? She could never remember a life without it. She had been very young when she had first discovered that her mother wasn't like other mothers. Even as a little girl, she had hated the oddly sweet smell of the liquor on her mother's breath that no mints could disguise, and she had dreaded the flushed face, the first slurred, affectionate, then angry tones that had drawn mocking stares or sympathetic glances from friends and neighbors.

Raven pressed her fingers against her brow. So many years. So much waste. And now her mother had disappeared again. Where was she? In what sordid hotel room had she holed herself up in to drink away what was left of her life? Raven made a determined effort to push her mother out of her mind, but the terrible images, the frightful scenes, played on in her mind.

It's my life! I have to get on with it, Raven told herself, but she could feel the bitter taste of sorrow and guilt rise in her throat. She started when the door across swung open and Wayne walked in.

He leaned against the knob. "Beautiful!" he said admiringly, surveying her. "Did you wear that for me?"

She made a sound that was somewhere between a laugh and a sob as she moved across the room to hug him. "Of course. Bless you!"

"If you were going to dress up for me, you might at least have worn something of mine," he complained but returned the embrace. He was tall, a thin reed of a man who had to bend over to give her the quick kiss. Not yet thirty, he had a scholarly attractive face with hair and eyes the same rich shade of brown. A small white scar marred his left eyebrow and gave him, he preferred to think, a rakish profile.

"Jealous?" Raven grinned and drew away from him. "I thought you were too big for that."

"You're never too big for that." He released her, then made his way across to the bar. "Well, at least take off your hat and coat."

Raven obliged, tossing them aside with a carelessness that made Wayne wince. He gazed at her for a long moment as he poured out a Perrier. She grinned again and did a slow model's turn. "How am I holding up?" she demanded.

"I should have seduced you when you were eighteen." He sighed and drank the sparkling water. "Then I wouldn't be constantly regretting that you slipped through my fingers."

She came back for her ginger ale. "You had your chance, fella."

"I was too exhausted in those days." He lifted his scarred brow in a practiced gesture that always amused her. "I get more rest now."

"Too late," she told him and touched her glass to his. "And you're much too busy with the model-of-the-week contest."

"I only date all those skinny girls for the publicity." He reached for a cigarette and lit it elegantly. "I'm basically a very retiring man."

"The brilliance of the pun I could make is terrifying, but I'll pass."

"Wise," he concluded, then blew out a delicate trail of smoke. "I hear Brand Carstairs is in town."

Raven's smile fled, then returned. "He never could keep a low profile."

"Are you okay?"

She shrugged her shoulders. "A minute ago I was beautiful, now you have to ask if I'm okay?"

"Raven." Wayne laid a hand on top of hers. "You folded up when he left. I was there, remember?"

"Of course I remember." The teasing note left her voice. "You were very good to me, Wayne. I don't think I would have made it without you and Julie."

"That's not what I'm talking about, Raven. I want to know how you feel now." He turned her hand over and laced his fingers through hers. "I could renew my offer to go try to break all his bones, if you like."

Touched and amused, she laughed. "I'm sure you're a real killer, Wayne, but it isn't necessary." The straightening of her shoulders was unconscious, a gesture of pride that made Wayne smile. "I'm not going to fold this time."

"Are you still in love with him?"

She hadn't expected such a direct question. Dropping her gaze, she took a moment to answer. "A better question is, Did I ever love him?"

"We both already know the answer to that one," Wayne countered. He took her hand when she would have turned away. "We've been friends a long time. What happens to you matters to me."

"Nothing's going to happen to me." Her eyes were back on his, and she smiled. "Absolutely nothing. Brandon is the past. Who knows better than I that you can't run away from the past, and who knows better how to cope with it?" She squeezed his hand. "Come on, show me the costumes that are going to make me look sensational."

After a quick, final glance at her face, Wayne walked over to a gleaming Chippendale table and pushed the button on an intercom. "Bring in Ms. Williams's designs."

Raven had approved the sketches, of course, and the fabrics, but still the completed designs took her by surprise. They had been created for the spotlights. She knew she'd sparkle on stage. It felt odd wearing blood red and silver sequins in Wayne's brightly lit, elegant room with mirrors tossing her image back at her from all angles. But then, she remembered, it was an odd business.

Raven stared at the woman in the mirrors and listened with half an ear to Wayne's mumbling as he tucked and adjusted. Her mind could not help but wander. Six years before, she'd been a terrified kid with an album shooting off the top of the charts and a whirlwind concert tour to face. It had all happened so fast: the typical overnight success—not counting the years she had struggled in smoke-choked dives. Still, she'd been young to make a name for herself and determined to prove she wasn't a one-shot fluke. The romance with Brand Carstairs, while she had still been fresh, hot news, hadn't hurt her career. For a brief time it had made her the crown princess of popular music. For more than six months their faces appeared on every magazine cover, dominating the news-stands. They'd laughed about it, Raven remembered, laughed at the silly, predictable headlines: "Raven and Brand Plan Love Nest"; "Williams and Carstairs Make Their Own Music."

Brand had complained about his billing. They had ignored the constant flare and flash of cameras because they had been happy and saw little else but each other. Then, when he had gone, the pictures and headlines had continued for a long time—the cold, cruel words that flashed the intimacies of private hurts for the public eye. Raven no longer looked at them.

Over the months and years, she had grown from the crown princess to a respected performer and celebrity in her own right. That's what's important, she reminded herself. Her career, her life. She'd learned about priorities the hard way.

Raven slipped into the glistening black jumpsuit and found it fit like a second skin. Even her quiet breathing sent sequins flashing. Light streaked out from it at the slightest movement. It was, she decided after a critical survey, blisteringly sexy.

"I'd better not gain a quarter of an ounce before the tour," she remarked, turning to view her slim, sleek profile. Thoughtfully, she gathered her hair in her hand and tossed it behind her back. "Wayne..." He was kneeling at her feet, adjusting the hem. His answer was a grunt. "Wayne, I don't know if I have the nerve to wear this thing."

"This thing," he said mildly as he rose to pluck at the sleeve, "is fantastic."

"No artistic snub intended," she returned and smiled as he stepped back to survey her up and down in his concentrated, professional gaze. "But it's a bit..." She glanced at herself again. "Basic, isn't it?"

"You've got a nice little body, Raven." Wayne examined his creation from the rear. "Not all my clients could wear this without a bit of help here and there. Okay, take it off. It's perfect just as it is."

"I always feel like I've been to the doctor when I've finished here," she commented as she slipped back into her white slacks and orchid blouse. "Who knows more about our bodies' secrets than our dressmakers?"

"Who else knows more about *your* secrets, darling?" he corrected absently as he made notes on each one of the costumes. "Women tend to get chatty when they're half-dressed."

"Oh, what lovely gossip do you know?" Fastening her belt, Raven walked to him, then leaned companionably on his shoulder. "Tell me something wonderfully indiscreet and shocking, Wayne."

"Babs Curtin has a new lover," he murmured, still intent on his notes.

"I said shocking," Raven complained. "Not predictable."

"I've sworn an oath of secrecy, written in dressmaker's chalk."

"I'm very disappointed in you." Raven left his side to fetch her coat and hat. "I was certain you had feet of clay."

"Lauren Chase just signed to do the lead in *Fantasy*."

Raven stopped on her way to the door and whirled. "What?" She dashed back across the room and yanked the notebook from Wayne's hand.

"Somehow I thought that would get your attention," Wayne observed dryly.

"When? Oh, Wayne," she went on before he could answer. "I'd give several years of my young life for a chance to write that score. Lauren Chase…oh, yes, she's so right for it. Who's doing the score, Wayne?" Raven gripped his shoulders and closed her eyes. "Go ahead, tell me, I can take it."

"She doesn't know. You're cutting off the circulation, Raven," he added, disengaging her hands.

"Doesn't know!" she groaned, crushing the hat down on her head in a way that made Wayne swear and adjust it himself. "That's worse, a thousand times worse! Some faceless, nameless songwriter who couldn't possibly know what's right for that fabulous screenplay is even now sitting at a piano making un-forgivable mistakes."

"There's always the remote possibility that whoever's writing it has talent," he suggested and earned a lethal glare.

"Whose side are you on?" she demanded and flung the coat around her shoulders.

He grinned, grabbed her cheeks and gave her a resounding kiss. "Go home and stomp your feet, darling. You'll feel better."

She struggled not to smile. "I'm going next door and buy a Florence DeMille," she threatened him with the name of a leading competitor.

"I'll forgive you that statement," Wayne said with a hefty sigh. "Because along with my feet of clay I've a heart of gold."

She laughed and left him with her rack of costumes and his notebook.

The house was quiet when Raven returned. The faint scent of lemon oil and pine told her that the house had just been cleaned. As a matter of habit, she peeked into her music room and was satisfied that nothing there had been disturbed. She liked her disorganization just as it was. With the idle thought of making coffee, Raven wandered toward the kitchen.

She had bought the house for its size and rambling openness. It was the antithesis of the small, claustrophobic rooms she had grown up in. And it smelled clean, she decided. Not antiseptic; she would have hated that, but there was no lingering scent of stale cigarettes, no sickly sweet odor of yesterday's bottle. It was her house, as her life was hers. She'd bought them both with her voice.

Raven twirled once around the room, pleased with herself for no specific reason. I'm happy, she thought, just happy to be alive.

Grabbing a rose from a china vase, she began to sing as she walked down the hall. It was the sight of Julie's long, narrow bare feet propped up on the desk in the library that stopped her.

Raven hesitated, seeing Julie was on the phone, but was quickly gestured inside.

"I'm sorry, Mr. Cummings, but Ms. Williams has a strict policy against endorsements. Yes, I'm sure it's a marvelous product." Julie lifted her eyes from her pink-tinted toenails and met Raven's amused grin. She rolled her eyes to the ceiling, and Raven settled cross-legged in an overstuffed leather chair. The library, with its warm, mahogany paneling and stately furnishings, was Julie's domain. And, Raven thought, snuggling down more comfortably, it suited her.

"Of course, I'll see she gets your offer, but I warn you, Ms. Williams takes a firm stand on this." With one last exasperated glance at the ceiling, Julie hung up. "If you didn't insist on being nice to everybody who calls you, I could have thought of a few different words for that one," Julie snapped.

"Trouble?" Raven asked, sniffing her rose and smiling.

"Get smart and I'll tell them you'll be thrilled to endorse his Earth Dubble Shampoo." She laced her fingers behind her head as she made the threat.

"Mercy," Raven pleaded, then kicked off her elegant, orchid-toned shoes. "You look tired," she said, watching Julie stretch her back muscles. "Been busy?"

"Just last-minute nonsense to clear things for the tour." A shrug dismissed the complications she had handled. "I never did ask you how the recording went. It's finished, isn't it?"

"Yeah." Raven took a deep breath and twirled her rose by the stem. "It went perfectly. I haven't been happier with a session since the first one. Something just clicked."

"You worked hard enough on the material," Julie remarked, thinking of the endless nights Raven had spent writing and arranging.

"Sometimes I still can't believe it." She spoke softly, the words hardly more than thoughts. "I listen to a playback, and it's all there, the strings, the brass, the rhythm and backups, and I can't believe it's me. I've been so incredibly lucky."

"Talented," Julie corrected.

"Lots of people have talent," Raven reminded her. "But they're not sitting here. They're still in some dreary piano bar, waiting. Without luck, they're never going to be anywhere else."

"There are also things like drive, perseverance, guts." Raven's persistent lack of self-confidence infuriated Julie. She'd been with her almost from the beginning of Raven's start in California six years before. She'd seen the struggles and the disappointments. She knew about the fears, insecurities and work behind the glamour. There was nothing about Raven Williams that Julie didn't know.

The phone interrupted her thoughts on a lecture on self-worth. "It's your private line," she said as she pressed the button. "Hello." Raven tensed but relaxed when she saw Julie smile. "Hi, Henderson. Yes, she's right here, hold on. Your illustrious agent," Julie stated as she rose. She slipped her feet back into her sandals. Raven got up from her chair just as the doorbell chimed.

"I guess that's Brandon." With admirable ease, she flopped into the chair that Julie had just vacated. "Would you tell him I'll be along in a minute?"

"Sure." Julie turned and left as Raven's voice followed her down the hall.

"I left it where? In your office? Henderson, I don't know why I ever bother carrying a purse."

Julie smiled. Raven had a penchant for losing things: her purse, her shoes, her passport. Vital or trivial, it simply didn't matter. Music and people filled Raven's thoughts, and material objects were easily forgotten.

"Hello, Brand," Julie said as she opened the front door. "Nice to see you again." Her eyes were cool, and her mouth formed no smile.

"Hello, Julie."

There was warmth in his greeting. She sensed it and ignored it. "Come in," she invited. "Raven's expecting you; she'll be right out."

"It's good to be here again. I've missed this place."

"Have you?" Her tone was sharp.

His grin turned into a look of appraisal. Julie was a long-stemmed woman with a sleek cap of honey-blond hair and direct brown eyes. She was closer to Brand's age than Raven's and was the sort of woman he was usually attracted to: smart, sophisticated and coolly sexy. Yet, there could never have been anything between them but friendship. She was too fiercely devoted to Raven. Her loyalty, he saw, was unchanged.

"Five years is a long time, Julie."

"I'm not sure it's long enough," she countered. Old resentments came simmering back to the surface. "You hurt her."

"Yes, I know." His gaze didn't falter at the confession, and there was no plea for understanding in his eyes. The lack of it touched off respect in Julie, but she dismissed it. She shook her head as she looked at him.

"So," she said softly, "you've come back."

"I've come back," he agreed, then smiled. "Did you think I wouldn't?"

"She didn't," Julie retorted, annoyed with herself for warming to him. "That's what matters."

"Julie, Henderson's sending over my purse." Raven came down the hall toward them in her quick, nervous stride. "I told him not to bother; I don't think there's anything in it but a comb and an expired credit card. Hello, Brandon." She offered her hands as she had at the recording studio, but now she felt more able to accept his touch.

She hadn't bothered to put her shoes back on or to repaint her mouth. Her smile was freer, more as he remembered it. "Raven." Brand brought her hands to his lips. Instantly she stiffened, and Brand released her. "Can we talk in the music room?" His smile was easy, friendly. "I was always comfortable in there."

"Of course." She turned toward the doorway. "Would you like something to drink?"

"I'd have some tea." He gave Julie his quick, charming grin. "You always made a good cup of tea."

"I'll bring it in." Without responding to the grin, Julie moved down the hall toward the kitchen. Brand followed Raven into the music room.

He touched her shoulder before she could cross to the sofa. It was a gesture that asked her to wait. Turning her head, Raven saw that he was giving the room one of his long, detailed studies. She had seen that look on his face before. It was a curious aspect of what seemed like a casual nature. There was an intensity about him at times that recalled the tough London street kid who'd once fought his way to the top of his profession. The key to his talent seemed to be in his natural gift for observation. He saw everything, remembered everything. Then he translated it into lyric and melody.

The fingers on her shoulder caressed once, almost absently, and brought back a flood of memories. Raven would have moved away, but he dropped the hand and turned to her. She had never been able to resist his eyes.

"I remember every detail of this room. I've pictured it from time to time when I couldn't do anything but think of you." He lifted his hand again to brush the back of it against her cheek.

"Don't." She shook her head and stepped away.

"It's difficult not to touch you, Raven. Especially here. Do you remember the long evenings we spent here? The quiet afternoons?"

He was moving her—with just his voice, just the steady spell of his eyes. "It was a long time ago, Brandon."

"It doesn't seem so long ago at the moment. It could be yesterday; you look the same."

"I'm not," she told him with a slight shake of her head. He saw her eyes darken before she turned away. "If I had known this was why you wanted to see me, I wouldn't have let you come. It's over, Brandon. It's been over for a long time."

"Is it?" Raven hadn't realized he was so close behind her. He turned her in his arms and caught her. "Show me, then," he demanded. "Just once."

The moment his mouth touched hers, she was thrown back in time. It was all there—the heat, the need, the loving. His lips were so soft, so warm; hers parted with only the slightest pressure. She knew how he would taste, how he would smell. Her memory was sharper than she had thought. Nothing was forgotten.

He tangled his fingers in the thickness of her hair, tilting her head further back as he deepened the kiss. He wanted to luxuriate in her flavor, in her scent, in her soft, yielding response. Her hands were trapped between their bodies, and she curled her fingers into the sweater he wore. The need, the longing, seemed much too fresh to have been dormant for five years. Brand held her close but without urgency. There was a quiet kind of certainty in the way he explored her mouth. Raven responded, giving, accepting, remembering. But when she felt the pleasure drifting toward passion, she resisted. When she struggled, he loosened his hold but didn't release her. Raven stared up at him with a look he well remembered but had never been able to completely decipher.

"It doesn't seem it's altogether finished after all," he murmured.

"You never did play fair, did you?" Raven pushed out of his arms, furious and shaken. "Let me tell you something, Brandon. I won't fall at your feet this time. You hurt me before, but I don't bruise so easily now. I have no intention of letting you back into my life."

"I think you will," he corrected easily. "But perhaps not in the way you mean." He paused and caught her hair with his fingers. "I can apologize for kissing you, Raven, if you'd like me to lie."

"Don't bother. You've always been good at romance. I rather enjoyed it." She sat down on the sofa and smiled brightly up at him.

He lifted a brow. It was hardly the response he had expected. He drew out a cigarette and lit it. "You seem to have grown up in my absence."

"Being an adult has its advantages," Raven observed. The kiss had stirred more than she cared to admit, even to herself.

"I always found your naiveté charming."

"It's difficult to remain naive, however charming, in this business." She leaned back against the cushion, relaxing deliberately. "I'm not wide-eyed and twenty anymore, Brandon."

"Tough and jaded are you, Raven?"

"Tough enough," she returned. "You gave me my first lesson!"

He took a deep drag on his cigarette, then considered the glowing tip of it. "Maybe I did," he murmured. "Maybe you needed it."

"Maybe you'd like me to thank you," she tossed back, and he looked over at her again.

"Perhaps." He walked over, then dropped down beside her

on the sofa. His laugh was sudden and unexpected. "Good God, Raven, you've never had this bloody spring fixed."

The tension in her neck fled as she laughed with him. "I like it that way." She tossed her hair behind her back. "It's more personal."

"To say nothing of uncomfortable."

"I never sit on that spot," she told him.

"You leave it for unsuspecting guests, I imagine." He shifted away from the defective spring.

"That's right. I like people to feel at home."

Julie brought in a tea tray and found them sitting companionably on the sofa. Her quick, practiced glance found no tension on Raven's face. Satisfied, she left them again.

"How've you been, Brandon? Busy, I imagine." Raven crossed her legs under her and leaned over to pour the tea. It was a move Brandon had seen many times. Almost savagely, he crushed out his cigarette.

"Busy enough." He understated the five albums he had released since she'd last seen him and the three grueling concert tours. There'd been more than twenty songs with his name on the copyright in the past year.

"You've been living in London?"

"Mostly." His brow lifted, and she caught the gesture as she handed him his tea.

"I read the trades," she said mildly. "Don't we all?"

"I saw your television special last month." He sipped his tea and relaxed against the back of the sofa. His eyes were on her, and she thought them a bit more green than blue now. "You were marvelous."

"Last month?" She frowned at him, puzzled. "It wasn't aired in England, was it?"

"I was in New York. Did you write all the songs for the album you finished up yesterday?"

"All but two." Shrugging, she took up her own china cup. "Marc wrote 'Right Now' and 'Coming Back.' He's got the touch."

"Yes." Brand eyed her steadily. "Does he have you, too?" Raven's head whipped around. "I read the trades," he said mildly.

"That comes under a more personal heading." Her eyes were dark with anger.

"More bluntly stated, none of my business?" he asked, sipping again.

"You were always bright, Brandon."

"Thanks, love." He set down his cup. "But my question was professional. I need to know if you have any entanglements at the moment."

"Entanglements are usually personal. Ask me about my dancing lessons."

"Later, perhaps. Raven, I need your undivided devotion for the next three months." His smile was engaging. Raven fought his charm.

"Well," she said and set her cup beside his. "That's bluntly stated."

"No indecent proposal at the moment," he assured her. Settling back in the hook of the sofa's arm, he sought her eyes. "I'm doing the score for *Fantasy*. I need a partner."

3

To say she was surprised would have been a ridiculous understatement. Brand watched her eyes widen. He thought they were the color of peat smoke. She didn't move but simply stared at him, her hands resting lightly on her knees. Her thoughts had been flung in a thousand different directions, and she was trying to sit calmly and bring them back to order.

Fantasy. The book that had captured America's heart. A novel that had been on the bestseller list for more than fifty weeks. The sale of its paperback rights had broken all records. The film rights had been purchased as well, and Carol Mason, the author, had written the screenplay herself. It was to be a musical; *the* musical of the nineties. Speculation had been buzzing for months on both coasts as to who would write the score. It would be the coup of the decade, the chance of a lifetime. The plot was a dream, and the reigning box-office queen had the lead. And the music… Raven already had half-formed songs in her head. Carefully she reached back and poured more tea. Things like this don't just fall in your lap, she reminded herself. Perhaps he means something entirely different.

"You're going to score *Fantasy*," she said at length, cautiously. Her eyes met his again. His were clear, confident, a little puzzled. "I just heard that Lauren Chase had been signed. Everywhere I go, people are wondering who's going to play Tessa, who's going to play Joe."

"Jack Ladd," Brand supplied, and the puzzlement in Raven's eyes changed to pure pleasure.

"Perfect!" She reached over to take his hands. "You're going to have a tremendous hit. I'm very happy for you."

And she was. He could see as well as hear the absolute sincerity. It was typical of her to gain genuine pleasure from someone else's good fortune, just as it was typical of her to suffer for someone else's misfortune. Raven's feelings ran deep, and he knew she'd never been afraid to show emotion. Her unaffectedness had always been a great part of her appeal. For the moment, she had forgotten to be cautious with Brand. She smiled at him as she held his hands.

"So that's why you're in California," she said. "Have you already started?"

"No." He seemed to consider something for a moment, then his fingers interlaced with hers. Her hands were narrow-boned and slender, with palms as soft as a child's. "Raven, I meant what I said. I need a partner. I need you."

She started to remove her hands from his, but he tightened his fingers. "I've never known you to need anyone, Brandon," she said, not quite succeeding in making her tone light. "Least of all me."

His grip tightened quickly, causing Raven's eyes to widen at the unexpected pain. Just as quickly, he released her. "This is business, Raven."

She lifted a brow at the temper in his voice. "Business is

usually handled through my agent," she said. "You remember Henderson."

He gave her a long, steady look. "I remember everything." He saw the flash of hurt in her eyes, swiftly controlled. "Raven," his tone was gentler now. "I'm sorry."

She shrugged and gave her attention back to her tea. "Old wounds, Brandon. It does seem to me that if there was a legitimate offer, Henderson would have gotten wind of it."

"There's been an offer," Brand told her. "I asked him to let me speak to you first."

"Oh?" Her hair had drifted down, curtaining her face, and she flipped it behind her back. "Why?"

"Because I thought that if you knew we'd be working together, you'd turn it down."

"Yes," she agreed. "You're right."

"And that," he said without missing a beat, "would be incredibly soft-headed. Henderson knows that as well as I do."

"Oh, does he?" Raven rose, furious. "Isn't it marvelous the way people determine my life? Did you two decide I was too feeble-brained to make this decision on my own?"

"Not exactly." Brand's voice was cool. "We did agree that left to yourself, you have a tendency to be emotional rather than sensible."

"Terrific. Do I get a leash and collar for Christmas?"

"Don't be an idiot," Brand advised.

"Oh, so now I'm an idiot?" Raven turned away to pace the room. She had the same quicksilver temper he remembered. She was all motion, all energy. "I don't know how I've managed all this time without your pretty compliments, Brandon." She whirled back to him. "Why in the world would you want an emotional idiot as a collaborator?"

"Because," Brandon said and rose, "you're a hell of a writer. Now shut up."

"Of course," she said, seating herself on the piano bench. "Since you asked so nicely."

Deliberately he took out another cigarette, lit it and blew out a stream of smoke, all the while his eyes resting on her face. "This is an important project, Raven," he said. "Let's not blow it. Because we were once very close, I wanted to talk to you face to face, not through a mediator, not through a bloody telephone wire. Can you understand that?"

She waited a long moment before answering. "Maybe."

Brand smiled and moved over to her. "We'll add stubborn to those adjectives later, but I don't want you mad again."

"Then let me ask you something before you say anything I'll have to get mad about." Raven tilted her head and studied his face. "First, why do you want a collaborator on this? Why share the glory?"

"It's also a matter of sharing the work, love. Fifteen songs."

She nodded. "All right, number two, then. Why me, Brandon? Why not someone who's scored a musical before?"

He answered her by walking around her and slipping down on the piano bench beside her. Without speaking, he began to play. The notes flooded the room like ghosts. "Remember this?" he murmured, glancing over and into her eyes.

Raven didn't have to answer. She rose and walked away. It was too difficult to sit beside him at the same piano where they had composed the song he now played. She remembered how they had laughed, how warm his eyes had been, how safe she had felt in his arms. It was the first and only song they had written and recorded together.

Even after he had stopped playing, she continued to prowl

the room. "What does 'Clouds and Rain' have to do with anything?" she demanded. He had touched a chord in her; he heard it in the tone of her voice. He felt a pang of guilt at having intentionally peeled away a layer of her defense.

"There's a Grammy over there and a gold record, thanks to that two minutes and forty-three seconds, Raven. We work well together."

She turned back to look at him. "We did once."

"We will again." Brand stood and came to her but this time made no move to touch her. "Raven, you know how important this could be to your career. And you must realize what you'd be bringing to the project. *Fantasy* needs your special talents."

She wanted it. She could hardly believe that something she wanted so badly was being offered to her. But how would it be to work with him again, to be in constant close contact? Would she be able to deal with it? Would she be sacrificing her personal sanity for professional gain? But I don't love him anymore, she reminded herself. Raven caught her bottom lip between her teeth in a gesture of indecision. Brand saw it.

"Raven, think of the music."

"I am," she admitted. "I'm also thinking of you—of us." She gave him a clear, candid look. "I'm not sure it would be healthy for me."

"I can't promise not to touch you." He was annoyed, and his voice reflected it in its crisp, concise tone. "But I can promise not to push myself on you. Is that good enough?"

Raven evaded the question. "If I agreed, when would we start? I've a tour coming up."

"I know, in two weeks. You'll be finished in six, so we could start the first week in May."

"I see." Her mouth turned up a bit as she combed her fingers through her hair. "You've looked into this thoroughly."

"I told you, it's business."

"All right, Brandon," she said, conceding his point. "Where would we work? Not here," she said quickly. There was a sudden pressure in her chest. "I won't work with you here."

"No, I thought not. I have a place," he continued when Raven remained silent. "It's in Cornwall."

"Cornwall?" Raven repeated. "Why Cornwall?"

"Because it's quiet and isolated, and no one, especially the press, knows I have it. They'll be all over us when they hear we're working together, especially on this project. It's too hot an item."

"Couldn't we just rent a small cave on the coast somewhere?"

He laughed and caught her hair in his hand. "You know how poor the acoustics are in a cave. Cornwall's incredible in the spring, Raven. Come with me."

She lifted a hand to his chest to push back, not certain if she was about to agree or decline. He could still draw too much from her too effortlessly. She needed to think, she decided; a few days to put it all in perspective.

"Raven."

She turned to see Julie in the doorway. "Yes?"

"There's a call for you."

Vaguely annoyed, Raven frowned at her. "Can't it wait, Julie? I…"

"It's on your private line."

Brand felt her stiffen and looked down curiously. Her eyes were completely blank.

"I see." Her voice was calm, but he detected the faintest of tremors.

"Raven?" Without thinking, he took her by the shoulders and turned her to face him. "What is it?"

"Nothing." She drew out of his arms. There was something remote about her now, something distant that puzzled him. "Have some more tea," she invited and smiled, but her eyes remained blank. "I'll be back in a minute."

She was gone for more than ten, and Brand had begun to pace restlessly through the room. Raven was definitely no longer the malleable young girl she had been five years before; he knew that. He wasn't at all certain she would agree to work with him. He wanted her—for the project and yes, for himself. Holding her, tasting her again, had stirred up much more than memories. She fascinated him and always had. Even when she had been so young, there had been an air of secrecy about her. There still was. It was as if she kept certain parts of herself locked in a closet out of reach. She had held him off five years before in more than a physical sense. It had frustrated him then and continued to frustrate him.

But he was older, too. He'd made mistakes with her before and had no intention of repeating them. Brand knew what he wanted and was determined to get it. Sitting back at the piano, he began to play the song he had written with Raven. He remembered her voice, warm and sultry, in his ear. He was nearly at the end when he sensed her presence.

Glancing up, Brand saw her standing in the doorway. Her eyes were unusually dark and intense. Then he realized it was because she was pale, and the contrast accentuated the gray of her irises. Had the song disturbed her that much? He stopped immediately and rose to go to her.

"Raven…"

"I've decided to do it," she interrupted. Her hands were folded neatly in front of her, her eyes direct.

"Good." He took her hands and found it chilled. "Are you all right?"

"Yes, of course." She removed her hands from his, but her gaze never faltered. "I suppose Henderson will fill me in on all the details."

Something about her calm disturbed him. It was as if she'd set part of herself aside. "Let's have dinner, Raven." The urge to be with her, to pierce her armor, was almost overwhelming. "I'll take you to the Bistro; you always liked it there."

"Not tonight, Brandon, I...have some things to do."

"Tomorrow," he insisted, knowing he was pushing but unable to prevent himself. She looked suddenly weary.

"Yes, all right, tomorrow." She gave him a tired smile. "I'm sorry, but I'll have to ask you to leave now, Brandon. I didn't realize how late it was."

"All right." Bending toward her, he gently kissed her. It was an instinctive gesture, one that demanded no response. He felt the need to warm her, protect her. "Seven tomorrow," he told her. "I'm at the Bel-Air; you only have to call me."

Raven waited until she heard the front door shut behind her. She pressed the heel of her hand to her brow and let the tide of emotions rush through her. There were no tears, but a blinding headache raged behind her eyes. She felt Julie's hand on her shoulder.

"They found her?" Julie asked, concerned. Automatically she began kneading the tension from Raven's shoulders.

"Yes, they found her." She let out a long, deep breath. "She's coming back."

4

The sanitarium was white and clean. The architect, a good one, had conceived a restful building without medical overtones. The uninformed might have mistaken it for an exclusive hotel snuggled in California's scenic Ojai. It was a proud, elegantly fashioned building with several magnificent views of the countryside. Raven detested it.

Inside, the floors were thickly carpeted, and conversation was always low-key. Raven hated the controlled silence, the padded quiet. The staff members wore street clothes and only small, discreet badges to identify themselves, and they were among the best trained in the country, just as the Fieldmore Clinic was the best detoxification center on the west coast. Raven had made certain of its reputation before she had brought her mother there for the first time over five years before.

Raven waited in Justin Karter's paneled, book-lined, tasteful office. It received its southern exposure through a wide, thick-paned window. The morning sunlight beamed in on a thriving collection of leafy green plants. Raven wondered idly why her own plants seemed always to put up only a halfhearted struggle for life, one they usually lost. Perhaps she should ask Dr. Karter what his secret was. She laughed a little and rubbed her fingers on the nagging headache between her brows.

How she hated these visits and the leathery, glossy smell of his office. She was cold and cupped her elbows, hugging her arms across her midriff. Raven was always cold in the Fieldmore Clinic, from the moment she walked through the stately white double doors until long after she walked out again. It was a penetrating cold that went straight to the bone. Turning away from the window, she paced nervously around the room. When she heard the door open, she stopped and turned around slowly.

Karter entered, a small, youthful man with a corn-colored beard and healthy pink cheeks. He had an earnest face, accentuated by tortoise-rimmed glasses and a faint smattering of freckles. Under other circumstances, Raven would have liked his face, even warmed to it.

"Ms. Williams." He held out a hand and took hers in a quick, professional grip. It was cold, he realized, and as fragile as he remembered. Her hair was pinned up at the nape of her neck, and she looked young and pale in the dark tailored suit. This woman was far different from the vibrant, laughing entertainer he had watched on television a few weeks before.

"Hello, Dr. Karter."

It always amazed him that the rich, full-toned voice belonged to such a small, delicate-looking woman. He had thought the same years before when she had been hardly more than a child. He was an ardent fan but had never asked her to sign any of the albums in his collection. It would, he knew, embarrass them both.

"Please sit down, Ms. Williams. Could I get you some coffee?"

"No, please." She swallowed. Her throat was always dry when she spoke to him. "I'd like to see my mother first."

"There are a few things I'd like to discuss with you."

He watched her moisten her lips, the only sign of agitation. "After I've seen her."

"All right." Karter took her by the arm and led her from the room. They walked across the quiet, carpeted hallway to the elevators. "Ms. Williams," he began. He would have liked to have called her Raven. He thought of her as Raven, just as the rest of the world did. But he could never quite break through the film of reserve she slipped on in his presence. It was, Karter knew, because he knew her secrets. She trusted him to keep them but was never comfortable with him. She turned to him now, her great, gray eyes direct and expressionless.

"Yes, Doctor?" Only once had Raven ever broken down in his presence, and she had promised herself she would never do so again. She would not be destroyed by her mother's illness, and she would not make a public display of herself.

"I don't want you to be shocked by your mother's appearance." They stepped into the elevator together, and he kept his hand on her arm. "She had made a great deal of progress during her last stay here, but she left prematurely, as you know. Over the past three months, her condition has…deteriorated."

"Please," Raven said wearily, "don't be delicate. I know where she was found and how. You'll dry her out again, and in a couple of months she'll leave and it'll start all over. It never changes."

"Alcoholics fight a continuing battle."

"Don't tell me about alcoholics," she shot back. The reserve cracked, and the emotion poured through. "Don't preach to me about battles." She stopped herself, then, shaking her head, pressed her fingers to the concentrated source of her headache. "I know all about alcoholics," she said more calmly. "I haven't your dedication or your optimism."

"You keep bringing her back," he reminded Raven softly.

"She's my mother." The elevator doors slid open, and Raven walked through them.

Her skin grew colder as they moved down the hallway. There were doors on either side, but she refused to think of the people beyond them. The hospital flavor was stronger here. Raven thought she could smell the antiseptic, the hovering medicinal odor that always made a hint of nausea roll in her stomach. When Karter stopped in front of a door and reached for a knob, Raven laid a hand on top of his.

"I'll see her alone, please."

He sensed her rigid control. Her eyes were calm, but he had seen the quick flash of panic in them. Her fingers didn't tremble on his hand but were stiff and icy. "All right. But only a few minutes. There are complications we need to discuss." He took his hand from the knob. "I'll wait for you here."

Raven nodded and twisted the knob herself. She took a moment, struggling to gather every ounce of strength, then walked inside.

The woman lay in a hospital bed on good linen sheets, dozing lightly. There was a tube feeding liquid into her through a needle in her arm. The drapes were drawn, and the room was in shadows. It was a comfortable room painted in soft blue with an ivory carpet and a few good paintings. With her fingers dug into the leather bag she carried, Raven approached the bed.

Raven's first thought was that her mother had lost weight. There were hollows in her cheeks, and her skin had the familiar unhealthy yellow cast. Her dark hair was cropped short and streaked liberally with gray. It had been lovely hair, Raven remembered, glossy and full. Her face was gaunt, with deathly circles under the eyes and a mouth that seemed dry and pulled in. The helplessness stabbed at Raven, and for a minute she closed her eyes against it. She let them fall while she looked down on the sleeping woman. Without a sound, without moving, the woman in bed opened her eyes. They were dark and gray like her daughter's.

"Mama." Raven let the tears roll freely. "Why?"

By the time Raven got to her front door, she was exhausted. She wanted bed and oblivion. The headache was still with her, but the pain had turned into a dull, sickening throb. Closing the door behind her, she leaned back on it, trying to summon the strength to walk up the stairs.

"Raven?"

She opened her eyes and watched Julie come down the hall toward her. Seeing Raven so pale and beaten, Julie slipped an arm around her shoulders. Her concern took the form of a scolding. "You should have let me go with you. I should never have let you go alone." She was already guiding Raven up the stairs.

"My mother, my problem," Raven said tiredly.

"That's the only selfish part of you," Julie said in a low, furious voice as they entered Raven's bedroom. "I'm supposed to be your friend. You'd never let me go through something like this alone."

"Please, don't be angry with me." Raven swayed on her feet as Julie stripped off the dark suit jacket. "It's something I feel is my responsibility, just mine. I've felt that way for too long to change now."

"I am angry with you." Julie's voice was tight as she slipped the matching skirt down over Raven's hips. "This is the only thing you do that makes me genuinely angry with you. I can't stand it when you do this to yourself." She looked back at the pale, tired face. "Have you eaten?" Raven shook her head as she stepped out of the skirt. "And you won't," she concluded, brushing Raven's fumbling hands away from the buttons of the white lawn blouse. She undid them herself, then pushed the material from Raven's shoulders. Raven stood, unresisting.

"I'm having dinner with Brandon," Raven murmured, going willingly as Julie guided her toward the bed.

"I'll call him and cancel. I can bring you up something later. You need to sleep."

"No." Raven slipped between the crisp, cool sheets. "I want to go. I need to go," she corrected as she shut her eyes. "I need to get out; I don't want to think for a while. I'll rest now. He won't be here until seven."

Julie walked over to pull the shades. Even before the room was darkened, Raven was asleep.

It was some minutes past seven when Julie opened the door to Brandon. He wore a stone-colored suit with a navy shirt open at the throat. He looked casually elegant, Julie thought. The nosegay of violets was charming rather than silly in his hands. He lifted a brow at the clinging black sheath she wore.

"Hello, Julie. You look terrific." He plucked one of the violets out of the nosegay and handed it to her. "Going out?"

Julie accepted the flower. "In a little while," she answered. "Raven should be down in a minute. Brand…" Hesitating, Julie shook her head, then turned to lead him into the music room. "I'll fix you a drink. Bourbon, isn't it? Neat."

Brand caught her arm. "That isn't what you were going to say."

She took a deep breath. "No." For a moment longer she

hesitated, then began, fixing him with her dark brown eyes. "Raven's very important to me. There aren't many like her, especially in this town. She's genuine, and though she thinks she has, she hasn't really developed any hard edges yet. I wouldn't like to see her hurt, especially right now. No, I won't answer any questions," she said, anticipating him. "It's Raven's story, not mine. But I'm going to tell you this: She needs a light touch and a great deal of patience. You'd better have them both."

"How much do you know about what happened between us five years ago, Julie?" Brandon asked.

"I know what Raven told me."

"One day you ought to ask me how I felt and why I left."

"And would you tell me?"

"Yes," he returned without hesitation. "I would."

"I'm sorry!" Raven came dashing down the stairs in a filmy flutter of white. "I hate to be late." Her hair settled in silky confusion over the shoulders of the thin voile dress as she stopped at the foot of the stairs. "I couldn't seem to find my shoes."

There was a becoming blush of color on her cheeks, and her eyes were bright and full of laughter. It passed through Brand's mind quickly, and then was discarded, that she looked a little too bright, a little too vibrant.

"Beautiful as ever." He handed her the flowers. "I've never minded waiting for you."

"Ah, the golden Irish tongue," she murmured as she buried her face in the violets. "I've missed it." Raven held the flowers up to her nose while her eyes laughed at him over them. "And I believe I'll let you spoil me tonight, Brandon. I'm in a mood to be pampered."

He took her free hand in his. "Where do you want to go?"

"Anywhere. Everywhere." She tossed her head. "But dinner first. I'm starving."

"All right, I'll buy you a cheeseburger."

"Some things do stay the same," she commented before she turned to Julie. "You have fun, and don't worry about me." She paused a moment, then smiled and kissed her cheek. "I promise I won't lose my key. And say hello to…" She hesitated as she walked toward the door with Brandon. "Who is it tonight?"

"Lorenzo," Julie answered, watching them. "The shoe baron."

"Oh, yes." Raven laughed as they walked into the cool, early spring air. "Amazing." She tucked her arm through Brandon's. "Julie's always having some millionaire fall in love with her. It's a gift."

"Shoe baron?" Brand questioned as he opened the car door for Raven.

"*Mmm.* Italian. He wears beautiful designer suits and looks as though he should be stamped on the head of a coin."

Brand slid in beside her and in an old reflex gesture brushed the hair that lay on her shoulder behind her back. "Serious?"

Raven tried not to be moved by the touch of his fingers. "No more serious than the oil tycoon or the perfume magnate." The leathery smell of the upholstery reminded her abruptly of Karter's office. Quickly she pushed away the sensation. "What are you going to feed me, Brandon?" she asked brightly—too brightly. "I warn you, I'm starving."

He circled her throat with his hand so that she had no choice but to meet his eyes directly. "Are you going to tell me what's wrong?"

He'd always seen too much too quickly, she thought. It was one of the qualities that had made him an exceptional songwriter.

Raven placed her hand on top of his. "No questions, Brandon, not now."

She felt his hesitation. Then he turned his hand over and gripped hers. Slowly, overriding her initial resistance, he brought her palm to his lips. "Not now," he agreed, watching her eyes. "I can still move you," he murmured and smiled as though the knowledge pleased him. "I can feel it."

Raven felt the tremors racing up her arms. "Yes." She drew her hand from his but kept her eyes steady. "You can still move me. But things aren't the same anymore."

He grinned, a quick flash of white teeth, then started the engine. "No, things aren't the same anymore."

As he pulled away, she had the uncomfortable impression that they had said the same words but meant two different things.

Dinner was quiet and intimate and perfect. They ate in a tiny old inn they had once discovered by chance. Here, Brand knew, there would be no interruptions for autographs, no greetings and drinks from old acquaintances. Here there would be just the two of them, a man and a woman amidst candlelight, wine, fine food, and an intimate atmosphere.

As the evening wore on, Raven's smile became more spontaneous, less desperate, and the unhappiness he had seen deep in her eyes before now faded. Though he noticed the transition, Brand made no comment.

"I feel like I haven't eaten in a week," Raven managed between bites of the tender roast beef that was the house speciality.

"Want some of mine?" Brand offered his plate.

Raven scooped up a bit of baked potato; her eyes seemed to laugh at him. "We'll have them wrap it up so I can take it home. I want to leave room for dessert. Did you see that pastry tray?"

"I suppose I could roll you to Cornwall," Brand considered, adding some burgundy to his glass.

Raven laughed, a throaty sound that appealed and aroused. "I'll be a bag of bones by the time we go to Cornwall," she claimed. "You know what those whirlwind tours can do." She shook her head as he offered her more wine.

"One-night stands from San Francisco to New York." Brand lifted his glass as Raven gave him a quizzing look. "I spoke to Henderson." He twirled a strand of her hair around his finger so absently, Raven was certain he was unaware of the gesture. She made no complaint. "If it's agreeable with you, I'll meet you in New York at the end of the tour. We'll fly to England from there."

"All right." She took a deep breath, having finally reached her fill of the roast beef. "You'd better set it up with Julie. I haven't any memory for dates and times. Are you staying in the States until then?"

"I'm doing a couple of weeks in Vegas." He brushed his fingers across her cheek, and when she would have resisted, he laid his hand companionably over hers. "I haven't played there in quite a while. I don't suppose it's changed."

She laughed and shook her head. "No. I played there, oh, about six months ago, I guess. Julie won a bundle at the baccarat table. I was a victim of the slots."

"I read the reviews. Were you as sensational as they said?" He smiled at her while one finger played with the thin gold bracelet at her wrist.

"Oh, I was much more sensational than they said," she assured him.

"I'd like to have seen you." His finger drifted lazily to her pulse. He felt it jump at his touch. "It's been much too long since I've heard you sing."

"You heard me just the other day in the studio," she pointed out. She took her hand from his to reach for her wine. He easily took her other one. "Brandon," she began, half-amused.

"I've heard you over the radio as well," he continued, "but it's not the same as watching you come alive at a concert. Or," he smiled as his voice took on that soft, intimate note she remembered, "listening to you when you sing just for me."

His tone was as smooth as the burgundy she drank. Knowing how easily he could cloud her brain, she vowed to keep their conversation light. "Do you know what I want right now?" She lowered her own voice as she leaned toward him, but he recognized the laughter in her eyes.

"Dessert," he answered.

"You know me so well, Brandon." She smiled.

She wanted to go dancing. By mutual consent, when they left the restaurant they avoided the popular, trendy spots in town and found a crowded, smoky hole-in-the-wall club with a good band, much like the dozens they had both played in at the beginnings of their respective careers. They thought they wouldn't be recognized there. For almost twenty minutes they were right.

"Excuse me, aren't you Brand Carstairs?" The toothy young blond stared up at Brand in admiration. Then she glanced at Raven. "And Raven Williams."

"Bob Muldroon," Brand returned in a passable Texas drawl. "And my wife Sheila. Say howdy, Sheila," he instructed as he held her close and swayed on the postage-sized dance floor.

"Howdy," Raven said obligingly.

"Oh, Mr. Carstairs." She giggled and thrust out a cocktail napkin and a pencil. "Please, I'm Debbie. Could you write, 'To my good friend Debbie'?"

"Sure." Brand gave her one of his charming smiles and told Raven to turn around. He scrawled quickly, using her back for support.

"And you, too, Raven," Debbie asked when he'd finished. "On the other side."

It was typical of her fans to treat her informally. They thought of her as Raven. Her spontaneous warmth made it difficult for anyone to approach her with the awe normally reserved for superstars. Raven wrote on her side of the napkin when Brand offered his back. When she had finished, she noted that Debbie's eyes were wide and fixed on Brand. The pulse in her throat was jumping like a jackhammer. Raven knew what fantasies were dancing in the girl's mind.

"Here you are, Debbie." She touched her hand to bring the girl back to reality.

"Oh." Debbie took the napkin, looked at it blankly a moment, then smiled up at Brand. "Thanks." She looked at Raven, then ran a hand through her hair as if she had just realized what she had done. "Thanks a lot."

"You're welcome." Brand smiled but began to edge Raven toward the door.

It was too much to expect that the incident had gone unnoticed or that no one else would recognize them. For the next fifteen minutes they were wedged between the crowd and the door, signing autographs and dealing with a barrage of questions. Brand made certain they weren't separated from each other as he slowly maneuvered a path through the crowd.

They were jostled and shoved a bit but he judged the crowd to be fairly civilized. It was still early by L.A. standards, and there hadn't been too much drinking yet. Still he wanted her out. This type of situation was notoriously explosive; the mood could change abruptly. One overenthusiastic fan and it could all be different. And ugly. Raven signed and signed some more while an occasional hand reached out to touch her hair. Brand felt a small wave of relief as he finally drew her out into the fresh air. Only a few followed them out of the club, and they were able to make their way to Brand's car with just a smattering of extra autographs.

"Damn it. I'm sorry." He leaned across her to lock her door. "I should have known better than to have taken you there."

Raven took a long breath, combing her hair back from her face with her fingers as she turned to him. "Don't be silly; I wanted to go. Besides, the people were nice."

"They aren't always," he muttered as the car merged with Los Angeles traffic.

"No." She leaned back, letting her body relax. "But I've been pretty lucky. Things have only gotten out of hand once or twice. It's the hype, I suppose, and it's to be expected that fans sometimes forget we're flesh and blood."

"So they try to take little chunks of us home with them."

"That," Raven said dryly, "can be a problem. I remember seeing a film clip of a concert you gave, oh, seven or eight years ago." She leaned her elbow on the back of the seat now and cupped her cheek in her palm. "A London concert where the fans broke through the security. They seemed to swallow you whole. It must have been dreadful."

"They loved me enough to give me a couple of broken ribs."

"Oh, Brandon." She sat up straight now, shocked. "That's terrible. I never knew that."

He smiled and moved his shoulders. "We played it down. It did rather spoil my taste for live concerts for a while. I got over it." He turned, heading toward the hills. "Security's tighter these days."

"I don't know if I'd be able to face an audience after something like that."

"Where else would you get the adrenaline?" he countered. "We need it, don't we? That instant gratification of applause." He laughed and pulled her over beside him. "Why else do we do it, Raven? Why else are there countless others out there scrambling to make it? Why did you start up the road, Raven?"

"To escape," she answered before she had time to think. She sighed and relaxed against his shoulder when he didn't demand an explanation. "Music was always something I could hold on to. It was constant, dependable. I needed something that was wholly mine." She turned her head a bit to study his profile. "Why did you?"

"For most of the same reasons, I suppose. I had something to say, and I wanted people to remember I said it."

She laughed. "And you were so radical at the start of your career. Such pounding, demanding songs. You were music's bad boy for some time."

"I've mellowed," he told her.

"'Fire Hot' didn't sound mellow to me," she commented. "Wasn't that the lead cut on your last album?"

He grinned, glancing down at her briefly. "I have to keep my hand in."

"It was number one on the charts for ten consecutive weeks," she pointed out. "That isn't bad for mellow."

"That's right," he agreed as if he'd just remembered. "It knocked off a little number of yours, didn't it? It was kind of a sweet little arrangement, as I recall. Maybe a bit heavy on the strings, but…"

She gave him an enthusiastic punch on the arm.

"Raven," Brand complained mildly. "You shouldn't distract me when I'm driving."

"That sweet little arrangement went platinum."

"I said it was sweet," he reminded her. "And the lyrics weren't bad. A bit sentimental, maybe, but…"

"I like sentimental lyrics," she told him, giving him another jab on the arm. "Not every song has to be a blistering social commentary."

"Of course not," he agreed reasonably. "There's always room for cute little ditties."

"Cute little ditties," Raven repeated, hardly aware that they had fallen back into one of their oldest habits by debating each other's work. "Just because I don't go in for showboating or lyrical trickery," she began. But when he swung off to the side of the road, she narrowed her eyes at him. "What are you doing?"

"Pulling over before you punch me again." He grinned and flicked a finger down her nose. "Showboating?"

"Showboating," she repeated. "What else do you call that guitar and piano duel at the end of 'Fire Hot'?"

"A classy way to fade out a song," he returned, and though she agreed with him, Raven made a sound of derision.

"I don't need the gadgetry. My songs are…"

"Overly sentimental."

She lifted a haughty brow. "If you feel my music is overly sentimental and cute, how do you imagine we'll work together?"

"Perfectly," he told her. "We'll balance each other, Raven, just as we always did."

"We're going to have terrible fights," she predicted.

"Yes, I imagine we will."

"And," she added, failing to suppress a smile, "you won't always win."

"Good. Then the fights won't be boring." He pulled her to him, and when she resisted, he cradled her head on his shoulder again. "Look," he ordered, pointing out the window, "why is it cities always look better at night from above?"

Raven looked down on the glittering Los Angeles skyline. "I suppose it's the mystique. It makes you wonder what's going on and you can't see how fast it's moving. Up here it's quiet." She felt his lips brush her temple. "Brandon." She drew away, but he stopped her.

"Don't pull away from me, Raven." It was a low, murmured request that shot heat up her spine. "Don't pull away from me."

His head lowered slowly, and his lips nibbled at hers, hardly touching, but the hand at the back of her neck was firm. He kept her facing him while he changed the angle of the kiss. His lips were persuasive, seductive. He kissed the soft, dewy skin of her cheeks, the fragile, closed eyelids, the scented hair at her temple. She could feel herself floating toward him as she always had, losing herself to him.

Her lips parted so that when his returned, he found them inviting him to explore. The kiss deepened, but slowly, as if he savored the taste of her on his tongue. Her hand slid up his chest until she held him and their bodies touched. He murmured something, then pressed his mouth against the curve of her neck. Her scent rose and enveloped him.

She moaned when he took her breast, a sound of both

hunger and protest. His mouth came back to hers, plundering now as he responded to the need he felt flowing from her. She was unresisting, as open and warm as a shaft of sunlight. Her body was yearning toward him, melting irresistibly. She thought his hand burned through the thin fabric of her dress and set fire to her naked skin. It had been so long, she thought dizzily, so long since she had felt anything this intensely, needed anything this desperately. Her whole being tuned itself to him.

"Raven." His mouth was against her ear, her throat, the hollow of her cheek. "Oh, God, I want you." The kiss was urgent now, his hands no longer gentle. "So long," he said, echoing her earlier thought. "It's been so long. Come back with me. Let me take you back with me to the hotel. Stay with me tonight."

Passion flooded her senses. His tongue trailed over her warmed skin until he came again to her mouth. Then he took possession. The heat was building, strangling the breath in her throat, suffocating her. There was a fierce tug of war between fear and desire. She began to struggle.

"No." She took deep gulps of air. "Don't."

Brand took her by the shoulders and with one quick jerk had her face turned back up to his. "Why?" he demanded roughly. "You want me, I can feel it."

"No." She shook her head, and her hands trembled as she pushed at his chest. "I don't. I can't." Raven tried to deepen her breathing to steady it. "You're hurting me, Brandon. Please let me go."

Slowly he relaxed his fingers, then released her. "The same old story," he murmured. Turning away from her, he carefully drew out a cigarette and lit it. "You still give until I'm halfway mad, then pull away from me." He took a long, deep drag. "I should have been better prepared for it."

"You're not fair. I didn't start this; I never wanted…"

"You wanted," he tossed back furiously. "Damn it, Raven, you wanted. I've had enough women to know when I'm holding one who wants me."

She stiffened against the ache that was speeding through her. "You're better off with one of your many women, Brandon. I told you I wouldn't fall at your feet this time, and I meant it. If we can have a professional relationship, fine." She swallowed and straightened the hair his fingers had so recently caressed. "If you can't work with things on that level, then you'd best find another partner."

"I have the one I want." He tossed his cigarette through the open window. "We'll play it your way for a while, Raven. We're both professionals, and we both know what this musical's going to do for our careers." He started the engine. "I'll take you home."

5

Raven hated to be late for a party, but there was no help for it. Her schedule was drum tight. If it hadn't been important that she be there, to rub elbows with Lauren Chase and a few other principals from the cast and crew of *Fantasy,* she'd have bowed out. There were only two days left before the start of her tour.

The truth was, Raven had forgotten about the party. Rehearsals had run over, then she had found herself driving into Beverly Hills to window shop. She hadn't wanted to buy anything but had simply wanted to do something mindless. For weeks there had been nothing but demand after demand, and she could look forward only to more of the same in the weeks to come. She would steal a few hours. She didn't want to think about her mother and the clean white sanitarium or song lists and cues or her confusion over Brand as she browsed through the treasures at Neiman-Marcus and Gucci. She looked at everything and bought nothing.

Arriving home, she was met by a huge handwritten note from Julie tacked on her bedroom door.

Party at Steve Jarett's. I know—you forgot. IMPORTANT!
Get your glad rags together, babe, and go. Out with Lorenzo for dinner, we'll see you there. J.

Raven swore briefly, rebelled, then capitulated before she
stalked to the closet to choose an outfit. An hour later she was
cruising fast through the Hollywood Hills. It was important
that she be there.

Steve Jarett was directing *Fantasy*. He was, at the moment,
the silver screen's boy wonder, having just directed three major
successes in a row. Raven wanted *Fantasy* to be his fourth as
much as he did.

The party would be crowded, she mused, and looked wistfully at the open, star-studded sky. And noisy. Abruptly she
laughed at herself. Since when did a noisy, crowded party
become a trial by fire? There had been a time when she had
enjoyed them. And there was no denying that the people who
haunted these parties were fascinating and full of incredible
stories. Raven could still be intrigued. It was just that… She
sighed, allowing herself to admit the real reason she had dragged
her feet. Brandon would be there. He was bound to be.

Would he bring a date? she wondered. Why wouldn't he? She
answered herself shortly, downshifting as she took a curve. Unless
he decided to wait and take his pick from the women there.
Raven sighed again, seeing the blaze of lights that told her she
was approaching Jarett's house. It was ridiculous to allow herself
to get tied up in knots over something that had ended years before.

Her headlights caught the dull gleam of sturdy iron gates,
and she slowed. The guard took her name, checked his list,
then admitted her. She could hear the music before she was
halfway up the curving, palm-lined drive.

There was a white-jacketed teenager waiting to hand her out of the Lamborghini. He was probably a struggling actor or an aspiring screenwriter or cinematographer, Raven thought as she smiled at him.

"Hi, I'm late. Do you think I can slip in without anybody noticing?"

"I don't think so, Ms. Williams, not looking like that."

Raven lifted her brows, surprised that he had recognized her so quickly in the dim light. But even if he had missed the face and hair, she realized, he would never have mistaken the voice.

"That's a compliment, isn't it?" she asked.

"Yes, ma'am," he said so warmly that she laughed.

"Well, I'm going to do my best, anyway. I don't like entrances unless they're on stage." She studied the sprawling, white brick mansion. "There must be a side door."

"Around to the left." He pointed. "There's a set of glass doors that lead into the library. Go through there and turn left. You should be able to slip in without being noticed."

"Thanks." She went to take a bill out of her purse, discovered she had left it in the car and leaned in the window to retrieve it. After a moment's search, she found a twenty and handed it to him.

"Thank *you!* Raven," he enthused as she turned away. Then he called to her, "Ms. Williams?" Raven turned back with a half smile. "Would you sign it for me?"

She tossed back her hair. "The bill?"

"Yeah."

She laughed and shook her head. "A fat lot of good it would do you then. Here." She dug into her bag again and came up with a slip of paper. One side was scrawled on, a list of groceries Julie had given her a few weeks before, but the other side was blank. "What's your name?" she demanded.

"Sam, Sam Rheinhart."

"Here, Sam Rheinhart," she said. Dashing off a quick line on the paper, she gave him the autograph. He stared after her, the twenty in one hand and the grocery list in the other, as she rushed off.

Raven found the glass doors without trouble. Though they were closed, the sounds of the party came clearly through. There were groups of people out back listening to a very loud rock band and drifting around by the pool. She stayed in the shadows. She wore an ankle-length skirt and a dolman-sleeve pullover in a dark plum color with silver metallic threads running through which captured the moonlight. Entering through the library, she gave herself a moment to adjust to the darkness before groping her way to the door.

There was no one in the hall immediately outside. Pleased with herself, Raven stepped out and gravitated slowly toward the focus of noise.

"Why, Raven!" It was Carly Devers, a tiny blond fluff of an actress with a little-girl voice and a rapier sharp talent. Though they generally moved in different circles, Raven liked her. "I didn't know you were here."

"Hi, Carly." They exchanged obligatory brushes of the cheek. "Congratulations are in order, aren't they? I heard you were being signed as second lead in *Fantasy*."

"It's still in the working stage, but it looks like it. It's a gem of a part, and of course, working with Steve is *the* thing to do these days." As she spoke, she gave Raven a piercing look with her baby blue eyes. "You look fabulous," she said. Raven knew she meant it. "And of course, congratulations are in order for you as well, aren't they?"

"Yes, I'm excited about doing the score."

Carly tilted her head, and a smile spread over her face. "I was thinking more about Brand Carstairs than the score, darling." Raven's smile faded instantly. "Oops." Carly's smile only widened. "Still tender." There was no malice in her amusement. She linked her arm with Raven's. "I'd keep your little collaboration very tight this time around, Raven. I'm tempted to make a play for him myself, and I guarantee I'm not alone."

"What happened to Dirk Wagner?" Raven reminded herself to play it light as they drew closer to the laughter and murmurs of the party.

"Old news, darling, do try to keep up." Carly laughed, a tinkling bell of a sound that Raven could not help but respond to. "Still, I don't make it a habit to tread on someone else's territory."

"No signs posted, Carly," Raven said carelessly.

"Hmm." Carly tossed back a lock of silver-blond hair. A waiter passed by with a tray of glasses, and she neatly plucked off two. "I've heard he's a marvelous lover," she commented, her eyes bright and direct on Raven's.

Raven returned the look equably and accepted the offered champagne. "Have you? But then, I imagine that's old news, too."

"Touché," Carly murmured into her glass.

"Is Brandon here?" she asked, trying to prove to herself and her companion that the conversation meant nothing.

"Here and there," Carly said ambiguously. "I haven't decided whether he's been trying to avoid the flocks of females that crawl around him or if he's seeking them out. He doesn't give away much, does he?"

Raven uttered a noncommittal sound and shrugged. It was time, she decided, to change the subject. "Have you seen Steve? I suppose I should fight my way through and say hello."

It was a typical enough party, Raven decided. Clothes ranged from Rive Gauche to Salvation Army. There was a steady drum beat from the band by the pool underlying the talk and laughter. The doors to the terrace were open wide, letting out the clouds of smoke and allowing the warm night air to circulate freely. The expansive lawns were ablaze with colored lights. Raven was more interested in the people but gave the room itself a quick survey.

It was decorated stunningly in white—walls, furniture, rugs—with a few vivid green accents slashed here and there. Raven decided it was gorgeous and that she couldn't have lived in it in a million years. She'd never be able to put her feet up on the elegant, free-form glass coffee table. She went back to the people.

Her eyes sought out Julie with her handsome Italian millionaire. She spotted Wayne with one of his bone-thin models hanging on his arm. Raven decided that the rumors that he would design the costumes for *Fantasy* must be true. There were others Raven recognized: producers, two major stars whom she had watched countless times in darkened theaters, a choreographer she knew only by face and reputation, a screenwriter she had met before socially and several others whom she knew casually or not at all. She and Carly were both drawn into the vortex of the party.

There were dozens of greetings to exchange, along with hand-kissing and cheek-brushing, before Raven could begin to inch her way back toward the edges. She was always more comfortable with one or two people at a time than with a crowd, unless she was onstage. At a touch on her arm, she turned and found herself facing her host.

"Well, hello." Raven smiled, appreciating the chance for a tête-à-tête.

"Hi. I was afraid you weren't going to make it."

Raven realized she shouldn't have been surprised that he had noticed her absence in the crowds of people. Steve Jarett noticed everything. He was a small, slight man with a pale, intense face and dark beard who looked ten years younger than his thirty-seven years. He was considered a perfectionist, often a pain when shooting, but the maker of beautiful films. He had a reputation for patience—enough to cause him to shoot a scene over and over and over again until he got precisely what he wanted. Five years before, he had stunned the industry with a low-budget sleeper that had become the unchallenged hit of the year. His first film had received an Oscar and had opened all the doors that had previously been firmly shut in his face. Steve Jarett held the keys now and knew exactly which ones to use.

He held both of her hands and studied her face. It was he who had insisted on Brand Carstairs as the writer of the original score for *Fantasy* and he who had approved the choice of Raven Williams as collaborator. *Fantasy* was his first musical, and he wasn't going to make any mistakes.

"Lauren's here," he said at length. "Have you met her?"

"No, I'd like to."

"I'd like you to get a real feel for her. I've copies of all of her films and records. You might study them before you begin work on the score."

Raven's brow rose. "I don't think I've missed any of her movies, but I'll watch them again. She is the core of the story."

He beamed suddenly, unexpectedly. "Exactly. And you know Jack Ladd."

"Yes, we've worked together before. You couldn't have picked a better Joe."

"I'm making him work off ten pounds," Jarett said, plucking a canape from a tray. "He has some very unflattering things to say about me at the moment."

"But he's taking off the ten pounds," Raven observed.

Jarett grinned. "Ounce by ounce. We go to the same gym. I keep reminding him Joe's a struggling writer, not a fulfilled hedonist."

Raven gave a low, gurgling laugh and popped a bite of cheese into her mouth. "Overweight or not, you're assembling a remarkable team. I don't know how you managed to wrangle Larry Keaston into choreographing. He's been retired for five years."

"Bribes and perseverance," Jarett said easily, glancing over to where the trim, white-haired former dancer lounged in a pearl-colored armchair. "I'm talking him into doing a cameo." He grinned at Raven again. "He's pretending dignified reluctance, but he's dying to get in front of the cameras again."

"If you can even get him to do a time step on film, you'll have the biggest coup of the decade," Raven observed and shook her head. And he'd do it, she thought. He has the touch.

"He's a big fan of yours," Jarett remarked and watched Raven's eyes widen.

"Of mine? You're joking."

"I am not." He gave Raven a curious look. "He wants to meet you."

Raven stared at Jarett, then again at Larry Keaston. Such

things never ceased to amaze her. How many times, as a child, had she watched his movies on fuzzy black and white TV sets in cramped rooms while she had waited for her mother to come home? "You don't have to ask me twice," she told Jarett. She linked her arm in his.

Time passed quickly as Raven began enjoying herself. She talked at length with Larry Keaston and discovered her girlhood idol to be personable and witty. He spoke in a string of expletives delivered in his posh Boston accent. Though she spoke briefly with Jack Ladd, she had yet to meet Lauren Chase when she spotted Wayne drinking quietly in a corner.

"All alone?" she asked as she joined him.

"Observing the masses, my dear," he told her, sipping lightly from his whiskey and soda. "It's amazing how intelligent people will insist on clothing themselves in inappropriate costumes. Observe Lela Marring," he suggested, tilting his head toward a towering brunette in a narrow, pink minidress. "I have no idea why a woman would care to wear a place mat in public."

Raven suppressed a giggle. "She has very nice legs."

"Yes, all five feet of them." He swerved his line of vision. "Then, of course, there's Marshall Peters, who's trying to start a new trend. Chest hair and red satin."

Raven followed the direction of his gaze and this time did giggle. "Not everyone has your savoir-faire, Wayne."

"Of course not," he agreed readily and took out one of his imported cigarettes. "But surely, taste."

"I like the way you've dressed your latest protégée," Raven commented, nodding toward the thin model speaking to a current hot property in the television series game. The model was draped in cobwebby black and gold filigree lace. "I swear, Wayne, she can't be more than eighteen. What do you find to talk about?"

He gave Raven one of his long, sarcastic looks. "Are you being droll, darling?"

She laughed in spite of herself. "Not intentionally."

He gave her a pat on the cheek and lifted his glass again. "I notice Julie has her latest conquest with her, a Latin type with cheekbones."

"Shoes," Raven said vaguely, letting her eyes drift around the room. They rested in disbelief on a girl dressed in skin-tight leather pants and a spangled sweatshirt who wore heart-shaped glasses over heavily kohl-darkened eyes. Knowing Wayne would be horrified, she started to call his attention to her when she spotted Brand across the room.

His eyes were already on hers. Raven realized with a jolt that he had been watching her for some time. It had been at just such a party that they had first met, with noise and laughter and music all around them. Their eyes had found each other's then also.

It had been Raven's first Hollywood party, and she had been unashamedly overwhelmed. There had been people there whom she had known only as voices over the radio or faces on the screen. She had come alone then, too, but in that case it had been a mistake. She hadn't yet learned how to dodge and twist.

She remembered she had been cornered by an actor, though oddly she couldn't recall his name or his face. She hadn't had the experience to deal with him and was slowly being backed against the wall when her eyes had met Brand's. Raven remembered how he had been watching her then, too, rather lazily, a half smile on his mouth. He must have seen the desperation in her eyes, because his smile had widened before he had started to weave his way through the crowd toward her. With perfect aplomb, Brand had slid between Raven and the actor, then had draped his arm over her shoulders.

"Miss me?" he had asked, and he had kissed her lightly before she could respond. "There're some people outside who want to meet you." He had shot the actor an apologetic glance. "Excuse us."

Before another word could be exchanged, he had propelled Raven through the groups of people and out to a terrace. She could still remember the scent of orange blossoms that had drifted from an orchard nearby and the silver sprinkle of moonlight on the flagstone.

Of course Raven had recognized him and had been flustered. She had managed to regain her poise by the time they were alone in the shadows on the terrace. She had brushed a hand through her hair and smiled at him. "Thanks."

"You're welcome." It had been the first time he had studied her in his direct, quiet fashion. She could still remember the sensation of gentle intrusion. "You're not quite what I expected."

"No?" Raven hadn't known exactly how to take that.

"No." He'd smiled at her. "Would you like to go get some coffee?"

"Yes." The agreement had sprung from her lips before she had given it a moment's thought.

"Good. Let's go." Brand had held out his hand. After a brief hesitation, Raven had put hers into it. It had been as simple as that.

"Raven…Raven."

She was tossed back into the present by the sound of Wayne's voice and his hand on her arm.

"Yes…what?" Blandly Raven looked up at him.

"Your thoughts are written all over your face," he murmured. "Not a wise move in a room full of curious people." Taking a fresh glass of champagne from a tray, he handed it to her. "Drink up."

She was grateful for something to do with her hands and took the glass. "I was just thinking," she said inadequately, then made a sound of frustration at Wayne's dry look. "So," she tried another tactic, "it seems we'll be working on the same project."

"Old home week?" he said with a crooked grin.

She shot him a direct look. "We're professionals," she stated, aware that they both knew whom she was speaking of.

"And friends?" he asked, touching a finger to her cheek.

Raven inclined her head. "We might be; I'm a friendly sort of person."

"Hmm." Wayne glanced over her shoulder and watched Brand approach. "At least he knows how to dress," he murmured, approving of Brand's casual but perfectly cut slate-colored slacks and jacket. "But are you sure Cornwall's necessary? Couldn't you try Sausalito?"

Raven laughed. "Is there anything you don't know?"

"I certainly hope not. Hello, Brand, nice to see you again."

Raven turned, smiling easily. The jolt of the memory had passed. "Hello, Brandon."

"Raven." His eyes stayed on her face. "You haven't met Lauren Chase."

With an effort Raven shifted her eyes from his. "No." She smiled and looked at the woman at his side.

Lauren Chase was a slender wisp of a woman with a thick mane of dark, chestnut hair and sea-green eyes. There was something ethereal about her. Perhaps, Raven thought, it was that pale, almost translucent skin or the way she had of walking as though her feet barely touched the ground. She had a strong mouth that folded itself in at the corners and a long, slender neck that she adorned with gold chains. Raven knew she was well into her thirties and decided she looked it. This was a woman who needn't rely on dewy youth for her beauty.

She had been married twice. The first divorce had become an explosive affair that had received a great deal of ugly press. Her second marriage was now seven years old and had produced two children. Raven recalled there was little written about Lauren Chase's current personal life. Obviously, she had learned to guard her privacy.

"Brand tells me you're going to put the heart in the music." Lauren's voice was full and rich.

"That's quite a responsibility." Raven shot Brand a glance. "Generally Brand considers my lyrics on the sentimental side; often I consider him a cynic."

"Good." Lauren smiled. "Then we should have a score with some meat in it. Steve's given me final word on my own numbers."

Raven lifted a brow. She wasn't altogether certain if this had been a warning or a passing remark. "Then I suppose we should keep you up to date on our progress," she said agreeably.

"By mail and phone," Lauren said, slanting a glance at Brand, "since you're traipsing off halfway around the world to write."

"Artistic temperament," Brand said easily.

"No question, he has it," Raven assured her.

"You should know, I suppose." Lauren lifted a shoulder. Abruptly she fixed Raven with a sharp, straight look. "I want a lot out of this score. This is the one I've been waiting for." It was both a challenge and a demand.

Raven met the look with a slow nod. Lauren Chase was, she decided, the perfect Tessa. "You'll get it."

Lauren touched her upper lip with the tip of her tongue

and smiled again. "Yes, I do believe I will at that. Well," she said, turning to Wayne and linking her arm through his, "why don't you get me a drink and tell me about the fabulous costumes you're going to design for me?"

Raven watched them move away. "That," she murmured, toying with the stem of her glass, "is a woman who knows what she wants."

"And she wants an Oscar," Brand remarked. Raven's eyes came back to his. "You'll remember she's been nominated three times and edged out three times. She's determined it isn't going to happen again." He smiled then, fingering the dangling amethyst Raven wore at her ear. "Wouldn't you like to bag one yourself?"

"That's funny, I'd forgotten we could." She let the thought play in her mind. "It sounds good, but we'd better get the thing written before we dream up an acceptance speech."

"How're rehearsals going?"

"Good. Very good." She sipped absently at her champagne. "The band's tight. You leave for Vegas soon, don't you?"

"Yes. Did you come alone?"

She glanced back at him, confused for a moment. "Here? Why, yes. I was late because I'd forgotten about it altogether, but Julie left me a note. Did she introduce you to Lorenzo?"

"No, we haven't crossed paths tonight." As she had begun to search the crowd for Julie, Brand took her chin to bring her eyes back to his. "Will you let me take you home?"

Her expression shifted from startled to wary. "I have my car, Brandon."

"That isn't an answer."

Raven felt herself being drawn in and struggled. "It wouldn't be a good idea."

"Wouldn't it?" She sensed the sarcasm before he smiled, bent down and kissed her. It was a light touch—a tease, a promise or a challenge? "You could be right." He touched her earring again and set it swinging. "I'll see you in a few weeks," he said with a friendly grin, then turned and merged back into the crowd.

Raven stared after him, hardly realizing she had touched her lips with her tongue to seek his taste.

6

The theater was dark and quiet. The sound of Raven's footsteps echoed, amplified by the excellent acoustics. Very soon the quiet would be shattered by stagehands, grips, electricians, all the many backstage people who would put together the essential and hardly noticed details of the show. Voices would bounce, mingling with hammering and other sounds of wood and metal. The noise would have a hollow, empty tone, almost like her footsteps. But it was an important sound, an appealing sound, which Raven had always enjoyed.

But she enjoyed the quiet, too and often found herself roaming an empty theater long before she was needed for rehearsals, hours before the fans started to line up outside the main doors. The press would be there then, with their everlasting, eternal questions. And Raven wasn't feeling too chummy with the press at the moment. Already she'd seen a half dozen different stories about herself and Brandon—speculation about their pending collaboration on *Fantasy* and rehashes of their former relationship. Old pictures had been dredged up and reprinted. Old questions were being asked again. Each time it was like bumping the same bruise.

Twice a week she put through a call to the Fieldmore Clinic and held almost identical conversations with Karter. Twice a week he transferred her to her mother's room. Though she knew it was foolish, Raven began to believe all the promises again, all the tearful vows. She began to hope. Without the demands of the tour to keep her occupied and exhausted, she knew she would have been an emotional wreck. Not for the first time in her life, she blessed her luck and her voice.

Mounting the stage, Raven turned to face an imaginary audience. The rows of seats seemed to roll back like a sea. But she knew how to navigate it, had known from the first moment of her first concert. She was an innate performer, just as her voice was natural and untrained. The hesitation, the uncertainty she felt now, had to do with the woman, not the singer. The song had hovered in her mind, but she still paused and considered before bringing it into play. Memories, she felt, could be dangerous things. But she needed to prove something to herself, so she sang. Her voice lifted, drifting to the far corners of the theater; her only accompaniment was her imagination.

Through the clouds and the rain
You were there,
And the sun came through to find us.

Oversentimental? She hadn't thought so when the words had been written. Now Raven sang what she hadn't sung in years. Two minutes and forty-three seconds that bound her and Brand together. Whenever it had played on the radio, she had switched it off, and never, though the requests had been many, had she ever incorporated it in an album or in a concert. She sang it now as a kind of test, remembering the drifting, almost aching harmony of her own low tones combined with Brand's clean, cool voice. She needed to be able to face the memory of working with him if she was to face the reality of doing so. The tour had reached its halfway point. There were only two weeks remaining.

It didn't hurt the way she had been afraid it would; there was no sharp slap across the face. There was more of a warm ache, almost pleasant, somehow sexual. She remembered the last time she had been in Brand's arms in the quiet car in the hills above L.A.

"I've never heard you sing that."

Caught off-guard, Raven swung around to stage right, her hand flying in quick panic to her throat. "Oh, Marc!" On a laugh, she let out a long breath. "You scared the wits out of me. I didn't know anyone was here."

"I didn't want you to stop. I've only heard the cut you and Carstairs made of that." He came forward now out of the shadows, and she saw he had an acoustic guitar slung over his shoulder. It was typical; she rarely saw him without an instrument in his hands or close by. "I've always thought it was too bad you never used it again; it's one of your best. But I guess you didn't want to sing it with anyone else."

Raven looked at him with genuine surprise. Of course, that had been the essential reason, but she hadn't realized it herself until that moment. "No, I guess I didn't." She smiled at him. "I guess I still don't. Did you come here to practice?"

"I called your room. Julie said you'd probably be here." He walked to her, and since there were no chairs, he sat on the floor. Raven sat with him. She crossed her legs in the dun-colored trousers and let her hair fall over the soft shoulders of her topaz angora sweater. She was relaxed with him, ready to talk or jam like any musician.

Raven smiled at Marc as he went through a quick, complicated lick. "I'm glad you came by. Sometimes I have to get the feel of the theater before a performance. They all begin to run together at this part of a tour." Raven closed her eyes and tilted her head, shaking her hair back. "Where are we, Kansas City? God, I hate the thought of getting back on that airplane. Shuttle here, shuttle there. It always hits me like this at the halfway point. In a couple of days I'll have my second wind."

Marc let her ramble while he played quick, quiet runs on the guitar. He watched her hands as they lay still on her knees. They were very narrow, and although they were tanned golden brown, they remained fragile. There was a light tracing of blue vein just under the skin. The nails were not long but well-shaped and painted in some clear, hardening polish with a blush of pink. There were no rings. Because they were motionless, he knew she was relaxed. Whatever nerves he had sensed when he had first spoken to her were stilled now.

"It's been going well, I think," she continued. "The Glass House is a terrific warm-up act, and the band's tight, even though we lost Kelly. The new bass is good, don't you think?"

"Knows his stuff," Marc said briefly. Raven grinned and reached over to tug his beard.

"So do you," she said. "Let me try."

Agreeably Marc slipped the strap over his head, then handed Raven his guitar. She was a better-than-average player, although she took a great deal of ribbing from the musicians in her troupe whenever she attempted the guitar. Periodically she threatened them with a bogus plan to incorporate her semiskillful playing into the act.

Still she liked to make music with the six strings. It soothed her. There was something intimate about holding an instrument close, feeling its vibrations against your own body. After hitting the same wrong note twice, Raven sighed, then wrinkled her nose at Marc's grin.

"I'm out of practice," she claimed, handing him back his Gibson.

"Good excuse."

"It's probably out of tune."

He ran quickly up and down the scales. "Nope."

"You might be kind and lie." She changed position, putting her feet flat on the floor and lacing her hands over her knees. "It's a good thing you're a musician. You'd have made a lousy politician."

"Too much traveling," he said as his fingers began to move again. He liked the sound of her laughter as it echoed around the empty theater.

"Oh, you're right! How can anyone remain sane going from city to city day after day? And music's such a stable business, too."

"Sturdy as a crap table."

"You've a gift for analogy," she told him, watching the skill of his fingers on the strings. "I love to watch you play," she continued. "It's so effortless. When Brandon was first teaching me, I…" but the words trailed off. Marc glanced up at her face, but his fingers never faltered. "I—it was difficult," she went on, wondering what had made her bring up the matter, "because he was left-handed, and naturally his guitar was, too. He bought me one of my own, but watching him, I had to learn backwards." She laughed, pleased with the memory. Absently she lifted a hand to toy with the thick, dangling staff of her earring. "Maybe that's why I play the way I do. I'm always having to twist it around in my head before it can get to my fingers."

She lapsed into silence while Marc continued to play. It was soothing and somehow intimate with the two of them alone in the huge, empty theater. But his music didn't sound lonely as it echoed. She began to sing with it quietly, as though they were at home, seated on a rug with the walls close and comforting around them.

It was true that the tour had tired her and that the midway point had her feeling drained. But the interlude here was lifting her, though in a different way than the audience would lift her that night. This wasn't the quick, dizzying high that shot endurance back into her for the time she was on stage and in the lights. This was a steadying hand, like a good night's sleep or a home-cooked meal. She smiled at Marc when the song was over and said again, "I'm glad you came."

He looked at her, and for once his hands were silent on the strings. "How long have I been with you, Raven?"

She thought back to when Marc had first become a semi-regular part of her troupe. "Four—four and a half—years."

"Five this summer," he corrected. "It was in August, and you were rehearsing for your second tour. You had on baggy white pants and a T-shirt with a rainbow on it. You were barefoot. You had a lost look in your eyes. Carstairs had gone back to England about a month before."

Raven stared at him. She had never heard him make such a long speech. "Isn't it strange that you would remember what I was wearing? It doesn't sound very impressive."

"I remember because I fell in love with you on the spot."

"Oh, Marc." She searched for something to say and found nothing. Instead, she reached up and took his hand. She knew he meant exactly what he said.

"Once or twice I've come close to asking you to live with me."

Raven let out a quick breath. "Why didn't you?"

"Because it would have hurt you to have said no and it would have hurt me to hear it." He laid the guitar across his lap and leaning over it, kissed her.

"I didn't know," she murmured, pressing both of his hands to her cheeks. "I should have. I'm sorry."

"You've never gotten him out of your head, Raven. It's damn frustrating competing with a memory." Marc squeezed her hands a moment, then released them. "It's also safe. I knew you'd never make a commitment to me, so I could avoid making one to you." He shrugged his well-muscled shoulders. "I think it always scared me that you were the kind of woman who would make a man give everything because you asked for nothing."

Her brows drew together. "Am I?"

"You need someone who can stand up to you. I'd never have been able to. I'd never have been able to say no or shout at you or make crazy love. Life's nothing without things like that, and we'd have ended up hurting each other."

She tilted her head and studied him. "Why are you telling me all this now?"

"Because I realized when I watched you singing that I'll always love you but I'll never have you. And if I did, I'd lose something very special." He reached across to touch her hair. "A fantasy that warms you on cold nights and makes you feel young again when you're old. Sometimes might-have-beens can be very precious."

Raven didn't know whether to smile or to cry. "I haven't hurt you?"

"No," he said so simply she knew he spoke the truth. "You've made me feel good. Have I made you uncomfortable?"

"No." She smiled at him. "You've made me feel good."

He grinned, then rose and held out a hand to her. "Let's go get some coffee."

Brand changed into jeans in his dressing room. It was after two in the morning, but he was wide-awake, still riding on energy left over from his last show. He'd go out, he decided, and put some of it to use at the blackjack table. He could grab Eddie or one of the other guys from the band and cruise the casinos.

There'd be women. Brand knew there'd be a throng of them waiting for him when he left the privacy of his dressing room. He could take his pick. But he didn't want a woman. He wanted a drink and some cards and some action; anything to use up the adrenaline speeding through his system.

He reached for his shirt, and the mirror reflected his naked torso. It was tight and lean, teetering on being thin, but there were surprising cords of muscles in the arms and shoulders. He'd had to use them often when he'd been a boy on the London streets. He always wondered if it had been the piano lessons his mother had insisted on that had saved him from being another victim of the streets. Music had opened up something for him. He hadn't been able to get enough, learn enough. It had been like food, and he had been starving.

At fifteen Brand had started his own band. He was tough and cocky and talked his way into cheap little dives. There had been women even then; not just girls, but women attracted by his youthful sexuality and arrogant confidence. But they'd only been part of the adventure. He had never given up, though the living had been lean in the beer-soaked taverns. He had pulled his way up and made a local reputation for himself; both his music and his personality were strong.

It had taken time. He had been twenty when he had cut his first record, and it had gone nowhere. Brand had recognized that its failure had been due to a combination of poor quality recording, mismanagement and his own see-if-I-care attitude. He had taken a few steps back, found a savvy manager, worked hard on arrangements and talked himself into another recording session.

Two years later he had bought his family a house in the London suburbs, pushed his younger brother into a university and set off on his first American tour.

Now, at thirty, there were times he felt he'd never been off the merry-go-round. Half his life had been given over to his career and its demands. He was tired of wandering. Brand wanted something to focus his life, something to center it. He knew he couldn't give up music, but it wasn't enough by itself anymore. His family wasn't enough, and neither was the money or the applause.

He knew what he wanted. He had known five years before, but there were times he didn't feel as sure of himself as he had when he had been a fifteen-year-old punk talking his way past the back door of a third-rate nightclub. A capacity crowd had just paid thirty dollars a head to hear him, and he knew he could afford to take every cent he made on that two-week gig and throw it away on one roll of the dice. He had an urge to do it. He was restless, reckless, running on the same nerves he had felt the night he'd taken Raven home from their dinner date. He'd only seen her once after that—at Steve Jarett's house. Almost immediately afterward he had flown to Las Vegas to begin polishing his act.

It was catching up with him now—the tension, the anger, the needs. Not for the first time, Brand wondered whether his unreasonable need for her would end if he could have her once, just once. With quick, impatient movements, he thrust the tail of his shirt into the waist of his jeans. He knew better, but there were times he wished it could be. He left the dressing room looking for company.

For an hour Brand sat at the blackjack table. He lost a little, won a little, then lost it again. His mind wasn't on the cards. He had thought the noise, the bright lights, the rich smell of gambling was what he had wanted. There was a thin, intense woman beside him with a huge chunk of diamond on her finger and sapphires around her neck. She drank and lost at the same steady rhythm. Across the table was a young couple he pegged as honeymooners. The gold band on the girl's finger looked brilliantly new and untested. They were giddy with winning what Brand figured was about thirty dollars. There was something touching in their pleasure and in the soft, exchanged looks. All around them came the endless chinkity-chink of the slots.

Brand found himself as restless as he had been an hour before in his dressing room. A half-empty glass of bourbon sat at his elbow, but he left it as he rose. He didn't want the casino, and he felt an enormous surge of envy for the man who had his woman and thirty dollars worth of chips.

When he entered his suite, it was dark and silent, a sharp contrast to the world he had just left. Brand didn't bother hitting the switches as he made his way into the bedroom. Taking out a cigarette, he sat on the bed before lighting it. The flame made a sharp hiss and a brief flare. He sat with the silence, but the adrenaline still pumped. Finally he switched on the small bedside lamp and picked up the phone.

Raven was deep in sleep, but the ringing of the phone shot

panic through her before she was fully awake. Her heart pounded in her throat before the mists could clear. She'd grown up with calls coming in the middle of the night. She forgot where she was and fumbled for the phone with a sense of dread and anticipation.

"Yes…hello."

"Raven, I know I woke you. I'm sorry."

She tried to shake away the fog. "Brandon? Is something wrong? Are you all right?"

"Yes, I'm fine. Just unbelievably inconsiderate."

Relaxing, Raven sank back on the pillows and tried to orient herself. "You're in Vegas, aren't you?" The dim light told her it was nearing dawn. He was two hours behind her. Or was it three? She couldn't for the life of her remember what time zone she was in.

"Yes, I'm in Vegas through next week."

"How's the show going?"

It was typical of her, he mused, not to demand to know why the hell he had called her in the middle of the night. She would simply accept that he needed to talk. He drew on the cigarette and wished he could touch her. "Better than my luck at the tables."

She laughed, comfortably sleepy. The connection was clean and sharp; he didn't sound hundreds of miles away. "Is it still blackjack?"

"I'm consistent," he murmured. "How's Kansas?"

"Where?" He laughed, pleasing her. "The audience was fantastic," she continued, letting her mind wander back to the show. "Has been straight along. That's the only thing that keeps you going on a tour like this. Will you be there in time for the show in New York? I'd love you to hear the warm-up act."

"I'll be there." He lay back on the bed as some of the superfluous energy started to drain. "Cornwall is sounding more and more appealing."

"You sound tired."

"I wasn't; I am now. Raven…"

She waited, but he didn't speak. "Yes?"

"I missed you. I needed to hear your voice. Tell me what you're looking at," he demanded, "what you see right now."

"It's dawn," she told him. "Or nearly. I can't see any buildings, just the sky. It's more mauve than gray and the light's very soft and thin." She smiled; it had been a long time since she had seen a day begin. "It's really lovely, Brandon. I'd forgotten."

"Will you be able to sleep again?" He had closed his eyes, the fatigue was taking over.

"Yes, but I'd rather go for a walk, though I don't think Julie would appreciate it if I asked her to come along."

Brand pried off his shoes, using the toe of one foot, then the other. "Go back to sleep, and we'll walk on the cliffs one morning in Cornwall. I shouldn't have woken you."

"No, I'm glad you did." She could hear the change; the voice that had been sharp and alert was now heavy. "Get some rest, Brandon. I'll look for you in New York."

"All right. Good night, Raven."

He was asleep almost before he hung up. Fifteen hundred miles away, Raven laid her cheek on the pillow and watched the morning come.

7

Raven tried to be still while her hair was being twisted and knotted and groomed. Her dressing room was banked with flowers; they had been arriving steadily for more than two hours. And it was crowded with people. A tiny little man with sharp, black eyes touched up her blusher. Behind her, occasionally muttering in French, was the nimble-fingered woman who did her hair. Wayne was there, having business of his own here in New York. He'd told Raven that he'd come to see his designs in action and was even now in deep discussion with her dresser. Julie opened the door to another flower delivery.

"Have I packed everything? You know, I should have told Brandon to give me an extra day in town for shopping. There're probably a dozen things I need." Raven turned in her seat and heard the swift French oath as her partially knotted hair flew from the woman's fingers. "Sorry, Marie. Julie, did I pack a coat? I might need one." Slipping the card from the latest arrangement of flowers, she found it was from a successful television producer with whom she'd worked on her last TV special. "They're from Max.... There's a party tonight. Why don't you go?" She handed the card to Julie and allowed her lip liner to be straightened by the finicky makeup artist.

"Yes, you packed a coat, your suede, which you could need this early in the spring. And several sweaters," Julie said distractedly, checking her list. "And maybe I will."

"I can't believe this is it, the last show. It's been a good tour, hasn't it, Julie?" Raven turned her head and winced at the sharp tug on her hair.

"I can't remember you ever getting a better response or deserving one more...."

"And we're all glad it's over," Raven finished for her.

"I'm going to sleep for a week." Julie found space for the flowers, then continued to check off things in her notebook. "Not everyone has your constant flow of energy."

"I love playing New York," she said, tucking up her legs to the despair of her hairdresser.

"You must hold still!"

"Marie, if I hold still much longer, I'm going to explode." Raven smiled at the makeup artist as he fussed around her face. "You always know just what to do. It looks perfect; I feel beautiful."

Recognizing the signal, Julie began nudging people from the room. Eventually they went, and soon only Julie and Wayne were left. The room quieted considerably; now the walls hummed gently with the vibrations of the warm-up act. Raven let out a deep sigh.

"I'll be so glad to have my face and body and hair back," she said and sprawled in the chair. "You should have seen what he made me put all over my face this morning."

"What was it?" Wayne asked absently as he smoothed the hem of one of her costumes.

"Green," she told him and shuddered.

He laughed and turned to Julie. "What are you going to do when this one takes off to the moors?"

"Cruise the Greek Islands and recuperate." She pushed absently at the small of her back. "I've already booked passage on the ninth. These tours are brutal."

"Listen to her." Raven sniffed and peered at herself critically in the glass. "She's the one who's held the whip and chair for four weeks. He certainly makes me look exotic, doesn't he?" She wrinkled her nose and spoiled the effect.

"Into costume," Julie commanded.

"See? Orders, orders." Obediently Raven rose.

"Here." Wayne lifted the red and silver dress from the hanger. "Since I nudged your dresser along, I'll be your minion."

"Oh, good, thanks." She stepped out of her robe and into the dress. "You know, Wayne," she continued as he zipped her up, "you were right about the black number. It gets a tremendous response. I never know if they're applauding me or the costume after that set."

"Have I ever let you down?" he demanded as he tucked a pleat.

"No." She turned her head to smile at him over her shoulder. "Never. Will you miss me?"

"Tragically." He kissed her ear.

There was a brief, brisk knock at the door. "Ten minutes, Ms. Williams."

She took a long breath. "Are you going to go out front?"

"I'll stay back with Julie." He glanced over at her, lifting a brow in question.

"Yes, thanks. Here, Raven, don't forget these wonderfully

gaudy earrings." She watched Raven fasten one. "Really, Wayne, they're enough to make me shudder, but they're fabulous with that dress."

"Naturally."

She laughed, shaking her head. "The man's ego," she said to Raven, "never ceases to amaze me."

"As long as it doesn't outdistance the talent," he put in suavely.

"New York audiences are tough." Raven spoke quickly, her voice jumping suddenly with nerves and excitement. "They scare me to death."

"I thought you said you loved playing New York." Wayne took out a cigarette and offered one to Julie.

"I do, especially at the end of a tour. It keeps you sharp. They're really going to know if I'm not giving them everything. How do I look?"

"The dress is sensational," Wayne decided. "You'll do."

"Some help you are."

"Let's go," Julie urged. "You'll miss your cue."

"I never miss my cue." Raven fussed with the second earring, stalling. He'd said he'd be here, she told herself. *Why isn't he?* He could have gotten the time mixed up, or he could be caught in traffic. Or he could simply have forgotten that he'd promised to be here for the show.

The quick knock came again. "Five minutes, Ms. Williams."

"Raven." Julie's voice was a warning.

"Yes, yes, all right." She turned and gave them both a flippant smile. "Tell me I'm wonderful when it's over, even if I wasn't. I want to end the tour feeling marvelous."

Then she was dashing for the door and hurrying down the hall where the sounds of the warm-up band were no longer gentle; now they shook the walls.

"Ms. Williams, Ms. Williams! Raven!"

She turned, breaking the concentration she'd been building and looked at the harried stage manager. He thrust a white rose into her hand.

"Just came back for you."

Raven took the bud and lifted it, wanting to fill herself with the scent. She needed no note or message to tell her it was from Brand. For a moment she simply dreamed over it.

"Raven." The warm-up act had finished; the transition to her own band would take place on the darkened stage quickly. "You're going to miss your cue."

"No, I'm not." She gave the worried stage manager a kiss, forgetful of her carefully applied lipstick. Twirling the rose between her fingers, she took it with her. They were introducing her as she reached the wings.

Big build-up; don't let the audience cool down. They were already cheering for her. *Thirty seconds; take a breath.* Her band hit her introduction. Music crashed through the cheers. *One, two, three!*

She ran out, diving into a wave of applause.

The first set was hot and fast, staged to keep the audience up and wanting more. She seemed to be a ball of flame with hundreds of colored lights flashing around her. Raven knew how to play to them, play with them, and she pumped all her energy into a routine she had done virtually every night for four weeks. Enthusiasm and verve kept it fresh. It was hot under the lights, but she didn't notice. She was wrapping herself in the audience, in the music. The costume sizzled and sparked. Her voice smoked.

It was a demanding forty minutes, and when she rushed offstage during an instrumental break, she had less than three minutes in which to change costumes. Now she was in white, a brief, shimmering top covered with bugle beads matched with thin harem pants. The pace would slow a bit, giving the audience time to catch their breath. The balance was in ballads, the slow trembling ones she did best. The lighting was muted, soft and moody.

It was during a break between songs, when she traditionally talked to the audience, that someone in the audience spotted Brand in their midst. Soon more people knew, and while Raven went on unaware of the disturbance, the crowd soon became vocal. Shielding her eyes, she could just make out the center of the commotion. Then she saw him. It seemed they wanted him up on stage.

Raven was a good judge of moods and knew the value of showmanship. If she didn't invite Brand on stage, she'd lose the crowd. They had already taken the choice out of her hands.

"Brandon." Raven spoke softly into the mike, but her voice carried. Though she couldn't see his eyes with the spotlight in her own, she knew he was looking at her. "If you come up and sing," she told him, lightly, "we might get you a refund on your ticket." She knew he'd grin at that. There was an excited rush of applause and cheers as he rose and came to the stage.

He was all in black: trim, well-cut slacks and a casual polo sweater. The contrast was striking as he stood beside her. It might have been planned. Smiling at her, he spoke softly, out of the range of the microphone. "I'm sorry, Raven, I should have gone backstage. I wanted to watch you from out front."

She tilted her head. It was, she discovered, more wonderful to see him than she had imagined. "You're the one being put to work. What would you like to do?"

Before he could answer, the demands sprang from the crowd. Once the idea formed, it was shouted over and over with growing enthusiasm. Raven's smile faded. "Clouds and Rain."

Brand took her wrist and lifted the rose she held. "You remember the words, don't you?"

It was a challenge. A stagehand rushed out with a hand mike for Brand.

"My band doesn't know it," she began.

"I know it." Marc shifted his guitar and watched them. The crowd was still shouting when he gave the opening chords. "We'll follow you."

Brand kept his hand on Raven's wrist and lifted his own mike.

Raven knew how it needed to be sung: face to face, eye to eye. It was a caress of a song, meant for lovers. The audience was silent now. Their harmony was close, intricate. Raven had once thought it must be like making love. Their voices flowed into each other. And she forgot the audience, forgot the stage and for a moment forgot the five years.

There was more intimacy in singing with him than she had ever allowed in any other aspect of their relationship. Here she could not resist him. When he sang to her, it was as if he told her there wasn't anyone else, had never been anyone else. It was more moving than a kiss, more sexual than a touch.

When they finished, their voices hung a moment, locked together. Brand saw her lips tremble before he brought her close and took them.

They might have been on an island rather than on stage, spotlighted for thousands. She didn't hear the tumultuous applause, the cheers, the shouting of their names. Her arms went around him, one hand holding the mike, the other the rose. Cameras flashed like fireworks, but she was trapped in a velvet darkness. She lost all sense of time; her lips might have moved on his for hours or days or only seconds. But when he drew her away, she felt a keener sense of loss than any she had ever known before. Brand saw the confusion in her eyes, the dazed desire, and smiled.

"You're better than you ever were, Raven." He kissed her hand. "Too bad about those sentimental numbers you keep sticking into the act."

Her brows rose. "Try to boost your flagging career by letting you sing with me, and you insult me." Her balance was returning as they took a couple of elaborate bows, hands linked.

"Let's see if you can carry the rest on your own, love. I've warmed them back up for you." He kissed her again, but lightly now, on the cheek, before he waved to the audience and strolled offstage left.

Raven grinned at his back, then turned to her audience. "Too bad he never made it, isn't it?"

Raven should have been wrung dry after the two hours were over. But she wasn't. She'd given them three encores, and though they clamored for more, Brand caught her hand as she hesitated in the wings.

"They'll keep you out there all night, Raven." He could feel the speed of her pulse under his fingers. Because he knew how draining two hours onstage could be, he urged her back down the hall toward her dressing room.

There were crowds of people jammed in together in the hallway, congratulating her, touching her. Now and then a reporter managed to elbow through to shoot out a question. She answered, and Brandon tossed off remarks with quick charm while steering her determinedly toward her dressing room. Once inside, he locked the door.

"I think they liked me," she said gravely, then laughed and spun away from him. "I feel so good!" Her eyes lit on the bucket of ice that cradled a bottle. "Champagne?"

"I thought you'd need to console yourself after a flop like that." Brand moved over and drew out the bottle. "You'll have to open the door soon and see people. Do try to put on a cheerful front, love."

"I'll do my best." The cork popped, and the white froth fizzed a bit over the mouth of the bottle.

Brand poured two glasses to the rim and handed her one. "I meant it, Raven." He touched his glass to hers. "You were never better."

Raven smiled, bringing the glass to her lips. Again, he felt the painful thrust of desire. Carefully Brand took the glass from her, then set both it and his own down again. "There's something I didn't finish out there tonight."

She was unprepared. Even though he drew her close slowly and took his time bringing his mouth to hers, Raven wasn't ready. It was a long, deep, kiss that mingled with the champagne. His mouth was warm on hers, seeking. His hands ran over her hips, snugly encased in the thin black jumpsuit, but she could sense he was under very tight control.

His tongue made a thorough, lengthy journey through the moist recesses of her mouth, and she responded in kind. But he wanted her to do more than give; he wanted her to want more. And she did, feeling the pull of need, the flash of passion. She could feel the texture of his long, clever fingers through the sheer material of her costume, then flesh to flesh as he brought them up to caress the back of her neck.

Her head was swimming with a myriad of sensations: excitement and power still clinging from her performance; the heady, heavy scent of mixed flowers which crowded the air; the firm press of his body against her; and desire, more complex, more insistent than she had been prepared for.

"Brandon," she murmured against his lips. She wanted him, wanted him desperately, and was afraid.

Brand drew her away, then carefully studied her face. Her eyes were like thin glass over her emotions. "You're beautiful, Raven, one of the most beautiful women I know."

She was unsteady and tried to find her balance without clinging to him. She stepped back, resting her hand on the table that held their glasses. "One of the most?" she challenged, lifting her champagne.

"I know a lot of women." He grinned as he lifted his own glass. "Why don't you take that stuff off your face so I can see you?"

"Do you know how long I had to sit still while he troweled this stuff on?" Moving to the dressing table, she scooped up a generous glob of cold cream. Her blood was beginning to settle. "It's supposed to make me glamorous and alluring." She slathered it on.

"You make me nervous when you're glamorous, and you'd be alluring in a paper sack."

She lifted her eyes to his in the mirror. His expression was surprisingly serious. "I think that was a compliment." She smeared the white cream generously over her face and grinned. "Am I alluring now?"

Brand grinned back, then slowly let his eyes roam down her back to focus on her snugly clad bottom. "Raven, don't fish. The answer is obvious."

She began to tissue off the cream and with it the stage

makeup. "Brandon. It was good to sing with you again." After removing the last of the cream from her face, Raven toyed with the stem of her champagne glass. "I always felt very special when I sang with you. I still do." He watched her chew for a moment on her bottom lip as if she was unsure about what she should say. "I imagine they'll play up that duet in the papers. They'll probably make something else out of it, especially—especially with the way we ended it."

"I like the way we ended it." Brand came over and laid his hands on her shoulders. "It should always be ended that way." He kissed the back of her neck while his eyes smiled into hers in the glass. "Are you worried about the press, Raven?"

"No, of course not. But, Brandon…"

"Do you know," he interrupted, brushing the hair away from her neck with the back of his hand, "no one else calls me that but my mother. Strange." He bent, nuzzling his lips into the sensitive curve of her neck. "You affect me in an entirely different way."

"Brandon…"

"When I was a boy," he continued, moving his lips up to her ear, "and she called me Brandon, I knew that was it. Whatever crime I'd committed had been found out. Justice was about to strike."

"I imagine you committed quite a few crimes." She forced herself to speak lightly. When she would have moved away, he turned her around to face him.

"Too many to count." He leaned to her, but instead of the kiss she expected and prepared for, he caught her bottom lip between his teeth. She clutched at his shirt as she struggled for breath and balance. Their eyes were open and on each other's, but his face dimmed, then faded, as passion clouded her vision.

Brand released her, then gave her a quick kiss on the nose. Raven ran a hand through her hair, trying to steady herself. He was tossing her back and forth too swiftly, too easily.

"Do you want to change before we let anyone in?" he asked. When she could focus again, Raven saw he was drinking champagne and watching her. There was an odd look on his face, as if, she thought, he were a boxer checking for weaknesses, looking for openings.

"I—yes." Raven brought herself back. "Yes, I think I would, but…" She glanced around the dressing room. "I don't know what I did with my clothes."

He laughed, and the look was gone from his face. Relieved, Raven laughed with him. They began to search through the flowers and sparkling costumes for her jeans and tennis shoes.

8

It was late when they arrived at the airport. Raven was still riding on post-performance energy and chattered about everything that came into her head. She looked up at a half-moon as she and Brand transferred from limo to plane. The private jet wasn't what she had been expecting, and studying the comfortably lush interior of the main cabin helped to allay the fatigue of yet one more flight.

It was carpeted with a thick, pewter-colored shag and contained deep, leather chairs and a wide, plush sofa. There was a padded bar at one end and a doorway at the other which she discovered led into a tidy galley. "You didn't have this before," she commented as she poked her head into another room and found the bath, complete with tub.

"I bought it about three years ago." Brand sprawled on the sofa and watched her as she explored. She looked different than she had a short time before. Her face was naked now, and he found he preferred it that way. Makeup seemed to needlessly gloss over her natural beauty. She wore faded jeans and sneakers, which she immediately pried off her feet. An oversize yellow sweater left her shapeless. It made him want to run his hands under it and find her. "Do you still hate to fly?"

Raven gave him a rueful grin. "Yes. You'd think after all this time I'd have gotten over it, but…" She continued to roam the cabin, not yet able to settle. If she had to, Raven felt she could give the entire performance again. She had enough energy.

"Strap in," Brand suggested, smiling at the quick, nervous gestures. "We'll get started, then you won't even know you're in the air."

"You don't know how many times I've heard that one." Still she did as he said and waited calmly enough while he told the pilot they were ready. In a few minutes they were airborne, and she was able to unstrap and roam again.

"I know the feeling," Brand commented, watching her. She turned in silent question. "It's as though you still have one last burst of energy to get rid of. It's the way I felt that night in Vegas when I called and woke you up."

She caught back her hair with both hands. "I feel I should jog for a few miles. It might settle me down."

"How about some coffee?"

"Yes." She wandered over to a porthole and pressed her nose against it. It was black as pitch outside the glass. "Yes, coffee would be nice, then you can tell me what marvelous ideas you have forming for the score. You've probably got dozens of them."

"A few." She heard the clatter of cups. "I imagine you've some of your own."

"A few," she said, and he chuckled. Turning away from the dark window, she saw him leaning against the opening between the galley and the main cabin. "How soon do you think we'll start to fight?"

"Soon enough. Let's wait at least until we're settled into the house. Is Julie going back to L.A., or have you tied up all your loose ends there?"

A shadow visited her face. Raven thought of the one brief visit she had paid to her mother since the start of the tour. They had had a day's layover in Chicago, and she had used the spare time to make the impossible flight to the coast and back. There had been the inevitable interview with Karter and a brief, emotional visit with her mother. Raven had been relieved to see that the cast had gone from her mother's skin and that there was more flesh to her face. There had been apologies and promises and tears, just as there always were, Raven thought wearily. And as she always did, she had begun to believe them again.

"I never seem to completely tie up the loose ends," she murmured.

"Will you tell me what's wrong?"

She shook her head. She couldn't bear to dwell on unhappiness now. "No, nothing, nothing really." The kettle sang out, and she smiled. "Your cue," she told him.

He studied her for a moment while the kettle spit peevishly behind him. Then, turning, he went back into the galley to fix the coffee. "Black?" he asked, and she gave an absent assent.

Sitting on the sofa, Raven let her head fall back while the energy began to subside. It was almost as if she could feel it draining. Brand recognized the signs as soon as he came back into the room. He set down her mug of coffee, then sipped thoughtfully from his own as he watched her. Sensing him, Raven slowly opened her eyes. There was silence for a moment; her body and her mind were growing lethargic.

"What are you doing?" she murmured.

"Remembering."

Her lids shuttered down, concealing her eyes and their expression. "Don't."

He drank again, letting his eyes continue their slow, measured journey over her. "It's a bit much to ask me not to remember, Raven, isn't it?" It was a question that expected no answer, and she gave it none. But her lids fluttered up again.

He didn't have her full trust, nor did he believe he had ever had it. That was the root of their problems. He studied her while he stood and drank his coffee. There was high, natural color in her cheeks, and her eyes were dark and sleepy. She sat, as was her habit, with her legs crossed under her and her hands on her knees. In contrast to the relaxed position, her fingers moved restlessly.

"I still want you. You know that, don't you?"

Again Raven left his question unanswered, but he saw the pulse in her throat begin to thump. When she spoke, her voice was calm. "We're going to work together, Brandon. It's best not to complicate things."

He laughed, not in mockery but in genuine amusement. She watched his eyes lose their brooding intensity and light. "By all means, let's keep things simple." After draining his coffee, he walked over and sat beside her. In a smooth, practiced move, he drew her against his side. "Relax," he told her, annoyed when she resisted. "Give me some credit. I know how tired you are. When are you going to trust me, Raven?"

She tilted her head until she could see him. Her look was long and eloquent before she settled into the crook of his shoulder and let out a long sigh. Like a child, she fell asleep quickly, and like that of a child, the sleep was deep. For a long moment he stayed as he was, Raven curled against his side. Then he laid her down on the sofa, watching as her hair drifted about her.

Rising, Brand switched off the lights. In the dark he settled into one of the deep cabin chairs and lit a cigarette. Time passed as he sat gazing out at a sprinkle of stars and listening to Raven's soft, steady breathing. Unable to resist, he rose, and moving to her, lay down beside her. She stirred when he brushed the hair from her cheek, but only to snuggle closer to him. Over the raw yearning came a curiously sweet satisfaction. He wrapped his arm around her, felt her sigh, then slept.

It was Brand who awoke first. As was his habit, his mind and body came together quickly. He lay still and allowed his eyes to grow accustomed to the darkness. Beside him, curled against his chest, Raven slept on.

He could make out the curve of her face, the pixie sharp features, the rain straight fall of hair. Her leg was bent at the knee and had slipped between his. She was soft and warm and tempting. Brand knew he had experience enough to arouse her into submission before she was fully awake. She would be drowsy and disoriented.

The hazy gray of early dawn came upon them as he watched her. He could make out her lashes now, a long sweep of black that seemed to weigh her lids down. He wanted her, but not that way. Not the first time. Asleep, she sighed and moved against him. Desire rippled along his skin. Carefully Brand shifted away from her and rose.

In the kitchen he began to make coffee. A glance at his watch and a little arithmetic told him they'd be landing soon. He thought rather enthusiastically about breakfast. The drive from the airport to his house would take some time. He remembered an inn along the way where they could get a good meal and coffee better than the instant he was making.

Hearing Raven stir, he came to the doorway and watched her wake up. She moaned, rolled over and unsuccessfully tried to bury her face. Her hand reached out for a pillow that wasn't there, then slowly, on a disgusted sigh, she opened her eyes. Brand watched the stages as her eyes roamed the room. First came disinterest, then confusion, then sleepy understanding.

"Good morning," he ventured, and she shifted her eyes to him without moving her head. He was grinning at her, and his greeting was undeniably cheerful. She had a wary respect for cheerful risers.

"Coffee," she managed and shut her eyes again.

"In a minute." The kettle was beginning to hiss behind him. "How'd you sleep?"

Dragging her hands through her hair, she made a courageous attempt to sit up. The light was still gray but now brighter, and she pressed her fingers against her eyes for a moment. "I don't know yet," she mumbled from behind her hands. "Ask me later."

The whistle blew, and as Brand disappeared back into the galley, Raven brought her knees up to her chest and buried her face against them. She could hear him talking to her, making bright, meaningless conversation, but her mind wasn't yet receptive. She made no attempt to listen or to answer.

"Here, love." As Raven cautiously raised her head, Brand held out a steaming mug. "Have a bit, then you'll feel better." She accepted with murmured thanks. He sat down beside her. "I've a brother who wakes up ready to bite someone's—anyone's—head off. It's metabolism, I suppose."

Raven made a noncommittal sound and began to take tentative sips. It was hot and strong. For some moments there was silence as he drank his own cream-cooled coffee and watched her. When her cup was half empty, she looked over and managed a rueful smile.

"I'm sorry, Brandon. I'm simply not at my best in the morning. Especially early in the morning." She tilted her head so that she could see his watch, made a brave stab at mathematics, then gave up. "I don't suppose it matters what time it actually is," she decided, going back to the coffee. "It'll take me days to adjust to the change, anyway."

"A good meal will set you up," he told her, lazily sipping at his own coffee. "I read somewhere where drinking yeast and jogging cures jet lag, but I'll take my chances with breakfast."

"Yeast?" Raven grimaced into her mug, then drained it. "I think sleep's a better cure, piles of it." The mists were clearing, and she shook back her hair. "I guess we'll be landing soon, won't we?"

"Less than an hour, I'd say."

"Good. The less time I spend awake on a plane, the less time I have to think about being on one. I slept like a rock." With another sigh, Raven stretched her back, letting her shoulders lift and fall with the movement. "I made poor company." Her system was starting to hum again, though on slow speed.

"You were tired." Over the rim of his cup he watched the subtle movements of her body beneath the oversize sweater.

"I turned off like a tap," she admitted. "It happens that way sometimes after a concert." She lifted one shoulder in a quick shrug. "But I suppose we'll both be better today for the rest. Where did you sleep?"

"With you."

Raven closed her mouth on a yawn, swallowed and stared at him. "What?"

"I said I slept with you, here on the couch." Brand made a general gesture with his hand. "You like to snuggle."

She could see he was enjoying her dismayed shock. His eyes were deep blue with amusement as he lifted his cup again. "You had no right…" Raven began.

"I always fancied being the first man you slept with," he told her before draining his cup. "Want some more coffee?"

Raven's face flooded with color; her eyes turned dark and opaque. She sprang up, but Brand managed to pluck the cup from her hand before she could hurl it across the room. For a moment she stood, breathing hard, watching him while he gave her his calm, measuring stare.

"Don't flatter yourself," she tossed out. "You don't know how many men I've slept with."

Very precisely, he set down both coffee cups, then looked back up at her. "You're as innocent as the day you were born, Raven. You've barely been touched by a man, much less been made love to."

Her temper flared like a rocket. "You don't know anything about who I've been with in the last five years, Brandon." She struggled to keep from shouting, to keep her voice as calm and controlled as his. "It's none of your business how many men I've slept with."

He lifted a brow, watching her thoughtfully. "Innocence isn't something to be ashamed of, Raven."

"I'm not…" She stopped, balling her fists. "You had no right to—" She swallowed and shook her head as fury and embarrassment raced through her. "—While I was asleep," she finished.

"Do what while you were asleep?" Brandon demanded, lazing back on the sofa. "Ravish you?" His humor shimmered over the old-fashioned word and made her feel ridiculous. "I don't think you'd have slept through it, Raven."

Her voice shook with emotion. "Don't laugh at me, Brandon."

"Then don't be such a fool." He reached over to the table beside him for a cigarette, then tapped the end of it against the surface without lighting it. His eyes were fixed on hers and no longer amused. "I could have had you if I'd wanted to, make no mistake about it."

"You have colossal nerve, Brandon. Please remember that you're not privy to my sex life and that you wouldn't have had me because I don't want you. I choose my own lovers."

She hadn't realized he could move so fast. The indolent slouch on the sofa was gone in a flash. He reached up, seizing her wrist, and in one swift move had yanked her down on her back, trapping her body with his. Her gasp of surprise was swallowed as his weight pressed down on her.

Never, in all the time they had spent together past and present, had Raven seen him so angry. An iron taste of fear rose in her throat. She could only shake her head, too terrified to struggle, too stunned to move. She had never suspected he possessed the capacity for violence she now read clearly on his face. This was far different from the cold rage she had seen before and which she knew how to deal with. His fingers bit into her wrist while his other hand came to circle her throat.

"How far do you think I'll push?" he demanded. His voice was harsh and deep with the hint of Ireland more pronounced. Her breathing was short and shallow with fear. Lying completely still, she made no answer. "Don't throw your imaginary string of lovers in my face, or, by God, you'll have a real one quickly enough whether you want me or not." His fingers tightened slightly around her throat. "When the time comes, I won't need to get you drunk on champagne or on exhaustion to have you lie with me. I could have you now, this minute, and after five minutes of struggle you'd be more than willing." His voice lowered, trembling along her skin. "I know how to play you, Raven, and don't you forget it."

His face was very close to hers. Their breathing mixed, both swift and strained, the only sound coming from the hum of the plane's engines. The fear in her eyes leaped out, finally penetrating his fury. Swearing, Brand pushed himself from her and rose. Her eyes stayed on his as she waited for what he would do next. He stared at her, then turned sharply away, moving over to a porthole.

Raven lay where she was, not realizing she was massaging the wrist that throbbed from his fingers. She watched him drag a hand through his hair.

"I slept with you last night because I wanted to be close to you." He took another long, cleansing breath. "It was nothing more than that. I never touched you. It was an innocent and rather sweet way to spend the night." He curled his fingers into a fist, remembering the frantic flutter of her pulse under his hand when he had circled it around her throat. It gave him no pleasure to know he had frightened her. "It never occurred to me that it would offend you like this. I apologize."

Raven covered her eyes with her hand as the tears began. She swallowed sobs, not wanting to give way to them. Guilt and shame washed over her as fear drained. Her reaction to Brand's simple, affectionate gesture had been to slap his face. It had been embarrassment, she knew, but more, her own suppressed longing for him that had pushed her to react with anger and spiteful words. She'd tried to provoke him and had succeeded. But more, she knew now she had hurt him. Rising from the sofa, she attempted to make amends.

Though she walked over to stand behind him, Raven didn't

touch him. She couldn't bear the thought that he might stiffen away from her.

"Brandon, I'm so sorry." She dug her teeth into her bottom lip to keep her voice steady. "That was stupid of me, and worse, unkind. I'm terribly ashamed of the way I acted. I wanted to make you angry; I was embarrassed, I suppose, and..." The words trailed off as she searched for some way to describe the way she had felt. Even now something inside her warmed and stirred at the knowledge that she had lain beside him, sharing the intimacy of sleep.

Raven heard him swear softly, then he rubbed a hand over the back of his neck. "I baited you."

"You're awfully good at it," she said, trying to make light of what had passed between them. "Much better than I am. I can't think about what I'm saying when I'm angry."

"Obviously, neither can I. Look, Raven," Brand began and turned. Her eyes were huge, swimming with restrained tears. He broke off what he had been about to say and moved to the table for his cigarettes. After lighting one, he turned back to her. "I'm sorry I lost my temper. It's something I don't do often because it's a nasty one. And you've got a good aim with a punch, Raven, and it reminded me of the last time we were together five years ago."

She felt her stomach tighten in defense. "I don't think either of us should dwell on that."

"No." He nodded slowly. His eyes were calm again and considering. Raven knew he was poking into her brain. "Not at the moment, in any case. We should get on with today." He smiled, and she felt each individual muscle in her body relax. "It seems we couldn't wait until we settled in before having a fight."

"No." She answered his smile. "But then I've always been

impatient." Moving to him, Raven rose on her toes and pressed her lips tightly to his. "I'm really sorry, Brandon."

"You've already apologized."

"Yes, well, just remember the next time, it'll be your turn to grovel."

Brand tugged on her hair. "I'll make some more coffee. We should have time for one more cup before we have to strap in."

When he had gone into the galley, Raven stood where she was a moment. The last time, she thought, five years ago.

She remembered it perfectly: each word, each hurt. And she remembered that the balance of the fault then had also been hers. They'd been alone; he'd wanted her. She had wanted him. Then everything had gone wrong. Raven remembered how she had shouted at him, near hysteria. He'd been patient, then his patience had snapped, though not in the way it had today. Then, she remembered, he'd been cold, horribly, horribly cold. Comparing the two reactions, Raven realized she preferred the heat and violence to the icy disdain.

Raven could bring the scene back with ease. They'd been close, and the desire had risen to warm her. Then it was furnace hot and she was smothering, then shouting at him not to touch her. She'd told him she couldn't bear for him to touch her. Brand had taken her at her word and left her. Raven could easily remember the despair, the regret and confusion—and the love for him outweighing all else.

But when she had gone to find him the next morning, he had already checked out of his hotel. He had left California, left her, without a word. And there'd been no word from him in five years. No word, she mused, but for the stories in every magazine, in every newspaper. No word but for the whispered comments at parties and in restaurants whenever she would walk in. No word but for the constant questions, the endless speculation in print as to why they were no longer an item— why Brand Carstairs had begun to collect women like trophies.

So she had forced him out of her mind. Her work, her talent and her music had been used to fill the holes he had left in her life. She'd steadied herself and built a life with herself in control again. That was for the best, she had decided. Sharing the reins was dangerous. And, she mused, glancing toward the galley, it would still be dangerous. *He* would still be dangerous.

Quickly Raven shook her head. Brandon was right, she told herself. It was time to concentrate on today. They had work to do, a score to write. Taking a deep breath, she walked to the galley to help him with the coffee.

9

Raven fell instantly in love with the primitive countryside of Cornwall. She could accept this as the setting for Arthur's Camelot. It was easy to imagine the clash of swords and the glint of armor, the thundering gallop of swift horses.

Spring was beginning to touch the moors, the green blooms just now emerging. Here and there was the faintest touch of pink from wild blossoms. A fine, constant drizzling mist added to the romance. There were houses, cottages really, with gardens beginning to thrive. Lawns were a tender, thin green, and she spotted the sassy yellow of daffodils and the sleepy blue of wood hyacinths. Brand drove south toward the coast and cliffs and Land's End.

They had eaten a country breakfast of brown eggs, thick bacon and oat cakes and had set off again in the little car Brand had arranged to have waiting for them at the airport.

"What's your house like, Brandon?" Raven asked as she rummaged through her purse in search of something to use to secure her hair. "You've never told me anything about it."

He glanced at her bent head. "I'll let you decide for yourself when you see it. It won't be long now."

NORA ROBERTS

Raven found two rubber bands of differing sizes and colors. "Are you being mysterious, or is this your way of avoiding telling me the roof leaks."

"It might," Brand considered. "Though I don't recall being dripped on. The Pengalleys would see to it; they're quite efficient about that sort of thing."

"Pengalleys?" Raven began to braid her hair.

"Caretakers," he told her. "They've a cottage a mile or so off from the house. They kept an eye on the place, and she does a bit of housekeeping when I'm in residence. He does the repairs."

"Pengalley," she murmured, rolling the name over on her tongue.

"Cornishmen, tried and true," Brand remarked absently.

"I know!" Raven turned to him with a sudden smile. "She's short and a bit stout, not fat, just solidly built, with dark hair pulled back and a staunch, rather disapproving face. He's thinner and going gray, and he tipples a bit from a flask when he thinks she's not looking."

Brand quirked a brow and shot her another brief glance. "Very clever. Just how did you manage it?"

"It had to be," Raven shrugged as she secured one braid and started on the next, "if any gothic novel I've ever read had a dab of truth in it. Are there any neighbors?"

"No one close by. That's one of the reasons I bought it."

"Antisocial?" she asked, smiling at him.

"Survival instinct," Brand corrected. "Sometimes I have to get away from it or go mad. Then I can go back and slip into harness again and enjoy it. It's like recharging." He felt her considering look and grinned. "I told you I'd mellowed."

"Yes," she said slowly, "you did." Still watching him, Raven twisted the rubber band around the tip of the second braid. "Yet you've still managed to put out quite a bit. All the albums, the double one last year; all but five of the songs were yours exclusively. And the songs you wrote for Cal Ripley—they were the best cuts on his album."

"Did you think so?" he asked.

"You know they were," she said, letting the rubber band snap into place.

"Praise is good for the ego, love."

"You've had your share now." She tossed both braids behind her back. "What I was getting at was that for someone who's so mellow, you're astonishingly productive."

"I do a lot of my writing here," Brand explained. "Or at my place in Ireland. More here, actually, because I've family across the channel, so there's visiting to be done if I'm there."

Raven gave him a curious look. "I thought you still lived in London."

"Primarily, but if I've serious work or simply need to be alone, I come here. I've family in London as well."

"Yes." Raven looked away again out into the misty landscape. "I suppose large families have disadvantages."

Something in her tone made him glance over again, but her face was averted. He said nothing, knowing from experience that any discussion of Raven's family was taboo. Occasionally in the past, he had probed, but she had always evaded him. He knew that she had been an only child and had left home at seventeen. Out of curiosity, Brand had questioned Julie. Julie knew all there was to know about Raven, he was certain, but she had told him nothing. It was yet another mystery about Raven which alternately frustrated and attracted Brand. Now he put the questions in the back of his mind and continued smoothly.

"Well, we won't be troubled by family or neighbors. Mrs. Pengalley righteously disapproves of show people, and will keep a healthy distance."

"Show people?" Raven repeated and turning back to him, grinned. "Have you been having orgies again, Brand?"

"Not for at least three months," he assured her and swung onto a back road. "I told you I'd mellowed. But she knows about actors and actresses, you see, because as Mr. Pengalley tells me, she makes it her business to read everything she can get her hands on about them. And as for musicians, *rock* musicians, well…" He let the sentence trail off meaningfully, and Raven giggled.

"She'll think the worst, I imagine," she said cheerfully.

"The worst?" Brand cocked a brow at her.

"That you and I are carrying on a hot, illicit love affair."

"Is that the worst? It sounds rather appealing to me."

Raven colored and looked down at her hands. "You know what I meant."

Brand took her hand, kissing it lightly. "I know what you meant." The laugh in his voice eased her embarrassment. "Will it trouble you to be labeled a fallen woman?"

"I've been labeled a fallen woman for years," she returned with a smile, "every time I pick up a magazine. Do you know how many affairs I've had with people I've never even spoken to?"

"Celebrities are required to have overactive libidos," he murmured. "It's part of the job."

"Your press does yours credit," she observed dryly.

Brand nodded gravely. "I've always thought so. I heard about a pool going around London last year. They were betting on how many women I'd have in a three-month period. The British," he explained, "will bet on anything."

Raven allowed the silence to hang for a moment. "What number did you take?"

"Twenty-seven," he told her, then grinned. "I thought it best to be conservative."

She laughed, enjoying him. He would have done it, too, she reflected. There was enough of the cocky street kid left in him. "I don't think I'd better ask you if you won."

"I wish you wouldn't," he said as the car began to climb up a macadam drive.

Raven saw the house. It was three stories high, formed of sober, Cornish stone with shutters of deep, weathered green and a series of stout chimneys on the roof. She could just make out thin puffs of smoke before they merged with the lead-colored sky.

"Oh, Brandon, how like you," she cried, enchanted. "How like you to find something like this."

She was out of the car before he could answer. It was then that she discovered the house had its back to the sea. There were no rear doors, she learned as she dashed quickly to the retaining wall on the left side. The cliff sheared off too close to the back of the house to make one practical. Instead, there were doors on the sides, set deep in Cornish stone.

Raven could look down from the safety of a waist-high wall and watch the water foam and lash out at jagged clumps of rock far below. The view sent a thrill of terror and delight through her. The sea roared below, a smashing fury of sound. Raven stood, heedless of the chill drizzle, and tried to take it all in.

"It's fabulous. Fabulous!" Turning, she lifted her face, studying the house again. Against the stone, in a great tangle of vines, grew wild roses and honeysuckles. They were greening, not yet ready to bloom, but she could already imagine their fragrance. A rock garden had been added, and among the tender green shoots was an occasional flash of color.

"You might find the inside fabulous, too," Brand ventured, laughing when she turned her wet face to him. "And dry."

"Oh, Brandon, don't be so unromantic." She turned a slow circle until she faced the house again. "It's like something out of *Wuthering Heights.*"

He took her hand. "Unromantic or not, mate, I want a bath, a hot one, and my tea."

"That does have a nice sound to it," she admitted but hung back as he pulled her to the door. She thought the cliffs wonderfully jagged and fierce. "Will we have scones? I developed a taste for them when I toured England a couple years ago. Scones and clotted cream—why does that have to sound so dreadful?"

"You'll have to take that up with Mrs. Pengalley," Brand began as he placed his hand on the knob. It opened before he could apply any pressure.

Mrs. Pengalley looked much as Raven had jokingly described her. She was indeed a sturdily built woman with dark hair sternly disciplined into a sensible bun. She had dark, sober eyes that passed briefly over Raven, took in the braids and damp clothing, then rested on Brandon without a flicker of expression.

"Good morning, Mr. Carstairs, you made good time," she said in a soft, Cornish burr.

"Hullo, Mrs. Pengalley, it's good to see you again. This is Ms. Williams, who'll be staying with me."

"Her room's ready, sir. Good morning, Miss Williams."

"Good morning, Mrs. Pengalley," said Raven, a trifle

daunted. This, she was sure, was what was meant by "a formidable woman." "I hope I haven't put you to too much trouble."

"There's been little to do." Mrs. Pengalley's dark eyes shifted to Brand again. "There be fires laid, and the pantry's stocked, as you instructed. I've done you a casserole for tonight. You've only to heat it when you've a mind to eat. Mr. Pengalley laid in a good supply of wood; the nights're cool, and it's been damp. He'll be bringing your bags in now. We heard you drive up."

"Thanks." Brand glanced over, seeing that Raven was already wandering around the room. "We're both in need of a hot bath and some tea, then we should do well enough. Is there anything you want in particular, Raven?"

She glanced back over at the sound of her name but hadn't been attentive to the conversation. "I'm sorry. What?"

He smiled at her. "Is there anything you'd like before Mrs. Pengalley sees to tea?"

"No." Raven smiled at the housekeeper. "I'm sure everything's lovely."

Mrs. Pengalley inclined her head, her body bending not an inch. "I'll make your tea, then." As she swept from the room, Raven shot Brand a telling glance. He grinned and stretched his back.

"You continually amaze me, Brandon," she murmured, then went back to her study of the room.

It was, Raven knew, the room in which they would be doing most of their work over the next weeks. A grand piano, an old one which, she discovered on a quick testing run, had magnificent tone, was set near a pair of narrow windows. Occasional rag rugs dotted the oak-planked floor. The drapes were cream-colored lace and obviously handworked. Two

comfortable sofas, both biscuit-colored, and a few Chippendale tables completed the furniture.

A fire crackled in the large stone fireplace. Raven moved
closer to examine the pictures on the mantel.

At a glance, she could tell she was looking at Brand's family.
There was a teenage boy in a black leather jacket whose features
were the same as Brand's though his dark hair was a bit longer
and was as straight as Raven's. He wore the same cocky grin as
his brother. A woman was next; Raven thought her about
twenty-five and astonishingly pretty with fair hair and slanted
green eyes and a true English rose complexion. For all the difference in coloring, however, the resemblance to Brand was
strong enough for Raven to recognize his sister. She was in
another picture along with a blond man and two boys. Both
boys had dark hair and the Carstairs mischief gleaming in their
eyes. Raven decided Brand's sister had her hands full.

Raven studied the picture of Brand's parents for some time.
The tall, thin frame had been passed down from his father, but
it seemed only one of the children had inherited his fair, English
looks. Raven judged it to be an old snapshot—twenty, perhaps
twenty-five, years old. It had been painstaking staged, with the
man and woman dead center, standing straight in their Sunday
best. The woman was dark and lovely. The man looked a bit self-
conscious and ill at ease having to pose, but the woman beamed
into the camera. Her eyes bespoke mischief and her mouth a hint
of the cockiness so easily recognized in her children.

There were more pictures: family groups and candid shots,
with Brand in several of them. The Carstairses were very
much a family. Raven felt a small stir of envy. Shaking it off,
she turned back to Brand and smiled.

"This is quite a group." She flicked her fingers behind her

toward the mantel. "You're the oldest, aren't you? I think I read that somewhere. The resemblance is remarkable."

"Sweeney genes from my mother's side," Brand told her, looking beyond her shoulder at the crowded grouping of frames. "The only one they slipped up on a bit was Alison." He ran a hand through his damp hair and came to stand beside her. "Let me take you upstairs, love, and get you settled in. The grand tour can wait until we're dry." He slipped an arm around her. "I'm glad you're here, Raven. I've never seen you with things that are mine before. And hotel rooms, no matter how luxurious, are never home."

Later, lounging in a steaming tub, Raven thought over Brand's statement. It was part of the business of being an entertainer to spend a great many nights in hotel rooms, albeit luxury suites, in their positions, but they were hotel rooms nonetheless. Home was a place for between concerts and guest appearances, and to her, it had become increasingly important over the years. It seemed the higher she rose, the more she needed a solid base. She realized it was the same with Brand.

They'd both been on the road for several weeks. He was home now, and somehow Raven knew already that she, too, would be at home there. For all its age and size, there was something comforting in the house. Perhaps, Raven mused as she lazily soaped a leg, it's the age and size. Continuity was important to her, as she felt she'd had little of it in her life, and space was important for the same reason.

Raven had felt an instant affinity for the house. She liked the muffled roar of the sea outside her window and the breathtaking view. She liked the old-fashioned porcelain tub with the curved legs and the oval, mahogany-framed mirror over the tiny pedestal sink.

Rising from the tub, she lifted a towel from the heated bar. When she had dried herself, she wrapped a thick, buff-colored towel around her before letting down her hair. The two braids fell from where she had pinned them atop of her head. Absently, as she wandered back into the bedroom, she began to undo them.

Her luggage still sat beside an old brass chest, but she didn't give much thought to unpacking. Instead she walked to the window seat set in the south wall and knelt on the padded cushion.

Below her the sea hurled itself onto the rocks, tossed up by the wind. There was a sucking, drawing sound before it crashed back onto the shingles and cliffs. Like the sky, they were gray, except for where the waves crested in stiff, white caps. The rain drizzled still, with small drops hitting her window to trail lazily downward. Placing her arms on the wide sill, Raven rested her chin on them and lost herself in dreamy contemplation of the scene below.

"Raven."

She heard Brand's call and the knock and answered both absently. "Yes, come in."

"I thought you might be ready to go downstairs," he said.

"In a minute. What a spectacular view this is! Come look. Does your room face the sea like this? I think I could sit here watching it forever."

"It has its points," he agreed and came over to stand behind her. He tucked his hands into his pockets. "I didn't know you had such a fondness for the sea."

"Yes, always, but I've never had a room where I felt right on top of it before. I'm going to like hearing it at night." She smiled over her shoulder at him. "Is your house in Ireland on the coast, too?"

"No, it's more of a farm, actually. I'd like to take you there." He ran his fingers through her hair, finding it thick and soft and still faintly damp. "It's a green, weepy country, and as appealing as this one, in a different way."

"That's your favorite, isn't it?" Raven smiled up at him. "Even though you live in London and come here to do work, it's the place in Ireland that's special."

He returned the smile. "If it wasn't that there'd have been Sweeneys and Hardestys everywhere we looked, I'd have taken you there. My mother's family," he explained, "are very friendly people. If the score goes well, perhaps we can take a bit of a vacation there when we're done."

Raven hesitated. "Yes…I'd like that."

"Good." The smile turned into a grin. "And I like your dress."

Puzzled, Raven followed his lowered glance. Stunned, she gripped the towel at her breasts and scrambled to her feet. "I didn't realize…I'd forgotten." She could feel the color heating her cheeks. "Brandon, you might have said something."

"I just did," he pointed out. His eyes skimmed down to her thighs.

"Very funny," Raven retorted and found herself smiling. "Now, why don't you clear out and let me change?"

"Must you? Pity." He hooked his hand over the towel where it met between her breasts. The back of his fingers brushed the swell of her bosom. "I was just thinking I liked your outfit." Without touching her in any other way, he brought his mouth down to hers.

"You smell good," he murmured, then traced just the inside of her mouth with his tongue. "Rain's still in your hair."

A roaring louder than the sea began in her brain. Instinctually she was kissing him back, meeting his tongue with hers, stepping closer and rising on her toes. Though her response was quick and giving, he kept the kiss light. She sensed the hunger and the strength under tight control.

Under the towel, his finger swept over her nipple, finding it taut with desire. Raven felt a strong, unfamiliar ache between her thighs. She moaned with it as each muscle in her body went lax. He lifted his face and waited until her eyes opened.

"Shall I make love to you, Raven?"

She stared at him, aching with the churn of rising needs. He was putting the decision in her hands. She should have been grateful, relieved, yet at that moment she found she would have preferred it if he had simply swept her away. For an instant she wanted no choice, no voice, but only to be taken.

"You'll have to be sure," he told her quietly. Lifting her chin with his finger, he smiled. His eyes were a calm blue-green. "I've no intention of making it easy for you."

He dropped his hand. "I'll wait for you downstairs, though I still think it's a pity you have to change. You're very attractive in a towel."

"Brandon," she said when he was at the door. He turned, lifting a brow in acknowledgment. "What if I'd said yes?" Raven grinned, feeling a bit more steady with the distance between them. "Wouldn't that have been a bit awkward with Mrs. Pengalley still downstairs?"

Leaning against the door, he said lazily, "Raven, if you'd said yes, I wouldn't give a damn if Mrs. Pengalley and half the country were downstairs." He shut the door carefully behind him.

10

Both Raven and Brand were anxious to begin. They started the day after their arrival and soon fell into an easy, workable routine. Brand rose early and was usually finishing up a good sized breakfast by the time Raven dragged herself downstairs. When she was fortified with coffee, they started their morning stretch, working until noon and Mrs. Pengalley's arrival. While the housekeeper brought in the day's marketing and saw to whatever domestic chores needed to be seen to, Brand and Raven would take long walks.

The days were balmy, scented with sea spray and spring. The land was rugged, even harsh, with patches of poor ground covered with heather not yet in bloom. The pounding surf beat against towering granite cliffs. Hardy birds built their nests in the crags. Their cries could be heard over the crash of the waves. Standing high, Raven could see down to the village with its neat rows of cottages and white church spire.

They'd work again in the afternoon with the fire sizzling in the grate at their backs. After dinner they went over the day's work. By the end of the week they had a loosely based outline for the score and the completed title song.

They didn't work without snags. Both Raven and Brand felt too strongly about music for any collaboration to run smoothly. But the arguments seemed to stimulate both of them; and the final product was the better for them. They were a good team.

They remained friends. Brand made no further attempt to become Raven's lover. From time to time Raven would catch him staring intently at her. Then she would feel the pull, as sensual as a touch, as tempting as a kiss. The lack of pressure confused her and drew her more effectively than his advances could have. Advances could be refused, avoided. She knew he was waiting for her decision. Underneath the casualness, the jokes and professional disagreements, the air throbbed with tension.

The afternoon was long and a bit dreary. A steady downpour of rain kept Raven and Brand from walking the cliffs. Their music floated through the house, echoing in corners here and there and drifting to forgotten attics. They'd built the fire high with Mr. Pengalley's store of wood to chase away the dampness that seemed to seep through the windows. A tray of tea and biscuits that they had both forgotten rested on one of the Chippendale tables. Their argument was reaching its second stage.

"We've got to bring up the tempo," Raven insisted. "It just doesn't work this way."

"It's a mood piece, Raven."

"Not a funeral dirge. It drags this way, Brandon. People are going to be nodding off before she finishes singing it."

"Nobody falls asleep while Lauren Chase is singing," Brand countered. "This number is pure sex, Raven, and she'll sell it."

"Yes, she will," Raven agreed, "but not at this tempo." She

shifted on the piano bench so that she faced him more directly. "All right, Joe's fallen asleep at the typewriter in the middle of the chapter he's writing. He's already believing himself a little mad because of the vivid dreams he's having about his character Tessa. She seems too real, and he's fallen in love with her even though he knows she's a product of his own imagination, a character in a novel he's writing, a fantasy. And now, in the middle of the day, he's dreaming about her again, and this time she promises to come to him that night."

"I know the plot, Raven," Brand said dryly.

Though she narrowed her eyes, Raven checked her temper. She thought she detected some fatigue in his voice. Once or twice she'd been awakened in the middle of the night by his playing. "'Nightfall' is hot, Brandon. You're right about it being pure sex, and your lyrics are fabulous. But it still needs to move."

"It moves." He took a last drag on his cigarette before crushing it out. "Chase knows how to hang on to a note."

Raven made a quick sound of frustration. Unfortunately he was usually right about such things. His instincts were phenomenal. This time, however, she was certain that her own instincts—as a songwriter and as a woman—were keener. She knew the way the song had to be sung to reap the full effect. The moment she had read Brand's lyrics, she had known what was needed. The song had flowed, completed, through her head.

"I know she can hang on to a note, and she can handle choreography. She'll be able to do both and still do the song at the right tempo. Let me show you." She began to play the opening bars. Brand shrugged and rose from the bench.

Raven moved the tempo to *andante* and sang to her own accompaniment. Her voice wrapped itself around the music.

Brand moved to the window to watch the rain. It was the song of a temptress, full of implicit, wild promises.

Raven's voice flowed over the range of notes, then heated when it was least expected until Brand felt a tight knot of desire in the pit of his stomach. There was something not quite earthy in the melody she had created. The quicker tempo made a sharp contrast, much more effective than the pace Brand had wanted. She ended abruptly in a raspy whisper without any fade-out. She tossed her hair, then shot him a look over her shoulder.

"Well?" There was a half smile on her face.

He had his back to her and kept his hands tucked into his pockets. "You have to be right now and again, I suppose."

Raven laughed, spinning around on the bench until she faced the room. "You've a way with compliments, Brandon. It sets my heart fluttering."

"She doesn't have your range," he murmured. Then, making an impatient movement, he wandered over to the teapot. "I don't think she'll get as much out of the low scale as you do."

"Mmm." Raven shrugged as she watched him pour out a cup of tea. "She's got tremendous style, though; she'll milk every ounce out of it." He set the tea down again without touching it and roamed to the fire. As she watched him, a worried frown creased Raven's brow. "Brandon, what's wrong?"

He threw another log on the already roaring fire. "Nothing, just restless."

"This rain's depressing." She rose to go to the window. "I've never minded it. Sometimes I like a dreary, sleepy day. I can be lazy without feeling guilty. Maybe that's what you should do, Brandon, be lazy today. You've got that marvelous chessboard in the library. Why don't you teach me to play?" She lifted her hands to his shoulders and feeling the tension, began to knead absently. "Of course, that might be hard work. Julie gave up playing backgammon with me. She says I haven't any knack for strategy."

Raven broke off when Brand turned abruptly around and removed her hands from his shoulders. Without speaking, he walked away from her. He went to the liquor cabinet and drew out a bottle of bourbon. Raven watched as he poured three fingers into a glass and drank it down.

"I don't think I've the patience for games this afternoon," he told her as he poured a second drink.

"All right, Brandon," she said. "No games." She walked over to stand in front of him, keeping her eyes direct. "Why are you angry with me? Certainly not because of the song."

The look held for several long moments while the fire popped and sizzled in the grate. Raven heard a log fall as the one beneath it gave way.

"Perhaps it's time you and I talked," Brandon said as he idly swirled the remaining liquor in the glass. "It's dangerous to leave things hanging for five years; you never know when they're going to fall."

Raven felt a ripple of disquiet but nodded. "You may be right."

Brand gave her a quick smile. "Should we be civilized and sit down or take a few free swings standing up?"

She shrugged. "I don't think there's any need to be civilized. Civilized fighting never clears the air."

"All right," he began but was interrupted by the peal of the bell. Setting down his glass, Brand shot her a last look, then went to answer.

Alone, Raven tried to control her jitters. There was a storm brewing, she knew, and it wasn't outside the windows. Brand was itching for a fight, and though the reason was unclear to her, Raven found herself very willing to oblige him. The tension between them had been glossed over in the name of music and peace. Now, despite her nerves, she was looking forward to shattering the calm. Hearing his returning footsteps, she walked back to the tea tray and picked up her cup.

"Package for you." Brand gestured with it as he came through the doorway. "From Henderson."

"I wonder what he could be sending me," she murmured, already ripping off the heavy packing tape. "Oh, of course." She tossed the wrappings carelessly aside and studied the album jacket. "They're sample jackets for the album I'm releasing this summer." Without glancing at him, Raven handed Brand one of the covers, then turned to another to read the liner notes.

For the next few minutes Brand studied the cover picture without speaking. Again, a background of white, Raven sitting in her habitual cross-legged fashion. She was looking full into the camera with only a tease of a smile on her lips. Her eyes were very gray and very direct. Over her shoulders and down to her knees, her hair spilled—a sharp contrast against the soft-focused white of the background. The arrangement appeared to be haphazard but had been cleverly posed nonetheless. She appeared to be nude, and the effect was fairly erotic.

"Did you approve this picture?"

"*Hmm?*" Raven pushed back her hair as she continued to read. "Oh, yes, I looked over the proofs before I left on tour. I'm still not completely sure about this song order, but I suppose it's a bit late to change it now."

"I always felt Henderson was above packaging you this way."

"Packaging me what way?" she asked absently.

"As a virgin offering to the masses." He handed her the cover.

"Brandon, really…how ridiculous."

"I don't think so," he said. "I think it's an uncannily apt description: virgin white, soft focus, and you sitting naked in the middle of it all."

"I'm not naked," she retorted indignantly. "I don't do nudes."

"The potential buyer isn't supposed to know that, though, is he?" Brand leaned against the piano and watched her through narrowed eyes.

"It's provocative, certainly. It's meant to be." Raven frowned down at the cover again. "There's nothing wrong with that. I'm not a child to be dressed up in Mary Janes and a pink pinafore, Brandon. This is business. There's nothing extreme about this cover. And I'm more modestly covered than I would be on a public beach."

"But not more decently," he said coldly. "There's a difference."

Color flooded her face, now a mixture of annoyance and embarrassment. "It's not indecent. I've never posed for an indecent picture. Karl Straighter is one of the finest photographers in the business. He doesn't shoot indecent pictures."

"One man's art is another's porn, I suppose."

Her eyes widened as she lowered the jackets to the piano bench. "That's a disgusting thing to say," she whispered. "You're being deliberately horrible."

"I'm simply giving you my opinion," he corrected, lifting a brow. "You don't have to like it."

"I don't need your opinion. I don't need your approval."

"No," he said and crushed out his cigarette. "You bloody well don't, do you? But you're going to have it in any case." He caught her by the arm when she would have turned away. The power of the grip contrasted the cool tone and frosty eyes.

"Let go of me," Raven demanded, putting her hand on top of his and trying unsuccessfully to pry it from her arm.

"When I'm finished."

"You have finished." Her voice was abruptly calm, and she stopped her frantic attempts to free herself. Instead she faced him squarely, emotion burning in her eyes. "I don't have to listen to you when you go out of your way to insult me, Brandon. I won't listen to you. You can prevent me from leaving because you're stronger than I am, but you can't make me listen." She swallowed but managed to keep her voice steady. "I run my own life. You're entitled to your opinion, certainly, but you're not entitled to hurt me with it. I don't want to talk to you now; I just want you to let me go."

He was silent for so long, Raven thought he would refuse. Then, slowly, he loosened his grip until she could slip her arm from his fingers. Without a word she turned and left the room.

Perhaps it was the strain of her argument with Brand or the lash of rain against the windows or the sudden fury of thunder and lightning. The dream formed out of a vague montage of childhood remembrances that left her with impressions rather than vivid pictures. Thoughts and images floated and receded against the darkness of sleep. There were rolling sensations of fear, guilt, despair, one lapping over the other while she moaned and twisted beneath the sheets, trying to force herself awake. But she was trapped, caught fast in the world just below consciousness. Then the thunder seemed to explode inside her head, and the flash of lightning split the room with a swift, white flash. Screaming, Raven sat up in bed.

The room was pitch dark again when Brand rushed in; he found his way to the bed by following the sounds of Raven's wild weeping. "Raven. Here, love." Even as he reached her, she threw herself into his arms and clung. She was trembling hard, and her skin was icy. Brand pulled the quilt up over her back and cuddled her. "Don't cry, love, you're safe here." He patted and stroked as he would for a child frightened of a storm. "It'll soon be over."

"Hold me." She pressed her face into his bare shoulder. "Please, just hold me." Her breathing was quick, burning her throat as she struggled for air. "Oh, Brandon, such an awful dream."

He rocked her and laid a light kiss on her temple. "What was it about?" The telling, he recalled from childhood, usually banished the fear.

"She'd left me alone again," Raven murmured, shuddering so that he drew her closer in response. The words came out as jumbled as her thoughts, as tumbled as the dream. "How I hated being alone in that room. The only light was from the building next door—one of those red neon lights that blinks on and off, on and off, so that the dark was never still. And so much noise out on the street, even with the windows closed. Too hot...too hot to sleep," she murmured into his shoulder. "I watched the light and waited for her to come back. She was drunk again." She whimpered, her fingers opening and closing against his chest. "And she'd brought a man with her. I put the pillow over my head so I wouldn't hear."

Raven paused to steady her breath. It was dark and quiet in Brand's arms. Outside, the storm rose in high fury.

"She fell down the steps and broke her arm, so we moved, but it was always the same. Dingy little rooms, airless rooms that smelled always of gin no matter how you scrubbed. Thin walls, walls that might as well not have existed for the privacy they gave you. But she always promised that this time, this time it'd be different. She'd get a job, and I'd go to school…but always one day I'd come home and there'd be a man and a bottle."

She wasn't clinging any longer but simply leaning against him as if all passion were spent. Lightning flared again, but she remained still.

"Raven." Brand eased her gently away and tilted her face to his. Tears were still streaming from her eyes, but her breathing was steadier. He could barely make out the shape of her face in the dark. "Where was your father?"

He could see the shine of her eyes as she stared at him. She made a soft, quiet sound as one waking. He knew the words had slipped from her while she had been vulnerable and unaware. Now she was aware, but it was too late for defenses. The sigh she made was an empty, weary sound.

"I don't know who he was." Slowly she drew out of Brand's arms and rose from the bed. "She didn't, either. You see, there were so many."

Brand said nothing but reached into the pocket of the jeans he had hastily dragged on and found a pack of matches. Striking one, he lit the bedside candle. The light wavered and flickered, hardly more than a pulse beat in the dark. "How long," he asked and shook out the match, "did you live like that?"

Raven dragged both hands through her hair, then hugged herself. She knew she'd already said too much for evasions. "I don't remember a time she didn't drink, but when I was very young, five or six, she still had some control over it. She used to sing in clubs. She had big dreams and an average voice, but she was very lovely…once."

Pausing, Raven pressed her fingers against her eyes and wiped away tears. "By the time I was eight, she was…her problem was unmanageable. And there were always men. She needed men as much as she needed to drink. Some of them were better than others. One of them took me to the zoo a couple of times…."

She trailed off and turned away. Brand watched the candlelight flicker over the thin material of her nightgown.

"She got steadily worse. I think part of it was from the frustration of having her voice go. Of course, she abused it dreadfully with smoking and drinking, but the more it deteriorated, the more she smoked and drank. She ruined her voice and ruined her health and ruined any chance she had of making something of herself. Sometimes I hated her. Sometimes I know she hated herself."

A sob escaped, but Raven pushed it back and began to wander the room. The movement seemed to make it easier, and the words tumbled out quicker, pressing for release. "She'd cry and cling to me and beg me not to hate her. She'd promise the moon, and more often than not, I'd believe her. 'This time'—that was one of her favorite beginnings. It still is." Raven let out a shaky sigh. "She loved me when she wasn't drinking and forgot me completely when she was. It was like living with two different women, and neither one of them was easy. When she was sober, she expected an average mother-and-daughter relationship. Had I done my homework? Why was I five minutes late getting home from school? When she

NORA ROBERTS

was drunk, I was supposed to keep the hell out of her way. I remember once, when I was twelve, she went three months and sixteen days without a drink. Then I came home from school and found her passed out on the bed. She'd had an audition that afternoon for a gig at this two-bit club. Later she told me she'd just wanted one drink to calm her nerves. Just one…" Raven shivered and hugged herself tighter. "It's cold," she murmured.

Brand rose and stooped in front of the fire. He added kindling and logs to the bed of coals in the grate. Raven walked to the window to watch the fury of the storm over the sea. Lightning still flashed sporadically, but the violence of the thunder and the rain were dying.

"There were so many other times. She was working as a cocktail waitress in this little piano bar in Houston. I was sixteen then. I always came by on payday so I could make certain she didn't spend the money before I bought food. She'd been pretty good then. She'd been working about six weeks straight and had an affair going with the manager. He was one of the better ones. I used to play around at the piano if the place was empty. One of my mother's lovers had been a musician; he'd taught me the basics and said I had a good ear. Mama liked hearing me play." Her voice had quieted. Brand watched her trail a finger down the dark pane of window glass.

"Ben, the manager, asked me if I wanted to play during the lunch hour. He said I could sing, too, as long as I kept it soft and didn't talk to the customers. So I started." Raven sighed and ran a hand over her brow. Behind her came the pop and crackle of flame. "We left Houston for Oklahoma City. I lied about my age and got a job singing in a club. It was one of Mama's worst periods. There were times I was afraid to leave her alone, but she wasn't working then, and…" She broke off with a sound of frustration and rubbed at an ache in her temple. She wanted to stop, wanted to block it all out, but she knew she had come too far. Pressing her brow against the glass, she waited until her thoughts came back into order.

"We needed the money, so I had to risk leaving her at night. I suppose we exchanged roles for a time," she murmured. "The thing I learned young, but consistently forgot, was that an alcoholic finds money for a bottle. Always, no matter what. One night during my second set she wove her way into the club. Wayne was working there and caught onto the situation quickly. He managed to quiet her down before it got too ugly. Later he helped me get her home and into bed. He was wonderful: no lectures, no pity, no advice. Just support."

Raven turned away from the window again and wandered to the fire. "But she came back again, twice more, and they let me go. There were other towns, other clubs, but it was the same then and hardly matters now. Just before I turned eighteen I left her." Her voice trembled a bit, and she took a moment to steady it. "I came home from work one night, and she was passed out at the kitchen table with one of those half-gallon jugs of wine. I knew if I didn't get away from her I'd go crazy. So I put her to bed, packed a bag, left her all the money I could spare and walked out. Just like that." She covered her face with her hands a moment, pressing her fingers into her eyes. "It was like being able to breathe for the first time in my life."

Raven roamed back to the kitchen. She could see the vague ghost of her own reflection. Studying it, listening to the steady but more peaceful drum of rain, she continued. "I worked my way to L.A., and Henderson saw me. He pushed me. I'm not certain what my ambition was before I signed with him. Just to survive, I think. One day and then the next. Then there were contracts and recording sessions and the whole crazy circus. Doors started opening. Some of them were trap doors, I've always thought." She gave a quick, wondering laugh. "God, it was marvelous and scary and I don't believe I could ever go through those first few months again. Anyway, Henderson got me publicity, and the first hit single got me more. And then I got a call from a hospital in Memphis."

Raven turned and began to pace. The light silk of her nightgown clung, then swirled, with her movements. "I had to go, of course. She was in pretty bad shape. Her latest lover had beaten her and stolen what little money she had. She cried. Oh, God, all the same promises. She was sorry; she loved me. Never again, never again. I was the only decent thing she'd ever done in her life." The tears were beginning to flow again, but this time Raven made no attempt to stop them. "As soon as she could travel, I brought her back with me. Julie had found a sanitarium in Ojai and a very earnest young doctor. Justin Randolf Karter. Isn't that a marvelous name, Brandon?" Bitterness spilled out with the tears. "A marvelous name, a remarkable man. He took me into his tasteful, leather-bound office and explained the treatment my mother would receive."

Whirling, Raven faced Brand, her shoulders heaving with sobs. "I didn't want to know! I just wanted him to do it. He told me not to set my hopes too high, and I told him I hadn't any hopes at all. He must have found me cynical, because he suggested several good organizations I could speak to. He reminded me that alcoholism is a disease and that my mother was a victim. I said the hell she was; *I* was the victim!" Raven forced the words out as she hugged herself tightly. "*I* was the victim; *I* had had to live with her and deal with her lies and her sickness and her men. It was so safe, so easy, for him to be sanctimonious and understanding behind that tidy white coat. And I *hated* her." The sobs came in short, quick jerks as she balled her hands and pressed them against her eyes. "And I loved her." Her breath trembled in and out as everything she had pent up over the weeks of her mother's latest treatment poured through her. "I still love her," she whispered.

Weary, nearly spent, she turned to the fire, resting her palms on the mantel. "Dr. Karter let me shout at him, then he sat with me when I broke down. I went home, and they started her treatment. Two days later I met you."

Raven didn't hear him move, didn't know he stood behind her, until she felt his hands on her shoulders. Without speaking she turned and went into his arms. Brand held her, feeling the light tremors while he stared down at the licking, greedy flames. Outside, the storm had become only a patter of rain against the windows.

"Raven, if you had told me, I might have been able to make things easier for you."

She shook her head, then buried her face against his chest. "No, I didn't want it to touch that part of my life. I just wasn't strong enough." Taking a deep breath, she pulled back far enough to look in his eyes. "I was afraid that if you knew you wouldn't want anything to do with me."

"Raven." There was hurt as well as censure in his voice.

"I know it was wrong, Brandon, even stupid, but you have to understand: everything seemed to be happening to me at once. I needed time. I needed to sort out how I was going to live my life, how I was going to deal with my career, my mother, everything." Her hands gripped his arms as she willed him to see through her eyes. "I was nobody one day and being mobbed by fans the next. My picture was everywhere. I heard myself every time I turned on the radio. You know what that's like."

Brand brushed her hair from her cheek. "Yes, I know what that's like." As he spoke, he could feel her relax with a little shudder.

"Before I could take a breath, Mama walked back into my life. Part of me hated her, but instead of realizing that it was a normal reaction and dealing with it, I felt an unreasonable guilt. And I was ashamed. No," she shook her head, anticipating him, "there's no use telling me I had no need to be. That's an intellectual statement, a practical statement; it has nothing to do with emotion. I don't expect you to understand that part of it. You've never had to deal with it. She's my mother. It isn't possible to completely separate myself from that, even knowing that the responsibility for her problem isn't mine." Raven gave him one last, long look before turning away. "And on top of everything that was happening to me, I fell in love with you." The flames danced and snapped as she watched. "I loved you," she murmured so quietly he strained to hear, "but I couldn't be your lover."

Brand stared at her back, started to reach for her, then dropped his hands to his sides. "Why?"

Only her head turned as she looked over her shoulder at him. Her face was in shadows. "Because then I would be like her," she whispered, then turned away again.

"You don't really believe that, Raven." Brand took her shoulders, but she shook her head, not answering. Firmly he turned her to face him, making a slow, thorough study of her. "Do you make a habit of condemning children for their parents' mistakes?"

"No, but I…"

"You don't have the right to do it to yourself."

She shut her eyes on a sigh. "I know, I know that, but…"

"There're no buts on this one, Raven." His fingers tightened until she opened her eyes again. "You know who you are."

There was only the sound of the sea and the rain and fire. "I wanted you," she managed in a trembling voice, "when you held me, touched me. You were the first man I'd ever wanted." She swallowed, and again he felt the shudder course through her. "Then I'd remember all those cramped little rooms, all those men with my mother…." She broke off and would have turned away again if his hands hadn't held her still.

Brand removed his hands from her arms, then slowly, his eyes still on hers, he used them to frame her face. "Sleeping with a stranger is different from making love with someone you care for."

Raven moistened her lips. "Yes, I know that, but…"

"Do you?" The question stopped her. She could do no more than let out a shaky breath. "Let me show you, Raven."

Her eyes were trapped by his. She knew he would release her if she so much as shook her head. Fear was tiny pinpoints along her skin. Need was a growing warmth in her blood. She lifted her hands to his wrists. "Yes."

Again Brand gently brushed the hair away from her cheeks. When her face was framed by his hands alone, he lowered his head and kissed her eyes closed. He could feel her trembling in his arms. Her hands still held his wrists, and her fingers tightened when he brought his mouth to hers. His was patient, waiting until her lips softened and parted.

The kisses grew deeper, but slowly, now moister until she swayed against him. His fingers caressed, his mouth roamed.

Firelight flickered over them in reds and golds, casting its own shadows. Raven could feel the heat from it through the silk she wore, but it was the glow inside of her which built and flamed hot.

Brand lowered his hands to her shoulders, gently massaging as he teased her lower lip with his teeth. Raven felt the gown slip down over her breasts, then cling briefly to her hips before it drifted to the floor. She started to protest, but he deepened the kiss. The thought spiraled away. Down the curve of her back, over the slight flare of her hips, he ran his hands. Then he picked her up in his arms. With her mind spinning, she sank into the mattress. When Brand joined her, the touch of his naked body against hers jolted her, bringing on a fresh surge of doubts and fears.

"Brandon, please, I…" The words were muffled, then died inside his mouth.

Easily, his hands caressed her, stroking without hurry. Somewhere in the back of her mind she knew he held himself under tight control. But her mind had relaxed, and her limbs were heavy. His mouth wandered to her throat, tasting, giving pleasure, arousing by slow, irresistible degrees. He worked her nipple with his thumb, and she moaned and moved against him. Brand allowed his mouth to journey downward, laying light, feathering kisses over the curve of her breast. Lightly, very lightly, he ran his tongue over the tip. Raven felt the heat between her thighs, and tangling her fingers in his hair, pressed him closer. She arched and shuddered not from fear but from passion.

Heat unlike anything she had ever known or imagined was building inside her. She was still aware of the flicker of the fire and candlelight on her closed lids, of the soft brush of linen sheets against her back, of the faint, pleasant smell of wood-smoke. But these sensations were dim, while her being seemed focused on the liquefying touch of his tongue over her skin, the feathery brush of his fingers on her thighs. Over the hiss of rain and fire, she heard him murmur her name, heard her own soft, mindless response.

Her breath quickened, and her mouth grew hungry. Suddenly desperate, she drew his face back to hers. She wrapped her arms around him tightly as the pressure of the kiss pushed her head deep into the pillow. Brand lay across her, flesh to flesh, so that her breasts yielded to his chest. Raven could feel the light mat of his hair against her skin.

His hand lay on her stomach and drifted down as she moved under him. There was a flash of panic as he slid between her thighs, then her breath caught in a heady rush of pleasure. He was still patient, his fingers gentle and unhurried as they gradually increased her rhythm.

For Raven, there was no world beyond the firelit room, beyond the four-poster bed. His mouth took hers, his tongue probing deeply, then moving to her ear, her throat, her neck and back to her lips. All the while, his hands and fingers were taking her past all thought, past all reason.

Then he was on top of her, and she opened for him, ready to give, to receive. She was too steeped in wonder to comprehend his strict, unwavering control. She knew only that she wanted him and urged him to take her. There was a swift flash of pain, dulled by a pleasure too acute to be measured. She cried out, but the sound was muffled against his mouth, then all was lost on wave after wave of delight.

11

With her head in the curve of Brand's shoulder, Raven watched the fire. Her hand lay over his heart. She could feel its quick, steady rhythm under her palm.

The room was quiet, and outside, the rain had slackened to a murmur. Raven knew she would remember this moment every time she lay listening to rain against windows. Brand's arm was under her, curled over her back with his hand loosely holding her arm. Since he had rolled from her and drawn her against his side, he had been silent. Raven thought he slept and was content to lie with him, watching the fire and listening to the rain. She shifted her head, wanting to look at him and found he wasn't asleep. She could see the sheen of his eyes as he stared at the ceiling. Raven lifted a hand to his cheek.

"I thought you were asleep."

Brand caught her hand and pressed it to his lips. "No, I…" Looking down at her, he broke off, then slowly brushed a tear from her lash with his thumb. "I hurt you."

"No." Raven shook her head. For a moment she buried her face in the curve of his neck, where she could feel his warmth, smell his scent. "Oh, no, you didn't hurt me. You made me feel wonderful. I feel...free." She looked up at him again and smiled. "Does that sound foolish?"

"No." Brand ran his fingers through the length of her hair, pushing it back when it would have hidden her face from him. Her skin was flushed. In her eyes he could see the reflected flames from the fire. "You're so beautiful."

She smiled again and kissed him. "I've always thought the same about you."

He laughed, drawing her closer. "Have you?"

She lay half across him, heated flesh to heated flesh. "Yes, I always thought you'd make a remarkably lovely girl, and I see by your sister's picture that I was right."

He lifted a brow. "Strange, I never realized the direction of your thoughts. Perhaps it's best I didn't."

Raven gave one of her low, rich chuckles and pressed her lips against the column of his throat. She loved the way his tones could become suddenly suavely British. "I'm sure you make a much better man."

"That's comforting," he said dryly as he began to stroke her back, "under the circumstances." His fingers lingered at her hip to caress.

"I'm sure I like you much better this way." Raven kissed the side of his throat again, working her way to his ear. Under her breast she felt the sudden jump and scramble of his heartbeat. "Brandon..." She sighed, nuzzling his ear. "You're so good to me, so kind, so gentle."

She heard him groan before he rolled over, reversing their positions. His eyes were heated and intense and very green, reminding her of the moment he had held her like this on the plane. Now again her pulse began to hammer, but not with fear.

"Love isn't always kind, Raven," he said roughly. "It isn't always gentle."

His mouth came down on hers crushingly, urgently, as all the restraints he had put on himself snapped. There was no patience in him now, only passion. Where before he had taken her up calmly, easily, now he took her plummeting at a desperate velocity. Her mouth felt bruised and tender from his, yet she learned hunger incited hunger. Raven wanted more, and still more, so she caught him closer.

Demanding, possessing, he took his hands over her. "So long," she heard him mutter. "I've wanted you for so long." Then his teeth found the sensitive area of her neck, and she heard nothing. She plunged toward the heat and the dark.

Brand felt her give and respond and demand. He was nearly wild with need. He wanted to touch all of her, taste all of her. He was as desperate as a starving man and as ruthless. Where before, responding to her innocence, he had been cautious, now he took what he had wanted for too many years. She was his as he had dreamed she would be: soft and yielding, then soft and hungry beneath him.

He could hear her moan, feel the bite of her fingernails in his shoulders as he took his mouth down the curve of her breast. The skin of her stomach was smooth and quivered under his tongue. He slipped a hand between her thighs, and she strained against him so that he knew she was as desperate as he. Yet he wouldn't take her, not yet. He felt an impossible greed. His tongue moved to follow the path of his hands. All the years he'd wanted her, all the frustrated passion, burst out, catching them both in the explosion. Not knowing the paths, Raven went where he led her and learned that desire was deeper, stronger, than anything she had known possible.

He was pulling her down—down until the heat was too intense to bear. But she wanted more. His hands were rough, bruising her skin. But she craved no gentleness. She was steeped in passion too deep for escape. She called out for him, desperately, mindlessly, for him to take her. She knew there couldn't be more; they'd gone past all the rules. Pleasure could not be sharper; passion could not be darker than it was at that moment.

Then he was inside her, and everything that had gone before paled against the color and the heat.

His mouth was buried at her neck. From far off he heard her gasps for breath merge with his own. They moved together like lightning, so that he could no longer think. There was only Raven. All passion intensified, concentrated, until he thought he would go mad from it. The pain of it shot through him, then flowed from him, leaving him weak.

They lay still, with Brand over her, his face buried in her hair. His breathing was ragged, and he gave no thought to his weight as he relaxed completely. Beneath him Raven shuddered again and again with the release of passion. She gripped his shoulders tightly, not wanting him to move, not wanting to relinquish the unity. If he had shown her the tenderness and compassion of loving the first time, now he had shown her darker secrets.

A log fell in the grate, scattering sparks against the screen. Brand lifted his head and looked down at her. His eyes were heavy, still smoldering, as they lowered to her swollen mouth. He placed a soft kiss on them, then, shifting his weight, prepared to rise.

"No, don't go." Raven took his arm, sitting up as he did.

"Only to bank the fire."

Bringing her knees to her chest, Raven watched as Brand stacked the fire for the night. The light danced over his skin as she stared, entranced. The ripple of muscles was surprising in one so lean. She saw them in his shoulders, his back, his thighs. The passion in the cool, easygoing man was just as surprising, but she knew the feel of it now, just as she knew the feel of the muscles. He turned and looked at her with the fire leaping at his back. They studied each other, both dazed by what had passed between them. Then he shook his head.

"My God, Raven, I want you again."

She held her arms out to him.

There was a brilliant ribbon of sunlight across Raven's eyes. It was a warm, red haze. She allowed her lids to open slowly before turning to Brand.

He slept still, his breathing deep and even. She had to suppress the urge to brush his hair away from his face because she didn't want to wake him. Not yet. For the first time in her life she woke to look at her lover's face. She felt a warm, settled satisfaction.

He *is* beautiful, she thought, remembering how he had been faintly distressed to hear her say so the night before. *And I love him.* Raven almost said the words aloud as she let herself think them. I've always loved him, right from the beginning, all through the years in between—and even more now that we're together. But no mistakes this time. She closed her eyes tight on the sudden fear that he could walk out of her life again. *No demands, no pressures.* We'll just be together; that's all I need.

She dropped her eyes to his mouth. It had been tender in the night, she remembered, then hungry, almost brutal. She hadn't realized how badly he had wanted her, or she him, until the barriers had shattered. *Five years, five empty years!* Raven pushed the thought away. There was no yesterday, no tomorrow; only the present.

Suddenly she smiled, thinking of the enormous breakfasts he habitually ate. She would usually stumble into the kitchen for coffee as he was cleaning off a plate. Cooking wasn't her best thing, she mused, but it would be fun to surprise him. His arm was tossed around her waist, holding her against him so that their bodies had warmed each other even in sleep. Carefully Raven slipped out from under it. Padding to the closet, she found a robe, then left Brand sleeping to go downstairs.

The kitchen was washed in sunlight. Raven went straight to the percolator. First things first, she decided. Strangely, she was wide-awake, there was none of the drowsy fogginess she habitually used coffee to chase away. She felt vital, full of energy, very much the way she felt when finishing a live concert, she realized as she scooped out coffee. Perhaps there was a parallel. Raven fit the lid on the pot, then plugged it in. She had always felt that performing for an audience was a bit like making love: sharing yourself, opening your emotions, pulling down the barriers. That's what she had done with Brand. The thought made her smile, and she was singing as she rummaged about for a frying pan.

Upstairs, Brand stirred, reached for her and found her gone. He opened his eyes to see that the bed beside him was empty. Quickly he pushed himself up and scanned the room. The fire was still burning. It had been late when he had added the last logs. The drapes were open to the full strength of the sun. It spilled across the bed and onto the floor. Raven's nightgown lay where it had fallen the night before.

Not a dream, he told himself, tugging a hand through his

hair. They'd been together last night, again and again until every ounce of energy had been drained. Then they had slept, still holding each other, still clinging. His eyes drifted to the empty pillow beside him again. *But where—where the devil is she now?* Feeling a quick flutter of panic, he rose, tugged on his jeans and went to find her.

Before Brand reached the bottom of the stairs, her voice drifted to him.

Every morning when I wake,
I'll see your eyes.
And there'll only be the love we make,
No more good-byes.

He recognized the song as the one he had teased her about weeks before when they had sat in his car in the hills above Los Angeles. The knot in his stomach untied itself. He walked down the hall, listening to the husky, morning quality of her voice, then paused in the doorway to watch her.

Her movements suited the song she sang: cheerful, happy. The kitchen was filled with morning noises and scents. There was the popping rhythm of the percolator as the coffee bubbled on the burner, the hiss and sizzle of the fat sausage she had frying in a cast-iron skillet, the clatter of crockery as she searched for a platter. Her hair was streaming down her back, still tumbled from the night, while the short terry robe she wore rode high up on her thighs as she stretched to reach the top shelf of a cupboard.

Raven stopped singing for a moment to swear good-naturedly about her lack of height. After managing to get a grip on the platter, she lowered her heels back to the floor and turned.

She gave a gasp when she spotted Brand, dropped the fork she held and just managed to save the platter from following it.

"Brandon!" Raven circled her throat with her hand a moment and took a deep breath. "You scared me! I didn't hear you come down."

Brand didn't answer her smile. He didn't move but only looked at her. "I love you, Raven."

Her eyes widened, and her lips trembled open, then shut again. The words, she reminded herself, mean so many different things. It was important not to take a simple statement and deepen its meaning. Raven kept her voice calm as she stooped to pick up the fork. "I love you, too, Brandon."

He frowned at the top of her head, then at her back as she turned away to the sink. She turned on the tap to rinse off the fork. "You sound like my sister. I've already two of those; I don't need another."

Raven took her time. She turned off the tap, composed her face into a smile, then turned. "I don't think of you as a brother, Brandon." The tension at the back of her neck made it difficult to move calmly back to the cupboard for cups and saucers. "It isn't easy for me to tell you how I feel. I needed your support, your compassion. You helped me last night more than I can say."

"Now you make me sound like a bloody doctor. I said I love you, Raven." There was a snap of anger in the words this time. When Raven turned back to him, her eyes were eloquent.

"Brandon, you don't have to feel obligated…" She broke off as his eyes flared. Storming into the room, he flicked off the gas under the smoking sausage, then yanked the percolator cord from the wall. Coffee continued to pop for a few moments, then subsided weakly.

"Don't tell me what I have to do!" he shouted. "I know what I have to do." He grabbed her by the shoulders and shook her. "I *have* to love you. It's not an obligation, it's a fact, it's a demand, it's a terror."

"Brandon…"

"Shut up," he commanded. He pulled her close, trapping the dishes she held between them before he kissed her. She tasted the desperation, the temper. "Don't tell me you love me in that calm, steady voice." Brand lifted his head only to change the angle of the kiss. His mouth was hard and insistent before it parted from hers. "I need more than that from you, Raven, much more than that." His eyes blazed green into hers. "I'll have more, damn it!"

"Brandon." She was breathless, dizzy, then laughing. This was no dream. "The cup's digging a permanent hole in my chest. Please, let me put the dishes down." He said something fierce about the dishes, but she managed to pull away from him enough to put them on the counter. "Oh, Brandon!" Immediately Raven threw her arms around his neck. "You have more; you have everything. I was afraid—and a fool to be afraid—to tell you how much I love you." She placed her hands on his cheeks, holding his face away from her so that he could read what was in her eyes. "I love you, Brandon."

Quick and urgent, their lips came together. They clung still when he swept her up in his arms. "You'll have to do without your coffee for a while," he told her as she pressed a kiss to the curve of his neck. She only murmured an assent as he began to carry her down the hall.

"Too far," she whispered.

"*Mmm?*"

"The bedroom's much too far away."

Brand turned his head to grin at her. "Too far," he agreed, taking a sharp right into the music room. "Entirely too far." They sank together on a sofa. "How's this?" He slipped his hands beneath the robe to feel her skin.

"We've always worked well together here." Raven laughed into his eyes, running her fingers along the muscles of his shoulders. It was real, she thought triumphantly, kissing him again.

"The secret," Brand decided, then dug his teeth playfully into her neck, "is a strong melody."

"It's nothing without the proper lyric."

"Music doesn't always need words." He switched to the other side of her neck as his hand roamed to her breast.

"No," she agreed, finding that her own hands refused to be still. They journeyed down his back and up again. "But harmony—two strong notes coming together and giving a bit to each other."

"Melding," he murmured. "I'm big on melding." He loosened the belt of her robe.

"Oh, Brandon!" she exclaimed suddenly, remembering. "Mrs. Pengalley…she'll be here soon."

"This should certainly clinch her opinion of show people," he decided as his mouth found her breast.

"Oh, no, Brandon, stop!" She laughed and moaned and struggled.

"Can't," he said reasonably, trailing his lips back up to her throat. "Savage lust," he explained and bit her ear. "Uncontrollable. Besides," he said as he kissed her, then moved to her other ear, "it's Sunday, her day off."

"It is?" Raven's mind was too clouded to recall trivial things like days of the week. "Savage lust?" she repeated as he pushed the robe from her shoulders. "Really?"

"Absolutely. Shall I show you?"

"Oh, yes," she whispered and brought his mouth back to hers. "Please do."

A long time later Raven sat on the hearth rug and watched Brand stir up the fire. She had reheated the coffee and brought it in along with the sausages. Brand had pulled a sweater on with his jeans, but she still wore the short, terry robe. Holding a coffee cup in both hands, she yawned and thought that she had never felt so relaxed. She felt like a cat sitting in her square of sunlight, watching Brand fix a log onto snapping flames. He turned to find her smiling at him.

"What are you thinking?" He stretched out on the floor beside her.

"How happy I am." She handed him his coffee, leaning over to kiss him as he took it. It all seemed so simple, so right.

"How happy?" he demanded. He smiled at her over the rim of the cup.

"Oh, somewhere between ecstatic and delirious, I think." She sought his hand with hers. Their fingers linked. "Border-ing on rapturous."

"Just bordering on?" Brand asked with a sigh. "Well, we'll work on it." He shook his head, then kissed her hand. "Do you know you nearly drove me mad in this room yesterday?"

"Yesterday?" Raven tossed her hair back over her shoulder with a jerk of her head. "What are you talking about?"

"I don't suppose you'll ever realize just how arousing your voice is," he mused as he sipped his coffee and studied her face. "That might be part of the reason—that touch of innocence with a hell-smoked voice."

"I like that." Raven reached behind her to set down her empty cup. The movement loosened the tie of her robe, leaving it open to brush the curve of her breasts. "Do you want one of these sausages? They're probably awful."

Brand lifted his eyes from the smooth expanse of flesh that the shift of material had revealed. He shook his head again and laughed. "You make them sound irresistible."

"A starving man can't be picky," she pointed out. Raven plucked one with her fingers and handed it over. "They're probably greasy."

He lifted a brow at this but took a bite. "Aren't you going to have one?"

"No. I know better than to eat my own cooking." She handed him a napkin.

"We could go out to eat."

"Use your imagination," she suggested, resting her hands on her knees. "Pretend you've already eaten. It always works for me."

"My imagination isn't as good as yours." Brand finished off the sausage. "Maybe if you tell me what I've had."

"An enormous heap of scrambled eggs," she decided, narrowing her eyes. "Five or six, at least. You really should watch your cholesterol. And three pieces of toast with that dreadful marmalade you pile on."

"You haven't tried it," he reminded her.

"I imagined I did," she explained patiently. "You also had five slices of bacon." She put a bit of censure in her voice, and he grinned.

"I've a healthy morning appetite."

"I don't see how you could eat another bite after all that. Coffee?" Raven reached for the pot.

"No, I imagine I've had enough."

She laughed and leaning over, linked her arms around his

neck. "Did I really drive you mad, Brandon?" She found the taste of her own power delicious and sweet.

"Yes." He rubbed her nose with his. "First it was all but impossible to simply be in the same room with you, wanting you as I did. Then that song." He gave a quiet laugh, then drew back to look at her. "Music doesn't always soothe the savage beast. And then that damn album jacket. I had to be furious, or I'd have thrown you down on the rug then and there."

He saw puzzlement, then comprehension, dawn in her eyes. "Is that why you…" She stopped, and the smile grew slowly. Raven tilted her head and ran the tip of her tongue over her teeth. "I suppose that now that you've had your way with me, I won't drive you mad anymore."

"That's right." He kissed her lightly. "I can take you or leave you." Brand set down his empty cup, then ruffled her hair, amused by her wry expression. "It's noon," he said with a glance at the clock. "We'd best get to it if we're going to get any work done today. That novelty number we were toying with, the one for the second female lead—I'd an idea for that."

"Really?" Raven unhooked her hands from behind his neck. "What sort of idea?"

"We might bounce up the beat, a bit of early forties jive tempo, you know. It'd be a good contrast to the rest of the score."

"*Hmmm,* could be a good dance number." Raven slipped her hands under his sweater and ran them up his naked chest. She smiled gently at the look of surprise that flickered in his eyes. "We need a good dance number there."

"That's what I was thinking," Brand murmured. The move had surprised him, and the light touch of her fingers sent a dull thud of desire hammering in his stomach. He reached for her, but she rose and moved to the piano.

"Like this, then?" Raven played a few bars of the melody they had worked with, using the tempo he had suggested. "A little boogie-woogie?"

"Yes." He forced his attention to the bouncing, repetitive beat but found his blood beating with it. "That's the idea."

She looked back over her shoulder and smiled at him. "Then all we need are the lyrics." She experimented a moment longer, then went to the coffeepot. "Cute and catchy." Raven drank, smiling down at Brand. "With a chorus."

"Any ideas?"

"Yes." She set down the cup. "I have some ideas." Raven sat down beside him, facing him, and thoughtfully brushed the hair back from his forehead. "If they're going to cast Carly, as it appears they're going to do, we need something to suit that baby-doll voice of hers. Her songs should be a direct foil for Lauren's." She pressed her lips lightly to his ear. "Of course, the chorus could carry the meat of it." Again she slipped a hand under his sweater, letting her fingertips toy with the soft mat of hair on his chest. She slid her eyes up to his. "What do you think?"

Brand took her arm and pulled her against him, but she turned her head so that the kiss only brushed her cheek. "Raven," he said after a laughing moan. But when she trailed her finger down to his stomach, she felt him suck in air. Again he moaned her name and crushed her against him.

Raven tilted her head back for the kiss. It was deep and desperate, but when he would have urged her down, she shifted so that her body covered his. She buried her mouth at his neck and felt the pulse hammering against her lips. Her hands were still under his sweater so that she was aware of the heating of his skin. He tugged at her robe, but she only pressed harder against him, lodging the fabric between them. She nipped at the cord of his neck.

"Raven." His voice was low and husky. "For God's sake, let me touch you."

"Am I driving you mad, Brandon?" she murmured, nearly delirious with her own power. Before he could answer, she brought her lips to his and took her tongue deep into his mouth. Slowly she hiked up his sweater, feeling the shudders of his skin as she worked it over his chest and shoulders. Even as she tossed it aside, Raven began journeying down his chest, using her lips and tongue to taste him.

It was a new sensation for her: the knowledge that he was as vulnerable to her as she was to him. There was harmony between them and the mutual need to make the music real and full. Before, he had guided her, but now she was ready to experiment with her own skill. She wanted to toy with tempos, to take the lead. She wanted to flow *pianissimo,* savoring each touch, each taste. Now it was her turn to teach him as he had taught her.

His skin was hot under her tongue. He was moving beneath her, but the first wave of desperation had passed into a drugged pleasure. Her fingers weren't shy but rather sought curiously, stroking over him to find what excited, what pleased. His taste was something she knew now she would starve without. She could feel his fingers in her hair tightening as his passion built. As she had the night before, she sensed his control, but now the challenge of breaking it excited her.

His stomach was taut and tightened further when she glided over it. She heard his breathing catch. Finding the snap to his jeans, she undid it, then began to tug them down over his hips. The rhythm was gathering speed.

Then her mouth was on his, ripping them both far beyond the gentle pace she had initiated. She was suddenly starving, trembling with the need. Pushing herself up, Raven let the robe fall from her shoulders. Her hair tumbled forward to drape her breasts.

"Touch me." Her eyes were heavy but locked in his. "Touch me now."

Brand's fingers tangled in her hair as they sought her flesh. When she would have swayed back down to him, he held her upright, wanting to watch the pleasure and passion on her face. Her eyes were blurred with it. The need built fast and was soon too great.

"Raven." There was desperate demand in his voice as he took her hips.

She let him guide her, then gave a sharp gasp of pleasure. Their bodies fused in a soaring rhythm, completely tuned to each other. Raven shuddered from the impact. Then, drained, she lowered herself until she lay prone on him. He brought his arms around her to hold her close as the two of them flowed from passion to contentment.

Tangled with him, fresh from loving in a room quiet and warm, Raven gave a long, contented sigh. "Brandon," she murmured, just wanting to hear the sound of his name.

"Hmm?" He stroked her hair, seemingly lost somewhere in a world between sleep and wakefulness.

"I never knew it could be like this."

"Neither did I."

Raven shifted until she could look at his face. "But you've been with so many women." She curled up at his side, preparing to rest her head in the curve of his shoulder.

Brand rose on his elbow, then tilted her face up to his. He

studied her softly flushed cheeks, the swollen mouth and drowsy eyes. "I've never been in love with my lover before," he told her quietly.

For a moment there was silence. Then she smiled. "I'm glad. I suppose I've never been sure of that until now."

"Be sure of it." He kissed her, hard and quick and possessively.

She settled against him again but shivered, then laughed. "A few moments ago I'd have sworn I'd never be cold again."

Grinning, Brand reached for her robe. "I seriously doubt we'll get any work done unless you get dressed. In fact, I'd suggest unattractive clothes."

After tugging her arms through the sleeves, Raven put her hands on his shoulders. Her eyes were light and full of mischief. "Do I distract you, Brandon?"

"You might put it that way."

"I'll probably be tempted to try all the time, now that I know I can." Raven kissed him, then gave a quick shrug. "I won't be able to help myself."

"I'll hold you to that." Brand lifted a brow. "Would you like to start now?"

She gave his hair a sharp tug. "I don't think that's very flattering. I'm going to go see about those unattractive clothes."

"Later," he said, pulling her back when she started to rise.

Raven laughed again, amazed with what she saw in his eyes. "Brandon, really!"

"Later," he said again and pressed her back gently to the floor.

12

Summer came to Cornwall in stages. Cool mornings turned to warm afternoons that had bees humming outside the front windows. The stinging chill of the nights mellowed. The first scent of honeysuckle teased the air. Then the roses, lush wild roses, began to bloom. And all through the weeks the countryside blossomed, Raven felt that she, too, was blooming. She was loved.

Throughout her life, if anyone had asked her what one thing she wanted most, Raven would have answered, "To be loved." She had starved for it as a child, had hungered as an adolescent when she had been shuffled from town to town, never given the opportunity to form lasting friendships and affections. It was this need, in part, that had made her so successful as a performer. Raven was willing to let the audience love her. She never felt herself beyond their reach when she stood in the spotlight. And they knew it. The love she had gained from her audiences had filled an enormous need. It had filled her but had not satisfied her as much, she discovered, as Brand's love.

As the weeks passed, she forgot the demands and responsibilities of the performer and became more and more in tune with the woman. She had always known herself; it had been important early that she grasp an identity. But for the first time in her life Raven focused on her womanhood. She explored it, discovered it, enjoyed it.

Brand was demanding as a lover, not only in the physical sense but in an emotional one as well. He wanted her body, her heart, her thoughts, with no reservations. His need for an absolute commitment was the only shadow in the summery passing of days. Raven found it impossible not to hold parts of herself in reserve. She'd been hurt and knew how devastating pain could be when you loved without guard. Her mother had broken her heart too many times to count, with always a promise of happiness after the severest blow. Raven had learned to cope with that, to guard against it to some extent.

She had loved Brand before, naively perhaps, but totally. When he had walked out of her life, Raven had thought she would never be whole again. For five years she had insulated herself against the men who had touched her life. They could be friends—loving friends—but never lovers. The wounds had healed, but the scar had been a constant reminder to be careful. She had promised herself that no man would ever hurt her as Brand Carstairs had. And Raven discovered the vow she had made still held true. He was the only man who would ever have the power to hurt her. That realization was enough to both exhilarate and frighten.

There was no doubt that he had awakened her physically. Her fears had been swept away by the tides of love. Raven found that in this aspect of their relationship she could indeed give herself to Brand unreservedly. Knowing she could arouse him strengthened her growing confidence as a woman. She learned her passions were as strong and sensitive as his. She had kept them restricted far too long. If Brand could heat her blood with a look, Raven was aware he was just as susceptible to her. There was nothing of the cool, British reserve in his lovemaking; she thought of him as all Irish then, stormy and passionate.

One morning he woke her at dawn by strewing the bed with wild rosebuds. The following evening he surprised her with iced champagne while she bathed in the ancient footed tub. At night he could be brutally passionate, waking and taking her with a desperate urgency that allowed no time for surprise, protest or response. At times he appeared deliriously happy; at others she would catch him studying her with an odd, searching expression.

Raven loved him, but she could not yet bring herself to trust him completely. They both knew it, and they both avoided speaking of it.

Seated next to Brand at the piano, Raven experimented with chords for the opening bars of a duet. "I really think a minor mode with a raised seventh." She frowned thoughtfully. "I imagine a lot of strings here, a big orchestration of violins and cellos." She played more, hearing the imagined arrangement rather than the solitary piano. "What do you think?" Raven turned her head to find Brand looking down at her.

"Go ahead," he suggested, drawing on a cigarette. "Play the lot."

She began, only to have him interrupt during a bridge. "No." He shook his head. "That part doesn't fit."

"That was your part," she reminded him with a grin.

"Genius is obliged to correct itself," he returned, and Raven gave an unladylike snort. He looked down his very straight British nose. "Had you a comment, then?"

"Who, me? I never interrupt genius."

"Wise," he said and turned back to spread his own fingers over the keys. "Like this." Brand played the same melody from the beginning, only altering a few notes on the bridge section.

"Did you change something?"

"I realize your inferior ear might not detect the subtlety," he began. She jammed her elbow into his ribs. "Well said," he murmured, rubbing the spot. "Shall we try again?"

"I love it when you're dignified, Brandon."

"Really?" He lifted an inquiring brow. "Now, where was I?"

"You were about to demonstrate the first movement from Tchaikovsky's Second Symphony."

"Ah." Nodding, Brand turned back to the keys. He ran through the difficult movement with a fluid skill that had Raven shaking her head.

"Show-off," she accused when he finished with a flourish.

"You're just jealous."

With a sigh she lifted her shoulders. "Unfortunately, you're right."

Brand laughed and put his hand palm to palm with hers. "I have the advantage in spread."

Raven studied her small, narrow-boned hand. "It's a good thing I didn't want to be a concert pianist."

"Beautiful hands," Brand told her, making one of his sudden and completely natural romantic gestures by lifting her fingers to his lips. "I'm quite helplessly in love with them."

"Brandon." Disarmed, Raven could only look at him. A tremble of warmth shot up her spine.

"They always smell of that lotion you have in the little white pot on the dresser."

"I didn't think you'd notice something like that." She shivered in response when his lips brushed the inside of her wrist.

"There's nothing about you I don't notice." He kissed her other wrist. "You like your bath too hot, and you leave your shoes in the most unexpected places. And you always keep time with your left foot." Brand looked back up at her, keeping one hand entwined with hers while he reached up with the other to brush the hair from her shoulder. "And when I touch you like this, your eyes go to smoke." He ran a fingertip gently over the point of her breast and watched her irises darken and cloud. Very slowly he leaned over and touched his lips to hers. Lazily he ran his finger back and forth until her nipple was taut and straining against the fabric of her blouse.

Her mouth was soft and opened willingly. Raven tilted her head back, inviting him to take more. Currents of pleasure were already racing along her skin. Brand drew her closer, one hand lingering at her breast.

"I can feel your bones melt," he murmured. His mouth grew hungrier, his hand more insistent. "It drives me crazy." His fingers drifted from her breast to the top button of her blouse. Even as he loosened it, the phone shrilled from the table across the room. He swore, and Raven gave a laugh and hugged him.

"Never mind, love," she said on a deep breath. "I'll remind you where you left off this time, too." Slipping out of his arms, she crossed the room to answer. "Hello."

"Hello, I'd like to speak with Brandon Carstairs, please," a voice said.

Raven smiled at the musical lilt in the voice and wondered vaguely how one of Brand's fans had gotten access to his number. "Mr. Carstairs is quite busy at the moment." She grinned over at him and got both a grin and a nod of approval before he crossed to her. He began to distract her by kissing her neck.

"Would you ask him to call his mother when he's free?"

"I beg your pardon?" Raven stifled a giggle and tried to struggle out of Brand's arms.

"His mother, dear," the voice repeated. "Ask him to call his mother when he has a minute, won't you? He has the number."

"Oh, please, Mrs. Carstairs, wait! I'm sorry." Wide-eyed, she looked up at Brand. "Brandon's right here. Your mother," Raven said in a horrified whisper that had him grinning again. Still holding her firmly to his side, he accepted the receiver.

"Hullo, Mum." Brand kissed the top of Raven's head, then chuckled. "Yes, I was busy. I was kissing a beautiful woman I'm madly in love with." The color rising in Raven's cheeks had him laughing. "No, no, it's all right, love, I intend to get back to it. How are you? And the rest?"

Raven nudged herself free of Brand's arm. "I'll make some tea," she said quietly, then slipped from the room.

Mrs. Pengalley had left the kitchen spotlessly clean, and Raven spent some time puttering around it aimlessly while the kettle heated on the stove. She found herself suddenly hungry, then remembered that she and Brand had worked straight through lunch. She got out the bread, deciding to make buttered toast fingers to serve with the tea.

Afternoon tea was one of Brand's rituals, and Raven had grown fond of it. She enjoyed the late afternoon breaks in front of the fireplace with tea and biscuits or scones or buttered toast. They could be any two people then, Raven mused, two people sitting in front of a fireplace having unimportant conversations. The kettle sang out, and she moved to switch off the flame.

Raven went about the mechanical domestic tasks of brewing

tea and buttering toast, but her thoughts kept drifting back to
Brand. There had been such effortless affection in his voice
when he had spoken to his mother, such relaxed love. And
Raven had felt a swift flash of envy. It was something she had
experienced throughout childhood and adolescence, but she
hadn't expected to feel it again. Raven reminded herself she
was twenty-five and no longer a child.

The chores soothed her. She loaded the tray and started back
down the hall with her feelings more settled. When she heard
Brand's voice, she hesitated, not wanting to interrupt his conversation. But the weight of the tray outbalanced her sense of
propriety.

He was sunk into one of the chairs by the fire when Raven
entered. With a smile he gestured her over so that she crossed
the room and set the tray on the table beside him. "I will,
Mum, perhaps next month. Give everyone my love." He
paused and smiled again, taking Raven's hand. "She's got big
gray eyes, the same color as the dove Shawn kept in the coop
on the roof. Yes, I'll tell her. Bye, Mum. I love you."

Hanging up, Brand glanced at the ladened tea tray, then up
at Raven. "You've been busy."

She crouched down and began pouring. "I discovered I was
starving." She watched with the usual shake of her head as he
added milk to his tea. That was one English habit Raven knew
she would never comprehend. She took her own plain.

"My mother says to tell you you've a lovely voice over the
phone." Brand picked up a toast finger and bit into it.

"You didn't have to tell her you'd been kissing me," Raven
mumbled, faintly embarrassed. Brand laughed, and she glared
at him.

"Mum knows I have a habit of kissing women," he explained gravely. "She probably knows I've occasionally done a bit more than that, but we haven't discussed that particular aspect of my life for some time." He took another bite of toast, studying Raven's face. "She wants to meet you. If the score keeps going along at this pace, I thought we might drive up to London next month."

"I'm not used to families, Brandon," she said. Raven reached for her cup, but he placed his hand over hers, waiting until she looked back up at him.

"They're easy people, Raven. They're important to me. You're important to me. I want them to know you."

She felt her stomach tighten, and lowered her eyes.

"Raven." Brand gave a short, exasperated sigh. "When are you going to talk to me?"

She couldn't pretend not to understand him. She could only shake her head and avoid the subject a little while longer. The time when they would have to return to California and face reality would come soon enough. "Please, tell me about your family. It might help me get used to being confronted with all of them if I know a bit more than I've read in the gossip columns." Raven smiled. Her eyes asked him to smile back and not to probe. Not yet.

Brand struggled with a sense of frustration but gave in. He could give her a little more time. "I'm the oldest of five." He gestured toward the mantel. "Michael's the distinguished-looking one with the pretty blond wife. He's a solicitor." Brand smiled, remembering the pleasure it had given him to send his brother to a good university. He'd been the first Carstairs to receive that sort of education. "There was nothing distinguished about him at all as a boy," Brand remarked. "He liked to give anyone within reach a bloody nose."

"Sounds like a good lawyer," Raven observed dryly. "Please go on."

"Alison's next. She graduated from Oxford at the top of her class." He watched Raven glance up at the photo of the fragile, lovely blonde. "An amazing brain," Brand continued, smiling. "She does something incomprehensible with computers and has a particular fondness for rowdy rugby matches. That's where she met her husband."

Raven shook her head, trying to imagine the delicate-looking woman shouting at rugby games or programming sophisticated computers. "I suppose your other brother's a physicist."

"No, Shawn's a veterinarian." Affection slipped into Brand's voice.

"Your favorite?"

He tilted his head as he reached for more tea. "If one has a favorite among brothers and sisters, I suppose so. He's simply one of the nicest people I know. He's incapable of hurting anyone. As a boy he was the one who always found the bird with the broken wing or the dog with a sore paw. You know the type."

Raven didn't, but she murmured something and continued to sip at her tea. Brand's family was beginning to fascinate her. Somehow, she had thought that people raised in the same house under the same circumstances would be more the same. These people seemed remarkably diverse. "And your other sister?"

"Moray." He grinned. "She's in school yet, claims she's going into finance or drama. Or perhaps," he added, "anthropology. She's undecided."

"How old is she?"

"Eighteen. She thinks your records are smashing, by the way, and had them all the last time I was home."

"I believe I'll like her," Raven decided. She let her gaze sweep the mantel again. "Your parents must be very proud of all of you. What does your father do?"

"He's a carpenter." Brand wondered if she was aware of the wistful look in her eyes. "He still works six days a week, even though he knows money isn't a problem anymore. He has a great deal of pride." He paused a moment, stirring his tea, his eyes on Raven. "Mum still hangs sheets out on a line, even though I bought her a perfectly good dryer ten years ago. That's the sort of people they are."

"You're very lucky," Raven told him and rose to wander about the room.

"Yes, I know that." Brand watched her move around the room with her quick, nervous stride. "Though I doubt I thought a great deal about it while I was growing up. It's very easy to take it all for granted. It must have been very difficult for you."

Raven lifted her shoulders, then let them fall. "I survived." Walking to the window, she looked out on the cliffs and the sea. "Let's go for a walk, Brandon. It's so lovely out."

He rose and walked to her. Taking her by the shoulders, Brand turned her around to face him. "There's more to life than surviving, Raven."

"I survived intact," she told him. "Not everyone does."

"Raven, I know you call home twice a week, but you never tell me anything about it." He gave her a quick, caring shake. "Talk to me."

"Not about that, not now, not here." She slipped her arms around him and pressed her cheek to his chest. "I don't want anything to touch us here—nothing from the past, nothing from tomorrow. Oh, there's so much ugliness, Brandon, so many responsibilities. I want time. Is that so wrong?" She held him tighter, suddenly possessive. "Can't this be our fantasy, Brandon? That there isn't anybody but us? Just for a little while."

She heard him sigh as his lips brushed the crown of her head. "For a little while, Raven. But fantasies have to end, and I want the reality, too."

Raven lifted her face, then framed his with her hands. "Like Joe in the script," she reflected and smiled. "He finds his reality in the end, doesn't he?"

"Yes." Brand bent to kiss her and found himself lingering over it longer than he had intended. "Proving dreams come true," he murmured.

"But I'm not a dream, Brandon." She took both of his hands in hers while her eyes smiled at him. "And you've already brought me to life."

"And without magic."

Raven lifted a brow. "That depends on your point of view," she countered. "I still feel the magic." Slowly she lifted his hand to the neckline of her blouse. "I think you were here when we left off."

"So I was." He loosened the next button, watching her face. "What about that walk?"

"Walk? In all that rain?" Raven glanced over to the sun-filled window. "No." Shaking her head, she looked back at Brand. "I think we'd better stay inside until it blows over."

He ran his finger down to the next button, smiling at her while he toyed with it. "You're probably right."

13

Mrs. Pengalley made it a point to clean the music room first whenever Raven and Brand left her alone in the house. It was here they spent all their time working—if what show people did could be considered work. She had her own opinion on that. She gathered up the cups, as she always did, and sniffed them. Tea. Now and again she had sniffed wine and occasionally some bourbon, but she was forced to admit that Mr. Carstairs didn't seem to live up to the reputation of heavy drinking that show people had. Mrs. Pengalley was the smallest bit disappointed.

They lived quietly, too. She had been sure when Brand had notified her to expect him to be in residence for three months that he would have plans to entertain. Mrs. Pengalley knew what sort of entertainment show business people went in for. She had waited for the fancy cars to start arriving, the fancy people in their outrageous clothes. She had told Mr. Pengalley it was just a matter of time.

But no one had come, no one at all. There had been no disgraceful parties to clean up after. There had only been Mr. Carstairs and the young girl with the big gray eyes who sang as pretty as you please. But of course, Mrs. Pengalley reminded herself, she was in *that* business, too.

Mrs. Pengalley walked over to shake the wrinkles from the drapes at the side window. From there she could see Raven and Brand walking along the cliffs. Always in each other's pockets, she mused and sniffed to prevent herself from smiling at them. She snapped the drape back into place and began dusting off the furniture.

And how was a body supposed to give anything a proper dusting, she wanted to know, when they were always leaving their papers with the chicken scratchings on them all over everywhere? Picking up a piece of staff paper, Mrs. Pengalley scowled down at the lines and notes. She couldn't make head nor tail out of the notations, she scanned the words instead.

Loving you is no dream / I need you here to hold on to / Wanting you is everything / Come back to me.

She clucked her tongue and set the paper back down. Fine song, that one, she thought, resuming her dusting. Doesn't even rhyme.

Outside, the wind from the sea was strong, and Brand slipped his arm around Raven's shoulders. Turning her swiftly to face him, he bent her backward and gave her a long, lingering kiss. She gripped his shoulders for balance, then stared at him when his mouth lifted.

"What," she began and let out a shaky breath, "was that for?"

"For Mrs. Pengalley," he answered easily. "She's peeking out the music room window."

"Brandon, you're terrible." His mouth came down to hers again. Her halfhearted protest turned into total response. With a quiet sound of pleasure, Brand deepened the kiss and dragged her closer to him. Raven could feel the heat of the sun on her skin even as the sea breeze cooled it. The wind brought them the scent of honeysuckle and roses.

"That," he murmured as his mouth brushed over her cheeks, "was for me."

"Have any other friends?" Raven asked.

Laughing, Brand gave her a quick hug and released her. "I suppose we've given her enough to cluck her tongue over today."

"So that's what you want me for." Raven tossed her head. "Shock value."

"Among other things."

They wandered to the sea wall, for some moments looking out in comfortable silence. Raven liked the cliffs with their harsh faces and sheer, dizzying drop. She liked the constant, boiling noise of the sea, the screaming of the gulls.

The score was all but completed, with only a few minor loose ends and a bit of polishing to be done. Copies of completed numbers had been sent back to California. Raven knew they were drawing out a job that could be finished quickly. She had her own reasons for procrastinating, though she wasn't wholly certain of Brand's. She didn't want to break the spell.

Raven wasn't sure precisely what Brand wanted from her because she hadn't permitted him to tell her yet. There were things, she knew, that had to be settled between them—things that could be avoided for the time being while they both simply let themselves be consumed by love. But the time would come when they would have to deal with the everyday business of living.

Would their work be a problem? That was one of the questions Raven refused to ask herself. Or if she asked it, she refused to answer. Commitments went with their profession, time-consuming commitments that made it difficult to establish any sort of a normal life. And there was so little privacy. Every detail of their relationship would be explored in the press. There would be pictures and stories, true and fabricated. The worst kind, Raven mused, were those with a bit of both. All of this, she realized, could be handled with hard work and determination if the love was strong enough. She had no doubt theirs was, but she had other doubts.

Would she ever be able to rid herself of the nagging fear that he might leave her again? The memory of the hurt kept her from giving herself to Brand completely. And her feelings of responsibility to her mother created yet another barrier. This was something she had always refused to share with anyone. She couldn't even bring herself to share it with the person she cared for most in the world. Years before, she had made a decision to control her own life, promising herself she would never depend too heavily on anything or anyone. Too often she had watched her mother relinquish control and lose.

If she could have found a way, Raven would have prolonged the summer. But more and more, the knowledge that the idyll was nearly at an end intruded into her thoughts. The prelude to fantasy was over. She hoped the fantasy would become a reality.

Brand watched Raven's face as she leaned her elbows on the rough stone wall and looked out to sea. There was a faraway look in her eyes that bothered him. He wanted to reach her, but their time alone together was slipping by rapidly. A cloud slid across the sun for a moment, and the light shifted and dimmed. He heard Raven sigh.

"What are you thinking?" he demanded, catching her flying hair in his hand.

"That of all the places I've ever been, this is the best." Raven tilted her head to smile up at him but didn't alter her position against the wall. "Julie and I took a break in Monaco once, and I was sure it was the most beautiful spot on earth. Now I know it's the second."

"I knew you'd love it if I could ever get you here," Brand mused, still toying with the ends of her hair. "I had some bad moments thinking you'd refuse. I'm not at all sure I could have come up with an alternate plan."

"Plan?" Raven's forehead puckered over the word. "I don't know what you mean. What plan?"

"To get you here, where we could be alone."

Raven straightened away from the wall but continued looking out to sea. "I thought we came here to write a score."

"Yes." Brand watched the flight of a bird as it swooped down over the waves. "The timing of that was rather handy."

"Handy?" Raven felt the knot start in her stomach. The clouds shifted over the sun again.

"I doubt you'd have agreed to work with me again if the project hadn't been so tempting," he said. Brand frowned up at a passing cloud. "You certainly wouldn't have agreed to live with me."

"So you dangled the score in front of my nose like a meaty bone?"

"Of course not. I wanted to work with you on the project the moment it was offered to me. It was all just a matter of timing, really."

"Timing and planning," she said softly. "Like a chess game. Julie's right; I've never been any good at strategy." Raven turned away, but Brand caught her arm before she could retreat.

"Raven?"

"How could you?" She whirled back to face him. Her eyes were dark and hot, her cheeks flushed with fury. Brand narrowed his eyes and studied her.

"How could I what?" he asked coolly, releasing her arm.

"How could you use the score to trick me into coming here?" She dragged at her hair as the wind blew it into her face.

"I'd have used anything to get you back," Brand said. "And I didn't trick you, Raven. I told you nothing but the truth."

"Part of the truth," she continued.

"Perhaps," he agreed. "We're both rather good at that, aren't we?" He didn't touch her, but the look he gave her became more direct. "Why are you angry? Because I love you or because I made you realize you love me?"

"Nobody *makes* me do anything!" She balled her hands into fists as she whirled away. "Oh, I detest being maneuvered. I run my own life, make my own decisions."

"I don't believe I've made any for you."

"No, you just led me gently along by the nose until I *chose* what was best for myself." Raven turned back again, and now her voice was low and vibrant with anger. "Why couldn't you have been honest with me?"

"You wouldn't have let me anywhere near you if I'd been completely honest. I had experience with you before, remember?"

Raven's eyes blazed. "Don't tell me what I would've done, Brandon. You're not inside my head."

"No, you've never let me in there." He pulled out a cigarette, cupped his hands around a match and lit it. Before speaking, he took a long, contemplative drag. "We'll say I wasn't in the mood to be taking chances, then. Will that suit you?"

His cool, careless tone fanned her fury. "You had no right!"

she tossed at him. "You had no right to arrange my life this way. Who said I had to play by your rules, Brandon? When did you decide I was incapable of planning for myself?"

"If you'd like to be treated as a rational adult, perhaps you should behave as one," he suggested in a deceptively mild tone. "At the moment I'd say you're being remarkably childish. I didn't bring you here under false pretenses, Raven. There was a score to be written, and this was a quiet place to do it. It was also a place I felt you'd have the chance to get used to being with me again. I wanted you back."

"*You* felt. *You* wanted!" Raven tossed back her hair. "How incredibly selfish! What about *my* feelings? Do you think you can just pop in and out of my life at your convenience?"

"As I remember, I was pushed out."

"You left me!" The tears came from nowhere and blinded her. "Nothing's ever hurt me like that before. Nothing!" Tears of hurt sprang to her eyes. "I'll be damned if you'll do it to me again. You went away without a word!"

"You mightn't have liked the words I wanted to say." Brand tossed the stub of his cigarette over the wall. "You weren't the only one who was hurt that night. How the hell else could I be rational unless I put some distance between us? I couldn't have given you the time you seemed to need if I'd stayed anywhere near you."

"Time?" Raven repeated as thoughts trembled and raced through her mind. "You gave me time?"

"You were a child when I left," he said shortly. "I'd hoped you'd be a woman when I came back."

"You had hoped…" Her voice trailed off into an astonished whisper. "Are you telling me you stayed away, giving me a chance to—to grow up?"

"I didn't see I had any choice." Brand dug his hands into his pockets as his brows came together.

"Didn't you?" She remembered her despair at his going, the emptiness of the years. "And of course, why should you have given me one? You simply took it upon yourself to decide for me."

"It wasn't a matter of deciding." He turned away from her, knowing he was losing his grip on his temper. "It was a matter of keeping sane. I simply couldn't stay near you and not have you."

"So you stayed away for five years, then suddenly reappeared, using my music as an excuse to lure me into bed. You didn't give a damn about the quality of *Fantasy*. You just used it—and the talent and sweat of the performers—for your own selfish ends."

"That," he said in a deadly calm voice, "is beyond contempt." Turning, he walked away. Within moments Raven heard the roar of an engine over the sound of the sea.

She stood, watching the car speed down the lane. If she had meant to deal a savage blow, she had succeeded. The shock of her own words burned in her throat. She shut her eyes tightly.

Even with her eyes closed, she could see clearly the look of fury on Brand's face before he had walked away. Raven ran a shaking hand through her hair. Her head was throbbing with the aftereffects of temper. Slowly she opened her eyes and stared out at the choppy green sea.

Everything we've had these past weeks was all part of some master plan, she thought. Even as she stood, the anger drained out of her, leaving only the weight of unhappiness.

She resented the fact that Brand had secretly placed a hand on the reins of her life, resented that he had offered her the

NORA ROBERTS

biggest opportunity in her career as a step in drawing her to him. And yet… Raven shook her head in frustration. Confused and miserable, she turned to walk back to the house.

Mrs. Pengalley met her at the music room door. "There's a call for you, miss, from California." She had watched the argument from the window with a healthy curiosity. Now, however, the look in the gray eyes set her maternal instincts quivering. She repressed an urge to smooth down Raven's hair. "I'll make you some tea," she said.

Raven walked to the phone and lifted the receiver. "Yes, hello."

"Raven, it's Julie."

"Julie." Raven sank down in a chair. She blinked back fresh tears at the sound of the familiar voice. "Back from the isles of Greece?"

"I've been back for a couple weeks, Raven."

Of course. She should have known that. "Yes, all right. What's happened?"

"Karter contacted me because he wasn't able to reach you this morning. Some trouble on the line or something."

"Has she left again?" Raven's voice was dull.

"Apparently she left last night. She didn't go very far." Hearing the hesitation in Julie's voice, Raven felt the usual tired acceptance sharpen into apprehension.

"Julie?" Words dried up, and she waited.

"There was an accident, Raven. You'd better come home." Raven closed her eyes. "Is she dead?"

"No, but it's not good, Raven. I hate having to tell you over the phone this way. The housekeeper said Brand wasn't there."

"No." Raven opened her eyes and looked vaguely around the room. "No, Brandon isn't here." She managed to snap herself back. "How bad, Julie? Is she in the hospital?"

Julie hesitated again, then spoke quietly. "She's not going to make it, Raven. I'm sorry. Karter says hours at best."

"Oh, God." Raven had lived with the fear all her life, yet it still came as a shock. She looked around the room again a little desperately, trying to orient herself.

"I know there's no good way to tell you this, Raven, but I wish I could find a better one."

"What?" She brought herself back again with an enormous effort. "No, I'm all right. I'll leave right away."

"Shall I meet you and Brand at the airport?"

The question drifted through Raven's mind. "No. No, I'll go straight to the hospital. Where is she?"

"St. Catherine's, intensive care."

"Tell Dr. Karter I'll be there as soon as I can. Julie…"

"Yes?"

"Stay with her."

"Of course I will. I'll be here."

Raven hung up and sat staring at the silent phone.

Mrs. Pengalley came back into the room carrying a cup of tea. She took one look at Raven's white face and set it aside. Without speaking, she went to the liquor cabinet and took out the brandy. After pouring out two fingers, she pressed the snifter on Raven.

"Here now, miss, you drink this." The Cornish burr was brisk. Raven's eyes shifted to her. "What?"

"Drink up, there's a girl."

She obeyed as Mrs. Pengalley lifted the glass to her lips. Instantly Raven sucked in her breath at the unexpected strength of the liquor. She took another sip, then let out a shaky sigh.

"Thank you." She lifted her eyes to Mrs. Pengalley again. "That's better."

"Brandy has its uses," the housekeeper said righteously.

Raven rose, trying to put her thoughts in order. There were things to be done and no time to do them. "Mrs. Pengalley, I have to go back to America right away. Could you pack some things for me while I call the airport?"

"Aye." She studied Raven shrewdly. "He's gone off to cool his heels, you know. They all do that. But he'll be back soon enough."

Realizing Mrs. Pengalley spoke of Brand, Raven dragged a hand through her hair. "I'm not altogether certain of that. If Brandon's not back by the time I have to go to the airport, would you ask Mr. Pengalley to drive me? I know it's an inconvenience, but it's terribly important."

"If that's what you want." Mrs. Pengalley sniffed. Young people, she thought, always flying off the handle. "I'll pack your things, then."

"Thank you." Raven glanced around the music room, then picked up the phone.

An hour later she hesitated at the foot of the stairs. Everything seemed to have happened at once. She willed Brand to return, but there was no sign of his car in the driveway. Raven struggled over writing a note but could think of nothing to say on paper that could make up for the words she had thrown at him. And how could she say in a few brief lines that her mother was dying and she had to go to her?

Yet there wasn't time to wait until he returned. She knew she couldn't risk it. Frantically she pulled a note pad from her purse. "Brandon," she wrote quickly, "I had to go. I'm needed at home. Please, forgive me. I love you, Raven."

Dashing back into the music room, she propped the note against the sheet of staff paper on top of the pile on the piano.

Then, hurrying from the room, she grabbed her suitcases and ran outside. Mr. Pengalley was waiting in his serviceable sedan to drive her to the airport.

14

Five days passed before Raven began thinking clearly again. Karter had been right about there only being a matter of hours. Raven had had to deal not only with grief but also with an unreasonable guilt that she hadn't been in time. The demand of details saved her from giving in to the urge to sink into self-pity and self-rebuke. She wondered once, during those first crushing hours, if that was why people tied so many traditions and complications to death: to keep from falling into total despair.

She was grateful that Karter handled the police himself in a way that ensured the details would be kept out of the papers.

After the first busy days there was nothing left but to accept that the woman she had loved and despised was gone. There was no more she could do. The disease had beaten them, just as surely as if it had been a cancer. Gradually she began to accept her mother's death as the result of a long, debilitating illness. She didn't cry, knowing she had already mourned, knowing it was time to put away the unhappiness. She had never had control of her mother's life; she needed the strength to maintain control of her own.

A dozen times during those days Raven phoned the house

in Cornwall. There was never an answer. She could almost hear the hollow, echoing sounds of the ring through the empty rooms. More than once she considered simply getting on a plane and going back, but she always pushed the thought aside. He wouldn't be there waiting for her.

Where could he be? she wondered again and again. *Where would he have gone? He hasn't forgiven me.* And worse, she thought again and again, *he'll never forgive me.*

After hanging up the phone a last time, Raven looked at herself in her bedroom mirror. She was pale. The color that had drained from her face five days ago in Cornwall had never completely returned. There was too much of a helpless look about her. Raven shook her head and grabbed her blusher. Borrowed color, she decided, was better than none at all. She had to start somewhere.

Yes, she thought again, still holding the sable brush against her cheek. I've got to start somewhere. Turning away from the mirror, Raven again picked up the phone.

Thirty minutes later she came downstairs wearing a black silk dress. She had twisted her hair up and was setting a plain, stiff-brimmed black hat over it as she stepped into the hall.

"Raven?" Julie came out of the office. "Are you going out?"

"Yes, if I can find that little envelope bag and my car keys. I think they're inside it." She was already poking into the hall closet.

"Are you all right?"

Raven drew her head from the closet and met Julie's look. "I'm better," she answered, knowing Julie wouldn't be satisfied with a clichéd reply. "The lecture you gave me after the funeral, about not blaming myself? I'm trying to put it into practice."

"It wasn't a lecture," Julie countered. "It was simply a state-ment of facts. You did everything you could do to help your mother; you couldn't have done any more."

Raven sighed before she could stop herself. "I did every-thing I knew how to do, and I suppose that's the same thing." She shook off the mood as she shut the closet door. "I *am* better, Julie, and I'm going to be fine." She smiled, then, glimpsing a movement, looked beyond Julie's shoulder. Wayne stepped out of the office. "Hello, Wayne, I didn't know you were here."

He moved past Julie. "Well, I can definitely approve of that dress," he greeted her.

"And so you should," Raven returned dryly. "You charged me enough for it."

"Don't be a philistine, darling. Art has no price." He flicked a finger over the shoulder of the dress. "Where are you off to?"

"Alphonso's. I'm meeting Henderson for lunch."

Wayne touched Raven's cheek with a fingertip. "A bit heavy on the blush," he commented.

"I'm tired of looking pale. Don't fuss." She placed a hand on each of his cheeks, urging him to bend so that she could kiss him. "You've been a rock, Wayne. I haven't told you how much I appreciate your being here the last few days."

"I needed to escape from the office."

"I adore you." She lowered her hands to meet his arms and squeezed briefly. "Now, stop worrying about me." Raven shot a look past his shoulder to Julie. "You, too. I'm meeting Hen-derson to talk over plans for a new tour."

"New tour?" Julie frowned. "Raven, you've been working nonstop for over six months. The album, the tour, the score." She paused. "After all of this you need a break."

"After all this the thing I need least is a break," Raven corrected. "I want to work."

"Then take a sabbatical," Julie insisted. "A few months back you were talking about finding a mountain cabin in Colorado, remember?"

"Yes." Raven smiled and shook her head. "I was going to write and be rustic, wasn't I? Get away from the glitter-glamour and into the woods." Raven grinned, recalling the conversation. "You said something about not being interested in anything more rustic than a margarita at poolside."

Julie lifted a thin, arched brow. "I've changed my mind. I'm going shopping for hiking boots."

Wayne's comment was a dubious *"hmmm."*

Raven smiled. "You're sweet," she said to Julie as she kissed her cheek. "But it isn't necessary. I need to do something that takes energy, physical energy. I'm going to talk to Henderson about a tour of Australia. My records do very well there."

"If you'd just talk to Brand…" Julie began, but Raven cut her off.

"I've tried to reach him; I can't." There was something final and flat in the statement. "Obviously he doesn't want to talk to me. I'm not at all sure I blame him."

"He's in love with you," Wayne said from behind her. Raven turned and met the look. "A few thousand people saw the sparks flying the night of your concert in New York."

"Yes, he loves me, and I love him. It doesn't seem to be enough, and I can't quite figure out why. No, please." She took his hand, pressing it between both of hers. "I have to get my mind off it all for a while. I feel as if I had been having a lovely picnic and got caught in a landslide. The bruises are still a bit sore. I could use some good news," she added, glancing from one of them to the other, "if the two of you are ever going to decide to tell me."

Raven watched as Wayne and Julie exchanged glances. She grinned, enjoying what she saw. "I've been noticing a few sparks myself. Isn't this a rather sudden situation?"

"Very," Wayne agreed, smiling at Julie over Raven's head. "It's only been going on for about six years."

"Six years!" Raven's brows shot up in amazement.

"I didn't choose to be one of a horde," Wayne said mildly, lighting one of his elegant cigarettes.

"And I always thought he was in love with you," Julie stated, letting her gaze drift from Raven to Wayne.

"With *me?*" Raven laughed spontaneously for the first time in days.

"I fail to see the humour in that," Wayne remarked from behind a nimbus of smoke. "I'm considered by many to be rather attractive."

"Oh, you are," she agreed, then giggled and kissed his cheek. "Madly so. But I can't believe anyone could think you were in love with me. You've always dated those rather alarmingly beautiful models with their sculpted faces and long legs."

"I don't think we need bring all that up at the moment," Wayne retorted.

"It's all right." Julie smiled sweetly and tucked her hair behind her ear. "I haven't any problem with Wayne's checkered past."

"When did all this happen, please?" Amused, Raven cut into their exchange. "I turn my back for a few weeks, and I find my two best friends making calf's eyes at each other."

"I've never made calf's eyes at anyone," Wayne remonstrated, horrified. "Smoldering glances, perhaps." He lifted his rakishly scarred brow.

"When?" Raven repeated.

"I looked up from my deck chair the first morning out on the cruise," Julie began, "and who do you suppose is sauntering toward me in a perfectly cut Mediterranean white suit?"

"Really?" Raven eyed Wayne dubiously. "I'm not certain whether I'm surprised or impressed."

"It seemed like a good opportunity," he explained, tapping his expensive ashes into a nearby dish, "if I could corner her before she charmed some shipping tycoon or handy sailor."

"I believe I charmed a shipping tycoon a few years ago," Julie remarked lazily. "And as to the sailor…"

"Nevertheless," Wayne went on, shooting her a glance. "I decided a cruise was a very good place to begin winning her over. It was," he remarked, "remarkably simple."

"Oh?" Julie's left brow arched. "Really?"

Wayne tapped out his cigarette, then moved over to gather her in his arms. "A piece of cake," he added carelessly. "Of course, women habitually find me irresistible."

"It would be safer if they stopped doing so. I might be tempted to wring their necks," Julie cooed, winding her arms around his neck.

"The woman's going to be a trial to live with." Wayne kissed her as though he'd decided to make the best of it.

"I can see you two are going to be perfectly miserable together. I'm so sorry." Walking over, Raven slipped an arm around each of them. "You will let me give you the wedding?" she began, then stopped. "That is, are you having a wedding?"

"Absolutely," Wayne told her. "We don't trust each other enough for anything less encumbering." He gave Julie a flashing grin that inexplicably made Raven want to weep.

Raven hugged them both again fiercely. "I needed to hear

something like this right now. I'm going to leave you alone. I imagine you can entertain yourselves while I'm gone. Can I tell Henderson?" she asked. "Or is it a secret?"

"You can tell him," Julie said, watching as Raven adjusted her hat in the hall mirror. "We're planning on taking the plunge next week."

Raven's eyes darted up to Julie's in the mirror. "My, you two move fast, don't you?"

"When it's right, it's right."

Raven smiled in quick agreement. "Yes, I suppose it is. There's probably champagne in the refrigerator, isn't there, Julie?" She turned away from the mirror. "We can have a celebration drink when I get back. I'll just be a couple of hours."

"Raven." Julie stopped her as she headed for the door. Raven looked curiously over her shoulder. "Your purse." Smiling, Julie retrieved it from a nearby table. "You won't forget to eat, will you?" she demanded as she placed it in Raven's hand.

"I won't forget to eat," Raven assured her, then dashed through the door.

Within the hour Raven was seated in the glassed-in terrace room of Alphonso's toying with a plate of scampi. There were at least a dozen people patronizing the restaurant whom she knew personally. A series of greetings had been exchanged before she had been able to tuck herself into a corner table.

The room was an elaborate jungle, with exotic plants and flowers growing everywhere. The sun shining through the glass and greenery gave the terrace a warmth and glow. The floor was a cool ceramic tile, and there was a constant trickle of water from a fountain at the far end of the room. Raven enjoyed the casual elegance, the wicker accessories and the pungent aromas of food and flowers that filled the place. Now, however, she gave little attention to the terrace room as she spoke with her agent.

Henderson was a big, burly man whom Raven had always thought resembled a logjammer rather than the smooth, savvy agent he was. He had a light red thatch of hair that curled thinly on top of his head and bright merry blue eyes that she knew could sharpen to a sword's point. There was a friendly smattering of freckles over his broad, flat-featured face.

He could smile and look genial and none too bright. It was one of his best weapons. Raven knew Henderson was as sharp as they came, and when necessary, he could be hard as nails. He was fond of her, not only because she made him so rich, but because she never resented having done so. He couldn't say the same about all of his clients.

Now Henderson allowed Raven to ramble on about ideas for a new tour, Australia, New Zealand, promotion for the new album that was already shooting up the charts a week after its release. He ate his veal steadily, washing it down with heavy red wine while Raven talked and sipped occasionally from her glass of white wine.

He noticed she made no mention of the *Fantasy* score or of her time in Cornwall. The last progress report he had received from her had indicated the project was all but completed. The conversations he had had with Jarett had been enthusiastic. Lauren Chase had approved each one of her numbers, and the choreography had begun. The score seemed to be falling into place without a hitch.

So Henderson had been surprised when Raven had returned alone so abruptly from Cornwall. He had expected her to phone him when the score was completed, then to take the week or two she had indicated she and Brand wanted to relax and do nothing. But here she was, back early and without Brand.

She chattered nervously, darting from one topic to another. Henderson didn't interrupt, only now and again making some noncommittal sounds as he attended to his meal. Raven talked nonstop for fifteen minutes, then began to wind down. Henderson waited, then took a long swallow of wine.

"Well, now," he said, patting his lips with a white linen napkin. "I don't imagine there should be any problem setting up an Australian tour." His voice suited his looks.

"Good." Raven pushed the scampi around on her plate. She realized she had talked herself out. Spearing a bit of shrimp, she ate absently.

"While it's being set up, you could take yourself a nice little vacation somewhere."

Raven's brows rose. "No, I thought you could book me on the talk-show circuit, dig up some guest shots here and there."

"Could do that, too," he said genially. "After you take a few weeks off."

"I want gigs, not a few weeks off." Her brows lowered suspiciously. "Have you been talking to Julie?"

He looked surprised. "No, about what?"

"Nothing." Raven shook her head, then smiled. "Gigs, Henderson."

"You've lost weight, you know," he pointed out and shoveled in some more veal. "It shows in your face. Eat."

Raven gave an exasperated sigh and applied herself to her lunch. "Why does everyone treat me like a dimwitted child?" she mumbled, swallowing shrimp. "I'm going to start being temperamental and hard to get along with until I get some star treatment." Henderson said something quick and rude between mouthfuls which she ignored. "What about Jerry Michaels? Didn't I hear he was lining up a variety special for the fall? You could get me on that."

"Simplest thing in the world," Henderson agreed. "He'd be thrilled to have you."

"Well?"

"Well what?"

"Henderson." Resolutely, Raven pushed her plate aside. "Are you going to book me on the Jerry Michaels show?"

"No." He poured more wine into his glass. The sun shot through it, casting a red shadow on the tablecloth.

"Why?" Annoyance crept into Raven's tone.

"It's not for you." Henderson lifted a hand, palm up, as she began to argue. "I know who's producing the show, Raven. It's not for you."

She subsided a bit huffily, but she subsided. His instincts were the best in the field. "All right, forget the Michaels gig. What, then?"

"Want some dessert?"

"No, just coffee."

He signaled the waiter, then, after ordering blueberry cheesecake for himself and coffee for both of them, he settled back in his chair. "What about *Fantasy?*"

Raven twirled her wineglass between her fingers. "It's finished," she said flatly.

"And?"

"And?" she repeated, looking up. His merry blue eyes were narrowed. "It's finished," she said again. "Or essentially finished. I can't foresee any problem with the final details. Brandon or his agent will get in touch with you if there are, I'm sure."

"Jarett will probably need the two of you off and on during the filming," Henderson said mildly. "I wouldn't consider myself finished with it for a while yet."

Raven frowned into the pale golden liquid in her glass. "Yes, you're right, of course. I hadn't thought about it. Well…" She shook her head and pushed the wine away. "I'll deal with that when the times comes."

"How'd it go?"

She looked at Henderson levelly, but her thoughts drifted. "We wrote some of the best music either one of us has ever done. That I'm sure of. We work remarkably well together. I was surprised."

"You didn't think you would?" Henderson eyed the blueberry cheesecake the waiter set in front of him.

"No, I didn't think we would. Thank you," this to the waiter before she looked at Henderson again. "But everything else apart, we did work well together."

"You'd worked well together before," he pointed out. "'Clouds and Rain.'" He saw her frown but continued smoothly. "Did you know sales on that have picked up again after your New York concert? You got yourself a lot of free press, too."

"Yes," Raven mumbled into her coffee. "I'm sure we did."

"I've had a lot of questions thrown at me during the last weeks," he continued blandly, even when her eyes lifted and narrowed. "From the inside," he said with a smile, "as well as the press. I was at a nice little soiree just last week. You and Brand were the main topic of conversation."

"As I said, we work well together." Raven set down her cup. "Brandon was right; we are good for each other artistically."

"And personally?" Henderson took a generous bite of cheesecake.

"Well." Raven lifted a brow. "You certainly get to the point."

"That's all right, you don't have to answer me." He swallowed the cake, then broke off another piece. "You can tell *him*."

"Who?"

"Brand," Henderson answered easily and added cream to his coffee. "He just walked in."

Raven whirled around in her chair. Instantly her eyes locked on Brand's. With the contact came a wild, swift surge of joy. Her first instinct was to spring from the table and run to him. Indeed, she had pushed the chair back, preparing to do so, when the expression on his face cut through her initial spring of delight. It was ice-cold fury. Raven sat where she was, watching as he weaved his way through the crowded restaurant toward her. There were casual greetings along the way which he ignored. Raven heard the room fall silent.

He reached her without speaking once or taking his eyes from her. Raven's desire to hold out a hand to him was also overcome. She thought he might strike it away. The look in his eyes had her blood beating uneasily. Henderson might not have been sitting two feet away.

"Let's go."

"Go?" Raven repeated dumbly.

"Now." Brand took her hand and yanked her to her feet. She might have winced at the unexpected pressure if she hadn't been so shocked by it.

"Brandon…"

"Now," he repeated. He began to walk away, dragging her behind him. Raven could feel the eyes following them. Shock, delight, anxiety all faded into temper.

"Let go of me!" she demanded in a harsh undertone.

"What's the matter with you? You can't drag me around like this." She bumped into a lunching comedian, then skirted around him with a mumbled apology as Brand continued to stalk away with her hand in his. "Brandon, stop this! I will not be dragged out of a public restaurant."

He halted then and turned so that their faces were very close. "Would you prefer that I say what I have to say to you here and now?" His voice was clear and cool in the dead silence of the room. It was very easy to see the violence of temper just beneath the surface. Raven could feel it in the grip of his hand on hers. They were spotlighted again, she thought fleetingly, but hardly in the manner in which they had been in New York. She took a deep breath.

"No." Raven struggled for dignity and kept her voice lowered. "But there isn't any need to make a scene, Brandon."

"Oh, I'm in the mood for a scene, Raven," he tossed back in fluid British tones that carried well. "I'm in the mood for a bloody beaut of a scene."

Before she could comment, Brand turned away again and propelled her out of the restaurant. There was a Mercedes at the curb directly outside. He shoved her inside it, slamming the door behind her.

Raven straightened in the seat, whipping her head around as he opened the other door. "Oh, you're going to get one," she promised and ripped off her hat to throw it furiously into the back seat. "How *dare* you…"

"Shut up. I mean it." Brand turned to her as she started to speak again. "Just shut up until we get where we're going, otherwise I might be tempted to strangle you here and be done with it."

He shot away from the curb, and Raven flopped back

against her seat. I'll shut up, all right, she thought on wave after wave of anger. I'll shut up. It'll give me time to think through exactly what I have to say.

15

By the time Brand stopped the car in front of the Bel-Air, Raven felt she had her speech well in order. As he climbed out of his side, she climbed out of hers, then turned to face him on the sidewalk. But before she could speak, he had her arm in a tight grip and was pulling her toward the entrance.

"I told you not to drag me."

"And I told you to shut up." He brushed past the doorman and into the lobby. Raven was forced into an undignified half-trot in order to keep up with his long-legged stride.

"I will *not* be spoken to like that," she fumed and gave her arm an unsuccessful jerk. "I will *not* be carted through a hotel lobby like a piece of baggage."

"I'm tired of playing it your way." Brand turned, grabbing both of her shoulders and dragging her against him. His fingers bit into her skin and shocked her into silence. "My game now, my rules."

His mouth came down hard on hers. It was a kiss of rage. His teeth scraped across her lips, forcing them open so that he could plunder and seek. He held her bruisingly close, as if daring her to struggle.

When Brand pulled away, he stared at her for a long, silent

moment, then swore quickly, fiercely. Turning, he pulled her to the elevators.

Though she was no longer certain if it was fear or anger, Raven was trembling with emotion as they took the silent ride up. Brand could feel the throbbing pulse as he held her arm. He swore again, pungently, but she didn't glance at him. As the doors slid open, he pulled her into the hall and toward the penthouse.

There were no words exchanged between them as he slid the key into the lock. He released her arm as he pushed the door open. Without protest, Raven walked inside. She moved to the center of the room.

The suite was elegant, even lush, in a dignified, old-fashioned style with a small bricked fireplace and a good, thick carpet. Behind her the door slammed—a final sound—and she heard Brand toss the key with a faint metallic jingle onto a table. Raven drew a breath and turned around.

"Brandon…"

"No, I'll do the talking first." He crossed to her, his eyes locked on hers. "My rules, remember?"

"Yes." She lifted her chin. Her arm throbbed faintly where his fingers had dug into it. "I remember."

"First rule, no more bits and pieces. I won't have you closing parts of yourself off from me anymore." They were standing close. Now that the first dazed shock and surprise were passing, Raven noticed signs of strain and fatigue on his face. His words were spilling out so quickly, she couldn't interrupt. "You did the same thing to me five years ago, but then we weren't lovers. You were always holding out, never willing to trust."

"No." She shook her head, scrambling for some defense. "No, that's not true."

"Yes, it's true," he countered and took her by the shoulders again. "Did you tell me about your mother all those years ago? Or how you felt, what you were going through? Did you bring me into your life enough to let me help you, or at least comfort you?"

This was not what she had expected from him. Raven could only press her hand to her temple and shake her head again. "No, it wasn't something…"

"Wasn't something you wanted to share with me." He dropped her arms and stepped away from her. "Yes, I know." His voice was low and furious again as he pulled out a cigarette. He knew he had to do something with his hands or he'd hurt her again. He watched as she unconsciously nursed her arm where he had gripped her. "And this time, Raven, would you have told me anything about it if it hadn't been for the nightmare? If you hadn't been half asleep and frightened, would you have told me, trusted me?"

"I don't know." She made a small sound of confusion. "My mother had nothing to do with you."

Brand hurled the cigarette away before he lit it. "How can you say that to me? How can you stand there and say that to me?" He took a step toward her, then checked himself and stalked to the bar. "Damn you, Raven," he said under his breath. He poured bourbon and drank. "Maybe I should have stayed away," he managed in a calmer tone. "You'd already tossed me out of your life five years ago."

"*I* tossed you out?" This time her voice rose. "You walked out on me. You left me flat because I wouldn't be your lover." Raven walked over to the bar and leaned her palms on it. "You walked out of my house and out of my life, and the only word I had from you was what I read in the paper. It didn't take you long to find other women—several other women."

"I found as many as I could," Brand agreed and drank again. "As quickly as I could. I used women, booze, gambling—anything—to try to get you out of my system." He studied the dregs of liquor in his glass and added thoughtfully, "It didn't work." He set the glass down and looked at her again. "Which is why I knew I had to be patient with you."

Raven's eyes were still dark with hurt. "Don't talk to me about tossing you out."

"That's exactly what you did." Brand grabbed her wrist as she turned to swirl away from him. He held her still, the narrow, mahogany bar between them. "We were alone, remember? Julie was away for a few days."

Raven kept her eyes level. "I remember perfectly."

"Do you?" He arched a brow. Both his eyes and voice were cool again. "There might be a few things you don't remember. When I came to the house that night I was going to ask you to marry me."

Raven could feel every thought, every emotion, pour out of her body. She could only stare at him.

"Surprised?" Brand released her wrist and again reached in his pocket for a cigarette. "Apparently we have two differing perspectives on that night. I *loved* you." The words were an accusation that kept her speechless. "And God help me, all those weeks we were together I was faithful to you. I never touched another woman." He lit the cigarette, and as the end flared, Raven heard him say softly, "I nearly went mad."

"You never told me." Her voice was weak and shaken. Her eyes were huge gray orbs. "You never once said you loved me."

"You kept backing off," he retorted. "And I knew you were innocent and afraid, though I didn't know why." He gave her

NORA ROBERTS

a long, steady look. "It would have made quite a lot of difference if I had, but you didn't trust me."

"Oh, Brandon."

"That night," he went on, "you were so warm, and the house was so quiet. I could feel how much you wanted me. It drove me crazy. Good God, I was trying to be gentle, patient, when the need for you was all but destroying me." He ran a tense hand through his hair. "And you were giving, melting, everywhere I touched you. And then—then you were struggling like some terrified child, pushing at me as if I'd tried to kill you, telling me not to touch you. You said you couldn't bear to have me touch you."

He looked back at her, but his eyes were no longer cool. "You're the only woman who's ever been able to hurt me like that."

"Brandon." Raven shut her eyes. "I was only twenty, and there were so many things…"

"Yes, I know now; I didn't know then." His tone was flat. "Though there really weren't so many changes this time around." Raven opened her eyes and started to speak, but he shook his head. "No, not yet. I've not finished. I stayed away to give you time, as I told you before. I didn't see any other way. I could hardly stay, kicking my heels in L.A., waiting for you to make up your mind. I didn't know how long I'd stay away, but during those five years I concentrated on my career. So did you."

Brand paused, spreading his long, elegant hands on the surface of the bar. "Looking back, I suppose that's all for the best. You needed to establish yourself, and I had a surge of productivity. When I started reading about you regularly in the gossip columns I knew it was time to come back." He watched her mouth fall open at that, and her eyes heat. "Get as mad as you damn well like when I've finished," he said shortly. "But don't interrupt."

Raven turned away to search for control. "All right, go on," she managed and faced him again.

"I came to the States without any real plan, except to see you. The solid idea fell into my lap by way of *Fantasy* when I was in New York. I used the score to get you back," he said simply and without apology. "When I stood up in that recording booth watching you again, I knew I'd have used anything, but the score did nicely." He pushed his empty glass aside with his fingertip. "I wasn't lying about wanting to work with you again for professional reasons or about feeling you were particularly right for *Fantasy*. But I would have if it had been necessary. So perhaps you weren't so far wrong about what you said on the cliffs that day." He moved from the bar to the window. "Of course, there was a bit more to it in my mind than merely getting you to bed."

Raven felt her throat burn. "Brandon." She swallowed and shut her eyes. "I've never been more ashamed of anything in my life than what I said to you. Anger is hardly an excuse, but I'd hoped—I'd hoped you'd forgive me."

Brand turned his head and studied her a moment. "Perhaps if you hadn't left, it would have been easier."

"I had to. I told you in the note…"

"What note?" His voice sharpened as he turned to face her.

"The note." Raven was uncertain whether to step forward or back. "I left it on the piano with the music."

"I didn't see any note. I didn't see anything but that you were gone." He let out a long breath. "I dumped all the music into a briefcase. I didn't notice a note."

"Julie called only a little while after you'd left to tell me about the accident."

His eyes shot back to hers again. "What accident?"

Raven stared at him.

"Your mother?" he said, reading it in her eyes.

"Yes. She'd had an accident. I had to get back right away."

He jammed his hands into his pockets. "Why didn't you wait for me?"

"I wanted to; I couldn't." Raven laced her fingers together to prevent her hands from fluttering. "Dr. Karter said it would only be a matter of hours. As it was…" She paused and turned away. "I was too late, anyway."

Brand felt the anger drain from him. "I'm sorry. I didn't know."

Raven didn't know why the simple, quiet statement should bring on the tears she hadn't shed before. They blinded her eyes and clogged her throat so that speech was impossible.

"I went a bit crazy when I got back to the house and found you'd packed and gone." Brand spoke wearily now. "I don't know exactly what I did at first; afterwards I got roaring drunk. The next morning I dumped all the music together, packed some things and took off for the States.

"I stopped off for a couple of days in New York, trying to sort things out. It seems I spend a great deal of time running after you. It's difficult on the pride. In New York I came up with a dozen very logical, very valid reasons why I should go back to England and forget you. But there was one very small, very basic point I couldn't argue aside." He looked at her again. Her back was to him, her head bent so that with her hair pulled up he could see the slender length of her neck. "I love you, Raven."

"Brandon." Raven turned her tear-drenched face toward

him. She blinked at the prisms of light that blinded her, then shook her head quickly when she saw him make a move to come to her. "No, please don't. I won't be able to talk if you touch me." She drew in a deep breath, brushing the tears away with her fingertips. "I've been very wrong; I have to tell you."

He stood away from her, though impatience was beginning to simmer through him again. "I had my say," he agreed. "I suppose you should have yours."

"All those years ago," she began. "All those years ago there were things I couldn't say, things I couldn't even understand because I was so—dazzled by everything. My career, the fame, the money, the perpetual spotlight." The words came quickly, and her voice grew stronger with them. "Everything happened at once; there didn't seem to be any time to get used to it all. Suddenly I was in love with Brandon Carstairs." She laughed and brushed at fresh tears. "*The* Brandon Carstairs. You have to understand, one minute you were an image, a name on a record, and the next you were a man, and I loved you."

Raven moistened her lips, moving to stare from the window as Brand had. "And my mother—my mother was my responsibility, Brandon. I've felt that always, and it isn't something that can be changed overnight. You were the genuine knight on a charger. I couldn't—wouldn't talk to you about that part of my life. I was afraid, and I was never sure of you. You never told me you loved me, Brandon."

"I was terrified of you," he murmured, "of what I was feeling for you. You were the first." He shrugged. "But you were always pulling back from me. Always putting up No Trespassing signs whenever I started to get close."

"You always seemed to want so much." She hugged her arms. "Even this time, in Cornwall, when we were so close. It didn't seem to be enough. I always felt you were waiting for more."

"You still put up the signs, Raven." She turned, and his eyes locked on hers. "Your body isn't enough. That isn't what I waited five years for."

"Love should be enough," she tossed back, suddenly angry and confused.

"No." Brand shook his head, cutting her off. "It isn't enough. I want a great deal more than that." He waited a moment, watching the range of expressions on her face. "I want your trust, without conditions, without exceptions. I want a commitment, a total one. It's all or nothing this time, Raven."

She backed away. "You can't own me, Brandon."

A quick flash of fury shot into his eyes. "Damn it, I don't want to own you, but I want you to belong to me. Don't you know there's a difference?"

Raven stared at him for a full minute. She dropped her arms, no longer cold. The tension that had begun to creep up the back of her neck vanished. "I didn't," she said softly. "I should have."

Slowly she crossed to him. She was vividly aware of every detail of his face: the dark, expressive brows drawn together now with thought, the blue-green eyes steady but with the spark of temper, the faint touch of mauve beneath them that told her he'd lost sleep. It came to her then that she loved him more as a woman than she had as a girl. A woman could love without fear, without restrictions. Raven lifted her fingertip to his cheek as if to smooth away the tension.

Then they were locked in each other's arms, mouth to mouth. His hands went to her hair, scattering pins until it tumbled free around them. He murmured something she had no need to understand, then plunged deep again into her mouth. Hurriedly, impatiently, they began to undress each other. No words were needed. They sought only touch, to give, to fulfill.

His fingers fumbled with the zipper of her dress, making him swear and her laugh breathlessly until he pulled her with him to the rug. Then, somehow, they were flesh to flesh. Raven could feel the shudders racing through him to match her own as they touched. His mouth was no more greedy than hers, his hands no less demanding. Their fire blazed clean and bright. Need erupted in them both so that she pulled him to her, desperate to have him, frantic to give.

Raw pleasure shot through her, rocking her again and again as she moved with him. His face was buried in her hair, his body damp to her touch. Air was forcing its way from her lungs in moans and gasps as they took each other higher and faster. Then the urgency passed, and a sweetness took its place.

Time lost all meaning as they lay together. Neither moved nor spoke. Tensions and angers, ecstasies and desperations, had all passed. All that was left was a soft contentment. She could feel his breath move lightly against her neck.

"Brandon," Raven murmured, letting her lips brush his skin. *"Hmm?"*

"I think I still had something to say, but it's slipped my mind." She gave a low laugh.

Brand lifted his head and grinned. "Maybe it'll come back to you. Probably wasn't important."

"You're right, I'm sure." She smiled, touching his cheek. "It had something to do with loving you beyond sanity or some such thing and wanting more than anything in the world to belong to you. Nothing important."

Brand lowered his mouth to hers and nipped at her still tender lip. "You were distracted," he mused, seeking her breast with his fingertip.

Raven ran her hands down his back. "I was in a bit of a hurry."

"This time…" He began to taste her neck and shoulder. "This time we'll slow down the tempo. A bit more orchestration, don't you think?" His fingers slid gently and teasingly over the point of her breast.

"Yes, quite a bit more orchestration. Brandon…" Her words were lost on a sound of pleasure as his tongue found her ear. "Once more, with feeling," she whispered.

* * * * *

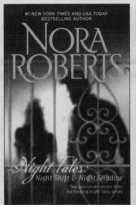 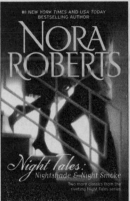 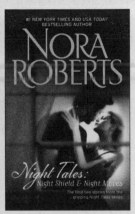

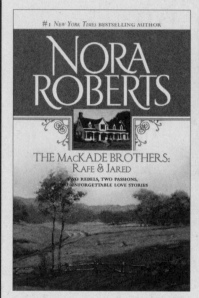
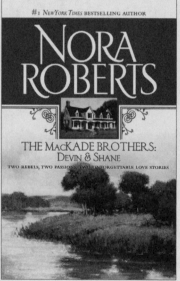